Another Family Reunion Novel
In The Wisdom of the Ancestors Series
— *Book 23* —

COUNTRY COOL, *City Chic,* Continental Class

ANN JEFFRIES

Published and distributed by
New View Literature
820 67th Avenue N, #7603
Myrtle Beach, South Carolina 29572
www.newviewliterature.com

Editor: Jessica Tilles

Cover and Interior Design: TWA Solutions

ISBN: 978-1-941603-07-9 Print
ISBN: 978-1-941603-08-6 eBook
Library of Congress Control Number 2014913787

First printing: November 2021

For inquiries, contact the publisher.

ACKNOWLEDGMENTS

The Creator

The Ancestors

Faithful family, friends, and fans

Reston Book Club, Reston, Virginia

Gourmet Book Club, Palm Coast, Florida

Aurora Book Club, Pittsburgh, Pennsylvania

African American Women's Book Club, Virginia

Alpha Kappa Alpha Book Club, Bowie, Maryland

F.R.E.S.H. Book Festival, Daytona Beach, Florida

Sweet Tea With A Chaser, Daytona Beach, Florida

Virginia Festival of the Book, Charlottesville, Virginia

Carolina Forest Authors' Club, Myrtle Beach, South Carolina

Carolina Forest Public Library, Horry County, South Carolina

ZORA! Festival: Zora Neale Hurston Book Festival, Jamesville, Florida

The journey continues and the struggle for literary perfection shall never end

I remain faithfully yours,

Ann Jeffries

Catherine H. Lowery, Author
Bella and the Muddy Puddle
Bella and the Bully
Bella and the Bear

Bella Fayre, Author
Maelstroms of the Silent
Sisters of the Scorned
Guardian of the Damned
Legacy of the Lost

"Stop all the clocks, cut off the telephone,
Prevent the dog from barking with a juicy bone,
Silence the pianos and with muffled drum
Bring out the coffin, let the mourners come.
The stars are not wanted now; put out every one,
Pack up the moon and dismantle the sun,
Pour away the ocean and sweep up the wood;
For nothing now can ever come to any good."

—"Funeral Blues" by W.H. Auden
Wystan Hugh Auden, born 21 February 1907, York, England
Died 29 September 1973, Vienna, Austria

"If you love someone, set them free. If they come back to you, your love is meant to be."
—Richard Bach

"Trust is the glue of life. It's the most essential ingredient in effective communication. It's the foundational principle that holds all relationships together."
—Stephen Covey

Chapter 1

Fiona Lizette Lowry sat on the roof of her serviceable old Jeep Cherokee, knees pulled into her chest, and arms loosely wrapped around her long, strong, shapely legs and thighs. It was a good angle and elevation to view the acreage stretching out toward the Chesapeake Bay in rural Bay County, Maryland. *Pristine land,* she thought, *that should remain undisturbed. Of course, it will change, as all things are destined to do over time.*

She sighed. Still, what a view it was!

In the distance offshore were boats with sails like unfurled wings, skimming the water. Their beauty was so incredible in the bright sunlight. Fiona guessed the Chase Brothers in Mitchell County, Maryland, likely built them. They were great boat builders with a growing reputation for excellence. Owning a boat was on Fiona's bucket list, but for now, to afford such a thing, she had to make money from her career as an architect. However, perks like this, being in the open air, enjoying Mother Nature's gifts, made her heart sing.

Still, she wanted a challenge, something to get her creative juices flowing. The last thing of that magnitude came from working with her cousin, JaiHonnah Hawkins Baylor, a few years ago. They completed a project in New York City, converting a twelve-story, former library building into a mixed-use, private residence, dance school, and studio. It was a thought-provoking and fun project for the recently wed, world-renowned prima ballerina Linda Montgomery Hamilton. Still, nothing, in no way, compared to creating something where nothing existed on the landscape. That was what she wanted now—the challenge of creativity and making her mark on the world's landscape.

11

Seagulls flew overhead, calling out their appreciation to Mother Nature for a day that could not have been more picture-perfect. Wild horses from the fourteen-thousand-acre Chincoteague National Wildlife Refuge grazed in the grassy meadow next to the farm. If she had been thinking instead of enjoying the scenery, she would have gathered carrots from the wild, overgrown garden to coax the horses into coming close enough to feed.

The O'Leary family, who had once farmed this land for generations, left a very productive vegetable garden that bloomed wild each year, as well as acres and acres of old, overgrown tobacco plants. Remnants of the farmhouse crumbled years ago. The only remaining sign that someone once lived there was a brick chimney that evidenced the history of this place, regardless of the ivy eating away at the mortar and bricks. The O'Leary family died out before her father was born, but vestiges of their lives remained, including descendants of the horses they once owned. Fiona loved horses and planned to own some. That, too, was on her bucket list.

The air, scented with a bit of brine, whipped teasingly across her gamine, sun-kissed, light-brown face and tugged at the baseball cap she wore backward. The cap barely covered the escaping perfusion of thick, dark red tresses of her long French braid hanging low on her back, lightly sweeping the top of the car.

Although the scenery was immaculate, she recognized Mother Nature was showing off her wares and wanted to be noticed. She deserved to have appreciative eyes cast upon her. Fiona, an ardent admirer, knew precisely what this parcel of land needed; a home that took in all of Mother Nature's gifts: earth, sun, sea, and air, but did not insult the senses or the scenery. The light, the glorious light, would bathe the home in rich, warm tones. *Glass*, she thought; inspired, she saw it in her mind's eye. Prisms of glass framed with girders and with local wood and rock used sparingly. Unobstructed, unobtrusive glass perched to float above the land, with gardens of seagrass and wild oats undulating in the frisky breeze, replacing the fields of tobacco. Tall weeping willows, and other deciduous trees, shading the home in the heat of summer, would be bare in winter so the sun would warm the house by day. *Yes,* she thought, *absolutely perfect.*

Fiona reached for her sketch iPad and began work on what was shaping up to be a six-thousand-square-foot, open concept home. A turn-of-the-century tobacco barn stood to her left through a cluster of old-growth trees. She'd make use of that, too, she decided. She'd take down a few Live Oaks to use in the house's foundation and the flooring in the barn conversion. The saplings she'd have her brother shred into mulch for the gardens. Fiona had the McKenna Mill in mind to convert the usable trees into lumber. They would do justice to the boards she needed for the barn studio. She preferred Brazilian Cherry for the house. It would be warm underfoot and hold heat longer when required. An order for the flooring would need to go in sooner rather than later. Space would have to be made in her warehouses for materials and supplies. Several projects would wrap up in the next few months and should provide the needed additional space. If not, she'd have to wheedle some space from one of her brothers' warehouses. That task went on her To-Do list.

She had walked through the old barn, checking for rot and rodents. If she couldn't convince the client to use this space strictly for relaxation, the old barn would make an adequate workspace. Though long beyond its natural life span, the foundation still appeared solid, and the standing-seam tin roof was free of leaks. Still, after digging out the basement for the house and the barn, she'd have an expert check and then treat the soil for termites. It would be a simple build and renovation to provide usable, year-round spaces.

The client, the son of an old military pal of her father's, was a music executive. He wanted a soundproof studio to record music, an office for his work, and a lounge and party room for entertaining. She liked that he didn't want to turn his house, his home, his sanctuary, into a typical three-ring showbiz arena. The barn structure, away from the house, would be perfect for the post-and-beam facility for work and entertainment she had in mind.

Here, she thought, looking up at the unblemished landscape. *Here would be the glass house—the crystal jewelry for Mother Nature's attire.*

A familiar Irish-accented voice, a deep brogue still prevalent in his tone, approached her. "What do you see, lass?"

Fiona didn't jolt at the intrusion. All her senses were alert. She heard her father's beefy, super-duty F-250 XL truck rumbling up the path toward her nearly an hour ago. He had left his truck and walked the land just as she had, getting a feel for the deconstruction and preconstruction plans; well and septic systems, utilities, etc. Generally, her dad would dispatch one of his foremen to handle this type of work, but his friend's son would get Alroy Lowry's full attention on this job. That meant it would get all of Fiona Lowry's best creative work and attention, too.

"Glass. Floating glass."

Alroy, Al to his friends, leaned against the front of his daughter's Jeep to view the land from her perspective, removed his cap, and idly scratched his still thick, wavy, red hair. "Huh, sure will make it tough to take a leak."

He was a tall, rawboned man with brawny arms and tight, ropy muscles. His hands were big and rough, evidencing the fact that he still rolled up his sleeves and worked side-by-side with his construction crews. He didn't need to, but the work was still gratifying after more than thirty years in the business. It pleased him that his seven children learned the construction trades from him, and, after college, each one returned home to open specialty construction businesses under his corporate umbrella. His Fiona Lizette, the only girl and the jewel in his crown, could work sunup to sundown by his and his sons' sides and had since she was knee-high to a duck. An architect and engineer by trade, she possessed insight and vision for the masterpieces she created.

"Are you going to dig the well over by the barn?"

He nodded. "Yep, best place for it. I think that's the site of the old well, anyway."

Fiona pointed toward her right, away from the tobacco barn. "A well should be dug over there, too."

"That's a long run for the water. Did you read the geology report?"

"I did, yes. It looks like one hundred fifty, maybe two hundred feet down in several places. I'm thinking a rain barrel system stored in an underground bunker as an additional water source. It will need several levels of purification to be potable. I'll put in two systems. One in the barn and the other in the house."

He thought that over and nodded his agreement. "Power?"

"Geothermal, wind, and passive and active solar for the house." She shrugged. "The windmill looks to still be in good shape. I'll ask Peter and Paul to check. Maybe bury propane in the bunker, too, for backup and gas appliances. It wouldn't do to lose power out here. Active solar and wind for the barn. Electrical run out to the county road is a stretch. Flynn said it would be costly. We'd have to bury it a long distance and use boosters along the way. He also said we'd need heavy-up boosters with three-hundred-amp service in both structures."

"I'll include a trench on my construction plan to the Maryland Gas and Electric Company. What's your HVAC source?"

"Radiant floors on two levels, ceiling fans, and high-velocity industrial air ducts, maybe exposed in the barn. I'll have to figure out how to filter out any noise. More industrial than chic ducts, depending on the client's preferences. Gannon said it's doable. As I understand, part of it's to be a soundproof music studio. I'll have to consult with an expert on that. Forced air systems can create noise."

Al grunted his agreement. He and his only daughter were often of like minds. They spoke a sort of shorthand conversation that vexed his wife and six sons. "The client has given you *Carte Blanche* to be creative and think outside the box."

Al leaned his six-foot-three-inch frame forward, dug his long, strong fingers into the soil, and lifted it to let the breeze take it. "Rich." He dusted the remaining dirt from his hands. "I hear tell this was once a nice farm. My granddad knew the O'Learys, but they had no kin to take on a life of farming. This tobacco farm took a hit when people stopped smoking cigarettes." He stood, arms folded across his toned, plaid-shirt-covered chest, regarding the view. "When can I have it?" He was referring to the house plans and scale model Fiona would design.

"Friday, early. Landscape plan might take a little longer. First, I want to rope off and preserve a wild vegetable and fruit garden over there before you bring in your heavy equipment. Next, I need to decide about the trees I want to take down and have milled for floorboards and siding. I'm thinking of having the siding in vertical panels and treated with linseed oil. There's also this process called Shou Sugi Ban used by the Japanese as a treatment to preserve wood. As I understand it, it's an artistic and unique finish that also improves durability. I've been looking for an opportunity to try it on one of my projects. There are a lot of cedar trees on the land I could use. I'll talk with AJ about it," referring to Alroy Junior, the oldest of her six brothers.

Al shrugged. "Never heard of it, but go for it. I trust you."

She looked at her dad with admiration and respect on her face. "Are you going to be able to sell it?"

"Max Kennard isn't the one buying it. It's his son's place. You should be the one to do the presentation. It's your concept."

"Can't. Got this thing with Aiden for his political campaign on Friday and Saturday."

With his head tilted down, Al squinted at his daughter over the top of his sunglasses. "Are you going to marry the boy?"

"I'm using him for sex, Daddy."

Her father laughed; the Irish in his brogue even more pronounced when talking with his offspring. "Not much of that going on, to hear your brothers tell it. Seems ole Aiden thinks you're about to kick him to the curb."

"Can't say the man's not perceptive." She eyed her father. "That's not going to cause you grief with Wilhelm McKenna, will it?"

Al shrugged a large, muscular shoulder. "Maybe, some. Probably. He's been planning to get you into his family for a long time, but then he's a Scot, not Irish, so who gives a damn?" He laughed.

"He may have to settle for getting his daughter married off to AJ. McKenna has visions of a McKenna-Lowry business merger. His mill and our construction businesses. He wants Aiden to manage it, instead of following a career in politics."

Fiona grinned at him, melting his heart just as it had the day she was born. He loved his sons fiercely, but next to his wife, his only daughter was his jewel. Al shook his head. "Let's go, Imp. Your mama wants me home early today. You know she also wants you to come by the house."

Fiona nimbly slid off the roof of the car to the hood and then down to the ground. She knew her mother despaired at her failed efforts to turn her only daughter into a proper young lady but having six rough-and-tumble older brothers had worked against that notion. "I'll be there Sunday for her birthday dinner with the rest of the offspring, uncles, aunts, and cousins."

"Your mother wants you to go shopping with her so that she can buy a dress for you to wear on her birthday."

Fiona gave an unladylike snort. "Not in this lifetime. I'd rather take a whipping."

Al barked a laugh. "That can be arranged." He hung a big, beefy arm around his daughter's shoulders. She was nearly as tall as he was. "If your mama orders up a can of whip ass, then that can certainly be arranged." He kissed her temple, released her, and then ambled toward his truck with his hands dug deep into his pockets.

For a moment, Fiona watched him go. She was unworried about the threat of a whipping from her father. He never used his hands to punish any of his children. However, her mother was a different thought altogether.

Chapter 2

"Glass?" Maxwell Bishop Kennard, the Third, Trey to his friends, uttered Friday morning more of a thought than as a question. The scale model of the house sitting on his conference table in his three-story New York City condo was undoubtedly intriguing but not particularly practical. Trey took a turn around the model to view it from a different angle. He shook his head. Nope. He still didn't know why he should like this glass house. There was no privacy to speak of. The thing was wide open and glass through and through. It was only held together by narrow, almost invisible steel girders. Then again, being surrounded by thousands of pristine, wooded acres would isolate him from view.

Yet, there was something about it that didn't let him dismiss it out of hand. It was certainly unique. He'd give it that. He had traveled widely, visited friends and acquaintances with extreme homes, but had seen nothing like this before. Of course, like most people who traveled a great deal, he had seen the Penthouse Glass Bank in Cocoa Beach, Florida, the Crystal Cathedral Church in California, and the Crystal Palaces in London, Germany, and Canada. The Palacio de Cristal, in Madrid, Spain, should have been considered one of the Seven Wonders of the World, along with the Wayfarers Chapel in Palos Verdes, California, but to put a glass house on the shores of the Chesapeake Bay in rural Bay County, Maryland? He wasn't so sure about that. Trey didn't want to draw attention to his retreat…but, damn it, this mind-bending concept had captured his attention.

Well, he needed a place where he could get away and relax. The Hamptons were out of the question; too many of his crowd spent time there. He would never have the privacy he wanted or be able to work when necessary. Purchasing a one-hundred-twenty-acre parcel, an old tobacco farm, on the eastern Chesapeake Bay coastline, was a good idea and a great deal four years ago. He loved to sail and swim, which the Bay offered. He enjoyed the occasional getaway with a lady friend *de jour*, too. However, although the land was isolated, he didn't consider himself an exhibitionist.

He sold his home on Martha's Vineyard because it didn't allow easy, year-round access and there wasn't enough land to build a state-of-the-art music studio on his property. He needed the studio sooner rather than later to score two feature-length movies he had contracted to complete and work with the music groups, songwriters, and vocal artists for videos. There was a band, Changelings, he had heard bits and pieces about. The band members lived in the Washington, DC, area and were still college students. It was fertile ground for musicians, as were nearby Annapolis and Baltimore, Maryland.

A friend with the rights to the remake of the once-popular television show, *New York Undercover*, asked him to give a new stylized update to the show's signature music. He also took on an executive producer role and scored a unique classical ballet titled *Goodwill*. The choreographer and co-executive producer was the world-renowned prima ballerina Linda Lewis. This new ballet was a departure from his usual and held the greatest excitement for him about now. She planned to create a contemporary ballet each year. Given the award-winning success of *Goodwill*, he wanted more opportunities to work with Ms. Lewis going forward. So, the acoustics in his new workspace had to be perfect to get the best results he wanted. Still, he saw nothing in this glass house resembling a studio.

His father laughed. "I can hear the wheels grinding in your head, son."

Green eyes rose to meet his father's identical ones. "In this house, you would be able to see them, too." Trey turned to look at his father's friend, Al Lowry. "What about my studio?"

"Lost in transport. A mishap at the airport, but there is an identical one back at the office. Any chance you can get down to Maryland to see it?"

"I don't know." Trey checked his watch. He would be in London for twenty days, or maybe a month. Then Madrid and Tokyo for equal amounts of time. He needed to squeeze in a trip to Paris, France, too, but if he didn't do this before he left the country, he wouldn't be back in the states for over three months. He had an opportunity to work with this hot, new artist, Loretta, and he wasn't going to pass it up. He worked hard to fit some of his plans into her schedule through his pal, Bill Chandler, who was also his and her agent and legal representative. He hoped, or more like prayed, to record the French Mariah in Paris at her club, so his schedule was tight.

"You could fly down with me and Al this afternoon, son. Then fly out of BWI or Dulles Airport on Monday morning."

Trey ran his fingers through his wavy, dark-blond hair. Damn, he needed a haircut. He didn't have time to go to Maryland, but he wouldn't see the studio if he did not. He had a date tonight with a leggy brunette, but his father had a point. Flying out of BWI Airport was just as convenient as flying out of a New York airport. He had studied the house and studio plans on paper and taken the virtual reality tour of the building on his laptop's view screen, but he needed to see the scale model of the entire site and the land he purchased sight unseen. Putting his hands on it to feel it was a necessity. Then he would know whether it was suitable for his needs. He could also talk with the architect more about this privacy-stealing glass house.

With an exasperated huff, he took his iPhone out of his pocket to scan his appointment calendar. Except for his date, he had only scheduled time for errands in preparation for his extended trip. The haircut would have to wait until he got to London.

Never one to ponder *ad nauseam*, he clicked on his executive assistant's number. "Sandra." As expected, she answered on the first ring. "I'm going down to Maryland this afternoon with my father and Al Lowry. Would you change the departure for the foreign tour to Baltimore-Washington International or whatever airport is closest to this address?" He rattled off the information. "Make it for as early on Monday morning as possible, and then have Henry grab my luggage and meet us at the heliport."

"Yes, sir. Anything else?"

"Yes, two dozen long-stem roses for Glenda with my apology for tonight."

Sandra laughed. "Better make that three dozen and some expensive little bobble, too. In the past two months, this will be the third time you've canceled a date with Glenda."

Trey chuckled. "Yeah, you're right. Call my jeweler and take care of that detail, too, would you please?"

"Got it. I'll have the limo out front in ten."

"Thanks, babe. You're a jewel."

"Yeah, I hear that a lot. Now I want something beautiful and expensive from Madrid *and* Tokyo."

"You got it, babe. See you Monday morning."

Hours later, the trio arrived at the Bay County home of Alroy and Mavis Hawkins Lowry.

Maxwell Kennard, the Second, smiled broadly at the woman he held at arm's length. "How is it possible you are even more beautiful today than you were thirty-five years ago, Mavis?" She was a statuesque five-foot-eight-inch, light-brown bombshell with lush, mature curves descendant from her Louisiana *gens du couleur libre* ancestry. Her dark eyes sparkled like polished onyx in her oval face with high cheekbones. Ink black hair and sculptured eyebrows showed no signs of gray. Her brilliant, white-teeth smile hinted at the joy she felt at seeing Maxwell Kennard again after all these years.

"You're worse than ever with your blarney, Max," Mavis Ramilles Hawkins Lowry chided with a wink, and then, turning to the tall, handsome lad at his side, she reached for Trey. "You look the spitting image of your papa, *Cher*." Creole whispered through her voice as she pulled him into a tight hug. "You couldn't deny this one if you had to, Max. He looks just as you did thirty-five years ago."

Maxwell chuckled and slung an arm over his son's broad shoulders. "Son, this is the woman who got away. She should have ended up being your momma. After Al and I were wounded, he carried me on his back out of the war zone. He and I were both in the field hospital for weeks. Mavis was our nurse. I tried everything I could to get a date with her, but she only had eyes for Al. Only Al was clueless. Finally, Mavis had to propose a date to Al before he caught a clue."

Having heard variations of this story many times over the years, Al gathered his wife to his side and kissed her waiting mouth. "What you didn't understand, Max, was that, unlike you, I was playing hard to get. I love it when a plan comes together."

They laughed, and Al introduced them to his six sons—all tall, athletically fit, young men.

"You have a lovely home, Mrs. Lowry." Trey was intrigued by the stunning architecture constituting the main house. Cottages led from a central courtyard like a peacock's tail fan and were just as colorful. The dark wood and stone exterior blended into the landscape so unobtrusively that the structures seemed part of nature.

Trey fell in love with the ambiance in the salon where they were having predinner cocktails. The walls were a warm butterscotch color with beautiful, wall-size, colorful paintings of New Orleans street scenes. He could just as easily imagine himself in a Louisiana courtyard with the large, leafy, tropical plants from Alroy Junior's garden nursery store strategically placed around the open floor plan. The vaulted ceiling beamed with pot lights and fans, adding to the ambiance. Round skylights added spots of light to further the warmth of the space.

Bougainvillea trailed over trellises off the lanai and perfumed the inside and outside air. The floor was a large composite slate in a random pattern. The sofas and chairs were a lush, mink-colored brown with accent pillows complementing the reds, oranges, yellows, blues, and greens in the pictures on the walls. *No dull grays or washed-out models for this home,* Trey thought. Instead, those who lived here were lively and vibrant people. As a result, the home managed to look comfortable and modern simultaneously. He recognized the Russell Greene originals hung in places of honor around the interior, envying the beauty the artist captured. It was the feeling he liked to capture with the music he created.

"Thank you, Trey, but this house and the cottages were one of Al and Fiona's early projects. I think she was about twelve years old when she decided she wanted her own cottage."

Gannon, Al and Mavis' second eldest son nodded. "More like eleven. I was in my senior year and sick of sharing a room with Gavin."

Gavin chuckled. "You weren't the only one. Flynn and Al, Junior, were getting on each other's nerves, too. The twins, Peter and Paul, were the only ones who could get along with each other in the same bedroom without fighting."

He gazed up as if in thought, remembering it all too well. "Fiona Lizette was tired of hearing the noise, so she proposed the two-bedroom, two-bath cottages with their own kitchenettes, salons, and plenty of outdoor space. Both Mavis and I loved the idea of having our home back without the constant bickering between the siblings. The boys and Fiona could also have sleepovers with their pals and not disturb the rest of the family. So before Gannon left for college, they built the cottages from the ground up, using their designs. I left them to it and remodeled the main house, using their former rooms for guest accommodations. It was a learning experience for them about careers in the construction industry. It was nirvana for Mavis and me."

Peter laughed with his twin, Paul, nodding in agreement about their sister. "Best idea the little vixen ever had."

Paul tapped Peter on the elbow. "Where is Fiona Lizette, anyway?"

Al faced his son, Paul. "She said something about an event with Aiden McKenna."

Nodding, Mavis recalled the event with an explanation to their guests. "Ah, Congressman Aiden Prescott McKenna is running for Maryland State's Attorney General. Fiona arranged a fundraiser in his honor. Many of those in attendance are her clients."

Maxwell's brow rose. "That's quite an undertaking for a friend."

Mavis smiled. "Fiona and Aiden have been best friends since the cradle."

"I hoped to have an opportunity to talk with your daughter about my studio and her house design while I was here. We've not found time to meet in person."

"She'll be here for Mavis' birthday party on Sunday." Al shook his head remorsefully. "However, I don't know whether I can get her here before then."

Mavis laughed. "You see, Fiona hates to shop, and Al made the mistake of telling her I wanted her to go shopping tomorrow with me."

Gannon shook his head. "Well, that settles it! You won't be able to get her anywhere near here if she thinks you're going to rope her into going shopping."

Paul elbowed Peter in the chest. "Maybe she'll be at the Rams Head Tavern tonight. Kemistry is performing. She loves Kem's music."

"You're right." Peter turned to the group at large. "She'll be there because she won't be able to resist. Bet money on it. Maybe we can catch up with her. Anyone game?"

Maxwell shook his head. "Not me."

Mavis looked at her husband of more than thirty-five years with a devilish smile curling her lips. "Us either."

Flynn looked at Trey. "You game, Trey?"

"Sure. I'd like to see Kemistry live. I'm always looking for talent."

Alroy nodded. "Great. Let's eat so these youngsters can get over to Annapolis."

Chapter 3

Fiona looked up into Aiden's handsome face and gave him a cross-eyed, frog-faced stare.

Aiden had just taken a sip of his drink and nearly burst out laughing at her antics. He didn't want to insult the group of financial supporters of his campaign. However, he knew Fiona was nearing her wit's end with the political jabbering they'd endured for the past two hours. He snaked one arm around her tiny waist and pulled her to his side. In his other hand, he held a drink that was more water than anything else. Tilting his wrist, he discretely looked at his watch. Only Fiona caught the subtle gesture. He knew she didn't have to remind him it was time to go. He could read her easier and better than a top-ten, best-selling novel.

"You gonna make this beautiful little lady your bride anytime soon, Congressman?" asked Hudson Callahan, a wealthy contributor.

He had spent the last few moments trying unsuccessfully to peek down the bodice of Fiona's dress. However, she stood five foot nine inches to his barely five-foot-five-inch height.

"Shh. Don't talk too loudly, Hudson. She might hear you. She's too smart to let me sneak up and catch her," Aiden joked.

The group laughed, and right on cue, the room lights flashed. Aiden's campaign manager, Harris Charles, took a microphone in hand and beckoned Aiden and Fiona to join him on the raised platform. After she did her duty, introducing him to the room full of contributors she invited to attend through her and her family's business contacts, she was done. Fifteen minutes of comments by the candidate, and they were saying their farewells to the contributors, the campaign coffers fatter for the two-and-a-half-hour grip-and-grin effort.

Thirty minutes later, Aiden parked his car in the public lot near the Rams Head Tavern and Restaurant in Annapolis, Maryland. He and Fiona walked hand-in-hand down the clean street and into the lobby of the bar. A hostess was showing them toward the VIP section where, surprise, surprise, she spotted her six brothers sitting with someone she hadn't seen before. Applause took her attention away from her family members. Delayed by patrons who recognized Aiden from his television ads and wanted to shake his hand or chat about politics, dutifully, she gripped and grinned along with him and his constituents. So, it took a while to reach their table, where her brothers and the stranger waited.

"Hey, fancy meeting you here." Paul smiled at his sister and friend, Aiden. He simultaneously held out his hand to his brothers, who all relinquished the dollar amount the bet called for.

"I didn't know you were coming." Standing, Aiden addressed the group at large while giving Fiona's brothers traditional knuckle-to-knuckle bumps. They grew up together as neighbors, classmates, and friends. His mother owned and operated a bed-and-breakfast and the McKenna Stables. From an early age, Mrs. McKenna taught the Lowry children to ride horses. As a result, Aiden was as close to the six Lowry men and their parents as he was to his own family.

Gannon knuckle-bumped Aiden. "Neither did the manager. However, when we introduced Trey Kennard and explained we were meeting you, the manager put us in the VIP section you reserved."

"Not a problem." Aiden extended his hand to Trey. "Aiden McKenna. Welcome."

"Trey Kennard. Thanks for letting us intrude, Congressman."

"Good to meet you, Trey, and this is—"

"Fiona Lizette Lowry, my architect." Trey was having a tough time catching his breath. He had to admit that never in his adult life had a woman's looks and demeanor literally taken his breath away. Still, Fiona Lizette Lowry did it the moment she walked into the club. Initially, the applause for the Congressman caught his attention. However, once Trey spotted her long, shapely legs in spiked heels and a sleeveless, maroon-colored, knee-length sheath, which left her shoulders bare, he couldn't look away.

It took Aiden and Fiona a while to advance through the crowded club, with many of their admirers stopping them along the way. Trey watched every step she took. Hailed by one group or another to shake hands or bust cheeks like a typical political candidate and power couple, they finally reached the raised platform where the VIP, rounded-back booth was located. When Fiona scaled the few steps up on the platform, her brothers stood and greeted her with a kiss or hug or some other form of affection. Trey noticed the Lowry brothers were equally affectionate with their parents before leaving the family compound and with Aiden McKenna. Now that he was standing face-to-face with Fiona, he still couldn't catch his breath. Nevertheless, Trey locked his eyes onto Fiona and had never strayed from her even to shake McKenna's hand.

Fiona smiled. "Hello, Trey. If I had known you were coming, I would have baked a cake."

"You cook?"

"Not a lick." Fiona grinned. She embraced him instead of shaking his hand. "Have a seat." She slid into the circular booth. Aiden secured her possessively into the crook of his side and then spread his arms out on the back of the seat cushion.

That was when Trey realized everyone was staring at him after they all took their seats. Awkwardly, he sat, still unable to stop looking at Fiona. Even in the dim, ambient club light, he could map her features with his eyes closed. Someone should have forewarned him, given that her six stair-step brothers were handsome men, like young Barack Obamas, and all looked very much alike. They were a cross between their interracial parents. The family resemblance was striking between the seven siblings, a blend of their Irish and African American ancestries.

"Seriously, Trey, did you come to Maryland to see me?"

"I did, yes. Your father brought the scale model of the house up to my office this morning. However, the model for the barn studio was damaged in transit. My father was already planning to come for the weekend and your mother's birthday party. So, I came along, too. We had dinner with your family."

"Ah, that must be why Mama was blowing up my cell phone. I thought she was trying to corral me into going shopping with her."

"That, too," Paul added dryly, "but primarily, she was trying to let you know Trey was coming to see the scale model of the barn studio."

Fiona turned her golden-brown-colored eyes on Trey. "Did you see it?"

His throat was beginning to unclog. "Your father showed it to me. I'm impressed. When would you have time to talk about the project?"

She turned her head and smiled up at Aiden over her left shoulder.

His groan was audible. "Okay. Okay. You've done your duty and paid your dues by pulling off a spectacular event today. Still, you don't have to be so happy about missing out on the political festivities tomorrow."

She turned back toward Trey. "Looks like my schedule for tomorrow just freed up. Now, if you can manage to keep my mama from getting her hands on me to go shopping, we'll have all day. After breakfast, we'll go out to the site. I haven't completed my take on the landscaping yet, but if AJ has time, maybe he can accompany us."

"AJ?" Trey asked.

"Alroy Junior. Yes, I've got time in the morning, but I'll have to drive. I've got other appointments in the afternoon, so I can't stay long."

Trey's brows rose in surprise. "You're the landscape architect?"

"Yep. You see, Trey, sitting at this table, you have all of the services needed to put you into your completed, new, custom, Lowry-built home and workspace. Fiona Lizette designs and engineers. Paul and Peter handle the carpentry work, including any metalwork. Flynn is our electrical designer and engineer. Gannon creates the plans for the plumbing and HVAC systems. Gavin handles finish work, like the wallboards, plastering, painting, and staining. Dad is the general contractor and we're his subcontractors for most of his projects. We each have our own businesses and crews, so we take on other projects and clients independently, particularly for our cousin, JaiHonnah Hawkins Baylor, and her husband, developer, J. Roderick Baylor."

"JRock?"

Gannon smiled at Trey. "You follow basketball?"

"With a passion, but who wouldn't know JRock? He's up there with the great icons of the sports industry like Derrick Jackson, Chuck Montgomery, and Gregory Alexander."

AJ nodded. "You'll get no argument from any of us. When JRock left basketball, he started a property development company. That's how he met our cousin, JaiHonnah Reise Hawkins. She's also an architect with solid credentials in architecture and civil and structural engineering. She consults on projects with us from time to time. We do the same for her and JRock when they're up against deadlines and need our help."

"I know. I tried for months to get on JaiHonnah's schedule with no luck. That's when my dad mentioned he had an old friend, your father, in the business in this area. I didn't know you were related to JaiHonnah Hawkins Baylor." Trey snapped his fingers as something occurred to him. *Whoa, wait!* Didn't JaiHonnah place second in the Miss America pageant years ago?"

Peter inclined his head. "First runner up, yes. When she was in her sophomore year in college at Spelman, but how did you know that?"

"I was one of the talent judges back then while I was still in grad school. I scored the music for a couple of movies and worked with the incredible Quincy Jones on a few albums. So, a friend of a friend of a friend—you know how that goes—got me in as a talent judge. I remembered your cousin's name because it is so unique. JaiHonnah. She's Indigenous American, isn't she?"

Paul smiled. "Half. Her mother was Navajo and her maternal grandmother, Kiavi Littlefeather, is a full-blooded Indigenous American. She still lives on the reservation near Ship Rock, New Mexico. She's a famous novelist who writes children's literature. Our uncle, Jake Hawkins, is our mother's only sibling. His first wife, Skai Littlefeather, was a nurse and our mother's inspiration to go into nursing as a career. Mom says that although Skai was her sister-in-law, she was more like a big sister. Mom is still a home health care nurse now. She travels around the county to check on patients who are unable to come into the county hospital. That's mom's way of honoring Aunt Skai, who used to do the same thing in rural Texas. Unfortunately, Aunt Skai died of breast cancer when JaiHonnah was still in school."

"Jake Hawkins is BlackHawk Global, a multibillion-dollar conglomerate, right?"

AJ nodded. "Yes, but he's currently an ambassador to the Republic of Seychelles in Africa, so he doesn't exercise control of his corporate interests."

"He recently married, didn't he?"

Flynn nodded. "He married JRock's sister, Kelley Baylor, a few years ago."

"He's got a couple of sons, too, I think."

Gavin nodded. "Jacob Junior and Adam."

"I've heard about Adam Hawkins. He's a Formula One race car driver."

The brothers laughed, and Gannon offered, "Sometimes. Our cousin is also an executive with BlackHawk Global. He's responsible for the philanthropic arm—the BlackHawk Foundation. Roderick and JaiHonnah are the co-directors of BlackHawk under their JR Baylor Holding company, the parent of BlackHawk. Jacob Junior is the president and Adam serves as vice president and the chairman of BlackHawk's foundation. You're well informed, Trey."

"I read a lot." What he didn't mention was that he had an eidetic or photographic memory. Once he saw, read, or heard something, he had total recall ability and couldn't forget it. It was an extremely rare capability and gift, and, thus, was a secret he and his father held tightly closed. The military-industrial complex or nefarious companies exploited people with his ability, sometimes without their consent. His father was in the military all his life, constituting the fourth generation of Army Rangers in his family, and knew the dangers of the revelation of Trey's secret.

Still, this eidetic capability immensely helped Trey when it came to his musical endeavors. He could play many musical instruments with perfection and recall every note in complicated compositions. Putting together scores of tunes challenged him with so many types of melodies constantly running through his head. He routinely scored songs for children's television shows. There was nothing he enjoyed more than watching a test market of little people respond to his tunes. They would get up on their short legs and bounce to his music with big smiles. It made him laugh, too. That partly was why he was looking forward to scoring more classical ballets like *Goodwill*. The performers and production would always feature children from Linda Lewis's New York School of Dance.

"Then you may have read about LaiLoni Skai."

Peter's statement brought Trey back from his musings. "Also known as Dakota Sinclair. It's a fascinating story and big news when an industrialist of your uncle's stature and background discovers his long, lost daughter after more than thirty years."

Peter nodded in agreement. "Yes, it was. LaiLoni Skai was kidnapped at birth from a medical clinic in Texas by a human trafficking ring. She grew up in an orphanage in North Dakota, not knowing anything about her family or heritage. LaiLoni and JaiHonnah were actually at Spelman College at the same time. LaiLoni was a senior who was given the name Dakota Sinclair by the orphanage personnel. JaiHonnah was a freshman. They were friendly toward each other even back then, but JaiHonnah didn't recognize the similarity to their mother. Years later, Uncle Jake spotted the resemblance to his deceased wife right away in a receiving line at his embassy in the Republic of Seychelles, Africa."

Trey nodded, intrigued. "That is quite a serendipitous story. As I understand it, LaiLoni Skai was known as Dakota Sinclair Chandler back then and was a part of the vice president's wife's entourage visiting African countries. I haven't read anything about her recently."

Gannon picked up the story. "She uses her birth name, LaiLoni Skai, now that she's married to Ambassador Jefferson Logan. They live in Summer County, South Carolina. Jefferson took over as dean of a prep school there. He and LaiLoni are busy raising their two energetic daughters, two girls they adopted, and the three sons the ambassador has from his first marriage."

"Yes, now I remember. Ambassador Logan was once married to the heiress to the Montrose family fortune who died tragically."

Paul laughed. "You're correct. You do read a lot."

Trey laughed, too. "You have no idea."

Trey shook hands in parting with the musical genius, Kem, and his band members. He enjoyed hearing them perform in the intimate club setting and talking with them after their set. Trey had some fresh ideas about several of Kemistry's ballads, particularly "When Love Calls," he wanted to work into one of the movies he would be scoring. Fiona Lizette inspired thoughts of new music he was itching to write and another movie score he contracted to do for Constantina "Tina" Justice Collins' Sweet Justice Productions. Tina and her husband, industrialist Nicholas "Nico" Collins, and their new addition, a bouncing baby boy, invited him to visit their winter retreat in a remote area on the Argentina coastline. They gave him a six-month window of opportunity to come and discuss the movie scheduled for production the following year. Trey felt he had enough material just by spending time with Fiona Lizette and her family to use as the inspiration for a new CD.

This impromptu trip was shaping up to be beneficial on several unexpected levels. *It is particularly true,* Trey thought, *when I can get an eyeful of the beautiful architect and engineer.*

Chapter 4

"Why don't we get married?"

In the act of getting out of her warm, comfortable bed, after having mind-bending sex, Fiona stopped and stared a moment into Aiden's dark-blue eyes, stumped. "Why, Aiden? We love each other and we have great sex together, but we're not *in love* with each other, are we?"

That she had to ask stung, but he wouldn't let on to her how he truly felt. He shrugged a naked shoulder because he had to keep this discussion light to feel her out on the topic of marriage. They hadn't discussed the possibilities before, but he felt that now was the time to introduce the topic of marriage before he got into the thick of stepped-up campaigning. "Yeah, I know we're still young, but we've been exclusive lovers since high school. We haven't been involved with anyone else. Everyone, your family and mine, expects us to take our relationship to the next level."

"When have we ever done what everyone else expects? It's true, you are my best friend and my first and only lover, but I don't want you to be my last." She rolled on top of him, digging her fingers through his lustrously thick, dark blond hair, kissing him briefly before rolling off him and out of bed.

He leaned up on his elbows to enjoy the view of her bare body. "I guess you don't want to be a politician's wife then?"

"Heck, no." She laughed while walking naked into her bathroom.

She wasn't particularly keen on being anyone's *wife*, Fiona ruminated, as she turned on the shower and stepped under the waterfall spray.

She and her future partner, whoever that person might turn out to be, would have to redefine the role of a wife before she would enter the bonds of holy matrimony. Even the word "bonds" gave her a low-grade headache. Marriage was high up there on the list of things she loathed, like shopping. Still, she had excellent role models from her parents. They, even now, acted like newlyweds, but theirs wasn't the typical love story. She had friends whose parents battled over the most asinine things in divorce settlements, rivaling world wars. So, if or when she did marry, she wanted to get it right the very first time.

Aiden was her best friend, confidant, and lover, but because of his chosen career trajectory in politics, he wasn't the man she wanted for the whole of her life. She didn't want to be the First Lady of Maryland or the First Lady of the United States. Yet, Fiona believed that was where Aiden's career could take him.

Marrying Aiden would be safe and predictable, but no challenge to keep her interested or intrigued. They would have the requisite two-point-five children and he would make an exceptional husband and father, but she would be bored out of her skull with his career requirements. A soccer mom, she was not and would never aspire to be. Moreover, she wondered whether she was mother material at all. Indeed, she couldn't come anywhere close to the type of woman her mother was. That fact saddened her because she believed that she wanted to have children at some point in her life. Her mother could be the poster image for what a mother should be, and as a grandmother, she would be phenomenal.

Because her thoughts were troublesome, she dismissed them and let the water wash away her unease. *In the meantime*, she thought, *for now*, as Aiden entered the shower and eased his arms around her from behind, *he nicely fills the bill as a creative lover.*

She liked the way his soapy hands caressed her breasts while kisses trailed up and down her neck. The feel of him hot and hard between her thighs never failed to elicit needful moans from her, which ignited him even more. She was aching with need when he turned her in his arms, hiked her up against the travertine marble wall, and drove into her while their mouths fused. Slow and steady, almost languidly, he moved inside her, talking all the time about how she made him feel. When his breathing quickened, so did hers until they reached nirvana together.

Trey sat at the long trestle table in the center of the expansive lanai with mechanical screens that were currently closed. The indoor/outdoor space included a large fireplace with sofas and chairs flanking the focal point. A flat-screen hung above the fireplace with high-end acoustical speakers strategically placed. The other end of the lanai held a kitchenette and a long quartz countertop bar with twelve tall chairs. Another flat-screen hung above the kitchenette space. He was having a second cup of excellent coffee and looking across the plaza which led to the cottages surrounding the Lowry's main house on three sides. The landscaping was extraordinary around the swimming pool and pebble-stone walkways that led into different little outdoor rooms, which constituted the entertainment spaces. He had never lived in a place like this where peace and tranquility reigned.

There were gazebos, water features, and a pool house within full view of the expansive, green-space yard. He liked the feel and comfort of the enclave, but he knew if he spent much more time there, he would enjoy it too much to get anything else accomplished. It was just that peaceful, yet it beckoned him to explore the little alcoves with unique outdoor furniture nestled among the flowers, shrubbery, and trees.

Then Fiona stepped out of what must have been her cottage, followed by Aiden McKenna. He playfully snatched the ball cap from her head before pulling her into his embrace for a quick farewell kiss. As Trey looked on, paying attention to whatever conversation Fiona and Aiden were having, Aiden then placed the cap on her head again in a reversed position before raising a hand to Trey in a friendly gesture. Aiden then said something else to Fiona that made her grin up at him before he stole another kiss and walked away to his parked car on the opposite side of Fiona's cottage.

Trey watched Fiona's loose-jointed saunter through one of the winding Pennsylvania bluestone and gravel paths toward the lanai. She was an absolute vision, with her tall, slim, but shapely body. She wore a nondescript white T-shirt and cut-off jeans that stopped just above her knees. Her dark-red hair under the inverted ball cap was ablaze in the bright sunlight in a damp braid down the center of her back. It ended in some type of twist-tie just above her finely sculptured butt. Last night at the club, he hadn't seen her hair color and, because she had it up in a topknot, he hadn't seen the length, but in the daylight, he could see it was long, a gorgeous shade of dark red, and thick.

She wore socks and hiking boots with loud blue and white polka-dot laces. His blood warmed at the sight of her.

"So, how are thee, Maxwell Bishop Kennard, the Third, this fine mornin'?" When she spoke, her merry Irish accent caressed his ears.

"Good and proper, Ms. Fiona Lizette. Good and proper. Top of the mornin' ta ya, lass." He, too, had a perfect, Irish brogue.

She gave him the pleasure of one of her quick grins before she proceeded to the kitchenette buffet to fill a plate with breakfast foods and to pour coffee and orange juice. Then she placed her tray on the table and sat across from him, blessed her food, and tucked into her healthy meal. She wasn't shy about the amount of food she consumed by any stretch of the imagination. He liked that about her, too. Looking at her full plate and side dishes, he sensed she had fueled up for a busy day, as if she may not have an opportunity for another meal until tomorrow. She seemed very much her own woman, self-possessed and very comfortable in her skin. Bare skin that, if he didn't miss his guess, bore no signs of underwear. Wearing no bra and the absence of a panty line—to his experienced eye for such things—alerted him she hadn't donned undergarments. She had a freshly scrubbed scent to her body and hair and body lotion that smelled of eucalyptus.

"So, where is everyone?" Fiona looked up at Trey as she ate. He was a feast for the eyes. In some ways, he reminded her of the actor, Augustus Prew, from one of her favorite shows back in the day, *Pure Genius*.

"They were all here an hour ago, and then when your mother started issuing orders, everyone seemed to disappear. Then your dad and mine got roped into taking your mother shopping at a farmers' market and craft village somewhere in Mitchell County."

"Ah, yes. Chase Brothers. My cousin, JaiHonnah, designed it, and we did subcontract work for her and her husband. The Farmers' Market is on newly built docks on the Chesapeake Bay, entertainment pavilions, and crafts village, including a boat-building business, and it's not too far from here. . Fishers unload their daily catches there and customers can have their meals cooked on-site at the Farmers' Market along with fresh steamed vegetables. It's an inspiring place with condos, villas, and townhomes with impressive water views. They were built primarily with shipping containers. It's a new, very walkable community, unique in every way. I enjoy going to lounge there to see the sights and hear the sounds. There is paddle boating in the summer and ice skating on their human-made lake in the winter. I pick up interesting pieces of handmade crafts for the homes I build or remodel, stage, and flip. My parents love it there, too, so I bet they'll eat at the Farmers' Market and be in the village for hours just seeing the sights. It's what passes for an interesting entertainment area short of driving to Annapolis, Baltimore, or Washington, DC."

Trey laughed. "I kept a low profile and was spared the experience, but I'd like to see it when I have more time. AJ said to tell you he would meet us at the site no later than noon, but probably sooner."

"That'll work." She polished off the plate of food and rose to get a second helping from the breakfast bar. "I'll text him and let him know when we leave here." She poured more coffee into his cup and hers and then cast an appreciative eye on him as she resumed her seat. "You look well-rested this morning."

"How could I not? I'm sitting here and marveling at how restful but still full of life this place is. There are beautiful butterflies in the gardens, and the birds are singing sweet sounds. I had visions of floating in your swimming pool in the open air. Back in New York, I live in a high-rise condo above my offices and studios. The building has great amenities, including a fully equipped gym, an Olympic-sized swimming pool, and restaurants. I have a view of the Hudson River and Central Park, but I don't make time to enjoy any of it. Here, I can't escape it. I'm forced to take time to be quiet and relax and energize simultaneously."

Fiona nodded and pointed her fork at him. "That's exactly right. That's why none of the Lowry clan has moved away. My father's siblings are scattered throughout Bay County. At day's end, we like to gather for dinner, conversation, games, a movie with popcorn, beer, or whatever. We have impromptu parties and invite a bunch of people over to join us. Mom loves to cook and, although she doesn't say it, I know she enjoys having us, our extended family, and her friends gather around her table to eat meals she prepares."

"She made breakfast for all of us this morning. She does this all by herself every day?"

Fiona nodded. "All of our lives, she's made sure we had a good breakfast before we left her house every day. Dinner is served promptly at six, and you dare not be late." She laughed. "Except, sometimes, Dad will take mom into Annapolis, or Baltimore, Maryland, or even Washington, DC, to stay at a nice five-star hotel and order room service. They still have a date night, at least twice a week, just the two of them. Otherwise, yes, mom does it all.

"Tomorrow is her birthday and we are having a houseful of guests, but she insists on doing all of the cooking. We are her dogsbodies, though. Dad has a company to come and clean the house from top to bottom as a gift for Mom. Nevertheless, she'll have us all up early and fed in preparation for her birthday party tomorrow afternoon, featuring authentic Louisiana cuisine. That will include," she pulled up the menu information on her iPad, "Étouffée, Creole onion soup, oyster soup, and tomato and okra gumbo. A tossed green salad and then the *pièce de résistance*: Trout Amandine, Chicken Esplanade, Blackened Redfish with crab meat, Crabs Béarnaise, shrimp creole with parsley rice and shrimp Scarlett with Andouille, chicken la zone, trout Kottwitz, Tournedos Rhys with Béarnaise and Marchand de Vin sauces and bouquetière vegetables.

"My personal favorites for desserts are Bananas Foster, Crepes Fitzgerald and Bridget, bread pudding, chocolate pecan pie, lemon curd tartlet, and cheesecake with fresh strawberry and raspberry sauce toppings. Pouilly-Fuisse and Louis Jadot will accompany each course. She got the menu from one of Angelique's cookbooks. It's one of the books I gave to her for Christmas last year. It's a menu created by one of Angelique's chefs, Pietro Alehandro. He's the principal chef of Angelique's New York City restaurant, and he's from New Orleans. Mom will have the Farmers' Market deliver everything fresh off the boat tomorrow.

"So, Maxwell Bishop Kennard, the Third, enjoy the quiet for as long as you can. By this time tomorrow, you'll probably be knee-deep in peeling potatoes or chopping onions and wishing you were back in your nice, sane condo in New York City. Chaos will rule in Chez Lowry."

His jaw had dropped at the beginning of her recitation of the fabulous specialty items on the menu. "*Laissez les bon temps rouler.*" His voice was as perfect in the French Creole accent as it had been with the Irish brogue.

She delighted and intrigued him with a raised eyebrow, a quick grin. "*Et trois.*"

They continued companionably chatting until she finished her meal and then took her dishes to the kitchenette, where the house cleaning crew was already beginning their work.

Trey and Fiona headed back toward her cottage and out to a parking pad where her dusty Jeep sat in desperate need of a good wash.

Trey appreciated the landscape before he entered the car. "I know Angelique very well. I live in the same building where she has a *pied-à-terre*. I usually eat my evening meal in the kitchen of her restaurant. It's in the same building where I live."

"I've eaten there, too." Fiona started her Jeep. Shortly they were amiably chatting while underway to his property, less than half an hour away, along back roads that saw little, if any, traffic. When they arrived, she steered her Jeep through an open gate, a narrow, nearly invisible black-topped path about a half-mile inland, right up to what looked like the middle of a grassy, overgrown site with an incredible view of the Chesapeake Bay a short distance away. Getting out of the car, they walked toward the sandy shore at the water's edge with its unobstructed view of the Bay.

Everything from big tankers and merchant vessels to small rowboats and Jet Skis shared the vast watery expanse. People were water skiing, while others were wind sailing with huge kites. Beautiful sailboats were skimming across the water, too. Fiona pointed out a Chase Brothers' J-Class sailing yacht. She was itching to go sailing but couldn't make the time considering all the projects she had underway. She even stepped in to help her cousin, JaiHonnah, when clients were geographically nearer to her on the eastern shore than to JaiHonnah.

Trey stood silently in awe of the beauty of nature. Nothing intruded on his view of the waterway for what looked like a mile in either direction. The Bay was so broad that the other shore was not easily visible to the naked eye.

Trey took a deep breath and closed his eyes, feeling the pleasure as he slowly exhaled. The frisky breeze blew across his face and body. He could imagine being on a three-mast yacht out in the bay with his sails full-blown and playing hide-and-go-seek with these gusts of wind. *Nirvana*, he thought. *This is precisely the type of atmosphere I've been searching for.* It would be a transcendental element for his state of mind, where he could work and play at his own choosing, unencumbered by others' demands on him. It would be the type of languid life he couldn't have found on Martha's Vineyard or in The Hamptons or the other adult playgrounds of the northeast. He could visualize that lifestyle here. To think he bought this land sight unseen simply based on a description in a real estate magazine?

With his career skyrocketing, he, like others, could have moved to the Left Coast, but he didn't want to get ensnared in the glitz and glitter of La La Land. He was a Right Coast kind of guy. He liked being able to be at 42nd Street and Broadway in a matter of minutes to join the theater crowds. Having a late dinner at some of the best restaurants within walking distance of his home and office was a plus.

His favorite restaurant, Angelique's Place, was right downstairs on the street level of his residence. The owner, Angelique Menendez-Gaza Alexander, a high-fashion model, and actress who became a Le Cordon Bleu-certified chef, was among his good friends. He became a dedicated patron the moment she opened the restaurant's doors. Angelique also owned the bar, The Run Way, adjacent to the restaurant, and hired musicians he recommended to her as entertainers. Trey enjoyed the ambiance she created so much that he once considered dating her. However, because she was very young and his intimate relationships typically were short-term, he decided against risking their friendship. When Angelique married basketball star, Gregory Alexander, who became a Wall Street tycoon, Trey was happy for her. Angelique still welcomed him into her establishments, even when she was full to overflowing. She would always accommodate him in her kitchen, at the staff tables, or in newly established private dining rooms.

Nevertheless, he felt maybe even that lifestyle might pale compared to what he found here on Maryland's eastern shore. He could easily make this his home base and use his New York facilities only when necessary. Here, just from the view of the natural scenery alone, he could create music that inspired the mind and soothed the soul.

Trey turned around to look at the building site where Fiona's Jeep and AJ's truck were parked. Now he could imagine the gardens as AJ described them. A red hone chestnut that only stood about ten inches tall would add a shocking red cluster to the otherwise hay-colored grasses. Serviceberry, a white flowering bush, bloomed in May. It had red berries and blackberries that ripened in July and attracted a colorful array of birds. Dogwoods, Magnolias, and something called a Golden Raintree, with large yellow panicles, bloomed in July and August. It would produce a large cluster of green Chinese lantern-like pods. He hadn't thought much about the landscaping, but as AJ continued to talk and show him pictures of the gardens as planned, Trey resolved he would have to study all of this to know what suited for pops of color in year-round foliage.

Then, as he looked up, he could see it: the glass house as it appeared on the scale model, with soaring peaks and angles geared to catch the sun as the seasons changed. It would appear to be floating above the tall, sweet grass and bulrush, waving and swaying in the energetic Bay breezes. The gardens would appear to be in bloom year-round, providing a kaleidoscope of colors. He could almost set music to what AJ described and he envisioned.

Fiona noticed the shift in the angles and planes of Trey's handsome face and read the excitement building in his eyes. "You see it now, don't you?"

Trey thoughtfully nodded. "Yes. In fact, I wonder whether I can shift my residence to Maryland and be here most of the year instead of in New York."

"If you mean as far as this becoming your primary residence, from a practical standpoint, the answer is yes. This would be a year-round home, not just a summer season retreat."

"It's what I'm thinking. We need to add apartments or dormitory space complete with a kitchen and other amenities to the barn to accommodate people I would need to work with for extended periods of time. Staff, too. I'll need a full-time cook and local household cleaning staff."

"Were I you, I would use this place as a sanctuary. A place to rest and relax; not work, but if you must, I can make it happen."

iPad in hand, Fiona pulled up the barn plan and began to sketch. In moments, she had added wings to the opposite side of the big red barn that was not within view of the glass house, but it would have a relaxing Bay view as well. She also planned to utilize outbuildings as guest quarters with an indoor/outdoor pool for his guests. Fiona handed her quickly-drafted work to Trey. "Something like this?"

For humming moments, Trey just stared before he nodded in amazement. "Exactly like that. How quickly can I have a scale model?"

"This may take me all of, oh, I don't know, maybe an hour once we get back to my cottage." She grinned at him. "I've sent the plan to my home office already. So the parts should be waiting for us when we get back. Then, with the magic of my glue gun, we should see the shape of things."

"Unreal." His breath backed up in his chest when Fiona Lizette smiled.

She stuck her left arm through his right one and proceeded to escort him around the site, pointing out the big, Live Oak trees she had already tagged for AJ to remove and send to the McKenna Mill and the saplings she would use for fragrant pine-scented mulch. She marked a few others with AJ's advice she would need to use for the additional timber-frame dormitory space and guest cabins.

Trey listened closely to her and AJ's running commentary about aspects of the revised plan. However, even with his superior recall abilities, he would be hard-pressed to repeat what they said. So instead, he just enjoyed listening to them feed off each other and hearing Fiona's voice.

A few hours later, AJ left before noon with a suggestion for Trey to come by his nursery to see the plants he had in mind. Then Trey and Fiona sat on the hood of her Jeep, just taking in the peace and tranquility of the site. When he looked off to his right, through the field of tall grasses and trees, he saw the horses grazing while younger colts played at the water's edge. Trey was utterly mesmerized by the sight of the horses in the fields. They remained in silent appreciation before making their way to AJ's nursery and then back to the Lowry compound.

Chapter 5

"Pardon me a moment, please, Trey. I've been waiting for this call." Fiona rose from her computer, where she and Trey were working on a CAD program, refining aspects of the floor plan for the new dormitory addition and other cabins. "Hi, Jai. Tell me something good," she teasingly begged.

JaiHonnah Hawkins Baylor, Fiona's first cousin, laughed. "Hi, Fiona. Mission accomplished. I spoke with Vivian, and she accepted the invitation to come with her family to Aunt Mavis' birthday party tomorrow. However, she is a little concerned about bringing her entire family because it would strain the menu."

"Tell her not to worry. Mama makes more than enough food to feed a starving army. I'll make sure to alert the people setting up the tables, chairs, and dishes. I am so happy, Jai. Mama is going to freak. This surprise visit is going to be such a treat for her. My mother friends Vivian Alexander Montgomery on CompuCorrect's social media site, Face-to-Face, watches her on television, and reads everything she writes. For Mama, this surprise will be right up there with meeting the President of the United States when Uncle Jake was named an ambassador. Thanks for making this happen, Jai."

"You're welcome, Fiona. I'm happy to do this for Aunt Mavis. However, I admit this wasn't hard. As you know, Vivian and I were roommates in college at Spelman, and she's still one of my best friends. We get together as often as possible, at least a couple of times a month for lunch and other occasions. Vivian and her husband, Chuck, think this will be an absolute pleasure for them, too. Vivian and my father have been good friends since she and I were roommates, but she's never met Aunt Mavis. I think you're going to like Vivian, her husband, and all their children.

"As I mentioned, Vivian already knows my dad very well, and she's looking forward to seeing him and Kelley. He taught Vivian how to play chess, and they've been playing long-distance since Viv and I were in college. In addition, Vivian used to be Roderick's attorney and worked closely with Kelley when she was a part of Roderick's company."

"Really? That's cool. However, Vivian doesn't look like she's old enough to have a lot of children."

JaiHonnah laughed. "You're right. Vivian's not that old. She and her first husband, Derrick Jackson, a noted pediatrician and pediatric surgeon, adopted orphans with medical challenges. They had one biological child together before Derrick died suddenly of a heart attack. Vivian and I are about the same age, and she had just passed the bar exam the year they married. After Derrick's death, Vivian inherited the lion's share of his medical practice and his entire estate, which was massive. She continued to adopt abandoned children with health issues. Then, Vivian and Chuck Montgomery married five years after Derrick died and, although they have several biological children, they still adopt orphaned, medically challenged children. Chuck is an Emergency Room doctor. He and several other doctors own and operate Physicians' Hospital in a rural county outside of DC in Maryland. They've lost some of the children they adopted who couldn't be saved, but they aren't giving up. Some of their children are off to college, so not everyone is still living at home on their farm."

Fiona snapped her fingers. "I remember now. You and I worked on their daughter, Linda's, library building conversion into a residence and dance studio in New York City five or six years ago. Still, I never met Linda's parents or siblings at the gala opening of the school. They must be very selfless people to open their home to abandoned children in need of medical attention."

"They are, but you'll get to meet them and their children tomorrow. Unfortunately, Linda and her husband, Will Hamilton, are out of the country visiting her biological half-brother, Bradley, in Manchester, England, so she won't be able to attend."

"I'm looking forward to meeting the rest of them. Thanks again, Jai, for arranging this."

"You're welcome, Fiona. I'll see you tomorrow."

After the call ended, Trey noticed Fiona sat for a moment, looking into near space, wearing a Mona Lisa smile. "You look pretty satisfied about something."

She looked up into his pretty green eyes and beamed. "I am, yes. My cousin, JaiHonnah, has arranged for Supreme Court Justice Vivian Alexander Montgomery, her husband, Doctor Charles Montgomery, and their children to come to Mama's birthday party. Mama is a huge fan of Justice Alexander Montgomery."

Trey snorted a laugh. "Are you kidding? Who isn't a big fan of hers? I was also a fan of her late-husband, Derrick 'Dunk and Jam' Jackson, and her current husband, Charles 'Chucky P' Montgomery. Derrick and Chuck were best friends from puberty. Actually, from what I've read, Derrick taught Chuck how to play basketball. They both had stellar, professional careers in the NBA, even winning championships and gold medals during the Olympic Games. Then they both left the game at the top of their careers to go into medicine. They were multi-billionaires when Derrick died in his mid-thirties. Judge Alexander Montgomery was, I think, in her early twenties when they married, and less than a year later, Derrick died. About five years after Derrick's death, Vivian married Chuck Montgomery.

"Just before Derrick died, she, and some of her law school friends, formed what is now one of the most prestigious, young law firms in the country: Alexander, Carter, Chandler, Charles, Lightfoot, and Towson, PA. I'm a client of theirs. Judge Alexander Montgomery was appointed to the DC Circuit Court of Appeals by the President, and now she has been appointed to the US Supreme Court. She is the youngest person ever to be appointed to the high court. What's even more incredible is that Vivian had little to no opposition from members of the United States Senate or public interest groups. She worked on Capitol Hill while she was in law school and after she graduated. So, Vivian was no stranger to the members of the Senate Judiciary Committee. Of course, some detractors could have held up her appointment because of her extraordinary wealth and property. Still, Vivian has lived such an exemplary life no one could raise any serious opposition other than the fact she's so young."

"Have you met her?"

"I haven't, no. However, my legal counsel at the firm is one of the founding partners, Bill Chandler."

"The actor and supermodel, Chandler?"

Trey chuckled. "Yes, he practices sports and entertainment law, too. Bill also sometimes accepts a role in a movie and produces them. In addition to modeling, he owns the magazines Risqué and Stallion. You've probably seen commercial ads for his products on television and in magazines. I've worked with him on several projects since I got into the music business back in grad school. Like me, he's a native New Yorker, though he spends most of his time in Washington, DC, and traveling abroad. So that's where we met. I was in Paris during Fashion Week when he was premiering his next season's clothing line under the Stallion label. I was brought in to score the music for one of the designers, Carlos Ortega.

"Chandler is stepping into the role of Executive Producer for a movie featuring one of his protégés, Miguel Menendez-Gaza. He's asked me to score the movie and write all the songs. Miguel's sister, Angelique, will also be in the movie. As you probably know, in addition to being a great chef, she's a high-fashion model and actress, too."

"Yes, I know about Angelique's career, but I didn't know about Bill Chandler and Miguel Menendez-Gaza. Wow! What a hot combination. We just saw Miguel in the new movie, Up Top. He should get an Academy Award for his performance, and he's only a kid."

"He's an incredible talent for a person his age. I've been working with him to develop his vocal ability, too. In addition, he plays the violin and a guitar. His home base is Washington, DC, so it should be an easy commute to work with him."

"Isn't he doing that remake of *New York Undercover*?"

"He is, yes, but when he's on hiatus, he's either in school at UPenn or at home in DC."

"He certainly has the natural charisma to pull off multiple careers."

"If we can get my new studios up and ready, I'll be working with him here."

"Then, if I can't convince you not to work while you're here, let's not waste any more time." She grinned. Just then, her phone rang again with a call from her brother, Gannon, about a framing change that needed her approval to allow for moving a wall. The client wanted the change, but it caused a problem with the plumbing and air conditioning runs.

While he waited, Trey turned and looked out of Fiona's expansive front windows at the plaza he had admired that morning from her parents' lanai. It was a beautiful setting from any angle.

He watched people transform the space to resemble a typical New Orleans courtyard, with accent lighting and staging no less meticulous than any movie set. A long, wide table would hold a feast in a screened-in area, and ten round tables of ten situated around two long buffets. A short man with a clipboard was orchestrating the placement of every piece of furniture. The set manager, Trey surmised.

Then Peter and Paul raced out of what must have been their cottage and dove into the pool, splashing water everywhere, much to the consternation of the manager. It made Trey smile to see Fiona's brothers racing each other in the warm afternoon sun. It looked like they were having fun, reminiscent of his childhood.

He didn't have siblings, but his parents ensured he constantly interacted with other children his age. Of course, it helped some when it was just his mom and him to be company for each other. His dad was often away for long deployments, fulfilling his military duty. Then, after his mom died, he was off to a private military boarding school in Connecticut until he went to college. He made one friend there, Daniel Connor, who was, coincidentally, from Mitchell County, on the eastern shore of Maryland, too, but he had lost touch with him many years ago.

Trey and his dad kept in touch, but it was not the kind of closeness he would have wanted or what he saw openly displayed between Al Lowry, his sons, and Fiona Lizette. Al and his boys were not just parent and children. They were a team and a loving one at that. It was clear they adored their mother, but their dad seemed to be equally dear to them.

He felt a little sad as he and his father lost so many years of being in each other's lives. They were still the same people they had been, but in fits and starts. They were now trying to make up for the lost time.

"So, what do you think?" Fiona asked as she resumed her position at the computer. She rotated the barn image on a large wall monitor that provided more detail. She manipulated the computer program to make it appear they were walking through finished, furnished, and decorated spaces.

Trey left his musings to study the revised floor plan for the barn studio and additional building structures. "I think they're perfect and that you're a genius. What's next?"

"I have to submit the revised plans to my brothers for review and approval so they can order supplies and material and schedule delivery. Then it goes to my dad. We will all sit down with him to iron out any details that need to be addressed. Once all of us have signed off on the final plan, my dad will handle the construction schedule and the process through the county for licenses and permits."

"What's the construction schedule?"

"If we have no delays with purchasing goods, labor, and building materials, we should have you in your home before Christmas. Dad is the best source on that aspect of the project, but he's eager to start with getting the underground utilities into place while the weather is still good. The only problem may be that we have a number of projects already underway or scheduled to launch. That means all of our crews will be stretched to the limit."

"You won't just leave the project, will you?"

"Oh, no. I'll be shepherding this from start to finish. Fortunately, we live in a virtual reality world where I don't have to be on-site to address any issues which may arise. However, I don't anticipate any problems with the construction. My other projects are in various stages of completion, but Dad has made it clear your project is to get our immediate and undivided attention."

"I appreciate that and the fact you changed your schedule with Aiden to work with me today."

"You're welcome, but frankly, I don't enjoy political campaigns. So, you actually saved me from having to chit and chat with Aiden's supporters today."

"You'll probably have to do more of that as Aiden's wife. He's a very popular political figure. I remember seeing him on various talk shows. He'll go far in his career. You must be very happy together."

She hooted a laugh. "If you're angling to determine the extent of my relationship with Aiden, just ask."

"Subtle, I'm not."

"Coy, I'm not. Aiden and I have been buddies since we were babies. His dad owns the McKenna Mill and Lumber Yard. We use them to mill trees we clear during construction and buy many of our building supplies and materials from them. In addition to the mill, Kathleen McKenna, Aiden's mother, manages their farm, which is also a bed-and-breakfast. She trains horses and teaches horseback riding. If you were just visiting the area as a tourist, I would have highly recommended that you stay at the McKenna Bed and Breakfast. It's a lovely place. Mrs. McKenna taught all the Lowry children to ride. Our families are also close friends back three or four generations, and the McKennas want me to bear Aiden's offspring. So they're questioning why I'm not already his wife. Also, Al Junior dates one of Aiden's sisters, Robinetta McKenna. That's an indication of how close our families are."

"The photojournalist Robinetta McKenna?"

"Yes." She seemed somewhat surprised at his knowledge.

Sometimes he chastised himself. He should just claim no knowledge of certain things and people, but when gazing at Fiona Lizette, he was hard-pressed to hold anything back from her. "How does that work with her always traveling?"

She listlessly shrugged. "AJ accepts commissions to design gardens for domestic and foreign clients. Usually, based on photos Robinetta, we call her Robin, takes during her travels. So many of the places she's been are places I've dreamed of going."

"You successfully sidestepped my question. Are you and Aiden—"

"We're friends with benefits. What about you?"

"Just benefits from time to time. No one special."

She laughed at his honesty and sent warmth coursing through his blood. "You are certainly direct."

"I have to be. There are no hidden agendas with me. I find you very intriguing, attractive, and engaging. I like your spirit, too." He was on the verge of asking her to go on tour with him on Monday, but didn't want to insult or embarrass her. He liked that she was quick and had no filters, but said exactly what was on her mind. No push, no pull, no bull, or other hidden agendas.

Fiona smiled, but wasn't ready to admit she found him interesting, too. After all, there was Aiden to consider. At a minimum, Aiden deserved to know another man had sparked her interest. For the time being, she would keep her own counsel. Trey Kennard would only be in her space for another day before he flew off to Europe. She had never traveled extensively and wished she could stow away on his flight. However, reality had set in. As interested as she was, she may not see Trey Kennard, with the beautiful green eyes, for another three to six months. Even then, he may have found a woman to spend time with during his travels.

By then, Aiden's campaign would be over, and, hopefully, he would have won the election in November. If so, he would be moving permanently to Baltimore City. He already had a waterfront townhouse in Annapolis, where he lived in the center of his Congressional district. Before becoming a US Congressional Representative, he was first elected to the Maryland State Senate in a tight race, replacing Julius Mitchell, Senior.

However, they found a riverfront condo in Baltimore's Inner Harbor within walking distance of popular places in the city to eat and shop. It even had a heliport on the roof. That would be convenient for Aiden to travel around the state as his duties would require. He had a panoramic view of the Patapsco River and the city skyline. The high-rise had the ideal concierge service for a single man. When he won the election, and she was sure, given the poll results, that he could win, his office would be within easy walking distance of the condo, too. He wouldn't often expect her to be his plus-one, and since they cleared the air about their nonexistent life together going forward, their paths to remain friends without benefits would be clear.

Then, and only then, might she entertain the idea of getting to know Maxwell Bishop Kennard, the Third, a little better. Then, at least, they wouldn't have an architect-client relationship to contend with, and, for some periods of time, he would be taking up residence in her neck of the woods, so to speak.

Chapter 6

Trey stood among the early arrivals, sampling an excellent glass of wine, finger foods, and chatting with Paul, AJ, and Robinetta McKenna. He had been introduced to Robinetta and Aiden's parents, Wilhelm and Kathleen O'Donnell McKenna. The day couldn't be more glorious for this afternoon event in the tented, transformed courtyard. Two long rows of buffet tables anchored two sides of the area, while ten round tables of ten circled the dance floor. There were little high-top tables tucked into nooks and crannies throughout the garden, where guests cheerfully gravitated from one group to another.

Jumpy zydeco filtering through hidden speakers had people snapping fingers to the beat while they mingled. A few had already taken to the dance floor and were rocking as if at Mardi Gras. Trey found the music intoxicating and picked up one of the group's business cards and brochures. He didn't have a project in mind where he could use this type of music, yet he'd keep up with their progress, maybe bring them into his studio to lay down some tracks.

Max Kennard appeared at his son's side. "Quite a gathering."

"Yes, it is," Trey agreed before he introduced his father to Robinetta McKenna. Then he and his father excused themselves to stroll the gardens.

"This is the life. This is the type of life I should have provided for you to grow up in. I just didn't know how to do this."

"My life wasn't so bad, Dad."

"You were shipped off to military school almost before you were out of diapers, son. That's no life for a child being away from home for so long, especially after we lost your mother. When I was younger than you,

I was sent to military school. Unlike me, you didn't even like the military life." On a windy sigh, he looked up and around at the Lowry offspring, except for Fiona Lizette, who had yet to make an appearance. "Having close family and friends around should have been a part of your early socialization."

"Stop beating yourself up, Dad. I didn't turn out so bad, did I? Besides, I have you and countless other military men and women to thank for keeping the rest of us safe to enjoy this type of life." He gestured with his wine glass at the beautiful surroundings. "You and my military ancestors put their lives on the line to save future generations."

"Thank you, son." Maxwell squeezed his son's bicep, noting the firmness. "Wow, you must have been working out."

"I have, and I should have mentioned to Fiona that I need an in-home gym." He scanned the grounds for a glimpse of her.

His father noticed. "She's out in front of the main house with her cousins, JaiHonnah and LaiLoni Skye, welcoming guests and waiting for Chuck and Vivian Alexander Montgomery to arrive with their family. Of course, they want the judge's arrival to be a complete surprise for Mavis."

"Oh, then that explains it. I wondered why Fiona wasn't out here yet."

"I noticed you seemed very taken with her."

Trey turned to his father and smiled. "I don't know, Dad, but I may have met my future bride."

A look of stunned surprise crossed the elder Maxwell's still handsome face. "Isn't she involved with the congressman?"

"She is, but not for long."

"Well, I have to admit her mother caught my attention almost exactly the same way years ago. However, from the beginning, she only had eyes for Al. I don't want you to experience the same disappointment I suffered. It caused me to rush headlong into a hasty marriage your grandparents arranged."

"Not to worry, Dad. I believe I know where I stand with Fiona and, more importantly for now, where Aiden McKenna stands with her. She admitted she doesn't fully grasp what I do and how I need my studio designed. She has also never traveled. So I'm going to ask her to go with me tomorrow."

Another stunned expression crossed his father's face. However, just then, there was a smattering of applause that grew in intensity as Alroy Lowry, Senior, squired his wife, Mavis, into the garden. They moved smoothly into a dance that showed they had danced together for many years. Trey and his father added their accolades to the handsome couple's flawless dance steps. Trey noted the absolute joy the gathered guests exhibited while the couple moved together. He also noted the wistful expression on his father's face. Obviously, his father had fallen hard for Mavis Hawkins Lowry and likely still carried a torch for her.

Then Fiona Lizette appeared out of the side garden, and Trey noted as his breath hitched. He took a mouthful of wine as his throat suddenly went dry from just gazing at her. Her sophisticated, yet earthy beauty was timeless in a simple, but elegant, strapless, sienna-colored tube-like sun gown. Her long hair wound like a rope around the top of her head, as if it were a crown, leaving her long neck clear. He was eager to place kisses there, just behind her ears to her collarbone and back again, to whisper his appreciation in her ear.

When Mavis squealed in delight at the sight of Chuck, Vivian, and their multicultural rainbow coalition of children, Fiona Lizette's face lit with such unadulterated love, joy, and pleasure, Trey felt it streak through his body from head to toe. Tears were in Mavis' eyes as the Supreme Court Justice embraced her. It was clear this was a very moving experience for all in attendance. Photographers and videographers were discreetly memorializing the occasion. Waitstaff circumnavigated the grounds, offering hot and cold hors d'oeuvres or red or white wines to the attendees. Servers distributed small, clever plate-sized clear trays that securely held a wine glass so guests could select an array of hors d'oeuvres from the trays and have a hand free to eat. The group of adolescents gravitated toward each other and formed their own cabal.

"Hello, again." Aiden offered his hand to Trey.

"Aiden, it's good to see you. May I present my father, Maxwell Bishop Kennard?"

"General Kennard. You probably don't remember me, but I'm on the US House of Representatives Select Committee, which oversees the military budget. I was in attendance when you testified on the issue of the need for more women in the upper ranks of the military. I believe your point was that the budget needed to be increased to allow the promotion of more women into command positions."

"Yes, I do remember you, Congressman. I believe you suggested that more of the senior members of the military should retire to make way for women and younger officers to advance. Fortunately, I believe Admiral Stacy Greene Alexander won the day for us before your committee. She suggested the military couldn't afford to see a mass exodus of seasoned officers; that too much institutional knowledge walking out the door would have a deleterious impact on national security and military readiness."

"The point was well taken by both of you. Were you aware the admiral is Judge Alexander Montgomery's sister-in-law?"

"I wasn't, no."

"The admiral is married to one of the justice's older brothers, five-star Air Force General and Astronaut Benjamin Alexander. He, the admiral, and their family are in the country for a few more weeks, and Fiona was able to convince them to attend Mavis' birthday party, too. I think you know them, don't you, Trey?"

Stunned and caught a little off guard, Trey looked directly into Aiden's eyes. "I, uh, do know Stacy and Benny," he acknowledged, but left it at that. It was a closely held secret that Benny and Stacy's four daughters constituted Ivy, one of the world's top ten music industry groups. Because their children were so young, and they and their parents were terrorist targets, Benny and Stacy permitted him to produce their albums only if he agreed to keep Ivy's identity secret. With the Alexanders' permission, his friend and talented vocalist, Matt Kennedy, brought Ivy to his attention with the proviso to never reveal the children's identities. If the young people did benefit appearances, they were always in costumes that hid their faces and camouflaged their bodies. He was to record them in Japan during his upcoming trip for the release of a new album.

Now Trey wondered how Aiden knew there was a connection between him and the Alexanders. This potential threat to the closely held secret caused red flags to raise in Trey's mind. He would have to notify his handler of the potential breach—immediately.

It took Fiona a while and a bit of maneuvering to extricate herself from her duties as co-host with her brothers for their mother's birthday bash. Her strategic part of the plan was to get Vivian and her family here as a surprise for her mother. Her brothers had other duties to perform and took on their roles, freeing her to mix and mingle with other guests.

She was extremely pleased both of her cousins, the sisters JaiHonnah and LaiLoni Skye, attended Spelman College with then-student Vivian Alexander. Though LaiLoni was a senior the year JaiHonnah and Vivian were freshmen, JaiHonnah and Vivian were roommates and friends with the then-senior known as Dakota Sinclair. She appreciated her cousins' efforts to get the Supreme Court Justice to the party on such short notice and to get Vivian's brother and sister-in-law, Benny and Stacy Alexander, to attend with their children as well. It was quite a coup to pull off, and her mother was beside herself with awe and joy. Arm-in-arm, her mother with Vivian, was introducing the judge and her husband to the other guests. Now Fiona felt she was free to relax a bit and enjoy the party at her leisure.

Earlier, she spotted Aiden chatting with Trey and his father. Then Aiden introduced his unmarried younger sisters to Trey, one of the record industry's top icons. Fiona Googled Trey Kennard just to get a better handle on who he was to enhance her plans for his home…or at least that was what she told herself to justify her heightened interest in him. Truth be told, she didn't need a dossier to convince her she wouldn't mind getting to know Trey better on a more personal level. He was eye candy of the most delicious type, with his cross between a youthful Robert Redford and Brad Pitt, good looks and English-Irish-Scottish ancestry. *He knows how to wear a suit of fashionable casual clothes, perfect for this event…to his best advantage, too,* she thought, as she watched him approach. However, beyond the minor surface qualities he possessed, she was fascinated with the way his mind worked. He was affable with a quick wit and a depth of knowledge that intrigued her.

Trey stood before Fiona, looking at her and inhaling her unique scent.

"Yes?" A corner of her wide, mobile mouth hitched up into a knowing grin.

"Uh, do you have a moment?"

"To do what?"

"I didn't mention I need an in-home gym."

"Yes, I presumed you would and a sauna, too. So I've included them in the below-ground level as a part of your in-home sports facility. I also included an exercise pool. If you recall the plan, the windows are high up on the walls and afford you natural light from all four directions. It's next to the space designated for a wine cellar and an in-home theater. You didn't notice?"

"I, uh, must have been distracted. You look absolutely amazing," Trey commented on a slow exhalation of breath.

Her grin broadened. "Do you need to go over the plan again before you leave in the morning?"

"I believe I would need to do anything to just look at you for a while longer."

She laughed at that and took his arm to stroll the garden cum courtyard. "I thought Aiden's sisters were enjoying your undivided attention."

"Were you watching?"

"Observing the flow of the party guests is a part of my party tasks."

"Good save." He smiled. "Still, it makes my day that you found time to 'observe.'"

"Aiden, at your three o'clock," she whispered.

He turned his back to Aiden's approach. "To be continued." Then, with one hand in his pocket, he leisurely strolled away.

Aiden watched Trey go as he approached Fiona. "Was it something I said?"

"I think we were discussing his exercise needs for his new home," she commented cryptically, still observing Trey's movements as he joined another cluster of guests.

Aiden turned from watching Trey's departure to look at Fiona. "I, uh, need you."

Surprised, she turned and looked up into Aiden's solemn but sincere face. "Aiden?" His simple statement caused her to pause with concern.

He shook his head. "Now that reality is setting in… Somehow, I never thought of my life without you in it, Fi. I guess I took it for granted we would always be a couple."

Sadness filled her eyes, he noted, so he shook off his disappointment and smiled at her while slinging a friendly arm around her bare shoulders. "For now, I need you to help with a potential donor whose ten-year-old son wants a custom-made tree house. The boy saw the one you designed and had built for one of his classmates. The kid now wants you to design one twice as big for him. If I could get you interested in the project, then the parents are willing to contribute handsomely to my campaign."

She laughed. "Point out this future Tarzan. I'll have the kid swinging from tree to tree as soon as the ink is dry on his parents' generous donation."

With his hand at the small of her bare back, Aiden steered Fiona toward the donors.

"Trey." Stacy Greene Alexander extended her hand.

"Admiral, General." He shook her hand, and then her husband's, Benjamin Alexander.

"It's a surprise to see you and your father here."

"I didn't know you were in town with your family, either. If I had, perhaps we could have arranged something."

"We were here for some business which we extended to celebrate my parents' forty-second wedding anniversary. How do you know the Lowrys?"

"My father and Al Lowry served together in combat many years ago. Al saved my dad's life, and they became close friends. My father also had a crush on Mavis Hawkins Lowry when she was a military nurse during their service. Al and Mavis's daughter, Fiona Lizette, is an architect and engineer. She's designing a custom home and studio for me here on the Chesapeake Bay shoreline. Al's sons are also the contractors who will complete the project."

"It's certainly a beautiful area," Benny offered when a few people moved close enough to overhear their conversation.

Trey noticed, too, and steered Stacy and Benny toward the main house. "Let me show you a copy of what I have planned."

They went into the house and directly to Trey's guestroom, closing the door behind them.

Fiona noticed when Trey, Benny, and Stacy went into the house and thought it curious. She didn't know Trey knew the Alexanders, but then again, he surprised her several times with how much he knew. Unfortunately, Kathleen McKenna, Aiden's mother, diverted her attention and buttonholed her on the pretense of having her address her book club. It was true Fiona had written a book, chronicling advances made in the construction industry and the new technologies employed to make homes and businesses more cost-effective, affordable, and efficient. Though met with critical acclaim, it was hardly something found on the *New York Times* Best Seller's List.

No, Kathleen was after a chance to move her relationship with Aiden along toward a Catholic Church wedding in the near future. Apparently, Aiden hadn't gotten around to mentioning to his family that he and she had come to a fork in the road. Fiona felt bad about that. She cared about the McKennas, but not enough to change her mind about marriage to the youngest of Kathleen's three sons. However, she did leave the question of whether she would address Kathleen's book club open. That was enough to have Mrs. McKenna, a dyed-in-the-wool society maven, licking her chops.

In the house, Trey spoke quietly to Benny and Stacy Alexander.

Benny leaned into Trey. "We didn't know you were here or even acquainted with the Lowrys."

"As I said, the connection to the Lowrys is through my father. He and Alroy Lowry served together as Army Rangers. As you know, my dad is an officer while Mr. Lowry was an enlisted man, a sergeant. In fact, according to my dad, he was severely injured, and Mr. Lowry carried him on his back for miles until they were rescued. He credits Mr. Lowry with saving his life. Alroy was injured, too, but never let on about his own injury until he got my father to safety. They ended up in the same field hospital where Mavis Hawkins was a military nurse. They've been friends since then.

"Don't concern yourselves about any possible connection between us. Your children handled being introduced to me as if we haven't known each other for several years."

Stacy nodded. "When we spotted you, we cautioned them not to react."

"There shouldn't be a problem. If anyone noticed us coming into the house, we could say I wanted to show you the house and studio Fiona Lizette Lowry is designing, and her father and brothers are going to build for me." He pointed to the mock-up scale model on the table in the bedroom suite.

Benny and Stacy moved to the table where the model sat.

Benny looked in awe. "Is that glass?"

"It is. I'm getting used to the concept. The studio is an existing tobacco barn Fiona will convert to living quarters and workspaces for whom I will be collaborating closely. These are other outbuildings to be used as guest cabins."

Stacy looked at Trey with concern. "Very innovative, but I'm not sure anyone is going to buy the story that we came into the house to see the scale model."

"Of course, they will, if you're looking for someone to design a home for you either in Japan or Summer County, South Carolina."

Stacy looked up over her shoulder into her husband's eyes. "That could work. Actually, we are thinking of building a home in Summer County. Benny has land there."

Benny nodded. "Then that's why we came into the house, if anyone asks."

Stacy nodded slowly. "Good, that's good. So then we're still set for your visit in the next few months for the recording sessions?"

Trey nodded. "We are, yes. Thanks, again, Benny, for arranging for me to meet your aunt Mariah. We've had several discussions. She's agreed to lay down some tracks if we can get our schedules to mesh."

"You're welcome, Trey. Our girls are excited about the possibility of doing duets with the French Mariah, their grandaunt. It's good of you to try to do this remotely. However, with our daughters in different locations and time zones, it's difficult to make this work with Aunt Mariah's schedule in Paris."

"Leave the logistics to me. First, I've gone over the music your girls wrote. Ivy's new album, *Ivy and Friends*, promises to be a great hit. Next, I want to get Whitney into a studio to lay down vocal tracks and with her on electric guitar, too. I know that it will be difficult now that she's married and living with her husband in Germany. I'll also be working with Miguel Menendez-Gaza on his introduction into the music industry."

Stacy's arched brow rose. "You'll still keep our daughters' participation secret."

"I will, yes. I'm equally concerned about keeping Whitney Ivy's identity and your triplets out of the public arena. I recognized how dangerous leaking their identity to the public could be for them and for you." He didn't mention his concern about Aiden McKenna's apparent knowledge that he and the Alexanders had a connection. He would contact his handler first before confiding that information to them.

"Thank you, Trey. Stacy and I can take care of ourselves. However, if the identity of the members of Ivy were to be discovered, it could prove problematic."

Trey nodded. "Believe me when I tell you, I know how critical this situation could be. If you ever feel their security has been compromised, I'll understand. Their protection is first and foremost in the big scheme."

Stacy leaned closer to Trey. "Your secret is safe with us, too, Trey."

"I know. Now, if you're comfortable with my explanation, that my presence here has nothing to do with my role as Ivy's producer, let's get back to the party."

It was almost time to sit down for dinner when Fiona looked up and around for her parents. When she spotted them, Gannon was escorting them with Uncle Jake and Aunt Kelley to the head table. Gavin also brought Chuck and Vivian to the head table with Maxwell Kennard, and...well, *hello*...Mom's good friend, Charlotte Everson. *Way to go, Mom*, Fiona thought. It was an excellent move, pairing Mrs. Everson, who was still an attractive woman, tall and statuesque, with Maxwell Kennard, the Second. A widow with three grown daughters who lived elsewhere, Mrs. Everson was the superintendent of the Bay County school system. Her husband died more than ten years ago. Mavis and Mrs. Everson have been friends since the days when she taught high school and then became the school's principal. After her husband died and her daughters were away in college, she went back to school and received her doctorate. Through the years, as Fiona and her brothers matriculated through high school, they each came through Mrs. Everson's English Literature class. Back in the day, Gannon took Mrs. Everson's eldest daughter to their high school prom. *Nicely played*, Fiona thought again, when Maxwell sat next to Mrs. Everson. They made quite a handsome couple and, if their smiles were any indication, they were enjoying each other's company.

Then chimes sounded, and everyone began moving to their assigned seats.

Trey stood behind Fiona. "Hungry?"

She smiled up at him over her shoulder. "Starving. Did you find your seat?"

"Well, yes, sort of." He grinned.

Turning to face him, she crossed her arms. "You changed the seating arrangements, didn't you?"

"Only slightly." The innocent look on his face was also unapologetic.

"Let me guess. You're no longer sitting at the table with Aiden's unattached sisters."

"I thought I'd learn more sitting with your brothers since I'll be working closely with them during the construction of my property. After all, we only have today to discuss the project. I'll be leaving early tomorrow morning, remember?"

"I suppose you're not sitting next to me."

"What a great idea. I wish I had thought of that." He grinned at her.

"Tell me. Were you this mischievous in your youth?"

"I'm still in my youth." He nodded, leaned in, and sniffed her perfume. "Aiden at twelve o'clock."

Aiden came up behind Fiona and between her and Trey. "Ready to be seated?"

"Yes, thank you." She turned and accepted the arm Aiden held out to her. As they began to move toward the table, she didn't have to look to note Trey's place card was to the right of hers where AJ's seat was supposed to be. Instead, Robin was to Trey's right, with AJ to Robin's right. Aiden sat to her left. Paul's job was to arrange the seating, so Fiona didn't recall the seating chart well enough to remember who was missing from the table. There were ten...no *twelve* seats. That was how he did it. He had the waitstaff add two additional settings to the table. Indeed, he was still mischievous...and fascinating. Very interesting indeed.

Chapter 7

"I guess it's time for me to say good night." Aiden slowly danced with Fiona. "I have an early morning Congressional breakfast. What are your plans for the week?"

"I haven't worked it out yet. I've got a lot of irons in the fire, including Trey's engineering and structural modifications to his studio and the monster tree house I agreed to do for your contributor's son."

He smiled down at her; their arms loosely locked around one another while they swayed to the music. "Thank you for that…and everything else you've done to support my election campaign." Leaning forward, he kissed her temple, nose, and when she rose on her toes, he took her mouth in a meltingly slow kiss. "I want to take you to bed, but I know you're tired. So am I. I had a hectic campaign schedule today before the party. I also had a constituent open house at my local office. I'll call you tomorrow. Maybe we can have a late dinner."

She could feel the state of his arousal against her and felt a twinge of regret. "Don't count on me for dinner this week. I've got to get with the boys and these changes to Trey's studio and guest cabins. We've all got tight schedules, so we'll probably have to work through dinner."

He nodded. "I know." He let her go but took her hand in his while raising his other hand to wave goodbye to the remaining guests. Then, he and Fiona strolled toward the parking lot in front of her cottage, where he had parked his car. When they reached his car, he took her in his arms and looked into her eyes. "I love you, Fi."

Her brow bunched as she looked quizzically up at him. "I know that, Aiden. I love you, too." An unreadable expression crossed his face and beautiful deep-blue eyes. "What is it? What's bothering you?"

I can't stand the feeling that I'm losing you, he thought, but shook his head as if nothing bothered him and smiled wanly at her. "Nothing. It's nothing. I don't tell you often enough how much I appreciate you."

She squeezed him, then stepped back, opening his car door for him. "Words aren't always necessary between us, Aiden. Drive safe."

He climbed into his car, and moments later, he watched her in his rearview mirror as she turned and headed back to the party in her amazing summer gown. He didn't tell her often enough how beautiful she was, both inside and out. For some awfully inexplicable moments, he feared he was losing his best friend, the love of his life. He could only hope and pray that, if he let her go, she would someday come back to him.

Fiona strolled back to the party where only her family, Robinette McKenna, and the Kennards remained.

"Well, there you are, lil' darlin'." The Texas drawl was apparent in Jake Hawkins' voice, her uncle and her mother's brother, as he grabbed her hand and teased her into a little do-si-do on the dance floor.

She laughed and danced with him and the others still on the makeshift dance floor until the music ended. They applauded as the band members took a final bow and began to break down their equipment. Recorded, mellow music began to play through the speaker system.

Gradually the group migrated to the lanai, where a lighted, traditional hot-and-cold buffet was located. They filled plates with shrimp and grits, warm waffles with fresh fruit compote, thick hot sausages, bacon, and fragrant stewed apples with raisins and cinnamon. Then, taking seats around the trestle table, they dug into the late-night meal with gusto and conversation.

"Have you been able to travel much in Africa, Aunt Kelley?" Gannon asked of their relatively new aunt, their uncle Jake's wife.

"Wow, have I ever. I think your uncle and I have visited nearly every country on the African continent. Your uncle stays on the go, so I have to keep a bag packed." Jake Hawkins was the US Ambassador to Seychelles, Africa. Although Jake put his legendary BlackHawk Global wealth in the hands of his children, particularly his daughter, JaiHonnah, and her husband, JRock, J. Roderick Baylor, he furtively used his wealth through his philanthropic foundation to improve the lives of indigent people in African nations where the need was greatest. Jake built schools and libraries, hospitals and clinics, sewer and water systems, instituted banks that offered low-cost loans to enterprising entrepreneurs, particularly women-owned and operated businesses. He also built housing in the poorest regions, each time giving jobs and creating career opportunities for the people.

Most of what Jake did, he did secretly through his BlackHawk Foundation, a not-for-profit non-government organization (NGO) managed by his son, Adam. Though Adam operated the Foundation independently, most observers suspected that the improvements in various countries' day-to-day existence came because of Jake's investments. For example, a recent project saw new refuse collection trucks and recycle facilities managed by an American businessman, Redmond Justice, from Chicago, Illinois, and his company, Justice Inc. It was also common knowledge that Redmond's daughter, Tina Justice Collins, was the reigning number one star of talk television. She was a multi-billionaire in her own right. Not to mention that her husband, Nico Collins, was even more wealthy than her.

"That must be so exciting." Fiona nodded wistfully at her aunt's opportunities to travel to exciting places.

"Indeed, it is. I hoped you were going to find time to come to visit for a while, Fiona."

"Believe me, Aunt Kelley, I want to, but I've been buried in projects. I've also been involved in my friend Aiden McKenna's political campaign. These things have been time-consuming."

Mavis ran a comforting hand down her daughter's arm. "You should make the time, Fi. You'll never see the wonders of the world if you only look out of one window for the whole of your life."

JaiHonnah, Jake's daughter from his previous marriage, nodded. "Aunt Mavis is right, Fiona. While I studied architecture and engineering abroad to receive my double doctorates, I made time to have excursions to places I only read about. Really, though, it has to be experienced, Fi."

"I've said the same thing to her," Robinetta offered. "I wanted her to go with me on my last tour, but then, Aiden started his campaign and drafted Fi to work with him, more or less, as his social secretary."

"You haven't traveled?" Maxwell asked.

She shrugged. "Not outside the states, except to Canada for a builders' convention in Montreal."

"Do you have a current passport?" Trey asked.

When she nodded in the affirmative and as the conversation continued around the lanai, the idea to ask Fiona to join him continued to form in Trey's very fertile mind. He'd avoided bringing women with him when he had work to complete. So, as the thought continued to grow and cause him to reconsider his long-held pledge, he found no reason not to ask her to go with him.

Chapter 8

Fiona's eyes slowly opened as the sleek, private, Adventurer Executive Airline (AEA) jet's wheels smoothly touched down on the runway at Heathrow International Airport, fourteen miles west of Central London, England. She sat up in her comfortable chaise-like seat and looked out of the window at the rain pouring on the tarmac. The jet taxied for quite a while toward a private terminal, passing a host of aircraft, bearing insignia for a multitude of other carriers and countries. She had read that more than seventy-five million passengers passed through Heathrow annually, making it one of the top ten busiest airports for international passenger traffic. However, if the number of jets arriving and departing was any indication, that number was underestimated.

Turning her attention away from the window, she unbuckled her seat restraints and removed the comfortable blanket someone had covered her with during the flight over the Atlantic. She found her laptop closed and secured in the netting beside her. Swinging her legs to the floor, she dug the heels of her hands in her eyes and then palmed her face. That was when she heard quiet voices coming from the front of the jet's well-appointed interior. Standing, she noted Trey sitting across from his incredibly beautiful and super-efficient Executive Assistant, Sandra Kent. Sandra was entering data on a laptop as Trey spoke and pointed out sections on the stack of papers on the table.

When Trey looked up, his eyes smiled at her before his mouth caught up. "Did you rest well?"

She nodded as the jet continued to taxi into docking position inside a covered area where a mobile arm swung into place. Just then, one of the two male flight attendants came forward to unlatch the door.

Fiona stifled a yawn. "I apologize for fading on you."

Trey shook his head. "No apology necessary. You had a full day yesterday, and a six A.M. departure takes a little getting used to. You'll probably be a little groggy and dehydrated during the rest of the day. My suggestion is to drink lots of water and get a good rest."

"The water, yes, but I have no intention of sleeping away this experience." She smiled at him.

"That-a-girl." Sandra closed the laptop and began to stack the papers in preparation for deplaning. "Stick with me, kiddo, and we'll see the sights."

The door opened and a rush of noise filled the cabin until the jet's engines slowly shut down. Two female pilots emerged from the cockpit and smiled at Trey.

"Nice flight." He grinned at them.

"Wouldn't know about that, Trey. We slept all the way," one pilot joked.

At least Fiona hoped they were joking. Trey introduced her to the pilots and flight attendants as well as Sandra at five-thirty in the morning when they boarded the flight at the small Bay County Municipal Airport near her home. She wasn't sure how she had let her family and Robinetta talk her into making this journey. Still, here she was on the first leg of a tour that included not only London, England, but also Madrid, Spain, and Tokyo, Japan, with a possible side trip to Paris, France. They would be traveling for at least two months and probably three before returning to the states. If her uncle and aunt, Jake and Kelley Hawkins, had anything to say about it, she'd also spend time in Seychelles, Africa, too.

"Ready?" Trey held out his arm to her.

Fiona drug herself out of her fugue state at the sound of his voice. "Oh, I need to get—"

"I've got it, Ms. Lowry." One of the two flight attendants held up her carry-on bag and laptop.

Resigned, with a bit of a shrug, she took Trey's arm, and he escorted her off the plane. They entered a terminal where customs officers waited to take and stamp passports.

"Welcome back, Mr. Kennard, Ms. Kent." The Customs Officer flipped through several pages to find a clear one to stamp. "And," he took her passport, "Ms. Lowry." He had no trouble finding a free page in her passport and gave her a bemused smile while handing back her credentials to her. "Enjoy your visit to our sunny country," he joked. The rain was still pouring like Niagara Falls.

Magically, her things were waiting on the other side of the security portal, as was her single piece of luggage. Her mother helped her pack and suggested she take along foldable duffel bags to carry all the new things she was told to purchase for this impromptu journey. Most of what she had were T-shirts and jeans, a couple of pairs of comfortable shoes, boots, and socks, along with assorted undergarments and sleepwear she rarely wore. She didn't use makeup much, but she added a couple of tubes of lip gloss and a mascara stick...at her mother's insistence. She didn't wear jewelry either, but her mother pressed a small, single cowrie shell on a necklace into her hand, a family heirloom passed down through many generations of the Hawkins family on the Louisiana Bayou.

The trip to the McCoy Royal Residential Hotel and Conference Center was slow in the pouring rain. Still, thirty minutes later, they pulled under the front portico, where hotel service personnel unloaded the luggage from the limo and led the way into the hotel. A concierge staff member met them at the entrance and led the way into a waiting elevator. Once on the upper floor, the elevator opened directly into the condo-like space. *It is indeed a space*, Fiona thought, as she looked up and up to the impossibly high ceilings, ornately and intricately designed and painted with frescos reminiscent of much earlier times in European history. Though the furniture was more modern, the jewel tones complemented the décor. She itched to grab her camera to record the enticing space.

Then she entered a suite of rooms she would use, and her jaw dropped. Waitstaff finished hanging her clothes and putting her underwear in a tall, wide Anwar in the bedroom. Her toiletries were on the marble sink stand in the en-suite, where big, fluffy, neatly stacked towels were in piles, and a long robe hung on a hook by the door. The generously wide, standing, glass-enclosed shower, with matching marble walls, could accommodate a quartet, while the deep soaker tub was wide enough to accommodate a family of three.

Trey leaned against the double-wide door jamb to Fiona's section of the suite, with his hands dug into the pockets of his slacks and his legs crossed at the ankles, watching Fiona flit from space to space. He got an enormous charge out of watching her expressions as her eyes lit with wonder at the architecture of the thirteenth-century castle remodeled to accommodate twenty-first-century lifestyles. Trey much preferred the old-world charm of the Royal to the other more modern, sleek residential hotels available through the McCoy chain. However, when he traveled, he always stayed at a McCoy property. The service was second to none and the ambiance enchanting. It was worth the cost to see the look on Fiona's face as she threw open a set of French doors that led to a balcony overlooking the London skyline. He strolled across her sitting room to find her with her eyes closed, face turned up to the spray of rain, and hugging herself.

Trey walked up behind her and took the time to look as she did over the city shrouded in a gray mist. Fiona unlocked her arms and reached behind her, pulling his arms around her and interlocking her fingers with his. She leaned back against him, placing her head on his broad, firm shoulder, and sighed. "Thank you."

He gave her a squeeze. "You're welcome." They continued to stand there as the misty rain dampened their clothes.

"Come on, you two," Sandra called from the open doors. "Supper is here."

Trey and Fiona took one last look at the mesmerizing sight and then uncoupled with arms around one another as they strolled into the dining salon.

"Thank you." Trey acknowledged the waitstaff. "Everything looks fine, but we'll serve ourselves."

The head waiter smiled, accepting the generous gratuity, and ushered the other waiters out of the suite.

"Mmmm." Sandra picked up a plate and served herself from the buffet's array of hot and cold foods. "I didn't know whether you have food allergies, Fiona, so if there is something you can't eat, let me know. Trey is a bottomless pit and will eat pretty much anything I order for him. Most of the time, he works so hard and long that he forgets to eat at all. We'll have to work together to make sure he's well-fed."

"You've worked for him for a long time?"

"She's been running my life for more than twelve years," Trey interjected, "and the Saints be praised that she'll never tire of the task. I'd be lost without her." He took her hand and kissed her knuckles.

Fiona thought the gesture intimate, but it didn't seem sexually motivated. Clearly, Sandra Kent was an extremely beautiful woman, but she didn't look at Trey as if he were her lover. She obviously cared for and about him, but otherwise, their relationship seemed to be strictly friendly, employer-employee-based.

"We're good as long as my wife doesn't complain about the long months I have to travel away from our family. You're safe."

A light bulb clicked on in Fiona's head. Sandra Kent was gay and in a long-term committed relationship. "You and your wife have children?" Fiona continued to eat.

"Two boys, ages nine and eleven. I could bore you to tears with pictures and stories, but they'll join us on the road when their schedules permit."

"I look forward to meeting them."

Sandra laughed. "Please try to remember that you said that after they show up."

They continued to talk over supper and coffee before Sandra checked her watch and called an end to the meal. She called the head waiter, and shortly the dining salon was put to right, and they retreated to their separate rooms to dress for the evening.

When Fiona walked into her sitting area, a woman was going through a rack of clothes and checking them off an electronic list she held in her hand.

"Ah, there you are, Miss." She had a noticeable cockney accent. "I be Thelma Grayson, come to get you ready for the evening's activities. You have time to shower if you have a mind to. It helps to shake off the jet lag, I'm told, though I've never traveled to the colonies myself. Me daughter has. She's a bright girl, my Carolee is, and tells me a shower helps."

"I thought I heard your voice, Thelma, my love." Trey came into the sitting room and hugged the middle-aged woman. "Thanks for the selection of clothes for me and for my friend, Fiona Lizette Lowry—"

"Lowry, you say? So that would be an Irish name?" Her eyes alight.

"Yes, my father's family migrated to America from Ireland."

"Well, I'll be. Me own grandda was from County Cork."

"Thelma, we'll be late if you don't let Fiona shower and dress."

"Aww, go on with yourself, Trey Kennard," she teased and ushered Fiona into the bathroom as if she were her mother.

Fiona had to laugh as she opened the glass shower door and did as instructed. The shower helped and her mother was right. Bringing her own shampoo and shower gel relaxed her considerably, particularly when she came into her bedroom to find Thelma choosing evening club clothes for her.

"Aww, what fine-looking hair! Let's see. I think the maroon color will go with your wonderful hair and skin tone." Thelma held up a swing dress to check the length, nodding her approval. "Yes, and these boots, I think." She passed the ankle boots with skyscraper heels to Fiona. "Now, leave your hair down, dear, and once you're dressed, I'll get that done." She breezed out of the room, pulling the rack of clothes into the walk-around closet.

Non-plus, Fiona looked from Thelma's retreating back to the beautiful maroon-colored confection she left draped across the king-size bed with the appropriate undergarments—a maroon thong and a strapless bra. She rarely needed to wear undergarments. They generally made her feel constrained and uncomfortable. However, she wasn't in Bay County, Maryland, anymore. So, she put on the bra and thong and tried not to feel too awkward. *Well, hell,* Fiona thought, while admiring the dress.

I can't argue with the woman's taste, but it has been a very long time since anyone picked out clothes for me. Nevertheless, she put on the dress.

"Yes, I know, Hugh. I don't think the time shift will be problematic." Trey spoke into his phone headset as he exited his section of the suite. "Yes, that should work and . . ." he trailed off when he looked up and saw Fiona standing by the salon bar, having a glass of wine with Sandra. The woman was simply gorgeous, with a waterfall of dark-red hair curling madly down her back. Decorative combs held her heavy hair away from her face. Intricately designed drop earrings hung from her lobes and shimmered in the ambient lighting. The dress she wore was perfection personified and as sexy as hell on her tall, shapely frame. It made her legs look as if they started at her earlobes and ended in a pair of man-killer ankle boots. She smiled at something Sandra said and took his breath away.

Trey was getting an annoying buzzing in his ear. Vaguely, he recalled having a conversation with Hugh Howard, his friend and stager, about the set-up for the London Philharmonic Orchestra. "Uh, yes, sorry, Hugh. I'm a bit distracted at the moment. Let's pick this conversation up at the club. I'll see you shortly." He disconnected the call and just stood with his hands linked together in front of him and stared.

Fiona blinked several times when Trey Kennard came into view. The man knew how to dress to his best advantage, and *hello*, his killer smile was awesome on his handsome face. He was a tall man without an ounce of unnecessary fat anywhere on his well-toned body. She continued to stare at him, mesmerized as he approached. She couldn't look away if her life depended on it.

His jaw dropped. "*Wow.* Just *wow!*"

"See, didn't I tell you that you look spectacular, Fiona?"

"You did, Sandra, but I rarely have to get dressed up like this, so I'm out of my element."

"Stick with us, kiddo, and it won't even faze you." Sandra laughed. "Now, let's go. The car is waiting and the night is young."

Chapter 9

People lined up outside the Ministry of Sound London, reputed to be the best club in the city.

"London has hundreds of nightclubs playing all kinds of music," Trey explained to Fiona as the car pulled to the curb. "At one time or another, I've visited the majority of them looking for talented musicians and innovative music."

"The Ministry of Sound London is his favorite," Sandra offered.

When the chauffeur opened the limo's rear door, Trey stepped out and reached back to assist Fiona and Sandra to their feet. The rain had stopped, but the water-soaked air was full of mist that dampened their faces, making them glisten and gleam in the club's changing lights. The paparazzi snapped a blizzard of flashbulbs in their faces and shouted questions before the club's doormen rushed forward to clear the path.

Once inside, Fiona thought the club to be electrifying, with high intensity. After bypassing the main queues, a hostess met them at the front gate, greeting Trey and Sandra by name. Trey introduced her to the hostess, Sophia, a petite, dark-eyed beauty who continually and salaciously smiled up at Trey. Sophia escorted their group to a reserved, private booth in the VIP lounge on the balcony level. *Security seems unusually tight in this area*, Fiona thought. The table already held a round of complimentary bottled shots. There was an unparalleled view of the iconic main room, one of three available from the VIP balcony where they sat.

They had barely sat down before the mingling began. *It seems Trey knows everyone or everyone wants to know him*, Fiona thought, as he had to rise repeatedly to greet people who approached the table to shake hands or extend a hug. She recognized these people as some she had seen in movies, television, or read about in magazines or newspapers. When the Royals stopped by on their way to the dance floor, Fiona realized why there was a need for extra security. They stood talking with Trey for quite a while. It was apparent that Sandra knew everyone Trey knew and introduced her to anyone who came to the table.

Fiona was sampling one of the mouth-watering cocktails sent to the table by some unknown patron when several attractive women approached with their escorts.

Trey nodded permission to the security team and again stood to greet the party before introducing her. "Fiona Lizette Lowry of America, may I have the honor of introducing you to Princess Blanche Harland of England, Princess Semina Surret Boviar of France, and Contessa Lolita Viejo Dela Porte of Spain." They nodded briefly and scathingly raked their eyes over her, but clearly, their attention immediately returned to Trey.

When she sat again, Sandra tapped her knee and dramatically rolled her eyes, making Fiona want to giggle. Instead, she held her face unreadable as she continued to sip her cocktail. Still, Fiona overheard the women shamelessly propositioning and flirting with Trey in front of their male escorts. She thought their behavior rude, but gave high points to Trey as he deftly avoided the sticky situation their conversation entailed. When the women departed, clearly disappointed they were unable to entice Trey to join them, two more men approached before he could retake his seat. Trey remained standing, again, signaling permission to his security team, but unlike the women, the men, who were clearly of Arab descent, raked their eyes over her. It was evident for entirely different reasons. She had the unmistakable feeling of being on an auction block.

Trey preferred not to make the introductions, but the sooner he did so, the sooner the men would take their leave. "Sheikh Al Ghalbi and his son, Prince Abdullah Ali Al Junaibi, I present Ms. Fiona Lizette Lowry of America."

Both the Sheikh and the Prince took her hand and kissed her knuckles, smiling unctuously at her, causing her to feel decidedly even more uncomfortable. Though they spoke with Trey, they continued to look at her as if she were a curiosity. She felt much better when they moved away, but they kept looking back at her and whispering to one another.

Later, Hugh Howard approached the table, shook Trey's hand, kissed Sandra's cheek, and began to sit until he spotted her. He stared while still suspended in mid-descent before he finally sat, and Trey introduced her. Tall and svelte, with a pelt of beautiful, dark-brown hair, loose and framing his handsome face, his blue eyes dark.

"Oh, man, where have you been all of my life?" Hugh asked Fiona on a breathy sigh.

Fiona smiled at Hugh for the compliment, but didn't take his words seriously. Though he and Trey were having a conversation, Fiona noticed Hugh glancing in her direction while she conversed with Sandra.

Over Hugh's shoulder, Fiona spotted a man...no, *a Greek god*, who was receiving a great deal of attention despite an entire club full of notables. She had seen him in movies, on magazine covers, billboards, and television as an occasional host of the *Sweet Justice* daily magazine show. She even subscribed to one of the monthly magazines he published. He was William "Bill" Chandler, Esquire, the spitting image of and often mistaken for Matt Bomer, star of the television series *White Collar* and *The Last Tycoon*. Like Bomer, Chandler, his stage name, is an American actor, producer, and director. He is known for his versatility in his performances in successful and independent films and his performances in the court of law. Chandler's accolades include Golden Globe and Emmy Awards. Voted the top male fashion model more than a few times, he produced and starred in several movies and television shows, which garnered high praise, and was a seasoned sports and entertainment attorney and agent to the stars.

Fiona remembered Chandler was also a founding member of one of America's most prestigious law firms: Alexander, Carter, Chandler, Charles, Lightfoot, and Towson. It was the law firm founded by Vivian Alexander when she and her law school pals graduated from Georgetown

Law and passed the bar. Although Vivian was now a US Supreme Court Justice, she and her former law partners, including Chandler, were rumored to still be very tight friends. So after meeting Vivian at her mother's birthday party, Fiona never thought she'd be privileged to meet anyone she admired as much. Still, here he came, striding purposely to the table.

"Trey, Hugh, Sandra," Bill Chandler acknowledged warmly. "This must be Fiona Lizette Lowry." He offered his hand to all and then to her. "I can't imagine you're not ready to hit the dance floor. Would you like to show them how it's done in the states?" He smiled at her.

Chandler has that movie-idol factor in spades, Fiona thought, as she accepted his hand and let him guide her to the dance floor. She wondered only briefly how he knew her name without the formal introduction. Then, *oh wow!* The man could *dance!*

Trey could have kicked himself for not asking Fiona to dance. Instead, he was listening to the band headlining tonight. They were good but sounded so much like other bands whose music they played instead of anything original. The musicians knew he was coming to the club and had asked Sophia to alert them when he arrived so they could highlight their best performances. If that was the best that they could offer, Trey wasn't particularly impressed. He continued to listen, but the only band member to spark his interest was the piano player. Still, they weren't terrible, so he'd bring them into the studio to give them another chance.

"Put them on the schedule," Trey told Hugh, who nodded his agreement. Since that was out of the way, he could pay more attention to Fiona.

Hugh pulled a business card from his pocket, consulted with Sandra, and then wrote a note, giving a date and time on the back, before calling over one of the hovering waiters. The card held the logo *III* and Hugh Howard on the front. He gave the card and a generous tip to the waiter with instructions to deliver it to one of the band members. The young man made his way to the stage and handed up the card just as the band ended that selection. A broad smile bowed the band leader's mouth, and, using the card, he made a tip-of-the-hat gesture, which Trey answered with a nod.

Trey and Hugh stood as Chandler slowly escorted Fiona back to the table. They were chatting and smiling broadly at each other, though Chandler seemed to be waylaid every step of the way by admiring fans. Finally, they reached the table, and Chandler, the consummate, urbane gentleman, seated her and thanked her for the dance before departing.

Trey waited a suitable amount of time before excusing himself and heading for the restroom. He entered and noted the two closed stall doors. Walking to a urinal, he took his time, waiting until one of the doors opened and a young man came out to wash his hands. When the other man left, Trey zipped up and washed his hands. Then, the other stall door opened, revealing his handler.

Trey passed the jump drive off and left the restroom.

"So, you're really an architect and an engineer?" Hugh asked of Fiona.

"I am, yes."

"So, how do you know Trey?"

"Why do you ask?"

Hugh shrugged. "Just checking to see whether the coast is clear."

"If I told you I was a lesbian lover of Sandra's, it really wouldn't matter, would it?"

"Oh…" Hugh slowly backed away, clearly disappointed.

Out of the corner of her eye, Fiona spotted Sandra desperately trying not to laugh. Then she spotted Trey working his way through the thick crowd back to the table. *He's quite a hunk and very intelligent, too*, she thought, watching him move. There wasn't anything about him that didn't appeal to her on every level. When he looked up and saw her watching him, he smiled, and her heart did a slow dive off a high pedestal.

"Enjoying yourself?" Trey's smile was still in place as he sat next to her.

"Immensely."

"Let's see whether we can improve on that. Where to next, Sandra?"

"Fabric, then Club Aquarium, KOKO, and, finally, Heaven. All of them have new acts performing tonight. So I alerted them you'd be in at some point this evening."

"Good. We'll do the club crawl and then wrap it up. Fiona has got to be tired."

Fiona tilted her head in question. "What's the club crawl?"

Trey stretched his arms out along the back of the booth. "We don't sit down. Rather, we grab a drink and slowly walk through the club in about thirty minutes or less. If we hear something unique, we may stay a while longer. If not, we move on to the next."

"Okay, so you're listening for what?"

"Sound quality, both instrumental and/or vocal. For example, the headlining band here at the Ministry of Sound kept people on the floor for every number, but they were only performing tried-and-true music, nothing new or novel."

"You're looking for something unique?"

"Exactly. London clubs each have a distinctive ambiance. It's reflected in the entertainment they bring in to perform. You'll see what I mean when we visit these next few clubs."

As the night progressed into the morning, she did understand. At Fabric, the bass came through the twenty-five-thousand-square-foot floors, making the clubbers feel the music, but it took a moment for Fiona to acclimate to the unisex toilets. At Club Aquarium, there were five different rooms, including a swimming pool, Jacuzzi, two dance floors, a chill-out room, and a VIP lounge. They crawled through the dance rooms, but Trey, Sandra, and Hugh agreed they heard nothing unique in the bands or house music.

At KOKO in Camden, where headliners like Coldplay, Madonna, My Chemical Romance, and Prince once performed, Trey felt they might have finally struck gold with the group known as History. Their sound was timeless, adding vocals and upbeat rhythms to classical music in a way Trey hadn't heard before. So this time, when the group took a break, Trey went backstage to speak with them.

The club Heaven was a huge, gay-straight-mixed nightspot under the railway arches at Charing Cross Station close to Trafalgar Square. Because of the large crowd and long line of chauffeured limos waiting to unload their passengers, Trey's car service couldn't get close before door attendants had to walk down the row to open car doors as much as a block away from the entrance. Everywhere they went, Fiona noted their treatment—like royalty, never having to wait to enter. Still, there was a rope line at Heaven, but patrons waiting to get in experienced the sounds from exterior speakers and a hot mulled wine punch. People were dancing in the street.

As they walked along the block to Heaven's front entrance, a cheer went up to the sound of a Reggae beat. Trey took Fiona's hand and teased her into dance moves as Hugh did the same with Sandra. Trey was a great dancer and showed her how to move with the unfamiliar beat. Inside the main floor, the dance space seemed to stretch endlessly and packed with beautiful, gyrating bodies of what seemed like all adult age groups. A level higher, scantily-clad go-go boys were on pedestals. Fiona heard different languages and dialects spoken at every turn.

As they began their crawl, Fiona recognized a familiar face. "Jacob!" she called out over the blaring music.

He turned and looked at her, a slight smile of recognition creasing his handsome face. "Fiona?" He curiously smiled while giving her a brief hug. "What in hell are you doing in England? You never leave the backwoods of Bay County, Maryland."

She grinned at him. "I'm on tour with friends for the summer. Trey Kennard, this is my cousin, Jacob Hawkins. Jacob, this is Trey, Hugh Howard, and Sandra Kent. Trey is in the music industry."

"Yes, I've heard of you. You were a judge for the Ms. America Pageant when my sister, JaiHonnah, was First Runner Up. How do you know each other?"

"Fiona's father and mine are longtime friends." Trey shook Jacob's hand. "Fiona is developing a property for me in Bay County. I was just there to witness her progress and was fortunate to be invited to attend your Aunt Mavis' birthday party. I met your father and stepmother there."

Fiona smiled up at her handsome cousin. "Why didn't you come, Jacob?"

"When Gavin called me, I told him I would be out of the country on business and couldn't attend the party. I sent a gift and an apology to Aunt Mavis."

"It was a great party," Trey offered.

"Adam couldn't make it, either," Jacob said defensively. "So, don't give me grief about it, Fiona."

"I wouldn't do that. You were missed, and we know Adam is in France getting ready for the Grand Prix. Gavin told me he sent his regrets, too."

Just then, the one person Fiona hoped never to see again joined them.

"Well, how the hell are you, Fiona Lizette?" Geneva Simpson was her cousin, JaiHonnah's nemesis and a former runner-up for Miss America. "You're looking…tasty." Geneva grinned salaciously, looking at her from the bottom up. "You remember me, don't you, kid? I was Miss Louisiana the same year JaiHonnah won Miss Texas. I own Geneva Cosmetics now."

"I've heard of the cosmetic line, but I don't need to wear much makeup."

Geneva stepped into Trey's personal space. "Why don't you join us?" She eyed him from the bottom up.

Fiona interjected, stepping in front of Trey. "Thank you, but no. We're on a schedule."

Geneva continued to gaze at Trey over Fiona's shoulder. "A pity. Maybe another time. By the way, how is Calvin's wife?" She grinned, shifting her gaze to Fiona.

"His *former* wife is happily married to J. Roderick Baylor, with wonderful children. You remember JRock, don't you?"

Fiona had to admit that she liked how the smile slipped from Geneva's face at the mention of JRock Baylor. There had been a physical attempt by Geneva to seduce Roderick away from her cousin, JaiHonnah, which had failed miserably. Calvin had not fared well either. The Russians killed him.

Geneva stepped closer into Fiona's personal space. "Had I known you'd shed your tomboyish demeanor and cleaned up to look like a supermodel, I would have bedded you."

Fiona didn't back down, getting up close and personal. "I'd have served you your balls sliced and diced on a silver tray with fava beans and rice," she coldly hissed at Geneva.

Jacob stepped between the two combatants. "That's enough, Geneva."

Fiona's malevolent eyes remained focused on Geneva. "You ought to find a better class of associates, Jacob."

"It was good to see you, Fiona. You said you're on tour. Where to from here?"

With an eye roll, Fiona turned her attention from Geneva to Jacob. "Trey has to go to France, Spain, and Japan before he returns to the states."

"I'm off to see my brother tomorrow in France," Jacob said of his brother Adam, "but I have a trip to Tokyo coming up in a few months. So I'll keep in touch. Maybe we can hook up there. I'm glad you're starting to spread your wings more." He hugged her.

"Thanks, Jacob." She returned the hug, but for Geneva, her eyes held nothing but disdain.

Jacob and Geneva walked away, but Geneva turned, grinned, and winked at Fiona.

Altercation forgotten, Trey, Fiona, Hugh, and Sandra danced for a solid hour as deejays continually hyped up the club music to the point of near pandemonium levels. However, Fiona didn't tire of the workout the music provided. When they left the insanity of Heaven, they went to the luxurious and stylish Club Boujis. It was a direct contrast to Heaven, a laid-back club with many of the same A-list, glamorous people they encountered earlier in the evening at the Ministry of Sound London. Here, like elsewhere, they occupied the VIP section and were treated to a late-night/early morning selection of delicious foods and drinks.

They relaxed and chatted over the meal and were back in the limo headed for the McCoy Royal just before the sun came up.

"So, you produce club music, too?" Fiona asked of Trey on the drive through the relatively deserted streets.

"I do, yes."

"He does it when he's bored and can't figure out something more creative to do. He has thirty-seven albums released so far," Sandra added. "Three of them this year. So, you can imagine he's been bored several times so far."

"I should hire her as my publicist," Trey said ruefully.

Fiona noted what looked like embarrassment on Trey's handsome face. He seemed almost vulnerable from the amount of praise heaped on him as Sandra and Hugh continued to extol his extraordinary accomplishments, hailing him as having the Midas touch of the music industry.

It wasn't long before they pulled in under the hotel's portico.

"Good night, Hugh," Fiona called out as she stepped out of the limo. "Or rather, good day to you."

"See you shortly," he called back as the doorman closed the car door.

Fiona turned to look as the car pulled away. "What did he mean, he'd see me shortly?"

"I have a seven o'clock session this morning. You don't have to go with us, Fi. You can stay at the hotel and rest. We should be back around noon or shortly thereafter. If you're up to it, I'll take you sightseeing."

"Noon? When are you going to sleep?"

Sandra laughed. "We're like sharks, Fiona. We have to keep moving or we'll die."

"We spend most of our time working at night and during the early morning," Trey offered as they walked through the quiet, deserted hotel lobby toward a waiting elevator. Once inside, Sandra inserted her key card into the slot and tapped security code keys on the panel. The door closed, and the box rose smoothly.

"May I go with you?"

"Certainly, if you feel up to it. If you get tired, you can always return to the hotel to rest." Trey was glad she wanted to come along. He thoroughly enjoyed her and her company. He hoped she enjoyed being with him, too. It was important to him. *She* was important to him.

"You may want to shower and put on comfortable clothes," Sandra advised.

"I'm with you there." Fiona laughed. She desperately wanted to shed the bra and thong. "I haven't danced like that since I was in college and certainly not on these stilts."

With those long, long legs, agile body, sparkling personality, and beautiful face, Trey hoped to have the pleasure of dancing with her a lot. However, he was impressed with the way she handled Geneva Simpson. He hoped he did nothing to get on Fiona's wrong side. She had guts and was no shrinking violet.

Chapter 10

When the car service pulled up to a building at six-forty-five in the morning, Fiona was surprised they were visiting such a nondescript place. It had none of the old-world charms of the surrounding age-old buildings. Instead, it looked like a three-story storage facility. As she followed, she looked around at the interesting architecture of other structures and snapped several pictures. Then, as they got closer to the extra tall, heavy, hammered-bronze front doors, Fiona noticed a small, copper placard with **III** etched into the medal. Once inside the thickly carpeted, silent building, they moved straight ahead, and Trey held open one wide theater door for them at what turned out to be the rear of an auditorium.

Inside, a host of people were milling about in the theater chairs, while others were tuning instruments on a graduating stage like bleachers, but broader.

Fiona spotted Hugh right away, his thick hair tied in a cue at the nape of his neck, wearing headphones, and an iPad in hand, directing porters as to how to arrange the musicians. As they advanced down the aisle, all commotion ceased, and applause rose.

Trey acknowledged the accolades by putting his hands together in a prayerful motion and bowing slightly over them. Then, taking a headset Hugh held out to him, he ascended a podium that looked like a lifeguard's perch facing the assembled musicians. He tapped his baton a few times, and the musicians immediately settled, each donning headsets. Lights above the heads of the over one-hundred-piece orchestra dimmed, and a three-hundred-sixty-degree screen lit on the walls around them, but no sound accompanied the movie scenes. Then Trey lifted his head, looking at each member of the orchestra as they looked at him. Then, baton in hand, he began, and the perfectly-pitched music flowed out.

Hours passed as Trey continued to conduct the orchestra, never stopping until after the closing credits rolled up on the screen.

On the Maryland eastern shore, Aiden finished his early morning run around his parents' quarter-mile racetrack on their horse farm and started the cooldown phase of his daily routine. With hands on hips, he walked in a figure-eight, his heart pumping hard in his chest.

He missed her. He missed Fiona like he would miss his arms if he ever had to lose them. He was devastated when he learned she left the country on an impromptu trip to visit foreign countries and ancient architecture up close and personal. Sleeping without her in his bed was an ache so deep; he wasn't sure he would survive the loss. Even more telling was missing having her to talk to every day. Because they shared so much of what went on in their lives each day, it was like half of his world had ceased to exist.

Her sudden departure for Europe with Trey Kennard was like a swift kick to his solar plexus. If he had known she wanted to travel, he would have made time to go with her, but she never expressed a desire...not that he recalled, but since his first campaign for public office, their lives together were about *his* political career aspirations. First, he went after the State Senate seat and won, soundly beating long-term State Senator Julius Mitchell, Senior. Then the US House of Representative's seat. Now it was the State's Attorney General's office. He was making strategic moves on his way to his ultimate goal and making a name for himself in the process. Eventually, he wanted to make a run for the governorship of Maryland. His aspirations didn't stop there. As a successful politician serving his constituency well, his party believed he'd be, at least, a contender for the Vice President's spot on any ticket. Maybe even a run for the President of the United States down the road. Fiona would be the quintessential First Lady. Now, painfully, he saw his mistake of not making time to share *her* dreams and desires. He took everything she offered but offered nothing in return.

Robinetta rode up on her horse, Peppa. After a moment, she asked, "Are you okay?"

He shook his head and then looked up at his sister. "No, I'm not okay."

"Fiona?"

He nodded. "I'm in love with her, Robin. I don't want to lose her, but I am so screwed."

"If you love someone —" Robin began.

Taking hold of Peppa's bridal and rubbing the horse's long neck, he nodded. "Let her go, and if it's to be, she'll come back to me," he finished the familiar phrase. "I know, but I haven't given her a reason to want to come back to me. I became too complacent."

"Believe it or not, little brother, this could be a good thing. We're country people, Aiden; us and the Lowrys. We've known each other all our lives. Fi hasn't been exposed to the bright lights and big cities. It's a cultural experience we all should have at least once in our lives."

He rubbed her horse's long jaw. "Has it helped you and AJ?"

She nodded. "AJ travels a lot, but he comes back here. This is home to him and for me, too. He could live anywhere, and so could I, but for us, this is the best place to grow up and someday maybe marry and have a family. However, regardless of how our parents feel, it's not preordained. There doesn't need to be a corporate merger between the families."

Aiden nodded his understanding. "I know this is a good opportunity for Fi to see more of the world. The problem is she doesn't want to be the wife of a politician."

"I know. You're a United States Congressman, and you're going to win the election as the next Maryland State Attorney General. Beyond that, you have your eye on the governor's mansion or the next senatorial election, whichever comes first. Maybe even higher office because you'd be a wonderful President of the United States. The question for you, dear brother, is whether Fiona is more important to you than your career aspirations? Do you think she sees herself as the First Lady of Maryland or the United States?"

Aiden thought about that for a moment before looking up at his sister. "Fiona is my best friend. She'd do almost anything for me that I asked of her, but yeah, no, now there's a question I don't believe I can ask of her and get a favorable answer."

With closed eyes, Fiona absorbed the unique sounds Trey and the members of the London Philharmonic Orchestra created. She and Sandra sat in the sound booth behind three rows of people who expertly played knobs and dials on mixing boards, capturing the sounds and syncing the music to the movie scenes.

She learned that Hugh rehearsed the orchestra for months before Trey arrived. This session was slated as a rehearsal to determine whether they were ready to record the final score of a movie in post-production. As she looked on, Fiona noticed that Trey stood with his eyes closed, the headset dangling around his neck, his arms up, and long fingers interlaced behind his head. Occasionally she could see him raising his baton for a quick instruction to a specific section of the orchestra, but otherwise, he seemed to let the music flow around him.

Fiona shook her head in awe. "Trey wrote this music?" Fiona asked in awe.

Sandra nodded. "He did, yes. This and more still. This isn't the only movie score he has in the works."

"How does he do this, Sandra? We were in and out of all of those clubs last night and here he is this morning creating a masterpiece."

Sandra smiled at her. "Pure genius, Fiona. You're in the presence of one of the world's top musical geniuses. He can play any instrument on that stage and hear it if any one piece of equipment or musician isn't performing at optimum levels. We've visited countries just because he wanted to hear native rhythms played by locals in some off-the-map environment. Learning what makes people respond to his treatment of sounds gives him pleasure. If he can sit for long periods of time and listen, like for a Broadway show or movie or dance to the music, without stopping, then he's in his element; in his zone."

"He doesn't do it for the accolades or awards, does he?"

Sandra smiled at her, amazed and pleased. "No." She shook her head. "He doesn't, and you're the first woman who recognized that about him." She searched Fiona's eyes, seeming to come to a mental conclusion. "Trey is an extraordinary man, Fiona. He's not delicate, but he's vulnerable because people usually only see the façade. He's handsome, wealthy, and charismatic, yet he's empathetic."

Fiona steadily gazed at Sandra. "He listens to what people say to him."

Solemnly, Sandra nodded. "Because everything, for Trey, is a learning experience. He's like a human sponge. He soaks up everything around him. In all the years I've known him, he has never brought anyone on tour with him. He's always said, *'It's too distracting, and it affects my ability to concentrate.'* However, the way he looks at you...I've never seen that look on his face for any other woman. He's never let any woman get this close to him or felt what I believe he feels for you."

Fiona looked away from Sandra and back through the glass partition at the man people in the music industry admired. She nodded. "I hear you, Sandra. I'll do my best work for him, building and designing his home and studio." She turned back to look into Sandra's eyes. "I promise you I'll never intentionally do anything that might hurt him."

After a humming moment, Sandra nodded and turned away. "Good, that's all I ask, Fiona. Try not to hurt him because, at this point, I believe you're the most special aspect of his life. You have the power."

The orchestra gave Trey another round of applause and boisterous cheers before they began to break down and store their instruments. Trey applauded them as well. This was an inspired session. If it sounded as exceptional in the mixing room as it sounded to him, he wouldn't have much tweaking to do before he could hand over a completed project to the client.

When he left his perch, as tradition dictated, he shook hands with the woman who was the first violinist and then Hugh as they pulled each other into a tight embrace.

"*Man!*" exclaimed Hugh. "You had them in a zone! *Awesome!*"

"Thanks to you. You built a solid sound."

Hugh nodded. "I'm a technician, Trey. I can put the ingredients together and bake a cake, but you frosted that cake and put the cherry on the icing. I didn't think we'd flow into the groove so fast."

Trey looked up at the second level where the sound booth was located and saw Fiona standing at the glass, looking down at him. "I had an unexpected inspiration."

Hugh followed Trey's line of sight. "Fiona?" He choked.

Trey nodded. "I, uh, like her...a lot."

Hugh shook his head as if to clear it. "She's a lesbian, man."

Trey turned his head, looking at Hugh, his brows bunched in confusion. Then he laughed. "What the hell gave you that impression?"

"She told me that last night."

Trey laughed again. "She just blurted out that she's gay?"

"Yes, I mean, no. What she said was 'If I told you . . .'" he trailed off and dramatically hit his forehead with the heel of his hand. "I'm daft!" He laughed. "She's good. She had me fooled."

Trey nodded again, looking up at the booth where Fiona stood.

"Man, am I right? Is she—"

"The one?" Trey finished.

"Yes."

Trey nodded. "Although we have been working on the plans for my home for several months, I met her for the first time last Friday night at the Ram's Head Tavern in Annapolis, Maryland. She created a masterpiece for me without doing more than walking into the club and talking with me for a while. Then when I met her the next day, she refined the building plans in the midst of planning a birthday party for her mother. She's a rare person, Hugh. Like the sounds we produced today, she feels very right to me."

It was broad daylight on the fourth day of the trip when Fiona readied herself for bed. She was pulling back the bedcovers when her phone beeped. Picking it up from the bedside table, Fiona checked her text message. Since her arrival, she sent pictures each day to her parents, brothers, and Aiden. It was much like journaling, except it was in real-time. Her family responded to the group messages, despite the time difference between her Maryland home and London. She enjoyed sharing this adventure with them and receiving their text messages and comments, some of which were hilarious.

It was a little strange not being with them every day, but they encouraged her to make the most of this experience. They were taking care of her workload, including having her cousin, JaiHonnah, help when necessary. She had done the same for Jai when she was in a pinch. Still, when Fiona found the time, she logged in to do a few hours of work on projects. She completed Trey's engineering and structural modifications and submitted them to her brothers for review. She also completed the monster tree house for Aiden's contributor, making it three houses in a triangle with zip lines between each one. They were only six feet off the ground, but the boy was only ten. When he was older, they could raise lines higher.

Fiona owed everyone an enormous debt of gratitude for their support. Although she missed them, she was having the time of her life. Each night she, Trey, Hugh, and Sandra hit five or six different clubs before returning to the hotel to shower, change, and go to Trey's music studio, ***III***.

Fiona was surprised that Trey owned the premier studio, which when he or Hugh weren't using it, he leased certain aspects to others. Sandra took her on a tour of the building, and she saw other smaller music rooms with sound booths in use, but from the hallway couldn't hear what was going on inside without using headphones to plug into mixing boards as each room was soundproof. Fiona made notes about the soundproofing techniques she would need to incorporate into the barn conversion. She also needed to discuss with Trey the size of the mixing booth he would want. Fiona had learned so much more about the technical aspects of what he did and how he did it. She would have to put more thought into not only the size of the studio but also the volume of space he should have to capture the sound.

Fiona consulted the audio technicians about the best way to achieve the results Trey expected from his workplace. First, she would study and learn how to block out white noise and other ambient annoyances so that what Trey could capture was clean and pure. Although his land was isolated and there was nothing close enough to disturb his peace and tranquility, it would not be enough. As a result, she decided to put Trey's sound studio on a lower level, causing her to deconstruct the tobacco barn and dig a deep basement with at least a twenty-foot ceiling. It would be large enough for him to seat an orchestra and account for the sound attenuation thick walls would afford them. Next, she'd use the original barnwood and more to redesign the rest of the workspace with an open concept main floor and two levels for sleep space above. Contacting her brothers and father, she had the changes entered into the CAD program and work diverted to make the plan work. The exterior would still resemble the old, red tobacco barn with more modern conveniences. She was pleased with the project so far.

After morning sessions ended, the foursome usually toured the city and surrounding areas, sightseeing for her benefit. On good days when it didn't rain, they even left the comfort of the car service and used the Tube, London's subway system, to go from place to place. It wasn't unusual for Trey to reach for and hold her hand as they did walking tours. Still, it excited her to know he wanted a physical connection to her. Likewise, it thrilled her to watch Trey in his element as he worked. He wore the pure joy he felt on his face for his work and for the musicians who performed their very best for him.

Each day they went to a different restaurant for lunch and discussed what had transpired the night before or in the studio that day. She liked how Trey, Hugh, and Sandra encouraged her to offer her opinion, making her a part of the discussion and accepting her suggestions. The process was beginning to make sense to her now. She now knew what to look and listen for when they went through the clubs and in the studio. The acts they saw and heard in the clubs came in for audition sessions. Trey wrote music quickly and gave the groups something new to play. The nine-member, mixed-raced, male and female singers and musicians' group, History, was so phenomenal they Trey immediately offered them a contract. With emotions brimming over with moist eyes, they accepted and were ready to sign on the dotted line. Still, Trey insisted they have an attorney review the contract with them before they sign it. The very next day, they and their attorney came back to the studio and signed the contract without making one change.

Sandra arranged for the members of History to meet with Trey's promotions team in New York City. With the group's agreement, he refined and recorded their sound before they left to tour America and four other countries over the next eight weeks. *It happened just that quickly,* Fiona thought, as she prepared for bed.

She answered a text from Aiden about his poll numbers, surprised she hadn't thought of his campaign much since she left home. Terribly glad, she was, that she didn't have to attend another of his fundraisers as his plus-one or political meetings. She was enjoying the contrast of London's nightlife much better than she did the big band sounds at a political rally.

Walking out of her bedroom suite to get bottled water, she entered the spacious kitchen to find Trey on his phone, talking with his father, and wearing only a pair of soft boxers. *Geeze-oh-flip, the man is ripped!*

"Really?" A smile grew on Trey's handsome face. "I think it's great... Yes." He looked up and watched Fiona stroll into the kitchen. He was hard-pressed to keep his mind on his conversation with his father as he tracked Fiona's movements.

"Yes, Dad, Fiona is fine. We're taking good care of her...Yes, she's right here if you...Yes, sir." He laughed and then held his phone out to her. "My father wants confirmation that we're treating you well."

She took the phone, laughing. "General, it's an emergency! Send troops to rescue me!" She giggled at Trey's look of astonishment and then menace as he lunged for her. She danced nimbly out of his grasp and backed away from him around the tall center-post island as he stalked her.

"Yes, Sir, he did drag me from one nightspot to the other, forcing me against my will to enjoy myself...Yes, Sir, he's a real taskmaster. Can you imagine that he makes me take naps in the middle of the day at my age, and then he drags me around sightseeing all these wonderful places? We went to Stonehenge, and I couldn't believe those stones were erected in 2500 BC. It was so absolutely awesome; it gave me chills...No, Sir, I never thought I'd ever actually touch one of the most important prehistoric sites in the world...Yes, Sir, he took me to Big Ben, and I actually touched it as that thirteen-ton bell sounded...Yes, we went to York Minster, and he, Sandra, and Hugh have plans to take me to every tourist attraction of note in England."

Fiona laughed at whatever Trey's father said and continued to evade Trey's capture. She faked right, and he almost had her, but the imp was quick moving left.

"Yes, Sir, I'll write a full report for you." Fiona laughed. "Promise me that you'll have him drawn and quartered." She laughed again, stopped evading Trey, and held out the phone to him.

When she would have scampered away, he caught her waist and pulled her into his embrace. "Yes, Dad?...Yes, she is a handful. She deserves a spanking for her bad behavior...Yes, Sir, I'll be gentle." He looked down into her beautiful eyes and mischievous expression. "Take care." He ended the call without taking his eyes off hers. "You're in big trouble," he feigned menace.

"So, I heard." She wrapped her arms around his waist. "Corporal punishment, is it?"

With her scantily-clad body flush against his, all thought of anything else but her left his mind. "At least."

They stared into each other's eyes until, somehow, there was no space left between their mouths. Fiona went up on her toes, and he bent to meet her halfway. Then, by all things holy, their tongues met and stroked. Fiona was like a fire igniting in his arms. The first taste of her was exhilarating. He bent slightly more to accommodate, her arms moving up, circling his neck, her fingers tunneling through his hair. Then, with his hands under her thighs, he lifted her until her long legs circled his waist, her pubis intimately against his swollen member.

"Fi," he breathed, her scent so intoxicating, he didn't want to stop, but he didn't want to go too far.

"No, don't stop," she breathed and, palming his face, deeply kissed Trey again.

That was all the permission he needed. Carrying her, wrapped around him, he managed to make it to his suite, close and lock his sitting-room door before entering his bedroom. Then, slowly, while his heart thundered in his chest, he lowered them to his bed.

Fiona's short robe fell open, revealing softly-scented skin, still a bit damp from her shower, and, Saints be praised, a hairless pubis. Shedding his shorts took a nanosecond and, after he reached into his nightstand, Fiona took the foil packet from his hand. She sat up as he knelt on the bed between her open thighs. Then, in agonizingly slow motion, she looked up into his eyes until she covered him and then brought him to her for another soul-stirring kiss.

He had other plans first, as he toured her body with fingertips and tongue. She tasted of everything exotic and necessary to sustain his life. Her body rose and fell in mindless abandon, further igniting his passion and desire for her alone. She was like the endless melody that played through his mind from the moment she entered the tavern in Annapolis, Maryland. Frame by frame, her image played in his head in little vignettes. He remembered her lazy, loose-jointed saunter as she approached the lanai to meet him for breakfast. Then she strolled around his property, pointing out the locations for his home and studio in the old tobacco barn. She outlined the wild patch of land she was preserving for his victory garden. Fiona explained how she planned to teach him the fine art of raising fruits and vegetables, and he laughed at the thought. They stood on the shore for a while, watching the waterway flow by while she caused him to envision the installation of the boat dock and helicopter landing platform. Then learning from her so much more about the site's history made him appreciate the property more than before. The birthday party when Fiona completely blew him away with her style and grace. Her eyes closed in complete, relaxed sleep as they flew over the Atlantic. The wonder on her gamine face as they danced and moved from club to club. Now the slumberous excitement in her eyes as he slowly buried himself deep inside her.

Fiona couldn't think. She could only feel and, what she felt, she cherished. Trey treated her body to a roller-coaster ride with all the sounds only consummate lovers voiced. She could hear his music in her head as he played her body as if it were one of his masterpieces. A concert pianist couldn't have had a better touch. She gave full voice to his direction as if she were the solo singer of the Hallelujah Chorus.

Later, when Trey woke to Fiona curled into his right side with her head on his shoulder and her right leg partially covering his body, he palmed her fleshy bottom, shifting her even closer. His fingers slipped between her thighs until he could insert two inside her hot, moist portal and play her clitoris with his thumb. She moaned long and deep before she latched on to his right nipple with her teeth and tongue and his rapidly swelling penis with her right hand. Then she kissed and licked her way down his body until she devoured him, making his sacks tighten to the size and consistency of golf balls. Ultimately, they ended up in the time-honored six-nine position. He scrambled to cover himself before he charged into her in response to her breathy cries for completion. Then, with her thighs crushing his waist and nearly asphyxiated from their heavy breathing, they climbed the peak again, as they had many times before, for the first time that day, their voices exploding into two-part harmony.

Trey could feel Fiona's heart thundering in her chest, and he knew she could feel his. Her thighs loosened from around his waist, falling open, but still cradling the sides of his hips. He was ensconced inside her and was not inclined to move. Instead, with foreheads pressed together, they comingled labored breaths. Then, when they could breathe nearly normally again, they kissed deeply.

"That was close," Trey sighed sated.

Fiona giggled. "Ya think? Have we had anything but close calls since I seduced you?"

He pulled back, his brows bunched, as he skeptically looked into her eyes. "You seduced me?" He laughed. "Whose bed are we in?"

"A mere technicality. Your bed was just closer." She grinned at him.

"As I recall, we almost had a close call when I wanted to take you on the kitchen counter."

"Details, details," she scoffed until he ground his rapidly inflating member deep inside her and began the slow, strong slides in and out of her still sensitive portal. He added to her aroused state, sucking, alternating breast tips in his warm mouth. Again, they were moving in sync to the music their damp bodies created for an extended time before they slept the sleep of the truly sated.

Chapter 11

On the weekend, they didn't frequent the city nightclubs. According to Hugh, too many tourists and weekenders flooded popular city venues to make the club crawls fun or beneficial. Rather, on Friday, after the session wrapped in the studio, they packed overnight bags to spend time in the English countryside. Hugh drove southwest of London in his comfortable and classic Mulsanne Range Bentley with Fiona in the front seat. Trey and Sandra rode in the back, going over details about various changes to their schedule. Because they finished the movie score so quickly, they were able to fit in other projects.

The countryside and back roads aren't much different from rural Bay County, Maryland. Yet, somehow it looks more calming the further away from the city we drive, Fiona thought, as she mindlessly gazed out of the windows until she saw horses grazing or romping in the open fields. She sat up in her seat as memories of early morning rides through the fields of the McKenna's picturesque farm, which was adjacent to the shore of the Chesapeake Bay, came to mind. Fiona thought of the McKenna's bed and breakfast, stables, and horses. Several bridle paths wound through the McKenna's property, but Fiona preferred the one that skirted the Bay not far from Trey's property line.

Though Wilhelm McKenna spent most of his time at the McKenna sawmill and lumber yard, his wife, Kathleen "Kathy" McKenna, a petite woman, ruled the roost. Kathy came from a long line of horse trainers and jockeys and still rode most days, rain or shine. She was the one to teach the Lowry children to ride and to care for the farm animals, particularly the horses.

Fiona thought of that now as they drove past one horse farm after the other or cattle or sheep farms less than two hours outside London. As teens, she and Aiden would often ride along the shore, find a place to picnic, and go for a swim while their horses grazed in the tall grasses. They would make love in the sunlight as the frisky, salt-water breezes dried their bodies. She closed her eyes, momentarily savoring the images of blue sky, warm sunshine, and cool air as they napped or talked of monumental or inconsequential things.

She and Aiden had such a long history between them that it was sometimes difficult to distinguish where he ended and she began. He had always been a part of her life from the very beginning. Their families were close, long-term friends and their fathers worked together on building projects. When they cleared land on a building site, it was the McKennas who they called to haul away the trees to mill into usable lumber. When a client asked for a specific building service, Wilhelm, without fail, recommended Lowry Construction. Their businesses and friendships fit together like yin and yang. Fiona hoped nothing would change now that it was clear she and Aiden weren't heading to the altar as everyone predicted, especially since there may still be a chance that AJ and Robinette were an item.

"A farthing for your thoughts." Hugh's voice pulled Fiona from her musings.

She smiled to her right at him. "A farthing? That's what, about equal to a quarter of a penny American? Surely my thoughts are worth far more than that."

He nodded and smiled, with his eyes on the road. "Every farthing counts and it's all I can spare at the moment." He smirked with a slight chuckle. "Homesick?"

She shook her head. "No, not yet. I'm in constant contact, via text message or e-mail, with my family. However, it's a little disconcerting to sit on this side of the car without a steering wheel in front of me, the driver's side of a car, and watch you drive on the wrong side of the road."

Hugh laughed. "I've been to the colonies many times, and there's nothing more frightening to me than to watch the demolition derby surrounding any major city there. You Yanks have to have talking cars to figure out where you're going and how to get there, and the cars don't speak the King's English."

Fiona laughed, too. "Not where I live, you don't. My home is in Bay County, a rural area, equal distance from Washington, DC, and Baltimore and Annapolis, Maryland, on the eastern shore of Maryland. We're not far from Ocean City, a big tourist area, and the State of Virginia. Bay County is an agricultural farming district with some large estates mixed in. The biggest things in the area are the county airport, where commuter aircraft are housed, and the county hospital."

"So, you're a country girl," Hugh teased.

"I am. Tried and true and proud of it," Fiona boasted with a grin.

"You must not have many opportunities to use your architectural and engineering skills then."

"On the contrary. My father owns a construction company, the only one of its kind in Bay County. My brothers and I work with him, and we're his subcontractors on most of his projects. We accept jobs from the surrounding counties and beyond, individually and/or as a group, but we like the pace in the rural countryside. My multitude of maternal lineage is based in Louisiana and Barbados before that. My father's family is large. We know everyone in our community because we've lived there for many generations. However, my many paternal great grandfathers came to the United States from Ireland a couple of centuries ago."

"Ah, so did mine, come from Ireland to England, I mean, but we don't still have connections in Ireland. What's your father's name?"

"Alroy Lowry."

"Ah, the red-headed boy. That's what the name, Alroy, means."

Fiona chuckled. "I didn't know that, but he does have red hair."

"As do you, though yours is a dark red." He smiled. "Like your ancestry, everyone in my immediate family has moved to larger cities, even other countries. I have a sister in Argentina and another in the south of France. Two brothers, one in the Royal Navy and the other in Quebec, Canada."

"Do you get together often?"

Hugh shrugged. "Not really. I haven't seen my siblings in about five, no six years now since our mum passed."

Fiona turned her head and looked at his left profile. Her brows bunched. "What about your father?"

"He remarried and lives in Australia. He's a pilot with a local airline there. I hear he married a flight attendant fifteen or twenty years his junior and has two children with her. The thing is, their children's births predate my mum's death."

"You haven't met your stepmother, his wife, and your new siblings?"

Hugh shook his head and shifted, seemingly uncomfortably in his seat. "I'm what you Yanks call 'old school' about some things. So, you no longer want a relationship? Okay, but you do it the right way. You get a divorce. He obviously disrespected our mum by starting another family while he and my mum were still married and living together. We had no idea he had another family in Australia. So, I never gave meeting his new family a thought. The funny thing is, he used to say *'Do as I say not as I do,'* whatever *that* means."

"It sounds like he's admitting he made mistakes in his life but wants to share what he learned so you won't make the same mistakes, too."

"Nice try." Hugh laughed. "He's a son-of-a-bitch, pure and simple."

Nor did Hugh share his grief with his own siblings, Fiona mused. She sensed that there was still a lot of hurt and anger below the surface. Because Hugh and Trey were such close friends, it made her wonder how Trey's early childhood socialization affected his growth and development. It is evident that he and Hugh were not only business associates, but also shared similar histories. Trey didn't talk about his relationship with his parents, so she wondered. Even on short acquaintance, it was clear to her that Trey and his father, the general, were struggling to create a closer relationship. *Family relations could be a sad state of affairs*, Fiona thought. She and her family were so tightly knit she could not imagine them not being in proximity for the rest of her life.

When Fiona went quiet, Hugh wanted to learn more about the woman his pal was falling in love with. "So, each of your brothers has a trade?"

Hugh's question brought her out of her woolgathering. "They do, yes." She told him about each one and, thereby, let him change the subject.

Trey listened to some of the conversation between Fiona and Hugh while Sandra was on her phone making arrangements to use their spare time for their side trip to Paris, France. He had known Hugh Howard for many years and hired Hugh to manage his European interests and London studio. The collaboration was an immediate success.

He also knew Hugh's family story. They shared similar disjointed family backgrounds. Like his father, Hugh's father was also a military man in the Royal Air Force, as Trey's father was a US Army Ranger; both men were rarely at home and both involved in foreign service in Vietnam, Iraq, and/or Afghanistan. In addition, Hugh's father was in service during England's foray into the Falklands. He provided a comfortable living environment for Hugh and his siblings to grow up in, but otherwise, he was an absentee parent. What Trey's father didn't do was disrespect his mother as Hugh's father had. So, it was no surprise that Trey and Hugh became chums.

They met in a London bar one night; two single young men about the same age. While listening to the music, they struck up a conversation about the quality of the sounds. They bonded over the history of music and recognized their kindred spirits. Hugh was working for a record producer, and each time Trey came to London looking for new or unique sounds, he sought Hugh.

After a few years, Trey shared his plan with Hugh to open a studio in London. He already had one in New York City. Hugh jumped at the chance to solidify his relationship with someone he respected, and the collaboration began.

Now, today, riding in the car, Trey's mind wandered back to his own childhood. It had often done that since he met Mavis Lowry, Fiona's mother, the woman his father had a serious crush on in his youth.

Although Trey's mother was a member of the Endicotts, a large, wealthy, old New England high-society family, he hadn't had close ties to that part of his relatives and ancestry. His grandparents arranged his parents' marriage. It was essentially a merger between the Kennards of Boston and Endicotts on both sides of the family tree. Though they were military families, his paternal great-grandparents were also high-society people too.

He was just a boy when his mother died, but he did not live with relatives during his father's deployments. Instead, he was sent to a military boarding school and, oh joy, wasn't that fun, he mused. He learned quickly, though; he obeyed the rules and, as expected, became an above-average student. Yet, on rare occasions when his father came to visit, only his father came, not his grandparents, uncles, aunts, or cousins. There were no warm hugs or kisses. Instead, he and his father shook hands, but didn't otherwise touch and were like two strangers each time meeting for the first time. Trey thought of his childhood dreams. He had hoped that his dad would come and take him home if he did well in school, but that never happened. So instead, Trey spent his time on campus with whoever was available during the holidays and summer vacations. By the time he hit his teen years, he knew there would be no warm hugs or kisses, so he learned to live without any warmth passing between him and his father.

Playing soccer became a passion, and he did it exceptionally well, consistently winning trophies and championships. Trainers scouted him for the Olympics and, because he was also constantly on the Dean's List, top colleges and universities made full-ride athletic or academic scholarship offers. He appeased his musical interest by playing in the military school band and writing music. Unfortunately, his father was rarely there to witness any of his accomplishments. He was not even front and center in the audience when Trey was valedictorian of his graduating class at age sixteen.

His father wanted him to continue his education at a military university. However, Trey refused his father's instructions, eschewed the offers from top universities to play soccer, and instead used his inheritance and trust fund to pay his way without his father's knowledge or consent, enrolling at Julliard in New York City. There he met young talented men and women who shared his love of music. He and a music virtuoso from Los Angeles, California, Mike Hall, became close friends. It was the first time Trey defied his father's directives, and his father took notice.

Trey was surprised when his father transferred to a command position at the United Nations instead of OCONUS, outside the continental United States. After that, they began to see each other more frequently, several times a month. However, it wasn't until one of his instructors mentioned to his father that he considered Trey a musical virtuoso when things began to change between them. That was when his father began to ask questions.

When his father learned he had total recall, eidetic abilities, he became very protective and cautioned him not to discuss his ability with anyone. Years later, after leaving Juilliard, his father introduced him to Bill Chandler. That was when the secrecy and covert missions began.

"We're all set." Sandra made a note on her iPad. "We'll have four days in Paris, maybe five, and Mariah's and Loretta's handlers agreed to the schedule. It'll be tight, but I've rearranged everything we have to do here and built in some downtime or flex time."

Trey nodded; his attention still focused on random memories from his past. That frequently happened after witnessing the closeness between the Lowrys. They were unabashedly demonstrative, hugging often and warmly. He and his father were still struggling to be comfortable in each other's company.

Because he had been too quiet, Sandra looked at Trey. "Something on your mind?"

"No, why?"

"I asked you whether you want me to arrange for more than a three-bedroom suite in Paris, and you didn't answer me."

He shook his head. "I, uh, think you should make it four bedrooms. I don't want to presume...you know." He desperately wanted Fiona to want to come to his bed again voluntarily. They had reservations for the weekend in Truro, the county seat of Cornwall, at the Bodream Manor Farm, a restored Cornish Longhouse with four bedrooms and four baths. It was the perfect location to get to know her better.

As the sun moved into mid-afternoon, the light shone through the car window directly onto Fiona's dark red hair, making it glow as she did in his arms the night before. She was fresh from her shower, her scent impossibly intoxicating. Touching every inch of her body with his tongue and fingertips became an absolute necessity. His desire for her was so intense he forced himself to take it slow, not wanting to frighten her with his neediness. However, thoroughly loving her was his new life's quest, as necessary as breathing in and out. His member thickened at the thought of repeating the cataclysmic eruptions they shared all afternoon long.

When they pulled into the narrow road, leading through the Village of Truro, where the centuries-old buildings encroached on paths of narrow sidewalks and then the even smaller drive up to the Bodream Manor, Fiona was thrilled to see the quaint architecture she immediately recognized as a longhouse. It was a proportionately narrow, single-room building introduced during the Neolithic period around 5,000 BCE. The farming settlements, built-in groups of about six to twelve, were home to large, extended families and kinships.

She got out of the car, her excitement growing. To her left were horses grazing in the lushly green fields, but to her right was a spectacular view of the Irish Sea, where it merged with the Bristol Channel. Behind her was a very walkable and picturesque English village with little shops, parks, and homes where the citizenry warmly greeted each other. When she turned back to look at the house that was centuries old, a smiling woman with bright gray eyes, salt-and-pepper hair, and pleasant features, including plump, pink cheeks, was coming out of the front entrance, drying her hands on an apron around her waist. She caught Trey up in a strong bear hug and giggled like a school girl when he lifted her off her feet. Her greeting for Hugh and Sandra was no less enthusiastic. Then it was Fiona's turn.

"Well, now, who have we here?" She smiled at Fiona; her English accent pronounced to Fiona's ears.

Trey clamped his hands on her shoulders. "Wendrona Ruman, my love, this is Fiona Lizette Lowry from America."

"You don't say?" She looked at Fiona from the bottom up. "All the way from the colonies, did ya say? And as pretty as an Irish lass. So don't be standing there teasing me with questions. Which one of these handsome lads has claimed your heart because surely, Sandra would never step out on her own true love, Harriet?"

Automatically, Fiona looked up over her right shoulder at Trey while Wendrona hooped in laughter.

"Well, now, the village girls will be sorely disappointed to have Maxwell off the market, but I can see why he would have eyes for only you. You've a beautiful aura, a glow around you, Fiona Lizette." She hugged her as enthusiastically as she had the others. "The lassies will, as always, swallow the bull shite Hugh and me own lad be feeding them."

"Thank you, Mrs. Ruman." Fiona enjoyed the warmth the middle-aged woman extended.

"No, no, now it's Wendrona or Wendy, as they called me in me youth, hon." Her Common Brittonic accent was a cross between distinctive neighboring Wales and Brittany.

Having heard so many English dialects in the weeks since their arrival, Fiona was beginning to distinguish the unique differences in each sound.

"I've never been married, but I've a good, strong, and handsome son about your age to brag about. He'll be over the top when he sees you and learns Maxwell already stole your heart."

Fiona blushed. "Yes, ma'am."

With their arms around each other's waists, Wendrona guided her into the farmhouse as Fiona asked questions about the architecture. The ceilings were much lower in the entrance, but the plastered, tapioca-colored walls gave the illusion of space in the long, narrow room. The large, comfortable-looking furniture took away the illusion. Yet, the intimately arranged groupings encouraged conversation. However, along one entire wall at the far end were unusually tall, diamond-shaped windows that offered an unobstructed, panoramic view of the water.

When Wendrona released Fiona to go check on her pots on the stove, Fiona walked to the ceiling-to-floor, diamond-shaped windows and just stared out. The Chesapeake Bay was broad, but, ultimately, she could see the western shore in some places from the eastern side of the bay. Here, it was so vast, Fiona was hard-pressed to distinguish the water from the sky.

Trey stood behind Fiona, just as awed at the sight, and, though he had seen it many times, as impressed as she seemed to be. Leaning forward around her, he unlatched the window, letting it swing out, and stepped through to the stone patio beyond. Trey reached for Fiona's hand, and she placed hers in his, following him out. He closed the window door behind them, and then they moved to the intricately designed, fenced iron railing.

Fiona stood before Trey, with his arms wrapped securely around her.

The brisk ocean breeze swung from one direction and then the other in an energetic dance, taking her loose, long hair with it.

"Chilled?"

She nodded. "A bit, but I could stand here in this spot for the rest of my life."

Trey nestled her inside his jacket, her back to his warm, solid chest, her head tucked under his chin and his arms crossed about her upper body. He kissed the top of her head and was content to spend the rest of his life standing like that, with her in his arms.

Fiona leaned her head back against the solid wall of Trey's chest, closed her eyes, luxuriating in his protective embrace, and drifted toward an exciting feeling for him in her heart.

Later, Fiona snapped pictures of the charmingly laid-out meal and sent them to her mother. They dined with Wendrona and her son, Cayden, on a leek-and-onion soup, smoked salmon, steamed vegetables, whipped garlic potatoes, roasted Cornish game hens with lemon and herbs, and Beef Wellington. They drank bottles of both red and/or white wines with each course. By the time they got to the Yorkshire pudding and coffee, Fiona was stuffed. Wendrona was a fine cook and reminded Fiona of her own mother's ability and cuisine. Sure enough, Mavis returned the text message requesting the recipe for each of the dishes.

Fiona was intrigued with the conversation as they lingered over coffee and port. "Wendrona, your name is unusual. Do you mind my asking where it came from?"

Wendrona hooted a laugh. "It is, and for as long as these three have been coming here to soak up the local culture, none have asked the origin."

Fiona shrugged. "It's the natural curiosity in me. After all, I'm a Yank."

Everyone laughed.

"Well, now, for your further English education about all things British, me da and mum named me for the Saint Wendrona, the patron saint of Wendron Parish Church. There is actually a village and civil parish here in Cornwall named Wendron many centuries ago. In the early Norman times, it is said that Saint Michael, the Archangel, was and is recognized by the Anglican Church as —."

"The Protector of Cornwall," Cayden, Wendrona's son, interjected. "So, me dear mum named me Cayden Michael to ensure I would never leave me roots here and would forever be the protector of our village and farm."

Everyone laughed at Wendrona's chagrin expression.

"He's a good lad, me son is! He sits on the Cornwall Council and the Crown Court, me son does. He makes his mum proud."

"'Tis true, what me mum says, but I prefer me farm duties to those required of me legal training."

Fiona's eyes widened in surprise. "You're a lawyer?"

"Barrister, yes. We're called barristers here and various other unsavory names." He took her hand to kiss her knuckles. "But, me beautiful Fiona Lizette, if you would but throw over Maxwell, The Magic Music Man, I would beg to be whatever it is you desire me to be."

She deftly removed her hand from his before his lips touched down again. "I think your mum already warned me about the bull shite you're capable of throwing."

Cayden grabbed his chest as if wounded, mimicking pulling an arrow from his heart with a pretense of anguish written on his handsome face. "You wound me, Fiona Lizette, my one true love, but would you perchance have a sister of the adult kind?"

Everyone again broke into gales of laughter.

To walk off their meal, Trey, Fiona, Hugh, and Sandra strolled through the narrow streets of the Village of Truro with others going in and out of quaint little shops. Cayden joined them, steering them to the most interesting sights in the village. As night fell, Trey led them to Ye Come Back Inn, an English pub and roadhouse. It smelled of yeast, beer, kidney pie, and fish and chips. There were rows of small tables and chairs in the long building with a dark mahogany bar that stretched the room's length. A quartet was wailing on an old mariner's folk song in the center of the room while the customers sang along, beating on tables or stomping their feet.

A roar went up when Trey entered the pub. Pats on his back followed him all the way to the bar. Women threw enticing looks at him, Hugh, and Cayden as the men made their way through the crowd.

"Well, if it isn't himself, come to visit," joked a tall, stocky man with electric blue eyes and a full red beard of obvious Cornish Celtic and Anglo-Saxon ancestry with a little Viking mixed in. He wore a battered watch cap and sat on a tall stool with a guitar slung across his broad body. Other members of the band hailed Trey by raising large, dark beer lagers in a toast. "Come give us a song, Yank."

Trey begged off, but the crowd started loudly beating on tables or stomping their feet on the ancient, scarred, hardwood floor covered with peanut shells and raising a racket. Finally, someone produced a guitar and a tall stool for Trey to sit on.

Trey only wanted to come and enjoy the pub's music with Fiona, but it was rare for him to do so without being cajoled into joining in. Two gentlemanly patrons offered Fiona and Sandra their seats at the bar, and their beer mugs were never empty. Trey settled in, quickly tuning the guitar, and selected an old John Denver song, "Sunshine on My Shoulders."

Fiona sat transfixed as she listened to his rendition of the song. This was yet another facet to the man she was coming to admire...and, perhaps, even love. Trey's voice and manner were mesmerizing. He sat on the tall stool, one booted foot hooked on a rung of the footrest, with the guitar resting on his firm thigh. The room quieted, and all activity stopped. No one moved, not the customers or the waitstaff.

He looked up at Fiona, their incisive gazes locked as he strummed the intro and, although the room was almost to capacity and more coming in, he sang only for her. *"If I had a day that I could give you, I'd give to you the day just like today. If I had a song that I could sing for you, I'd sing a song to make you feel this way."*

Fiona's chest was tight, her heart beating erratically and swelling as Trey continued to sing to her with his full, rich voice and expertly strumming the guitar, never taking his eyes from hers. When he finished, absolute silence reigned. He stood, closing the distance between them, and then leaned down, taking her mouth in a soul-stirring kiss.

The room erupted in loud, raucous applause, whistles, and stomping feet, but Fiona could only look up into Trey's pretty, green-eyed gaze. For ponderous moments, they stared at each other until she rose on her toes from her place at the bar, palmed his face, and kissed him back. Then the roar became even louder with boisterous cheers.

When Fiona released him, he smiled at her and winked. The crowd, however, was demanding another song. So, Trey reluctantly returned to the group and kept his eyes on her for the next few hours as they continued the jam session for the packed bar and standing-room-only patrons, who made room for dancing the jig.

Women clung to Hugh and Cayden like vines. It was certain they would not sleep alone tonight. As one song flowed into another, the crowd enthusiastically joined in.

Hugh shook his head while applauding at the end of another song. "You know, Fiona, I've been trying to get Trey to record his voice, but he refuses."

"He's extremely talented," Sandra offered, "but he's dedicated to using his gifts to promote other artists."

Hugh grinned. "You seem to have some influence with him, maybe—"

"No." Fiona shook her head with finality, not taking her eyes off Trey as the group of musicians performed an instrumental piece without voice.

Hugh laughed, as did Sandra. "How did I know you were going to say that?"

Because there is nothing I want to change about Maxwell Bishop Kennard the Third, Fiona thought. He was funny, talented, handsome, intelligent, and had more attributes that added up to near perfection in her eyes. That included their lovemaking. His touch electrified and soothed her, taking her to heights she had never experienced before. She was quickly becoming addicted to his taste.

Aiden stood on the dais with two other contenders for the State Attorney General's position. The televised debate was already in its second hour, and all he could think about was Fiona. For months, he had prepped for this second of three public debates and was ready to meet the challenge with his parents, siblings, and Fiona's family in attendance for moral support. However, it wasn't the same without Fiona by his side. When he took himself too seriously or went on a winding road that would put his audience into a coma, Fiona would be in his line of sight, making funny faces at him that could easily make him break into stifled laughter. He smiled at the memory and then sobered. This was the first time Aiden knew that he would not be able to swing by her place or have her meet him at his. He missed her in his space, in his bed, and, more importantly, in his life.

After the debate ended, and he was hailed far and away as the event's winner, his family and friends stood by patiently as the press and news media interviewed him. Aiden's entourage was going to a restaurant to eat and to wait for the critiques to hit the news and social media. However, one question threw him off course.

"Congressman McKenna, heretofore you've been seen at political events with your long-time girlfriend, architect Fiona Lowry. However, the last public events you've attended on your campaign trail, she has been noticeably absent. Still, according to the international press, Ms.

Lowry has been photographed in the constant company of popular music producer Trey Kennard. In fact, they are, apparently, living together in London, England. So is there trouble in paradise?"

He recognized the question for what it was: a fishing expedition and a means of getting back at him for spurning her advances. The female reporter, Chevon Ellis, who asked the question, had been coming on to him for years and trying to insinuate herself into his life. Ms. Ellis would often interview him on crucial issues pending before the US House of Representatives, but found he had to work hard to avoid meeting her outside of their professional relationship. However, since Fiona's departure, the television reporter had stepped up her game, and he was hard-pressed to find ways to avoid her.

Harris Charles, his campaign manager, stepped up. "The Congressman is running for the Maryland State Attorney General's office. All other matters have no place in this debate or this campaign. Next question?"

Aiden realized he was just standing there, forcing his surrogate to step in. He was ready with a concise answer to the next question, but Aiden noticed that Chevon had a Cheshire cat smile on her face. She knew she landed a blow to his heart. First, however, he would Google Trey Kennard to determine precisely what the media was reporting about the man and Fiona. He was far from willing to concede on this or any other campaign to get what he wanted. That included bringing Fiona back into his camp as his wife.

Chapter 12

The next morning, Trey woke early before dawn with Fiona warm and naked in his arms. They stayed the night before until the pub closed and enjoyed the local music, beer, and camaraderie. When they returned to the B&B, Fiona led the way to his room and began to undress him. It was pure heaven to help her disrobe as she helped him and then to make love with her. Even after they fell asleep, he reached for her, and she responded to his touch. He began to dream of a future with her in it, but he wondered whether she was with him on this magic carpet ride she had created for him.

In his entire thirty-plus years of life, he never had anyone offer precisely what he needed on an intimate level. She possessed such a warm and giving spirit, yet a delightfully impish personality that he adored. Her intimate responsiveness to him seemed as natural as breathing. Whenever they were together, his mating instincts took over and he couldn't seem to get enough of her. However, he combined his natural curiosity about a potential life with Fiona with caution. He never felt this overwhelming sense of the rightness of being with her. It...no, *she* was becoming the most important person in his life, and therein lay the trap. Anyone wanting to hurt him could use her by putting her in harm's way. As a result, he could very well lose her.

Turning his head toward the window, Trey raised his left hand to palm the back of his head. His fingers tangled in his unusually long hair. He had forgotten entirely about the haircut he needed, but Fiona enjoyed running her fingers through his long shoulder-length hair when they made love. So, to please her, he simply tied it in a queue at the nape of his neck. However, she liked it loose, nearly falling onto his shoulders. So, he hadn't bothered to cut it. If Fiona continued to touch him the way she liked to do, no barber would be getting his business anytime soon.

Outside the bedroom windows, the fingers of light began to illuminate the water and sky. Birds chorused a cacophony of sound, which was music to Trey's ears. Fishing boats, barely seen through the mist, made their way out to sea on the placid watery surface. The scene inspired a melody in his head, but he didn't move to make a note of it. Instead, he was more than content to stay where he was with Fiona in his arms.

He turned to look at her beautiful, *café au lait* complexion, reminding him of the actress Jennifer Beals of *Flashdance* fame. Fiona was not completely visible in the dim light, but he didn't need the sunshine to illuminate her features for him. His mind's eye had captured her for eternity. Her long, thick hair fanned out on his arm and the pillow the way he liked it, wavy and soft to the touch.

Then, as he continued to look his fill, he felt her hand move on his chest, slowly rubbing his left nipple between her fingertips. He kissed her temple, letting her play with his body while luxuriating in the warmth he felt with her pressed solidly into his right side. She cuddled even closer as her right hand roamed over him in question and need and found him hard and heavy, awaiting her special touch. Fiona didn't disappoint.

Her thick hair was loose around her, and, as he ran his fingers through the long strands, they feathered his abdomen and thighs, creating a curtain around her face as she took complete possession of him. He knew he would not last long with her skillful touch and reached for a foil packet on the nightstand.

Her clever fingers covered him, exercising him to a near explosion. Then, with him in hand, she guided him home while simultaneously latching onto his slightly raised chest tits. When she mounted him, riding him slowly, as if she was an experienced belly dancer, his hips seemed to move on their own volition. Fiona set the pace while he struggled to maintain control of his body.

Fiona felt that pecks like Trey's deserved to be worshipped and adored, and she did her best to meet the challenge. He moaned deeply, loudly, and long as her hands and mouth went to work, enjoying the pleasure of having him rock her world.

As Trey reversed positions, his body quickly and expertly brought her to and over another peak. He rolled his hips without losing their connection. "Fiona," he moaned like a mantra or a fervent prayer.

He was so thick, hot, and huge inside her, but didn't seem to need any direction. Instead, he read her body like it was fast-breaking news. Fiona moved with him, his strokes so firm inside her, consistently rubbing against her G-spot. She had incredible control of her PC muscles to the point his member felt as if it were in a velvet vice. Palming her breast, he molded her flesh until her nipples were as hard as pebbles. Her hands went up into her hair and loosened her locks by gliding her fingers through the strands, while his long, blunt fingers and thumb went to her sweet spot, aggressively massaging. Still, her internal muscles held him, shuddering through successive releases.

Trey could not seem to slow down because it felt so amazingly good to be inside her tight, wet portal. Even though she had cum several times in succession, she was still virginally tight. Her body still gripped him as tightly as if fisted in her hand. Each second he knew it couldn't get any better, but then it did when she tightened those female muscles even more, and he found himself near asphyxiation from his heavy breathing. Trey had never experienced what he heard called the Singapore Kiss before, and now that he had, he didn't know whether he would ever be satisfied with ordinary sex again.

Then she palmed his face, ravished his mouth, and pumped him harder and faster than before, this time sliding back and forth while on her knees to give her sweet spot the friction she needed. Grabbing her hips, he helped her glide, his penis slick with her creamy moisture. His nuts contracted into him before he lost control and came hard on a strangled cry. The spasms went on for what seemed like an eternity, his heart thundering in his chest and his muscles bunching taunt against the exquisite pain of a long, hard, pleasurable release.

In his haze, he felt Fiona follow within seconds of his earth-shattering discharge. Lightheaded from the rush, Trey thought he might pass out.

Eyes closed, he tried to focus on taking slow, deep breaths. However, her tightly flexing and spasming inner muscles were lethal on his still too sensitive penis, making him involuntarily tremble.

Fiona loved the way Trey made love with her. She clamped so tightly around him he couldn't pull out of her without hurting himself or her. For a while, the pleasure was so great, Fiona's muscles locked, causing a series of orgasms to flash over her in rapid succession. Once she released him, she took off the condom and mouthed him into life, tasting the remnants of his release and desiring more. Like so many other aspects of Trey, his recuperative ability and stamina were amazing. He wasn't a passive lover. Instead, he gave her wave after wave of unbridled and unbelievable pleasure. His warm hands glided over her body as if he couldn't get enough of her.

A while later, after another round of intimacy, the light was brighter, but Fiona, this time, was content to lie beneath Trey, lazily strumming his strong, muscular back while they tried to catch a normal breath. She could feel his heart thundering in his chest while his member rested snugly inside her. Again, she thoroughly enjoyed the intimacy they created and craved even more. Even under the light scent of sex, his natural smell was enticing and intoxicating.

"Come, I've a surprise for you." Trey slowly pulled out of her.

She languidly stretched and smiled up at him. "You mean another one?"

Geezus, Trey thought as he watched her lazily stretch with a contented smile. Fiona was so achingly beautiful, soft, and warm from making love that he was tempted to return to her warm embrace. Instead, he pulled her out of bed and into the adjacent bath.

They were in the barn twenty minutes later where Wendrona's son, Cayden, had a couple of horses saddled and waiting. Trey thought *the smile on Fiona's heartbreakingly beautiful face could have launched a thousand ships.*

It was still early when Trey led Fiona on a brisk ride across the fields on land that opened and rose and fell in mounds of thick, green grass.

It reminded her of the fourteen-thousand-acre Chincoteague wildlife preserve near her home, where wild ponies roamed. She and Trey crossed creeks and dales through sparse woodlands. Finally, they made their way down to the beach and narrow sandy shore with the tide incoming, splashing through the surf at the water's edge at break-neck speeds. Her mount, a beautiful Andalusian, had sure footing and a will to run, but he immediately responded to her direction when she signaled to slow down. He reminded her of the wild horses of the Chincoteague and Assateague Islands, not far from Trey's property. It wasn't unusual to wake to the sight of wild horses grazing on her own family's compound, too

She smiled to herself. Although he had seen the horses on his property, it was one of those local sights she failed to mention to Trey. Because his land was unoccupied for many generations, the horses took full advantage of the tall, sweet grasses his farmland afforded and the vegetable garden that continued to grow wild on the property. AJ would make allowances for that in his landscaping plan, she was sure.

Once on the hard-packed, sandy beach, riding side-by-side, they gave their mounts their heads and let them run full out for about a quarter-mile along the wide moorland landscapes, its long and varied coastline, and Bodmin Moor, a gift from Mother Nature. The coastline, composed mainly of resistant rock walls, gave rise in many places to impressive cliffs.

Her thick braid came loose and flowed as if in an airstream behind her as it dried. The horses raced neck-and-neck along the shore. Her eyes were intense, Trey noted, but she was laughing like a loon, her face radiant as she leaned forward over the horse's head, her knees bent and thighs holding her aloft over her saddle. Though the saddle was English, she rode American style like a jockey on a thoroughbred. Yet, Fiona intrigued him even more. She was one with her mount as if she didn't even need the saddle.

He had seen her gloriously naked, dressed to the nines, in sophisticated evening wear, chic club clothes, and dressed down in jeans and tennis shoes. Yet, in every view he had of her, she remained unchanged. She was simply Fiona Lizette Lowry, a self-possessed woman comfortable in any surroundings. Trey was coming to love that trait about her.

Later, Hugh looked up as he sat with the others gathered at the breakfast table. "Where did you two get off to so early?"

Trey shrugged. "I took Fiona riding along the coast."

Hugh looked at Fiona with a smile and tilted his head. "You ride?"

"I do, yes, since I was knee-high to a pony. Piccolo was my first mount. I was five."

Hugh chuckled and shook his head. "You truly are a country lass."

Fiona opened her napkin and placed it across her lap. "I told you. It was a great ride. Back home, I ride often."

Cayden smiled, blessed himself, and tucked into his food. "Well, we have a lot planned today after we break our fast, but we can walk most of it."

Of course, their early morning ride required Trey and Fiona to shower again, which took them longer because they were busy making love. Eventually, they put on clothes suitable for a day of sightseeing on foot in the area: boots and knee-length shorts with T-shirts.

They packed bottles of water and pieces of fruit into backpacks as they began their journey and struck out across the fields. In unexpected places, there were churches galore, dating back to the eleventh century and still in use, like St. German's Priory, a church built during the Norman invasion. The Church of St. Petroc at Bodmin, built in the late fifteenth century, was still stunning in its place on the wide-open landscape. Fiona snapped pictures from every conceivable angle while Cayden gave a running commentary on the history of each building. "In the early nineteenth century, Methodism was the leading form of Christianity in Cornwall County, but the little Poughill Methodist Church shows no grandeur as compared to its predecessors."

Fiona, who studied the changing architectures of religious buildings, still found actually seeing and touching the structures riveting.

"Here we have the Cornish Riviera," Cayden joked as they stood on the high cliffs overlooking the water and beaches.

"That's a picturesque fishing village." Fiona pointed far below and toward the north. "What's it called?"

"Polperro. It sits on the mouth of Pol River. There's also a fishing port called Looe on the River Looe just a little further north with the best fish stew you've ever tasted. I think we can make it there about tea time."

The spectacular dark green and red cliffs were impressive against the azure blue sky and deep blue sea. When Fiona saw a shadow on the ground and looked up, a red-billed chough flew low overhead. Its black wings spread impossibly wide in a buoyant acrobatic flight. The bird's glossy black plumage, long curved red bill, red legs, and loud, ringing call were startling to see up close.

"That's a chough," Cayden offered. "They nest in these cliffs."

"I know. My brother, Peter, is a stamp collector and he has that bird in his collection." She snapped pictures of the bird and immediately forwarded them to her brother.

Cayden looked up. "Well, now, it's a rare sight to see this bird so close. Nature is showing off for our Fiona Lizette. We usually have mostly rainy days, but since your arrival, we've had a bit of sunshine and balmy weather. Perchance we could induce you to stay and bring sunshine for a fortnight?"

"Thank you, no, but nice try." Fiona laughed as she continued to watch the huge bird's flight out over the ocean waters and quaint fishing village. "I happen to know Cornwall is one of the sunniest areas in the United Kingdom with more than seven hours of sunshine per day."

"*Ha!*" Sandra scoffed on a rolling laugh. "That's what comes of trying to flirt with an intelligent woman, Cayden Ruman. You get your bull shite handed to you."

"Nothing beats a try," a grinning Cayden offered.

On they walked, as Cayden continued to narrate the walking tour. They stopped at a curbside bistro in Looe with impressive views, including the female waitstaff whose pretty faces and buxom bodies were constantly on display for the three handsome men. Fiona and Sandra enjoyed the show the women put on to grab Hugh's, Trey's, and Cayden's attention. The ocean views, moist, mild air, and fish stew were all fresh and superb.

Both Hugh and Cayden left the bistro with phone numbers and promises to hook up later that night. Then the group was off again on their hike, this time to Penzance, the westernmost town in the county. They shopped there and moved on to the Cornwall Council's headquarters, where Cayden spent part of his time as a councilman. Once there, it was apparent, from the deference shown him, that Cayden was a man of influence and respect.

As they walked, Hugh and Cayden started a lively discourse over national politics. "The single council is our opportunity to maintain control over local issues from those of other regional and national government bureaucrats," Cayden argued with Hugh. "We are Cornish descendants forced to be subjugated to British rule."

"Cornwall is still a part of Great Britain and has to participate in national issues," Hugh countered.

"Ah, Rule, Britannia," Cayden scoffed. "Our issues are different here than in the . . ."

"Tired?" Trey put an arm around Fiona's shoulders as they continued their trek.

Fiona interlaced her fingers with his, her free arm circling his waist, and shook her head. "No, it's been a good walk. I even enjoy listening to Cayden and Hugh argue politics."

"You spent a considerable amount of time working on Aiden's campaign. So I imagine hearing Hugh and Cayden debate is second nature to you."

She slowed to a stop, turned toward him, seeming to search his eyes. "Are you concerned that I miss being with Aiden, Trey?"

Sticking his hands in his pockets, he looked down into her sun-tea-colored eyes but said nothing.

Placing a hand over his heart, she looked up into his eyes and tilted her head.

He shrugged and then shook his head.

Leaning up on her booted toes, she kissed him, snaked her arms around his waist, and smiled at him.

They didn't have to communicate verbally. It was all the reassurance he needed and what she could offer.

Cayden interrupted the intimate moment, seemingly without knowing it existed. He looped an arm around Fiona's shoulders, guiding her to where she could view the next exhibit of ancient Cornish culture and architecture.

By mid-afternoon, they had walked miles of the countryside and were back at the B&B, where Cayden had parked his van.

"We are off, lass, to the land where Maxwell will disappear into thin air."

Fiona laughed. "Oh? Where is that?"

"Newlyn, me darlin'. Home of the best food and music festival in all of Great Britain. I've tortured himself all the day long by taking you on a walking tour of our fair county. He's about champing at the bit to hear the Mummers Play, the Furry Dance played by the Helston Town Band, and the Obby Oss of Padstow."

"The what?" Fiona laughed. "You're making those names up."

"No bull shite, lass. The Obby Oss is a traditional part of May Day in Padstow. The festival starts at midnight tonight, May Eve. Townspeople will gather to sing the 'Night Song.' By morning, the towns will be dressed with greenery and flowers placed around a maypole."

"Folk music," Hugh supplied helpfully. "Some of the best can be found at the music festival here in Cornwall County. Last year, we contracted with a male voice choir for a movie score. The score is up for an Academy Award. This year, we wanted to hear the Camborne Youth Band to determine whether it's right for another classical ballet *III* has been contracted to score back in the colonies. The last ballet, *Goodwill,* is an all-young-people production. The new classical ballet is in preproduction but hasn't been titled yet. We plan to feature musical sounds from all around the world."

Fiona looked up sharply. "This ballet wouldn't happen to be for the prima ballerina Linda Lewis, would it?"

Trey's brows furrowed. "Yes, it is. How did you know?"

"I've not only met Linda, but I also helped my cousin, JaiHonnah Baylor, design and remodel Linda's mixed-use residence and dance studio in Manhattan last year."

Sandra crossed her arms over her chest. "Well, I'll be. Linda approached Trey last fall through a mutual friend, Angelique."

Nodding, Fiona grinned. "I know Angelique as well. She's a highly-respected restaurateur, Le Cordon Bleu chef, fashion model, and screen actress. Linda and Angelique have been best friends for many years. In fact, Angelique is the wife of the sport's icon, Gregory Alexander, Linda's uncle."

"It's a small world after all," Hugh sang in a really good voice, making the van's inhabitants laugh.

Once parked at the fairgrounds, they walked the acres of exhibits full of vibrant art and crafts. Several pieces of pottery caught Fiona's eye. She bought them, arranged to have them shipped, and took the artisan's brochure to be sure she could order additional pieces once she was back at home. She also bought gifts for her family and had them shipped as well.

As the sun began to sink, they purchased a picnic basket so full of food it took Cayden and Trey to carry it while Hugh carried a cooler with bottles of wine and water. Sandra and Fiona found a strategic spot on the grass to spread blankets in preparation for the cavalcade of forty or so bands scheduled to perform that evening.

It was nearing two in the morning when Trey, Fiona, and Sandra returned to the B&B. Hugh and Cayden hooked up with the women from the Looe bistro and had other plans. Trey and Fiona showered together before falling into bed. They made love slowly, languidly before sleep claimed them. Still, they were up early the following day for breakfast and a short walk to church services to hear a noted choir sing. Unfortunately, the church was near capacity, and they had to wedge themselves onto bench seats. Fiona noticed that when Trey was in intense listening mode, he closed his pretty green eyes, blocking out all forms of visual stimulation.

After services ended, Trey and Hugh approached the choir director and made his day. Animatedly, the director called the choir together, and, after a short conference, a boisterous cheer went up for Trey and

Hugh. Trey settled the singers down and had them resume their seats in the choir loft. Then, in an impromptu performance, Hugh took a seat at the church organ while Trey led the choir in an energetic and rousing reprise of the Hallelujah Chorus. Fiona took a seat with the others and just listened.

As they left the beautiful church, Trey shook hands with those still there and then put an arm around her shoulders as they began their walk back to the B&B. However, Fiona noticed that Trey's attention was inward, likely mentally working on some piece of music he was creating in his head. Though one arm was around her, his other was in his pocket as they quietly strolled. Then he suddenly kissed her temple, almost absentmindedly.

"Did you enjoy the service?"

"I did, yes. The music was great, too."

He nodded. "That it was." A beatific smile graced his face.

By ten in the morning, Trey, Hugh, and Cayden had donned sports clothes to play soccer on a nearby field. Now Fiona knew why there were so many people in Truro at early church services. Another favorite pastime drew an enormous crowd of city and county people on May Day. The players would choose sides by donning either a predominately black or a predominately white numbered jersey. The jerseys were reminiscent of the flag of Cornwall. Formerly known as the banner of Saint Piran, it was a white cross on a black background. Trey, Hugh, and Cayden were on the first team and wore white shirts with black crosses.

Wendrona grabbed seats at a vacant table with an umbrella beside the field near the center point of the action. She laid out sandwiches and snacks and cheered like a banshee on steroids. She knew the game well because she called soccer plays better than the radio announcer.

Fiona didn't need the play-by-play commentary because she kept her eyes on Trey. He had long, powerful legs and quick feet. Trey was fast, too, and accurate as he passed the ball back and forth between himself and his teammates. After a while, he was dripping in sweat, making his clothes stick to his very well-toned body, turning his white shorts almost translucent. *Oh, my*, she thought, as the game continued. *It is almost as if he is naked.* Her mouth went dry.

During timeouts, the team members would guzzle water but did nothing to shield their wet, nearly exposed bodies as they kept moving during breaks.

Trey's hair was dripping wet and plastered to his head. He poured a bottle of water over his head and shook it before tunneling his long, clever fingers through it and then securing it in a ponytail.

Fiona wore a pair of shorts and a T-shirt that shouldn't have been sexy by half, Trey noticed. Yet, her long, light-brown shapely legs, sandaled feet with pink polish, and hourglass figure had him in a constant state of semi-arousal. The game did the rest. It had been such a great weekend, and Fiona was mainly the reason why. Standing with her, overlooking the water on the first day; singing to her at the pub; horseback riding with her through the woods and along the shore; walking hand-in-hand with her on their tour of the county; sitting with her between his thighs with her back to his chest during the concert; and now looking at her looking at him, the images coalesced and made his heart slip further out of his control and into her hands. There was nothing about Fiona Lizette Lowry that didn't intrigue and please him. It was becoming more difficult not to fall face-first in love with her.

Chapter 13

Over the next two weeks, Fiona was treated to tours of some of the most iconic and fascinating attractions in Great Britain. For example, Hadrian's Wall, built in 122 AD, was at one time over seventy miles long and extended across England from the Irish Sea to the North Sea. The Romans built the wall to protect their colony, Britannia, from the tribes of Scotland. Although only stretches still existed, Fiona was thrilled to walk along a segment of it with Hugh, Trey, and Sandra, touching the massive stones that made up its girth and length.

Warwick Castle, another Roman construction built in the twelfth century during the Hundred Years' War, was a stunning example of military architecture. Fiona took pictures conceivably from every possible angle. Trey was delighted with her enthusiasm. However, he was even more touched by her reverent appreciation of the Lake District of Northwest England in Cumbria County. They walked the mountains and hills, enjoying scenery carved by glacial erosion that was awe-inspiring.

Fiona had a particular sensitivity to all things of natural beauty, Trey learned. It was easy to see why the glass house she created was so unique to her. Trey knew she wanted to maintain the natural splendor of nature. Now he understood that the glass house would preserve the beauty of the natural surroundings while, at the same time, permitting him to enjoy Mother Nature's gifts. She studied architecture as an academic necessity to practice her craft, but nature was her focal point, her guidepost in any construction.

They took a private, long boat ride on a stormy day to view the Tower of London, the home of the British Crown Jewels. Trey knew Fiona was disappointed about not being able to walk the grounds and the castle founded in 1066, but he had a secret he hoped would make up for it.

On a day trip, thankfully absent of rainy downpours, they roamed The Cotswolds, a range of gentle hills in south-central England famous for stone-built villages, historic towns, and stately homes and gardens. AJ asked Fiona to take lots of pictures of the gardens and parks if she had an opportunity to visit. She was happy to fulfill her brother's request and uploaded hundreds of photos of the flowers and green spaces to her cloud server earmarked for him.

They toured Durham Cathedral, cherished for its extraordinary architecture and incomparable setting. Then there was the Gothic York Minster, which, to Fiona's trained eye, incorporated all stages of architectural development in England.

One day, after an afternoon nap, Fiona noticed Trey was not in his bed with her. So, she showered and found Sandra at the kitchen island, talking on the phone to her wife. So as not to disturb Sandra, Fiona quietly prepared a snack of hard cheese, crisp green grapes, apple wedges, and freshly sliced salami with sea toast.

"I miss you, too." Sandra sighed as she disconnected the call. "That looks good. Is there enough to share?"

"There is, yes." Fiona sat the tray on the countertop for Sandra before going to the instant hot water and selecting her favorite brand of tea to steep. "Would you like coffee or tea?"

"Tea." Sandra yawned. "Did you rest well?"

"I slept so deeply I didn't notice when Trey left the room."

"He's been gone for several hours. Hugh picked him up."

"Did they have another session today?"

"They did, yes."

"Now I feel guilty about wanting to spend more time at York Minster. I didn't realize they had more work to do today."

"York Minster's been there for centuries." Sandra laughed. "It's not going anywhere anytime soon, so we can make time to go again if you'd like."

Fiona shook her head, brought the steeping pot of tea and a cup, and set it before Sandra. Then she retrieved another pot and cup for herself. "It's not necessary. We did get to tour a great deal of it."

"As often as I've been to England, I never took the time to go sightseeing or appreciated the architecture of buildings until you added why they are so noteworthy. I mean, I live in New York City around so many significant sights and I just don't see them. I'm either heading home to spend time with afternoon activities and my children or to work to ensure that Trey's schedule doesn't get royally screwed up. When I hear you talk about when these sights were constructed and why, it takes on a whole new dimension."

"It does for me as well, Sandra. I mean, I studied architecture at Carnegie Mellon University because Pittsburgh was close to home, but to actually touch these iconic buildings makes what I learned, as a purely academic exercise, come alive. Then I imagine all of the other sights I've only read about and I want to see even more."

"You should, Fiona. I've worked for Trey for many years. I've learned so much about the entertainment industry, which is a huge departure from my background in business administration. However, traveling has been the best classroom experience I could have had. I just wish I didn't have to leave Harriet and our children to enjoy the experience."

"I've been thinking along those same lines. I'm only in my mid-twenties and have no reason not to travel. Frankly, this trip has fired my creative imagination. I'd like to see more now rather than later. I really enjoy the creative process, but this trip has opened me to so much more of this world's natural wonders and this is only an infinitesimal portion of the whole."

"As I told you, stick with me, kid," Sandra joked as she got up to answer the chime at the elevator door.

Shortly, she returned with the personal shopper, Thelma Grayson.

"Well, hello, dearie," Thelma greeted.

"Hello, Thelma." Fiona was surprised to see the woman. Thelma provided so many changes of clothes that Fiona hardly chose to wear the clothes she brought on the trip with her. Instead, Fiona purchased almost everything Thelma recommended because they had two more months to go and three countries to visit before returning to her home in Maryland. Fiona had no idea what she would do with so many new outfits once she was back in Bay County. However, thankfully, she didn't have to decide now about the additional wardrobe for a while. They were flying on a private plane, so the amount of new luggage was not an issue. Still, it alone took up an incredible amount of space. So, Trey ordered trunks like his and Sandra's, which accommodated more clothes and shoes for her expanded wardrobe.

"Are we ready to dress for the evening?" Thelma asked.

"Fiona?" Sandra asked as she disposed of the remnants of their snack and the dishes in the washer.

"Certainly. I didn't realize we had an event planned for tonight." Fiona stood and headed to her rooms in the suite. "I've already showered, so I'll be ready in twenty minutes."

Fiona didn't take long to get ready, but when she reentered the bedroom, Thelma had just finished steaming the most beautiful forest-green, strapless, floor-length gown. Silver threads woven into the fabric caused the gown to shimmer, shine, and sparkle with movement. Then, she caught sight of a silver wrap with contrasting forest-green threads that matched the gown perfectly. She peeked at the label and her eyes popped wide. It was a Carlos Ortega original. The shoes were stilettos with a few webs of diamond-encrusted silver and forest-green straps across the toes and at the ankle. The shoes were also from the famous designer's collection. Thelma was a pure genius when it came to selecting clothes that suited her. Then she did Fiona's hair and makeup before assisting Sandra with a honeydew-melon-colored gown with a black cape. It made for a stunning contrast.

Sandra joined Fiona in the living area where Thelma, as usual, took pictures of the results of her efforts. The cherry on the icing was the simple but elegant drop diamond earrings and matching purses, which contained laced gloves and a tube of lip gloss.

"I think we're ready." Sandra led the way to the elevator doors.

"Don't we have to wait for Trey and Hugh?"

"They'll meet us."

Fiona shrugged. After weeks of the evening routine, she was accustomed to the glitz, glamour, and glitter, which sometimes was a requirement, so she and Sandra chatted amicably as the limo chauffeured them through the streets. However, unlike previous occasions, the window partition between the driver and the car's rear was up and the other windows were dark.

When the car pulled to a stop, the rear door opened, and Fiona followed Sandra out, expecting a host to greet her at another London club. However, when she looked up, and up, and up, her breath caught at the sight of Trey standing on the steps of none other than Buckingham Palace. Palace guards, resplendent in bright red, black, and white uniforms, squired her to where Trey waited with Hugh. Trey looked indescribably delicious in formal evening wear, his thick hair neatly trimmed and secured at the nape of his neck. His smile was pure sex appeal.

As she approached him, he reached for Fiona's hand and kissed her fingers. He wanted to do more, but proper decorum dictated that he exercised restraint. Fiona was a vision with her hair up in complicated twists and curls regally crowning her head, leaving her neck free. He pulled a box from his inside jacket pocket and opened it, revealing a spider web of tiny sparkling diamonds on silver threads that took her breath away.

"Trey," she was near breathless, "I can't. This is too much." Yet, as she searched his beautiful green eyes, her fingertips luxuriated in the sensual feel of the jewelry as he clasped it securely around her neck while looking into her eyes. She noted the disappointment her rejection seemed to cause him. "So, I'll just wear it tonight and only on very special occasions when you take me to your bed."

His face considerably brightened. "In that case, you'll never take it off." He kissed her. Protocol be damned. He offered his arm, and she took it.

They walked down the long, wide, room-size Ambassador's Entrance hall, one after another, and up a sweeping set of stairs until they reached ten-foot-tall, ornately-carved, wooden double doors, at which time they were told to put on their gloves. Then they positioned themselves before the doors, awaiting a signal. When it came, the doors opened to the throne room with pure-red carpet rolled out, bisecting the room leading to the thrones where their Majesties, the King and Queen of England, sat in royal splendor.

Fiona didn't realize until that moment the event was planned in Trey's honor until the trumpets began to blare in announcement. Then a loud, strong voice called out. "Your Majesties, present are Maxwell Bishop Kennard, the Third, and Ms. Fiona Lizette Lowry of America."

The king and queen stood while a man dressed in English ancestral garb and a long wooden staff preceded Trey and Fiona, advancing up the aisle. Hugh and Sandra were also announced and followed Trey and Fiona but moved off to seats in the front row. Once at the raised platform, Trey and Fiona stood while an elongated list of Trey's accomplishments was read. At the conclusion, a knighting bench was placed before Trey. He knelt and bowed his head as he had been instructed earlier. The king drew his sword and, with the flat side, tapped Trey on his right and then left shoulders, knighting him Sir Maxwell Bishop Kennard with the Royal Order of Artist. The king draped a wide, multicolored ribbon with a round, ornate medallion over Trey's head and around his neck. The ceremony continued for another thirty minutes as the king bestowed gifts on Trey, befitting his new position in the royal hierarchy.

The king and queen left the dais with Trey at the king's side and Fiona accompanying the queen. Hugh and Sandra followed ahead of the rest of the guests into another, even larger, chamber. There were giants from the music industry of England, Europe, and the Americas with whom Trey had worked. Also in attendance were people from other walks of life. Front and center, there, on graduated raised platforms, stood the Royal Philharmonic Orchestra. Also, among the musicians was the choir from the church in Truro.

Once the king, queen, and other guests took their seats, Trey mounted his unique perch, bringing the musicians to a stark silence with all eyes trained on him before the music began.

Some of the sounds, both instrumental and vocal, Fiona recognized. Other music was new to her, but the opera flowed seamlessly for over an hour. Fiona closed her eyes and simply absorbed and inhaled the extraordinary sounds the musicians flawlessly produced at Trey's direction. The finale was the Hallelujah Chorus, which brought tears of joy to many eyes, including the king and queen.

Shouts of *"Bravo"* accompanied thunderous applause at the event's conclusion. It took time for Fiona to stem the tide of her joyful tears, but she, too, stood, applauding and hailing Trey's genius.

Later that night, after a bout of mind-bending sex, Fiona settled comfortably in Trey's warm embrace.

Trey sleepily asked, "Did you enjoy the evening?"

"More than. I'm glad you didn't tell me beforehand about the ceremony. I didn't have time to be nervous. It was an incredible experience. When did you find out you would be knighted?"

"Several months ago." He sleepily yawned.

Fiona's brows bunched in confusion. "Did you tell your father about it?"

"No." He ran a lazy hand over Fiona's fleshy bottom.

She leaned up on her elbow and turned his head toward her. "Why not?"

He shrugged, his green gaze steady on her eyes. "I really didn't think of it."

"'Didn't think . . .'" she parroted. "I don't understand, Trey. This was a monumental event. Why wouldn't you want him to attend?"

"It's not our thing as it is in your family. I've seen how close you and your brothers are to your parents. It's apparent to any observer you not only love each other, but you also *like* each other. You're best friends to one another. My father and I never even shared events as I grew up. Most of the time, I didn't even know where he was or what he was doing other than I knew he was on duty doing something in the military.

"I have other relatives, cousins I wouldn't recognize if I saw them in a room. I believe the situation is mutual. They don't know me. You and your brothers are an integral part of the Lowry clan, your father's siblings, aunts, uncles, and cousins. None of my grandparents or other relatives visited when I was in school. I didn't even know when or if my father was coming to see me. It's only been more recently we've seen each other fairly regularly. So, for me, it was really no big deal that he wasn't there tonight. Besides, the most important people to me were in attendance." He kissed her mouth while rolling on top of her and sliding smoothly into her warmth. The lovemaking that ensued ended any additional conversation for the rest of the night. However, Fiona felt sad for the little boy whose talent is enormous, but no one recognized it until he made himself known to the world as an adult.

In the next few days, they packed, left London, and headed to Paris, France, for the impromptu session with The French Mariah and the incomparable songstress Loretta. They would also be in time to see Fiona's cousin, Adam Hawkins, compete in the Le Mans races.

Chapter 14

Trey ran through his mental gymnastics while setting the stage for this session. He didn't have the luxury of having an inordinate amount of time to plan for this event. This session had to be a one-and-done operation. Nevertheless, he recognized that it was an honor to do a live musical performance with the legendary French Mariah. She was Mariah Benson, the older divorced sister of Sylvia Benson Alexander from Goodwill, Summer County, South Carolina. Mutual friend, Loretta Hill McCoy, newly married wife of the hotelier, Justin Willis McCoy, joined them. The taping was held at Club Mariah in Paris' West End community, where a wealth of talented ex-pats and musical establishments were located. Jazz greats, like Josephine Baker, Ada Smith, Mickey Baker, Sidney Bechet, Nina Simone, Arthur Briggs, Johnny Griffin, Kenny Clarke, and Carole Fredericks lived, performed, and flourished there.

Other famed ex-pats, like basketball players Nicolas Batum, Tony Parker, Melvin Sanders, and Dominique Wilkins, joined the entertainers. Authors Richard Wright and James Baldwin called France their home, along with novelists Barbara Chase-Riboud and Chester Himes. The Parisian West End community was teeming with former Americans of great talent and notoriety.

Club Mariah's incredible acoustically perfect setting and sound system were the scene of many theatrical performances dating back to before World War I. Mariah and Sylvia Benson's many times' great grand ancestry left their sea island home on the shores of the South Carolina Low Country. They were performers in France, where Parisians accepted and revered them for their extraordinary talents. In later years, they performed with the great Josephine Baker until World War II chased them home. However, after the war, many of the Benson family members returned to France, preferring the warmth and acceptance of the French people to the hostilities they suffered in the post-war era in the United States.

In the late 1960s, a larger Benson family troupe again left Paris to return to the United States to raise families or send their children to colleges in America. Mariah, one of the great-grandchildren, was brought home to attend college. After her disastrous marriage to the good-for-nothing Reverend Obadiah Baker James ended, she immigrated back to France and reopened her family's club and home in Paris. Over time, Mariah made a name for herself, and her club was on the "must-see" list, as popular as the Eiffel Tower, Moulin Rouge, or Arc de Triomphe de l'Étoile. Club Mariah's was often booked months in advance and packed to the rafters when open. She kept the early nineteenth-century style when Paris was the place to be decadent.

However, Trey found it challenging to get all the video equipment into the space crowded around a dance floor with stately booth seating where Folies-Bergere dancers performed lively Las Vegas-like moves, like the can-can with precision. His vision was to shoot the session from many angles because this would be a one-and-done shot deal. No retakes or outtakes. So, Trey decided to shoot it with only spotlighting the singers and starlight the background as if the interview and vocals were floating in outer space. Though the club was at capacity, the sound mixing would be in the booth and be otherworldly.

Both women, Mariah and Loretta, played concert-level piano, so he brought in identical Baby Grands to shoot their duets with the camera constantly in motion circling them. No one questioned the need for four pianos wedged together facing each other, particularly when he put another camera in the center between the instruments.

It was a good thing the women knew each other before they became famous. Their easy camaraderie made the interview comfortable and relaxed. While playing one of the four pianos, Trey led the interview, starting with a question about how Mariah and Loretta became acquainted.

"I remember when Ms. Mariah led our choir for community benefits. I was still in high school." Loretta fingered keys on the piano, playing a familiar melody from that time and recalling her youthful experiences. "We sang all over our county back home in South Carolina, and in the summer, we went on road trips to sing in other churches as far away as Miami, Florida, and Washington, DC." She smiled to herself at the memory and sang a few stanzas of one of the songs they often sang.

Mariah played along and joined Loretta in song. "I admit, Loretta was one of my favorites. She has such an incredible vocal range; I enjoyed working with her in preparation for the Miss South Carolina pageant when she sounded better than Jennifer Hudson when she sang the torch song from *Dreamgirls*. Mariah sang the in introduction, '*I am telling you, I'm not going,*' and she won the contest hands down."

Loretta picked up the song, and a duet rocked the rafters, then Mariah continued. "I was thrilled when Loretta began to sing professionally. As you've heard on her many album releases, she has a sister, Kayla, who also has an outstanding voice, but I could never coax her into performing with us." Mariah laughed as she and Loretta continued to play the piano and respond to Trey's interview questions. "But leave it to Loretta to have her sister's voice blend so effortlessly with hers on her recent releases."

"I've heard your sister's voice, Loretta. She certainly has the talent," Trey offered as he, too, played one of the pianos and continued to lead the interview.

Then, out of the darkness, another voice emerged, bringing a surprised smile to the faces of Mariah and Loretta. Another spotlight focused on Kayla Hill, Loretta's older sister, who joined them in a piano concerto and led them all in song. At the same time, all three women continued to flawlessly play the pianos while the camera continued to capture them in a circular movement.

"We are two of six sisters, and our parents were strict about our upbringing," Kayla Hill contributed. "We all sang in the church choir from an early age, including our parents, but Loretta and I used to sneak away and sing popular rather than secular music."

"We couldn't let our parents hear us singing raunchy lyrics, like Grace Jones's *'Pull up to my bumper baby. And drive it in between'*" Loretta sang, followed by laughter. "We would have been grounded for months."

"We were the von Trapp family of South Carolina," Kayla joked without missing a chord.

"Are there others in your family, Mariah, who sing as they do in Loretta's family?" Trey asked as he played, and the interview continued.

"Oh, yes," Mariah answered. "My niece, Aretha Grace Alexander, plays the piano and has a vocal skill beyond belief."

"I had the honor of working with Aretha Grace from the time she was five years old up through her teen years," Loretta added. "We were invited to perform for the presidential inauguration several years ago. She also sang the "Star-Spangled Banner" at the opening ceremony of the baseball season. People are still talking about it. She's an even more accomplished pianist. In her youth, she won many piano competitions."

Though no one noticed, Trey had stopped playing and slipped off the piano bench in the darkness. "Does she sing or play professionally?"

Mariah shook her head. "No, she's a student at a university in England. She sings for fun with a Glee Club, but only for special events. I'd love to get her voice on a recording someday."

Then the opening sound of "I'm Every Woman" was so pure it sent chills up the spine because the voice sounded so much like the diva, Whitney Houston, and then grew in the darkness and intensity. Next, a widening, illuminating spotlight focused on the smiling face of Aretha Grace Alexander playing a fourth Baby Grand piano to the delight of Mariah, Loretta, and Kayla. Then Aretha torqued it up, and her aunt Mariah, Kayla, and Loretta were right there, all four in perfect pitch and harmony, singing the song Whitney Houston made famous.

"You tricked us, Trey." Mariah laughed and continued to play.

"I did, yes, and I won't apologize for the deception." He stood in the center of the four Baby Grand pianos as the women continued to play, but the narrow spotlights only illuminated the four women, not him. "I did my homework and when I discovered your niece was right there in London, I persuaded her to join us here today."

Aretha Grace smiled. "He didn't have to convince me that I needed to be with the three vocalists who most influenced me. So I jumped at the chance to do this."

For the next hour, the women, representing essentially several generations, played the pianos and sang together in perfect harmony.

They took turns playing and singing solos as the cameras continued to roll and circumnavigate around them with few questions, prompting them from Trey. He was content to let them take their jam sessions wherever they chose, and they did. They didn't need his direction. By the end of the performance, the women had executed a representative sample of a hundred years of significant, iconic music up to the current day. Again, they didn't need coaxing or directing; instinct took over to its best advantage. When the spotlights dimmed and faded to black, the audience leaped to their collective feet in roof-raising adoration.

Trey was pleased with the entire show, though it was not over. He still had another voice to add to the performance of the four exceptional women's sounds.

After the club cleared of patrons, Fiona sat amid the talented songstresses with Sandra, Hugh, and Trey, enjoying the club's superb cuisine.

With a linen napkin, Loretta wiped the corners of her mouth. "Trey, I have to admit that was fun."

Mariah nodded with a smile. "I agree. I've never had an interview like this or enjoyed one more, particularly since you've included my niece and dear friends from my home in Summer County, South Carolina."

"It was fun for me, too, Aunt Mariah. When Trey approached me while he was in London and asked whether I would be willing to come to Paris and surprise the three of you, I couldn't turn it down." She looked at Trey, beaming. "This was really a great opportunity to sing with my aunt, former choir director, and Kayla. Thank you for doing this, Trey, and including me."

"It is my pleasure, Aretha. If you ever decide you want a career in entertainment, I hope you'll give me a call. That goes for you, too, Kayla. Your voice is phenomenal."

"Not on a bet." Kayla laughed. "I'll keep my day job, working a regular nine-to-five for the US State Department." She didn't mention, but only Trey knew, that her job went far beyond the GS-level, her cover title as an aide to the Secretary of State would indicate. Her code name in The Nursery, an über secret G7 creation: Mata Hari. Her presence there was, in part, to alleviate Trey's concerns about what Aiden McKenna might know or uncover that would jeopardize Ivy's security.

"Your voices blended wonderfully, Trey, and I won't have to do any post-production work," Hugh added. "You've been quiet, Fiona. What did you think?"

"I'm still speechless, in absolute awe of the talent of these four women. I've never heard anything like it except when my father listens to the Celtic women from Ireland sing. He has an excellent voice, and he used to sing an Irish lullaby to me when . . ." Her words trailed off when she heard the four women begin to sing a capella.

"Goodnight, my angel. Time to close your eyes. And save these questions for another day. I think I know what you've been asking me. I think you know what I've been ..." The four women spontaneously sang the Celtic lullaby in perfect synchronization and four-part harmony.

Fiona's heart was in her throat hearing the song her father often sang to her as a child at bedtime. Tears flooded her eyes as she listened and smiled at the memory. "I can't wait until Trey releases this phenomenal show."

"Just for you, Fiona, and, if our artists are amenable, we'll record that lullaby as the closing song as the lights go out. So your father may enjoy it." The warmth of Trey's smile echoed in his voice.

"This production is scheduled for release during African American history month next year on PBS in the States and the BBC in England," Sandra offered. "Trey is calling the show Family Reunion."

"Of course, there are private showings for our performers and special guests." Trey smiled at Fiona.

If no one else sensed it, Fiona could see the heat in Trey's gaze. She felt the same and had to look away, her mouth suddenly dry. "You haven't sung together before?"

"No, not for something like this. My niece and I sing to entertain our family at holiday reunions, but I haven't sung with Loretta or Kayla in more than twenty years."

"That's amazing, Mariah. You sound as if you've sung together all along."

"No, actually, Mariah is right. We haven't done anything like this before, but I'm glad Trey brought us together."

Trey was glad, too, but he still had Ivy's voice to add to the production when they reached Tokyo, Japan. So, although Kayla assured him all was well, he would do the taping at an undisclosed location with just him and Ivy in attendance. He already had cut-ins in his plans to add the additional fifth voice and, if he was lucky, the voices of Whitney's triplet younger sisters.

Like England, France had a wealth of architectural natural wonders to tantalize Fiona's curiosity and professional enlightenment. Because they only had four days there, and since they had already seen Club Mariah, they chose to skip several other clubs and go sightseeing by day and see some of the countryside outside the city. They accomplished what they came to France to do, but Trey had a little surprise for Fiona.

In the meantime, Fiona took them to The Louvre Pyramid to see the large glass and metal structure surrounded by three smaller pyramids. Though Trey didn't care for the St. Mary Axe, the tallest structure in London's financial district made of glass, he was more amenable to The Louvre in France. Unfortunately, they didn't have time to visit the Sports and Leisure Center in Saint-Cloud, France, a glass building with bold colors and a modern cubism design. More importantly, she wanted Trey to see The Glass Home in Milano, Italy, with a covering of blue-tinted glass panels. Unfortunately, the schedule was too tight for another side trip.

Though Trey performed and lectured at The Sage, the center for the performing arts, music education, and conference in Gateshead, England, the glass structure reminded him of a gigantic, many-humped caterpillar. Nevertheless, it made him laugh each time he was there. So instead, he promised they would make time to visit the glass Basque Health Department building in Bilbao, Spain. The angular glass reportedly gave the building a unique and mesmerizing appearance.

A few days after the four women performed, Mariah invited them over for brunch at her home, Châteaux des Milandes, near Sarlat. First, she took them on a tour of the manor house built around 1489 and the extensive gardens. Then, just before they were ready to sit down to dine *al fresco,* Russell Greene, the young artist, who quickly rose to world-class notoriety, joined them. He, the younger brother of Admiral Stacy Greene Alexander, was also the guy friend of Aretha Grace. When they entered the sunny, tree-shaded plaza, they were holding hands. Though no one said it aloud, it was clear the young couple was very much in love.

Chapter 15

Constant news from Europe showed Trey and Fiona as a couple consistently in each other's company. The paparazzi caught candid shots of their trip to the Cornish countryside, at various clubs, and visiting sights of architectural wonder. However, pictures of Fiona at Trey's side during his knighting by the King of England struck fear in Aiden's heart.

Although there were many pictures of them together, they were usually in the company of Hugh Howard and Sandra Kent. Aiden Googled them and learned they were in Trey's employ. He learned everything he could about the musical genius, but found nothing to indicate Fiona should break her travel plans and return home. If his schedule were not so tight, he would have flown to England to gauge the depth of the relationship between Fiona and Trey. Now they were in Paris, the City of Love, together. Their next stop would be Spain and then Tokyo if their schedule didn't change in the interim. When he mentioned the possibility of going to Europe to Robinetta, she cautioned against such a plan.

When a camera light flashed, Aiden turned off his iPhone and paid closer attention to the representatives of newspapers and broadcasters who were discussing putting their weight behind his candidacy. They had finished dinner at the famed Angelique's Place restaurant in Washington, DC, and were talking over drinks and coffee. Fortunately, his campaign manager had the gift for gab and kept the media people enthralled… until…

"Gentlemen," came a recognizable female voice from behind him.

The men at the table smiled and began to stand. Aiden cursed under his breath but stood as well.

"Hi, Dad." Reporter Chevon Ellis greeted her father, who sat at Aiden's left.

"Sweetheart." Victor Ellis smiled. He was the son of Walter Ellis, the head of the Ellis Communications Group, and Chevon's grandfather. "I didn't know you were here?"

"I just finished an interview and my cameraman noticed you were here. Is this a private party or can anyone join?"

Of course, Victor had a waiter place a chair between him and Aiden, putting Chevon to his immediate left. Aiden had a feeling this was no chance meeting, and when the cameraman lined up to take shots of him with Chevon close to his side, he knew a setup when he saw one. So, he turned his face away to speak privately with Harris. "Isn't it about time to wrap this up?"

Harris sighed. "You need their support, Aiden. This would be a cakewalk if you'd just let the woman have a little of your time and attention."

"*Et tu, Brute?*"

Harris chuckled. "She wants your body, man. You could do worse. Hell, I'd bang her, and I wouldn't even have to put a bag over her face. On the other hand, she's not unattractive and might be good for a few laughs."

"I'm not laughing, Harris."

"Maybe it would take the edge off and at least give you a few giggles until Fiona returns. You've been a little uptight since she left. You're up in the polls, but with these media moguls behind you, you'd be a shoo-in. So, suck it up, boy-o, turn on the charm, and let's win this election. Remember, you've got miles to go to get to the presidency in the next eight to ten years."

"What do you think about . . ." Harris began aloud to get everyone's attention back into the discussion of Aiden's run for the Attorney General's office. The renewed discussion swirled around him for the next thirty minutes or so, but he was able to keep his head in the game and, as Harris instructed, turned on the charm.

He essentially ignored Chevon's presence and talked with the other people sitting around the dinner table. He knew that his long-term goals would likely need to include continued support from the communications people in attendance, so he convinced himself to be sociable. He ordered the next round of drinks, though he knew he was beyond his limit. He'd have to stay in town tonight. He was tired and needed to rest for another early start the next day.

Later, as the restaurant began to clear out, Aiden felt it was time to draw this dinner meeting to a close. So he discreetly signaled to Harris to wrap it up, and he did.

When he stood, the room seemed to tilt.

"Are you all right?" Harris quietly asked.

"I probably had a little more to drink than I should. I have an early morning meeting tomorrow. It's the Women's Guild my sister arranged. I'll check into the McCoy Hotel next door and drive to Fort Washington early for the breakfast event."

"Good idea. You have a twelve-thirty keynote appearance at the Maryland Women's Association luncheon in Bowie, Maryland, and then dinner with your Congressional business constituency in Upper Marlboro at four. Then, at seven in Baltimore . . ." he continued, but Aiden was having a hard time focusing.

How he was able to get into the hotel and sign for a room was a minor miracle in his state. Once he was in the room, he disrobed, put all his clothes into a laundry bag, and hung it on the door for pickup laundering by hotel personnel. His clothes would be returned, freshly cleaned to his room before five in the morning. Then he went into the shower and washed his hair and body with a lazy lassitude, remembering showering with Fiona.

She would scrub his back, and he would return the favor. Fiona was so embedded in his life; he couldn't take a breath without thinking of her. Now there wasn't anything that didn't remind him of Fiona. He leaned his hands against the marble shower walls and let the water beat down on his head. He wondered what Fiona was doing at that moment and planned to send a text message to her before going to sleep.

He dried himself, slid between the cool sheets, and picked up his phone. However, sleep instantly claimed him before he could send the text message to Fiona. Still, his vivid dreams were of her and the intimacy they shared. He never heard the door to his hotel room open. He also didn't realize that the warm body that slipped between the sheets was not Fiona's.

Even in the early morning, the two-hundred-thirty-mile trip from Paris, France, moving southwest to the area near the Town of Le Mans took nearly three hours on a well-traveled road. Still, it afforded Fiona a view of the countryside and iconic structures. She tried to absorb it all while her excitement grew. Trey surprised her with this side trip to see her cousin, Adam Hawkins, compete in the Le Mans, twenty-four hours of Le Mans being the world's oldest active sports car endurance race.

She listened intently as their French driver talked about the event; his accent pronounced.

"As it's considered one of the most prestigious automobile races in the world, it has been called the 'Grand Prix of Endurance and Efficiency.' This is because it represents one leg of the Triple Crown of Motorsport. The other events being the American Indianapolis 500 and the Monaco Grand Prix here on the eastern coast."

Long before their car approached the stadium, the roar of engines crushed the air. Nearly seventy cars began the race on the afternoon of the previous day. Now, only forty-two vehicles remained. Still, their unmuffled sound rivaled a continuous sonic boom.

At the security gate, credentials were handed over by the chauffeur. A golf cart marked SECURITY led them to a private VIP parking area.

Before exiting the car, Sandra handed out sound-deafening protectors. Fiona realized the loud sound reverberations could damage Trey's and Hugh's eardrums, yet he risked it so she could see her cousin and experience the world-renowned race. It was yet another indication that his support of her and her needs was without boundaries. That alone caused her to slip just a little bit more into love with him.

"This way," the security guy said and, because of the headgear, pantomimed his instructions.

They followed and came upon an area full of activity. Banners were everywhere proclaiming BlackHawk Motors racing. Flags indicated previous races the BlackHawk team won to be invited to participate. Upon their arrival in the pit, pamphlets were given to them, which proclaimed that the team had won championships in the European Le Mans Series, Asian Le Mans Series, and the Michelin GT3 Le Mans Cup. As second-place finishers in the European Le Mans Series championship, the placement also earned BlackHawk Motors an automatic invitation to participate. In addition, the missive noted that two participants from the WeatherTech Sports Car Championship were chosen by the series to be automatic entries by The Automobile Club de l'Ouest or ACO, the largest automotive group in France, regardless of their performance or category.

Fiona was enormously proud of her cousin Adam's achievements. She recalled that, from a young age, he was fascinated with aerodynamics. He was not even in his teens when he built his first racer, a boxcar with no engine. He progressed from there to stock car racing and then to drag racing, where he was known as The Hawk. When he qualified as a NASCAR driver, he raced in the Winston Cup Series, winning the championship several times. Although he only raced six months out of the year, he had an impressive winning record of two hundred races during his career so far. In his early thirties, he and his team had consistently won, placed, or showed in the Daytona 500. Statistically, according to the sports' car media, he is touted to be one of the youngest and most accomplished drivers currently on the motorsports circuit, already inducted into the NASCAR Hall of Fame.

When the sleek diamond-black race car with the fearsome-looking golden hawk pulled to a stop, pandemonium ensued. The driver peeled himself out of the vehicle as it was quickly hoisted off the ground. A unique blend of gas was filling the car from two different ports. With lightning-fast speed, mechanics removed the tires and installed new ones in less than sixty seconds. A different driver shoehorned himself into the car before it dropped to the ground and, in a flash, sped away.

Fiona watched as her cousin removed his helmet, face mask, and face shield before he guzzled a large bottle of water. Members of his team patted him on the back, and men with clipboards and iPads consulted with him. One of his team members pointed in her direction, and a warm smile bloomed on Adam's handsome Indigenous American and African American face. His ink-black hair was long and tied down at the nape of his neck. His eyes were diamond-sharp and black, but softened when he spotted her. When he reached her, he lifted her in his arms in a bear hug and swung her around. When she was on her feet again, he led her and her companions to a soundproof, glassed-in room.

Adam grinned and held Fiona at arm's length, looking her from the bottom up. "*Wow!* I could hardly believe it when Jacob told me he ran into you at a nightclub in England."

She nodded and turned to present her friends. "This is the reason I'm not in Maryland. Trey, Sandra, and Hugh, this is my cousin, Adam."

"A pleasure to meet you, Adam." Trey smiled, extending his hand. The others followed suit.

"Welcome, all of you. When my agent said you were coming today, I was thrilled that you could make the time."

"Actually, Trey arranged it as a surprise for me."

"That's what my agent told me. So, what do you think?"

Fiona shook her head. "I think you must be crazy to strap yourself into a missile and rocket around the track for twenty-four solid hours, but you're obviously having a lot of fun."

He laughed, slung an arm around her shoulders, and talked with the group at large. Though the noise was nearly nonexistent in the room, they kept their eyes on the monitors as other cars dropped out of the endurance race. They were on a tight schedule and couldn't stay until the end of the race, but only nineteen vehicles were still on the track before they left. BlackHawk's entry was one of them, still in contention and heading for the winning checkered flag.

Chapter 16

Madrid, Spain, was a balmy seventy-five degrees under cloudless, azure-blue skies with no humidity to speak of. They arrived at eight in the evening from an airport near Le Mans, France, giving them ample time to have a continental meal on the flight, so when they settled, Trey would be able to immediately go to work on his projects.

As before, the hotel, another McCoy Resort and Conference Center facility, had an abundance of charm, amenities, and space. Sandra arranged for the suite to have a media room and a salon with a couple of Baby Grand pianos. Trey's work was neatly organized and ready for his use. He tied back his hair and wasted no time starting.

Since Sandra and Hugh were both tied up the next day, Fiona perused the brochures in the suite and then struck out on her own to see the city. She didn't speak the language, but fortunately, the people spoke English in many of the places she visited.

It was after six in the evening when Trey looked up and checked his watch. He, Hugh, and Sandra worked from the time they arrived at the hotel without taking a real break other than to sleep for a few hours. That's how it often went with them. He and Hugh looked at the rough cut after his technicians finished syncing the movie to the audio. It was a masterful bit of work, so he sent a message of appreciation to his London crew, signed off on the final version, and had Sandra send it to the Executive Producer, Tina Justice Collins, at her Chicago Sweet Justice Production Office.

Next, they tackled the other musical discoveries he and Hugh made, wrapping up the work they started in London. The group, History, Sandra reported, was well received on their debut tour in the cities and universities where they performed. They also opened for other acts, but their popularity was growing by leaps and bounds. Trey had no doubt they would be the next group to top the music charts in the states. Now it would be his responsibility as their sponsor to keep them mentally and emotionally on track. He knew too many groups who fell apart on account of internal strife. He wanted History to avoid those pitfalls and to be around for many generations to come making music.

Next, he and Hugh previewed the rough cut of the interview they shot in France with the four women. Trey was extremely pleased with his decision to shoot the interview in virtual darkness with only the narrow spotlight focused down on each woman. They performed as if the cameras weren't constantly circling them or in the middle of the four Baby Grands to the last note of the lullaby they inserted after the club cleared. Now he had only to add the voice of Ivy to the mix and overlay it as if a celestial addition. He decided to release the interview as a video after it aired on PBS and the BBC, but to include the voices of the age-old original cuts if he could find them in a musical catalog and remix them to make a CD and DVD out of the old and new sounds and scenes. His creative juices were flowing like Niagara Falls on a good day when he looked up and around.

Concern masked his face. "Where is Fiona?"

"Sightseeing the last I know." Sandra noticed Trey hurriedly leaving the salon. She exchanged a knowing look with Hugh. They both smiled and went back to work.

"Fi!" Trey shouted as he searched the suite for her.

Fiona was working on her iPad, wearing earbuds. Initially, she didn't hear Trey calling her name, so she was surprised when he caught her up in a fierce hug and hungrily took her mouth. When he let her breathe, her brows bunched. "Hey, now." She soothed him, removing the earbuds and palming his face. "What's going on?"

He leaned his forehead against hers while catching his breath and closing his eyes, breathing in her unique scent. "I'm okay. I apologize for leaving you alone all day. I didn't think…Have you even eaten? Are you—"

She kissed his mouth, cutting his concern to the quick. "I'm fine, Trey. I had a great day while you were slaving away. Did you know there's an app that translates languages in real-time?"

"Si, Bella." He spoke the Spanish language like a native. His fear, that his benign neglect would make her angry enough to want to leave him, was still real and palpable.

Fiona didn't know what he said, but the look in his beautiful green eyes as he spoke had her blood warming. Then he kissed her into oblivion. An hour later, warm and satisfied, they lay naked in each other's arms.

"Trey?"

"Hmm?"

"You do know you're not expected to entertain me every moment."

He lazily ran his fingers through her hair. "I know, but—"

"No, buts, pal." She leaned up on her left elbow to look down into his eyes. "I'm fine on my own, particularly when you're working."

He looked at the concern on her pretty face. "I'm often obsessive when I work and need to be pulled back into the here and now. You do that for me, Fiona. You make me stop and smell the flowers without meaning to. I appreciate that. I make these tours sometimes two or three times a year, but I haven't enjoyed a previous tour as much as I have this time. That's because of you. I like looking at places I've seen many times through your eyes for a change. You add an entirely new dimension to the sights. Your insight inspires me like nothing else ever has. When I'm with you or think of you, I hear melodies running through my head."

She smiled, palming his serious expression and running her thumb over his enticing mouth. He was so achingly handsome and unique; she couldn't do anything at that moment but lay her mouth on his.

When Trey pulled her on top of him and parted her thighs, he covered himself and slipped slowly inside her. Fiona didn't think that now was the right time to tell him she didn't plan to be his muse forever.

Now that she had this taste of what the wonders of the world were like, she was eager to explore more.

Fiona had already contacted her uncle Jake and planned to visit him and her aunt Kelley when the couple returned to Africa. At her mother's party, her uncle asked her whether she would come to look at projects he had in mind to build in different African countries. He envisioned schools, hospitals, clinics, libraries, and communities. From time to time, his daughter, JaiHonnah, helped design facilities for him. Still, JaiHonnah was also busy raising her young family with her husband, Roderick, co-managing Baylor and Baylor, and helping to direct the activities of BlackHawk Industries.

Fiona hadn't considered it before, but just before Trey came to find her, she explored the possibilities with her cousin, Adam, and his father, her uncle Jake. Adam headed The BlackHawk Foundation, his father's philanthropic arm of his monolithic enterprise, BlackHawk Industries. Adam would split his time between the organization and his hobby of racing Formula One sports cars.

She couldn't think of that now as Trey levered up, taking her mouth. He had a firm grip on her hips, moving her to their needed satisfaction.

Later that night, the foursome made the Madrid club scene, starting at Club Joy Eslava, followed by Sala El Sol, Demode, and then the Shanghai Club. During the rest of the week, they visited tapas bars, cocktail clubs, jazz lounges, live music venues, and flamenco theatres which were plentiful. As more days passed into their second and third weeks, they attended live music shows, where up-and-coming artists, singer-songwriters, and jazz concerts showcased music at its best. They had toured the most popular nighttime destinations in the Madrid neighborhoods of Bilbao, Tribunal, Atocha, and Alonso Martinez. However, Trey found the District of Chueca the most popular, especially for the gay population. They hit several nightspots in that district over successive days and weren't disappointed by what they heard. Finally, Trey and Hugh brought seven groups into a leased studio for further auditions. They combined the members of two bands into one and signed them to contracts to tour the Americas. The remaining five bands were also put under contract, but Trey and Hugh felt their sound needed more work. Hugh would work with them in England for the next six months.

Three weeks after their arrival, the foursome left to immerse themselves in the Bohemian culture at twelve-thirty in the morning when most venues opened for business. They rarely made it back to their hotel before seven in the morning. They usually slept until after siesta ended and managed to go sightseeing before returning to the hotel to dress for dinner and to go to one of the Auditorio Nacional de Música classical music concerts.

This day, the Teatro Real, the main opera house in Madrid, was their after-dinner destination. It was located across the street from the Royal Palace, home of the royal family of Spain. As they stood in the lobby drinking wine and meeting and greeting other opera patrons, La Contessa Lolita Viero Dela Porte entered the lobby with her entourage. Native Spaniards still bowed or curtsied in the presence of royalty, causing silence to fall on the crowded lobby. She was an unmissable beauty and perfected a royal carriage as she silently advanced through the crowd that automatically parted for her.

However, when she stopped, her eyes landed on Trey with laser-like precision. She beckoned one of her minions, whispering something to him and dispatching him directly to Trey. The exchange was in rapid Spanish, but Fiona felt there was no need to understand the language to know what La Contessa expected Trey to do. However, when the messenger's eyes widened in surprise and concern for whatever Trey said, and he slightly shook his head, Fiona got the distinct impression royalty was in for a rude, twenty-first-century awakening.

The opera, *Rigoletto*, starring mezzo-soprano Karla Burns, whose voice compared to the great Leontyne Price, was more than Fiona could have imagined. Ms. Price, the cousin of famed American singers Whitney Houston, her mother, Cissy Houston, and Dionne Warwick, was still revered long after her death.

Later that night, after the opera, Trey lay awake with Fiona securely sleeping in his arms. They were midway through their European tour and would be heading for Asia in a few more days. As usual, Sandra was keeping them ahead of schedule. However, she was also making time for them to see the architecturally significant sights for Fiona's sake. He didn't mind so much the distraction. Watching Fiona's reactions was well worth the diversion. She was so excited by the architecture and ambiance of the areas they visited and the culture of the people. He was opening a whole new world to her and receiving her ardent affection in return. However, he had concerns about what would happen when the tour ended, and he returned to New York City.

He wanted to ask Fiona to move to the city and live with him. However, he wasn't at all sure that she would be willing to do that. He recognized that Fiona had a very close bond with her family, which would likely mitigate against her making that kind of decision. Fiona was a creative soul, and there wasn't much to be creative about in the concrete and steel canyons of the city he called home. The more he thought about it, the more the decision to make Maryland his home base made more sense in the long run. Fiona wouldn't have to decide between him and her family. There would be inconveniences to overcome. He would have to travel back to the city at least once a week, and he couldn't bring his essential staff members to live in Maryland.

Then there was the fact that Fiona would have to contend with the presence of Aiden McKenna back in her life. She shared that she and Aiden had been lovers since high school and that neither had relationships outside that bond. They went to the same college and lived together off-campus. Even in professional schools in different areas, they managed to keep their intimate bond intact. It was startling to Trey to know Fiona had only one lover before him. He didn't even remember the countless number of women he bedded in his life. However, Trey did know the one woman he wanted to sleep beside for the rest of his life. Lazily, he ran his fingers through her silky but thick hair and kissed her temple.

"What's wrong?" Fiona asked, now alert. "Can't you sleep?"

She rubbed her fingertips over his nipples, causing them to peak like raisins. Heat immediately infused his body, causing his member to thicken and grow before she reached down and took him in hand.

"You keep touching me like this and it's guaranteed to keep me awake," he teased. "Are you still cramping?"

"I took something for the pain. I'm fine." She yawned. "The problem is the pills make me sleepy. Let me see if I can figure out how to help you relax."

She parted his thighs and enlivened his body. Still, it was a long time before they slept.

Chapter 17

Aiden was dog-tired as he and his Capitol Hill staff finished a work meeting at nearly eight-thirty in the evening. The US House of Representatives was still in session, trying to tie up votes on various bills before the holiday season recess began. He had bills pending in multiple committees specifically geared to benefit his constituents. He had amassed enough votes to see them pass in this session of Congress rather than have them die in committees. Aiden was still on the ballot for his Congressional seat and simultaneously on the state ballot for the seat as the Attorney General. If he won both, he would have to choose which path to follow. If he decided to accept the Attorney General's position after the November election, they would be in a lame-duck session in the US House. He would have to clear up all his work and then be sworn in on January 20 of the following year. Several bills were in Conference Committees between the US House and the Senate. Still, more bills he introduced and championed were in the works and may need a quick vote tonight. The work never seemed to end.

He sat back in his desk chair, closed his eyes, and tried to relax for a few moments before he tackled the list of e-mails his assistant marked as priority items. He was on several committees in the House of Representatives and still had to participate in hearings on critical issues, particularly those which would impact his constituents. He had been campaigning nonstop for an average of fourteen hours a day and seven days a week. He usually had breakfast meetings and other conferences throughout the day to dinner meetings or other necessary grip-and-grin events often lasting past midnight. There were events he had to prioritize because he had multiple conflicts in his schedule. He couldn't complain because they kept him so busy he didn't have time to focus on how much he missed Fiona.

Every morning after his run, he checked social media sites for news of her. In Paris, France, she was spotted at various events and venues with Trey Kennard and then at the Le Mans sports car races with her cousin, Adam Hawkins. Days later, the press picked up pictures of her in Madrid, Spain. They must have been traveling by car because she sent videos and text messages home about all the places she had seen on the route. There was pure excitement in her messages, though she didn't mention much about Trey or her feelings for him. That fact puzzled him.

"Congressman?" Louise, his executive assistant, pulled him from his thoughts.

"Yes?" He opened his eyes and focused on her standing in his doorway.

"Ms. Chevon Ellis is here and would like to interview you on the clean water bill you introduced in Committee, HR 323."

He rolled his eyes, causing Louise to grin. "Is Bailey in the office?"

"Yes, but he's about to leave for the day."

"He's the contact person on that bill. Have him make time in his schedule to speak with her."

"Will do and, by the way, I received a thirty-minute warning on the vote for HR 833, the farm bill. You might want to start in that direction."

"Thanks, Louise. Hopefully, if all goes well, I'll have good news for my constituents tomorrow." He quickly rose from his seat, rolled down the sleeves of his shirt, buttoned the cuffs, and lifted his suit jacket from the back of his chair. "If there are no more bills scheduled tonight, I'm heading home after the vote. I believe I've got a full day of campaign stops tomorrow." He checked his appearance in the closet mirror and straightened the tie around his neck.

"Yes, you do. I've put tomorrow's schedule on your iPad. Sleep fast because you have an eight o'clock Congressional breakfast meeting in Cumberland. I've proofed your speech. It should go over well at several of your events tomorrow. Your flight leaves at six-thirty from the Bay

County Municipal Airport. You'll be met at the airport and driven to the Cumberland Gap's Club breakfast. There are over two hundred registered to attend."

"Of course, I do," he joked as he headed for his restroom to freshen up. Moments later, he hurried out the door of his office, only to be waylaid in the wide, busy hallway by the reporter, Chevon Ellis.

"Congressman, I need to speak with you." She blocked his way.

"I understand that you want to interview me about my clean water bill, HR 323. Bailey Coolidge is the point person on that legislation. He'll speak with you about it. Now, if you'll excuse me, a vote is about to be called, and I don't want to miss it." He tried to step around her, but again she stepped into his path.

"I want to speak with you on another matter."

"Please see Louise in my office, Ms. Ellis. I really don't have the time to—"

"I'm pregnant, it's your baby, and I can prove it. Now, do you have the time?"

Dumbfounded, Aiden just stopped and stared.

"Fiona?" Aiden breathed when she answered his call. He closed his eyes and listened to her voice.

"Hi, Aiden. It's good to hear from you, but it must be really late in your part of the world," she joked. "I'll bet real American money that you're still at your office in Washington," but then the solemn timbre of his voice had her stopping in her tracks. "Aiden, what's wrong? Did something happen?"

She knew him so well and, yes, something was terribly wrong. Could he share this with her? Could he tell her that a scheming woman was threatening his career, hell-bent on riding his political coattails into the highest public office in the country?

Initially, when Chevon said she was pregnant with his child, he laughed in her face. Every time he saw her nearby, he went the other way as quickly as possible. However, tonight in the crowded halls of Congress, she showed a video of him with her in bed having sex. He couldn't deny that it was him and her, but he had no idea how this could have happened. Her long blonde hair and blue eyes were unmistakable and as evident in the small screen iPhone video as when she appeared on news broadcasts and political television talk shows several times daily. Of course, these things could be photoshopped in pictures, but videos? He didn't know whether it was possible, but he recognized his image in the throes of ecstasy.

"Aiden? Aiden? Are you there?" Fiona demanded. "Is someone in my family or yours hurt? Tell me, what's going on?"

"Fi, no. No one is hurt. Everyone is well. I promise. I just…I just needed to hear your voice. I miss you. When are you coming home?"

Fiona sighed in relief. "I'm in the airport in Mallorca, Spain, now, waiting to board a flight to Tokyo, Japan. Did you know that Mallorca is the largest island in the Balearic Islands, which are part of Spain and located in the Mediterranean?"

"No." He smiled at her enthusiasm, although she couldn't see him. "Tell me more." He listened as she went on about the capital, Palma, and what she'd seen and done. On their first day on the island, they drove to Bellver Castle, a Gothic-style castle on a hill west of the center of Palma. It was built in the fourteenth century for King James II of Majorca and was one of the few circular castles in Europe. He could hear the unmistakable excitement in her voice for this journey of discovery.

The next day, they went to The Serra de Tramuntana, a mountain range running southwest-northeast, forming the northern backbone of the Spanish island of Mallorca. It was awarded World Heritage status by the United Nations Educational, Science, and Cultural Organization (UNESCO) as an area of great physical and cultural significance.

Next, the journey led them to Santuari de Lluc, a monastery and pilgrimage site located in the municipality of Escorca in northwest

Majorca. Fiona told him that every year, thousands of locals and tourists flock to the pilgrimage site of Lluc to worship the statue of the Black Madonna in the seventeenth-century basilica.

She went on about other iconic places she visited during the day and some nightspots playing music she had never heard before.

"After Japan, I think I'm going to Africa for a few weeks to visit with Uncle Jake and Aunt Kelley. I'll come home after that. So, I should be back in about six weeks."

Six weeks? he thought, disappointed. *She's already been away for more than two months.*

"Aiden? I have to go now. The flight is boarding. Hug everyone for me."

"Yes, I will. Have a safe trip, and keep the photos coming."

"I will. Are you sure everyone is okay?"

"Yes, now go, so you don't miss your flight."

"Okay. More soon. Hugs for you, too." She disconnected the call.

Aiden sat in his Baltimore condo, looking out at the panoramic view of the cityscape and the Patapsco River beyond. He couldn't tell his best friend and the love of his life that he was in serious trouble. So, he took another sip of his drink. The sun would be up soon. He hadn't slept, and he had a full schedule, but at that moment, he didn't know what he was going to do.

Chapter 18

"Is something wrong?" Sandra asked Fiona as she sat down beside her in the aircraft's lounge area.

Fiona shook her head and frowned. "No, I don't think so."

"Then why are you having a hard time getting some sleep?"

"Earlier, just before we boarded this flight, I got a call from my friend, Aiden McKenna. He sounded…I don't know, strange, I guess. At least, not his usual self. I haven't been able to shake the feeling that something was off-kilter with him. He's my best friend and a congressman from our district in Bay County and Mitchell County. He's also running for Maryland State Attorney General. I calculated the time difference between Maryland and where we were and he should have been sleeping. It's not like him to be awake at that hour."

"I presume that if you know his sleeping habits, he's more than your best friend."

Fiona nodded. "We were lovers, yes. Our families are very close. We've known each other since birth, but we came to an understanding before I left. I don't want to be the wife of a politician. He deserves to be with someone who can be on a perpetual campaign trail with him. I believe he has a great future ahead of him. Someday, he will be the Governor of Maryland and perhaps the President of the United States. He has every quality and qualification necessary to be successful in those roles."

"That's very selfless of you to give up that potential future and a man you obviously care deeply about for his benefit."

"'Selfless?' No, I wouldn't call it that. Realistic, I believe is more the case. I love Aiden and would do almost anything for him, but I'm not *in* love with him. He suggested that we marry, but I said no."

Sandra nodded her understanding, but was concerned about the longevity of Fiona and Trey's relationship. "You should go back to bed and try to get some sleep. It's an eighteen-hour flight to Japan's Narita International Airport. When we land, we'll have an hour's drive into Tokyo. It will be late at night when we get to the hotel, but we have several clubs to visit soon after we arrive."

"You're right, Sandra. I should get some rest. Good night." Fiona rose from the sofa, hugged Sandra, and made her way into the aircraft's master bedroom. She took off her robe and crawled into the king-sized bed behind Trey. Wrapping her right arm around his waist, she snuggled in tight against his back.

Sleepily, he took her hand and kissed her palm. "Are you okay?" Trey yawned.

Fiona nodded at his back. "Yes, I'm fine. Go back to sleep. I didn't mean to wake you."

He turned onto his back and brought her into a loose embrace against his right side, palming her fleshy bottom. "You're concerned about Aiden, aren't you?" He yawned again.

Fiona nodded against his shoulder. "Something about his call seems off to me."

"When we land, call one of your brothers or his sister, Robin, and ask that he or she check on him."

She leaned up and kissed his cheek. "That's a good idea. Thank you."

"You're welcome, but now you have to put me back to sleep." He brought her atop him.

Fiona grinned and positioned herself astride his torso, covering him before she guided him into her moist heat.

She and Trey sighed with pleasure as the aircraft cut down the distance between Spain and Japan.

The first view of Japan for Fiona was from forty-thousand feet in the air as their private jet circled the area and lined up for landing. Though the sky was pitch black, the landscape below seemed alive with thousands of diamonds on a dark velvet background. White and red ribbons of light snaked through the area and defined wide highways, which sometimes looped into huge cloverleaf patterns. Fiona sat in amazement and looked out of the portal window with her chin palmed in her hand. As the gear lowered and locked into place for landing, the multitude of lights became more distinct, and she could make out the shapes and heights of what appeared to be skyscrapers. Upon closer scrutiny, it became clear from the front view video that the landing strip was just that—a strip of land surrounded by water.

After landing, the aircraft taxied across a bridge for quite a distance before reaching terra firma. When she turned her head, Trey was watching her with an enigmatic smile on his face.

"What?" She smiled at him.

"Your emotions are clearly written on your face. This time, it is pure excitement."

"You can't possibly say that landing in Japan is passé for you, Trey. It's absolutely beautiful, even at night."

He nodded in agreement. "You're right, but I've done it so often that I forget to enjoy it. The countryside will be even more spectacular on the drive into Tokyo. The majority of the housing is in high-rise buildings. Even the clubs and other venues are stacked atop one another."

"Is that because Japan is about the size of California?"

"It is. It's an island of about one hundred forty-six thousand square miles, and only eighteen percent or an area of about the size of Los Angeles County is habitable. With a population of over one hundred twenty-seven million people, Japan has very tight living spaces. It's a good thing they're mostly small in stature. Compared to Los Angeles County's nearly five thousand square miles and ten million people, you can understand why the Japanese have to build vertically rather than horizontally the way we do in the states. However, just as California is prone to experience earthquakes, so is Japan."

Intrigued, Fiona cocked her head and studied Trey. She noticed his keen knowledge of facts on a broad range of topics, which might appear to be obscure to most people, were readily available to Trey. What an enigma he is, she thought. "Read much?" Fiona teased.

Damn it! Trey chastised himself, but his face held a smile. He often forgot to censor his commentary on anything that came so easily and quickly to his mind. He needed to keep his eidetic ability under wraps, but he lost all sense for self-preservation around Fiona. According to the way she was scrutinizing him, she was noticing his ability at total recall. "Private school education," he joked, in the hope that his comments would throw her off the track.

Fortunately, the jet came to a stop, and Hugh and Sandra began to prepare for deplaning. After the doors opened, the group made the short walk to the customs station and then through the private Adventurer Executive Airline terminal to the waiting car. After loading the luggage, they joined the heavy traffic racing along the broad highway toward the City of Tokyo.

As Trey mentioned, Fiona noticed that the tall buildings encroached upon the highway, making it appear to be a trail bending and twisting around canyon walls of every type and description. The cars moved as if they were low-flying jets with no regard for lanes or safety. While Sandra briefed Hugh and Trey on the places they were to visit, Fiona watched the insanity of the late-night traffic and the stratosphere of lights brighter than Broadway and 42nd Street on New Year's Eve.

Once settled in their suite of rooms, they had a meal of Okonomiyaki, better known as Japanese pizza, before dressing to go out.

"Tokyo is divided into nine distinct districts," Sandra explained while they waited for Hugh and Trey to finish dressing. She pointed out the different areas of the city on a paper map Fiona printed as a reference. "The Shibuya district is popular among the younger crowds while the Roppongi district is one of the more accessible ones for foreign travelers. Then, here," she pointed, "is the Shinjuku area where you'll find Japan's largest red-light district...Kabukichō." She laughed. "The Ginza is the more upscale district for nightlife. We'll start there tonight since it's where this hotel is located, and then in successive days, we'll fan out to the other districts to see whether we can find any new or novel music or performers. Once we've explored the city's clubs, we'll take side trips to other cities in Japan to see what they have to offer."

"Ready to go?" Trey, followed by Hugh, joined them in the living area.

To look at him is a marvel, Fiona thought. His casual wear screamed sophistication, wealth, and chic style. With his hair loose and just gracing his broad shoulders, he looked as if he could step into the pages of *GQ* magazine. When he grinned at her, his smile was a killer to any woman with a pulse. "Yes, we're ready." She accepted his outstretched hand.

Once on the street, they began to walk rather than take the chauffeured car that idled at the curb. A hand signal from Trey and the car's engine shut down.

The street lent itself to foot traffic, with sidewalks wide enough to walk four abreast, and every tree or bush beautifully covered with tiny, bright lights as if every day was Christmas. There were many upscale, fine dining restaurants, chic nightclubs, and lounges within feet of the McCoy Tokyo Ginza Hotel. Trey mentioned that some of the establishments only catered to those who could speak Japanese, but Trey and Hugh had no difficulty since they spoke the language as if they were natives. As in most of the clubs they visited, Trey and Hugh were shown deference in the seating arrangements. In one club, no sooner had they sat down than authentic Japanese cuisine and sake were set on the table.

"This is an Izakaya, which in Tokyo is basically a pub that serves food and typically a selection of sake," Hugh explained.

"It doesn't look like any pub I've ever been in." Fiona laughed. "Where are the peanut shells on the floor, like Ye Come Back Inn in Truro or the license plates from many states stapled to the walls as art deco? The plastic, red-and-white checkered table cloths are missing as well as the multi-colored nacho chips with jalapenos and greasy cheese gluing it together into a mountain of artery-clogging calories?"

"Hey, maybe I should be hanging out with you," Hugh joked.

They continued to joke with one another until the lights lowered, and a young, mixed-race woman began to play the piano.

Fiona noted how the young woman received Trey's undivided attention throughout her hour-long performance. There was a light in his gaze she hadn't noticed he had for anyone…except her. *Curious*, she thought and wondered whether he knew the woman. She had a Polynesian appearance with her hair shaved close to her scalp, outlining her perfectly-shaped head.

At the end of her performance, Trey excused himself, rose from their table, and approached the young woman as she was leaving the platform. Her face lit when she spotted Trey coming toward her and went easily into his arms.

"Her name is Amiria Kono," Hugh offered. "Trey met her years ago in a men's club where he went to listen to a few vocalists. Human traffickers also used the club to offer young girls as high-class prostitutes or long-term sex companions known here as a courtesans. She was only fifteen at the time of her abduction from her home on one of the islands in the Archipelago.

"Somehow, Trey found a way to get her freed, along with the other young women, but they didn't want to go back to the islands they came from. They were ashamed of what they had been forced to do and didn't want their families to know. In this culture, it's called losing face, which means to lose the respect of others, to experience humiliation or public disgrace. So, Trey arranged for them to stay in Japan and be educated at a private school in the nearby city of Kobe. They have all graduated now and, with Trey's help, have gone on to college or trade schools. Amiria trained in a music school and, as you've heard, she's very talented."

"She is," Fiona agreed as she watched Trey sitting and talking with the young woman while still holding her hands in his. It didn't take a genius to see that they had been more than just friends over the intervening years. She turned away and focused on the meal placed on the table.

"Tell me what I'm eating." Fiona tried using the chopsticks to capture the food and failed miserably.

"Well, let's see." Hugh pointed to each selection with chopsticks as he named them. "We have sushi and sashimi, which you're already familiar with. Ramen, which is the national dish. Tempura which is a Portuguese influence in Japan. Gyoza is a Japanese dumpling. Wagyu is Japanese beef, and Yaki udon is a noodle dish, the origin, and ingredients which I forget."

Sandra laughed. "Of course, no meal is complete without Mochi, and delicious Japanese treats like matcha matcha matcha."

"Hey, don't forget the Sake." Hugh held up the shot glass in a toast before swallowing it in one gulp. "It's the national beverage." He poured another from a squat, round pot.

"Much more of that, and you won't remember your name in the morning," Sandra joked.

Chapter 19

The next morning, when Fiona awoke, Trey had already dressed and left the hotel. She showered and dressed before ordering a continental breakfast and putting in a few hours of work on her projects. When she left the bedroom office, she noted that Hugh was in the music room of the suite working alone. Sandra had gone to the airport to meet her wife and children.

Shortly after noon, Sandra returned with her two boys, eleven-year-old Trevor and nine-year-old Kyle, and her wife, Harriet Stone. Also arriving were a few surprise guests, General Maxwell Kennard, the Second, and Fiona's former school teacher, Charlotte Everson, currently the superintendent of the Bay County School System.

"My, this is a surprise." Fiona smiled broadly and hugged Trey's father and her mother's close friend, Charlotte.

"It is certainly for me." Mrs. Everson smiled. "Much like you, I let your mother talk me into dropping everything and jumping on a flight at a moment's notice. I've never done anything like this before."

The general smiled broadly, seemingly pleased to have Charlotte join him. "It took quite a bit of encouragement from several sources, including Charlotte's daughters, to get her to agree."

After hugging Charlotte, Fiona turned to Trey's father. "Does Trey know that you were planning to come?"

"No, I didn't tell him. Sandra made all the arrangements and, since we were flying on a private jet, we didn't have to stick to a tight schedule. Harriet, the boys, and I flew into Bay County and picked up Charlotte. We've been in the air for nearly twenty hours."

Just then, Hugh came out of the music room to join the group. He lifted the boys, in turn, tucking each under his arms as if carrying sacks of grain. The boys' joy was evident at seeing him as they laughed and giggled, but didn't try to get away from Hugh. That was when Fiona noticed the boys had a striking resemblance to the general and Trey. Their hair was wheat-colored, like their mother's, but the shape and color of their eyes, nose, and mouth were very much like the Kennard men's. They seemed tall for their ages and lanky. It caused Fiona to wonder, but she said nothing.

General Kennard introduced Charlotte to Hugh since she had met Sandra at the airport. Harriet Stone was a slim woman with a military bearing, even in casual civilian clothes, Fiona thought, as they talked. She seemed to have a familiar relationship with Maxwell Kennard. When lunch arrived, they served themselves buffet-style.

"Where is Trey?" Harriet asked of no one in particular, between bites of food.

She handled the chopsticks like a pro, as did the boys and Sandra, Fiona noticed.

"He had an early morning appointment," Sandra said. "He should join us later tonight around dinner time."

Fiona thought that strange. He usually worked in lock-step with Hugh and Sandra, but to be away for a whole day without either of them was notable.

Maxwell Kennard turned his attention to Fiona. "So, have you been enjoying yourself?"

"I have, yes. It took a little getting used to, trading day time for nighttime events. Then to dress each evening to go out and sleep in the afternoon, I got a little turned around. This is usually the time of the day when we go to sleep until around eight when we eat dinner before we go out on the town."

"We're scheduled to go out tonight to the Shibuya district. It's popular among the younger crowds. Still, there's plenty to offer for pretty much anyone looking for a good time," Sandra said for Charlotte's benefit.

"We'll do a walking tour for a few hours to see the sights, but we'll make an early night of it. By then, jet lag will have the boys' eyes closing like walking zombies. Harriet and I will bring the boys back to the hotel, but the rest of you can keep going. You'll find numerous bars, dance clubs, nightclubs, lounges, and also great restaurants that stay open until the wee hours of the morning. It's a more accessible neighborhood for foreigners who don't know Japanese."

"Once upon a time, I was stationed here. So, I know the lay of the land," Maxwell assured Charlotte.

"I can't imagine it," Charlotte said in awe. She turned to Fiona. "I had dinner with your parents and brothers while Maxwell was in town last week. Gannon linked all your travel videos, and we looked at them after dinner. They were breathtaking views of both the cities and the countryside. You could have a career as a travel guide or reporter. You did a fine job, Fiona."

"Thanks, Mrs. Everson. Some of the time I was having so much fun, I forgot to take pictures." She laughed. "I saw places I had only read about, and we found iconic places I had never heard about before. This journey has been quite a wonderful and challenging learning experience."

"I can't believe you actually met the King and Queen," Charlotte enthused, again in awe.

"I did, twice. First at the nightclub, Ministry of Sound London, but Trey didn't tell me about the second event before I found myself on the steps of Buckingham Palace. I had very little time to be nervous."

"She handled it like a pro," Sandra chimed in.

Charlotte shook her head in wonder. "To be knighted had to be an awesome experience for Trey."

"Mrs. Everson, you would have thought it was something he did every day. He had a royal command performance after he was knighted." Fiona chuckled. "Now he's Sir Kennard."

Charlotte sighed. "Imagine doing all of that in such a short space of time."

"He's an organized bloke if ever there was one," Hugh offered. "Sometimes, like now, we're on a listening tour. He has a few acts he wants to bring into a studio to record before we leave the country, but for the most part, the schedule is lighter than in England and Spain. He has post-production work to complete, but nothing urgent."

Maxwell nodded. "While I was in Bay County, Fiona, I had an opportunity to look at his building site. I can't believe how much you've accomplished in a relatively short period of time. All the underground utilities are in place, and the foundations have been laid for all the buildings. Trey's studio is going to be huge. The old barn was deconstructed and the wood stored for reuse once the structure and framing are completed."

Fiona smiled. "Yes, we are on schedule. Dad has good relations with the zoning committee. As a result, he was able to get quick approval of the plans through the county board, and my brothers carved out time to work on their aspects of the project."

"All of that was worked into building those monster tree houses and zip lines for the Kenwood boy," Charlotte added with laughter.

"Would you build one like that for my brother and me?" Trevor piped up.

"Uh, no," Harriet interjected. "We live in Manhattan. The closest thing we have to a large yard is Central Park. The New York authorities frown on building tree houses and zip lines on public land."

"After watching the progress on some of the homes Fiona designed for her clients, I thought we might talk about buying or building a retreat somewhere outside the city," Sandra offered tentatively. "Someplace within a few hours of the city where we could maybe plant a garden and the boys can have a tree house."

Harriet tilted her head as if considering the possibility. Then she nodded. "We'll talk about it," she agreed, and the boys cheered. "Now, can we afford to get Fiona to design it for us?"

"Please! Please! Please, Ms. Lowry!" the boys begged in unison.

Fiona laughed. "That's a distinct possibility. I'm designing guest cottages on Trey's land using shipping containers that you might like to visit once they're done."

"Well, that's intriguing," Harriet said as if warming to the possibility.

"They're high quality, low-cost units and can be built to any scale. The ones for Trey's guests are four-bedroom, four-bath units with an open-concept kitchen and dining and living areas. We're using barnwood for the exteriors and some accent walls on the interior to mimic the studio so it will continue to resemble a barn. Except, however, the barn will have a full-sized, walk-out basement, while the cottages will be erected on slabs of concrete."

"The house is going to be a showpiece," Charlotte offered. "I saw renderings of it on the wall in Al's office and the scale models. It's being built on a deep, daylight basement, I noticed. AJ is already planting the trees, bushes, and flowers that will be the backdrop for the house and block the view of the other buildings."

Fiona nodded. "Yes, he didn't want to wait too late in the season to plant. Otherwise, he would have to delay planting until spring to begin putting in the gardens."

Nodding, Maxwell smiled. "Your family has accomplished quite a bit of work since you've been away."

"They have, and I owe them big time for springing me to come on this tour."

"Speaking of which, if we don't all go down for a nap, we won't be able to hang out tonight and tour the city." Sandra yawned.

Since the boys were already falling asleep, Hugh and Maxwell hefted them and carried them next door to the suite Sandra had reserved for her family. Everyone went to their separate rooms in the suite to sleep for the rest of the afternoon.

Chapter 20

When Fiona awoke late in the evening, Trey lay beside her, asleep. She hadn't heard him come into the bedroom or felt him get into bed. He lay on his back, his face relaxed. Rising onto her left elbow, she palmed her head and visually mapped his features. He looked like his father must have at the same age: a square jaw, firm mouth, and a handsome face. The more she thought about it, the more Sandra and Harriet's sons' features seemed to resemble Trey and his father.

Rather than disturb his sleep, she gingerly rolled out of bed and went into the shower.

Trey felt Fiona leave the bed. She tried not to wake him, but he was hard-pressed to sleep after seeing Amiria Kono again. There was such a stark difference in her appearance that, for a moment, he could only stare. Her innocence was compelling. She had such lovely feminine features and hair when he first met her; now, she sported a sheared head to the point that she looked like a boy. She was no more than a child when she offered him sex in the men's club. He wasn't there for a hookup. Rather, there were a few vocal soloists he wanted to hear. Yet, there was something about her other than her sensual beauty that intrigued him. He paid for her time and let her give him a lap dance, but did not accept her offer of sex. Instead, he spent the time talking with her. Because her handler was roaming the club, watching the girls, Amiria had to appear to be working so she could stay and talk. He wasn't a novice when it came to the crime syndicates who owned or operated some of the clubs or lounges he frequented in various cities. However, Amiria's situation was appalling, so he decided to do something about it.

The next day, he contacted his covert handler and described what he found out about the human trafficking ring headed by the very dangerous Yakuza, a transnational organized crime syndicate. A short time later, a story hit the world news like a bomb blast about the arrest of several highly placed individuals involved in human trafficking in many countries. The investigation, which had been ongoing for several years, had culminated in the most prominent criminal trials in The Hague the world had ever seen.

Amiria and the other young girls forced into involuntary prostitution were rounded up and kept in detention centers awaiting a determination to deport them back to their countries of origin. His handler suggested he could intervene and vouch for them. He did and arranged for them, eleven in all, to attend a private boarding school in the City of Kobe, Japan. He had seen Amiria off and on through the years and encouraged her musical aspirations. She was a virtuoso. Without prior formal training, she gravitated toward the piano, and, after a while, she could play complicated pieces of music by listening to him play it only once.

However, on her twenty-first birthday, they stepped over the line between teacher and student and became lovers. Their affair lasted only six weeks until Amiria expressed her desire to become pregnant with his child and move to New York to live with him.

He told her no and that it wasn't what he wanted. Then he broke off all ties with her and left the country. Although he continued to check on her progress as a pianist, he hadn't seen or talked with her again since he rejected her desire to have his child. Now, she asked him to help her get a passport to leave Japan. Unwittingly, she had attracted the attention of a young Yakuza lawyer. She was desperate to leave the country, to put distance between her and this gangster before he made good on his demand that she was to live under his roof.

Again, he appealed to his handler for assistance, and this morning, he saw Amiria off on a private flight off the island under an assumed name and a new identity. Her whereabouts had to remain a secret for a time until he could figure out the best place for her. He had contacts virtually worldwide, but he thought maybe somewhere in South America might be a good location for her. Tina Justice, a good friend of his, had a winter retreat in South America. He would speak with her when he had time to talk about the movie he had just finished scoring for her.

"Oh, you're awake," Fiona smiled as she came back into the bedroom while brushing her hair.

"Yes. What time is it?" He was a bit startled by her return. He had been so fixated in his thoughts; he had not heard her turn off the shower.

"Seven forty-five. You were up and out so early this morning; do you need to sleep longer? We could leave, let you rest, and then maybe you could catch up with us later."

"No, I'll shower and get dressed. That'll wake me up. We'll have dinner out, and then I have several places on the schedule I want to visit tonight." He was naked as he headed for the shower.

Fiona's brows beetled. She realized that it was odd for him to pass by her and not steal a kiss or hug her, particularly when she was naked. "Trey, is something wrong?"

"Uh, no. Just a lot on my mind." He returned to where she stood, kissed her mouth quickly, and went into the en suite bath.

Still confused, she watched him go but shrugged it off and went to the closet to select something appropriate to wear.

I am off my game, Trey chastised himself. The rush to get Amiria safely off the island had taken its toll on his concentration. He was waiting when Amiria snuck out of the back door of her building before dawn and got into the car with him. She laid her head in his lap, and he covered her with a blanket to conceal her from anyone who might be out and about at that early hour of the morning. He got Amiria to the US Yokota Air Force Base, forty-five kilometers northwest of Tokyo, at the foothills of the Okutama Mountains. Then he had to beat it back into Tokyo in time for his secret work with the sensational singing group, Ivy.

Because of the early morning clandestine machinations, his work with the solo performance using Whitney Ivy Alexander Cavanaugh's voice and her younger triplet sisters had suffered. Even after hours of work, Ivy was pitch-perfect, but he couldn't get it together until mid-afternoon. By the time they were satisfied with each cut on the new CD, they were all exhausted. Now, he couldn't get his shit together enough to pay proper attention to Fiona. Yet, she didn't demand an explanation for his uncharacteristic behavior. *Points in her favor*, he thought, as he continued to lather his body and then wash his hair.

Fiona was about to drop her damp robe in the laundry basket when she noticed a red smudge on Trey's shirt, and, curious, she picked it up. It was lipstick, and there wasn't just one smudge, but several. She only wore lip gloss, and it wasn't her shade. Women hugged or kissed Trey on his cheek all the time, so that wasn't unusual.

Then she noticed another smudge on the fly of his slacks. That was even more curious than the lipstick on his shirt. She dumped everything back in the laundry basket and began to dress.

Slipping into the thong confection, she wondered where Trey had been all day to have lipstick on his clothes. She wasn't a woman who cared over much about other females and the man with whom she was in a relationship. Certainly, she and Aiden had pledged their fidelity to one another since they were teenagers and became intimately involved in high school. They never strayed from that commitment. So, she had no worries where Aiden was concerned.

However, she had no such covenant with Trey. He confided that he had been in several intimate relationships since the age of fifteen. He was slightly more than twice that age now. Still, she was not so insecure that she had to know every detail of his life. If his feelings for her were changing or he was losing interest, she was still at a point that she could let go and walk away before either one of them became vested in the other. A two-month affair didn't necessarily portend a lifelong future together. For the time being, she would keep her own counsel, and, if necessary, she would take herself out of the equation.

When Trey reentered the bedroom, while towel-drying his hair, the sight of Fiona wearing only a thong caused his blood to warm and his member to grow thicker with need. She had her arms up, doing something with her hair. Tossing aside his towel, he eased up behind her and circled her narrow waist, intimately fitting his nude body to hers. Then, sliding his palms up, he cupped her grapefruit-sized breasts and marveled at their feel and texture. "Mmm, you smell good," he crooned in her right ear and then went to work kissing her neck, along her collar bone and shoulder.

"That shower really woke you up," she teased, and then sharply caught her breath when his right hand slipped under the front of her thong. Closing her eyes on a long moan, her head fell back against the solid wall of his firm pecs.

Trey nibbled his way up the column of her neck to her ear while luxuriating in her moist heat. "Would you leave your hair down? Maybe we don't need to go out tonight?"

"Then we would have to send Sandra, her wife, and boys out on their own." She breathlessly chuckled.

"*Christ!* I forgot they were coming today." He relaxed his forehead on her shoulder, his clever fingers stilled. "No, we have to go. The boys would be disappointed if we didn't take them out." He pulled her into a tight squeeze, burying his face in her hair. "I need a moment before I release you. I'm in a little bit of pain knowing that I can't make love with you the way I want to right now until later."

"Well, maybe the news that Charlotte Everson and your father are also here in the suite will help with the discomfort."

That news was tantamount to a bucket of ice-cold water on his heated need. He looked up, frowning into the mirror before them. "My father?" That was more of a statement than a question. "He's here?"

She nodded. "Yes, he wanted to surprise you. He, my mother, and Charlotte's daughters convinced her to take an impromptu vacation and accompany him. I think there's a budding relationship developing between them. Sandra put them in separate bedrooms, but I suspect that separation will be short-lived. How do you feel about that?"

He noncommittally shrugged. "I've never cared to question my father about his affairs. I assume he has them, but I've never met anyone he's been with."

"I wondered whether he had been involved with Harriet Stone. They seem particularly close."

Trey snorted a laugh as he released her and began to dress. "Not likely. She's his XO."

"XO?" Fiona queried. "You mean like lovers?"

Trey shook his head. "Executive Officer. His right-hand man, so to speak. They've risen through the ranks and been together for years."

"Oh, I didn't know. That must be why they seem so familiar with one another."

"Yes, because if there is one thing I know for sure about my father, he's strictly by the book. Duty first, last, and always." However, he didn't mention that his father, Harriet, Sandra, and he shared a secret they would keep until or unless absolutely necessary. "I'd better let you get dressed or I'll lose my resolve not to take you to bed to make love to you for the rest of the night."

"Promises, promises," she teased before slipping into a shimmering, pewter-colored, form-fitting sheath, hugging her curves like seal skin. She did leave her hair down but tied it in a knot at the nape of her neck.

When she bent at the waist to slip into her ankle boots, Trey groaned loud enough to make her laugh.

Chapter 21

The greeting between General Kennard and Trey could be considered awkward at best, Fiona noted. The father and son couldn't quite figure out whether to shake hands, embrace or pat one another on the back. So, they did a rather comical but sad combination of all three. Sandra and Harriet's boys, Trevor and Kyle, had no difficulties at all with that initial meeting. They simply climbed up on Trey as monkeys would scale a tree. There was pure joy on the three male faces, and hugs abounded. Harriet even received a strong hug and kiss on both cheeks from Trey.

Trey extended his hand to his father's companion. "Welcome to Japan, Mrs. Everson. I'm so glad you could join this merry band of nomads."

"I appreciate you for letting me intrude on what I understand is a working tour for you."

Trey nodded. "Occasionally, we do break to have some fun. That's what we're about for the next little while with the boys in town. So, you've come at a good time. If everyone is ready, let the fun begin." Trey ushered everyone out of the suite. "Where to first, Sandra?"

They entered the elevator and the boys fought over who would punch the down button.

Sandra took the boys' index fingers so they both punched the button. "We're heading for street vendors to find something to eat and then walk until our short friends' feet fall off," she joked as the elevator doors opened on the lobby level, and off the boys went at a sprint.

180

It's as if daylight occurred at eight o'clock at night, Fiona thought. Shinjuku was alive with brilliantly lit electronic billboards wrapped around skyscrapers, and each reader board was as tall as trees in the redwood forest. They advertised every conceivable thing in shocking vibrancy. The dazzling lights made Fiona wish for sunshades. She noted that some people, including Trey and Hugh, were wearing them.

The streets and sidewalks were teeming with people who walked in every direction. Trey suggested they abandon their car service since foot power was the best mode of transportation. However, even that was slow going along the sidewalks. So, like others, they took to the streets so they could stay together. The shops opened for twenty-four hours every day, as well as bars, pubs, restaurants, and almost anything she could think of was available for purchase.

They lucked up on some sort of food court with open-air dining. Snagging a table for nine took ingenuity, but General Kennard managed it with the help of efficient bussers, so by the time everyone had trays of food, seating together was available. The smell of good food was as overpowering as the cacophony of voices and many languages spoken at high decibels to be understood over the din.

"My, it's like the cafeteria of the United Nations in here," Charlotte remarked, seemingly in awe of her surroundings.

Maxwell nodded in agreement. "When Harriett and I were stationed in Japan, embassies from nearly every nation had consulates here. Because Tokyo is a global city that caters to all cultures, we, at the American consulate, had to have a working knowledge of protocols for each nation. Despite the high level of decorum practiced here by the Japanese Royals, parts of this city are like a perpetual party that never stops or sleeps."

Charlotte frowned. "I didn't realize that Japan still had a royal family."

Maxwell nodded. "Oh, yes, the Imperial House of Japan is comprised of those members of the reigning Emperor of Japan's extended family. They still undertake official and public duties. Under the present Constitution of Japan, the Emperor is the symbol of the state and the unity of the people. Other members of the Imperial Family perform ceremonial and social duties but have no role in government affairs. The duties as an Emperor are passed down the line to their children. Actually, the Japanese monarchy claims to be the oldest continuous hereditary monarchy in the world."

Charlotte looked at Maxwell with surprise. "You were a diplomat?"

Maxwell shrugged. "Military Attaché representing the US Army. I'm an Army Ranger by profession. The military services, such as the US Navy, Air Force, Marines, and others, are advisors to the US Ambassador to Japan. The Ambassador coordinates the activities not only of the Foreign Service Officers and staff, but also representatives of other US agencies in the country. Nearly thirty different US federal agencies are posted here and work in concert with embassy staff."

Charlotte nodded her understanding as they continued to eat. "Didn't I read somewhere that one of the military men is an astronaut?"

"Oh, yes. I believe you're referring to Air Force General Benjamin Alexander. He's one of the youngest to have been promoted to his rank in the US Air Force. He's an extraordinary jet fighter pilot, and he's flown missions to SPACEHOME, the geostationary space station.

"Actually, one of his nephews, Brian Montgomery, married a member of Japan's Royal family a few years ago in Summer County, South Carolina. It was quite a scandal here because the young woman refused to marry one of several men her family had chosen for her. So instead, there was a rather impromptu wedding held during the Alexander's Juneteenth family reunion. You see, the young bride, a graduate of Georgetown University, was in love, pregnant, and facing deportation. Brian was deeply in love, too. His mother, Supreme Court Justice Vivian Alexander Montgomery, and father, Dr. Charles Montgomery, weren't about to have their grandchild deported. Thus, the quick marriage.

"The general and admiral go to the states each year for their reunion. Because they were in the states for that event, they were able to attend Mavis' birthday party. Brian and his wife, KiLe Hakamora Alexander, were at the party, too, with their two young boys."

Charlotte's eyes widened. "Oh my, I believe I met him and his wife, Admiral Stacy Alexander, at Mavis' birthday party. There were so many people in attendance that, at the time, I didn't make the connection. It's hard to imagine, years ago, Japan attacked America at Pearl Harbor because it wanted to destroy the US Pacific Fleet. They declared war on the United States so we could not impede Japan's plans for expansion throughout the South Pacific. Now Japan has one of the largest US naval operations surrounding this island."

Maxwell nodded. "Japan also hoped to shatter the morale of Americans to prevent us from entering World War II. That approach didn't quite work out the way they planned. Since you're a student of history, Charlotte, I thought that you might like to see the cities of Nagasaki and Hiroshima, where America dropped atomic bombs from the Enola Gay, a Boeing B-29 Superfortress bomber. I'd also like to take you on a tour of several of the military bases while we're here."

"I would enjoy that. Are General and Admiral Alexander here in Japan? I'd like to say hello, if we could."

"Yes, Benjamin, who we call Benny, and his wife, Stacy, who we call The Admiral," Maxwell joked, "are both military attachés to the US Ambassador. They and their children are back on the island. I planned to see them and others while I'm here. I hoped you'd make time to join me." He smiled. "I love it when a plan comes together."

The smile blooming on Charlotte's face is beatific, Fiona thought, as she listened to the discussion between Maxwell and Charlotte. Fiona liked what she saw developing between Trey's father and her former school teacher. They asked her to join them to see the historical sites in Japan, and she agreed. However, when she turned to Trey, he was engrossed in a discussion with Trevor and Kyle.

For a moment, she simply watched as they put their heads together over plans for the time they would be in town. The sight made her wonder whether Trey would make a good father. Given the difficulty he and his father seemed to have with communicating, she had to wonder whether that factor would negatively impact his relations with a son or daughter of his own.

Then, too, he spent a substantial amount of his time touring the world searching for significant music to develop into masterpieces and performers to train to be headliners. Those facts alone would mitigate against a more sedentary lifestyle for him.

Since she wasn't searching for a father for any future children she might consider having, the thought was purely academic…and moot.

"If we're all finished with stuffing our faces, let's see what exciting things Shinjuku holds for us tonight," Hugh suggested.

At his signal, everyone rose. No sooner were they on their feet, it seemed an army of bussers swooped in to clear away the debris and seat more customers.

"Here's your hat, and what's your hurry?" Fiona joked, making the others laugh.

"Ya gotta keep up," Sandra parried. "A New York state-of-mind is a stroll in the countryside compared to Tokyo. The Japanese do not know the words slow down. They're very industrious people constantly in motion."

Trey offered his hand to Fiona. She took it, and together they led the way into the melee that was Tokyo after dark.

Trevor and Kyle almost made it to eleven o'clock before Sandra and Harriett called it a night and returned to the McCoy Hotel. The remaining five adults: Trey, Fiona, Hugh, Maxwell, and Charlotte, continued their enjoyment of Shinjuku, starting at What The Dickens, a laid-back ex-pat bar, and, according to Hugh, a great place to hear live music.

"The bands here play everything from rock to reggae, jazz, blues, folk, and even Dixieland jazz," Hugh said upon arrival. "They have British beer on tap, which is a nice change from Sake, as well as a menu of steak pie, fish and chips, and other pub fare I miss when we're on tour like this. It's sort of a dive," he said, with an apologetic shrug, "but it pleases my English soul to spend time here."

Trey clamped Hugh on the back. "We've tried to outlast the locals here without success."

Hugh grinned. "We've picked up a few good pieces of music though, and three recording artists we employ as backup singers."

"That we did," Trey agreed.

Hugh ordered sample platters of food for the table to share and a round of drinks before the next musical act began.

Trey looked up to answer the waiter's question about his preference for beer and squinted at someone who had just come into the club. The young man, whom Trey immediately recognized, seemed to be looking for someone. A whispered message to the waiter had him scurrying off in pursuit of the young man. When the waiter caught him and pointed in Trey's direction, a broad smile of recognition bloomed on both of their faces.

"Trey Kennard, how the hell are you, man?" said the tall, sturdy-built, handsome young man when they joined hands in a manly embrace. "I wasn't sure, but I thought I saw you very early this morning with a young woman on the Yokota Air Force Base. I was in physical training with a friend, Ginger Dixon. I broke ranks and tried to catch up with you, but I was too far away to get your attention."

"In any event, it's good to see you. Let me introduce you to my friends." Trey turned to the group at large and dismissed the fact that he had been spotted with Amiria. "Everyone, this is Daniel Connor from Mitchell County, Maryland. He and I were in private military school together. Daniel, this is Fiona Lizette Lowry and Charlotte Everson, both from Bay County, Maryland."

"Wow, that's practically next door to Mitchell County," Daniel enthused. "It's a pleasure to meet you."

"You, too, Daniel," they both acknowledged.

"This is my father, General Maxwell Kennard the Second, from New York City, and my music partner, Hugh Howard from London, England."

They shook hands and chatted for a moment about the fact that the general was once posted there.

"Join us," Trey suggested.

"Another time, I would, but I'm meeting people I'm working with. We just took a break and decided to get something to eat and take a breather."

Trey nodded. "We'll have to work out something. What are you doing these days?"

"I'm in the Navy. I've been accepted into Officer Candidate School in Newport, Rhode Island. I leave in a few weeks."

"That's great, man! You're following in your father's footsteps."

"I am, although he was a Master Sergeant. I want to become a Navy SEAL."

Trey smiled. "Everyone in your family doing well?"

"They are, yes, but let's catch up before you and I leave the island, okay?"

"Sure thing," Trey nodded as Daniel said his farewells and left to join other young military personnel at another table.

Trey could feel his father's eyes on him. Obviously, the fact that he was seen on the Air Force base didn't skip his father's notice. He hoped that no one else had picked up on it. Fortunately, when he rejoined the conversation around the table, the food was delivered, and the music began.

Chapter 22

"What's going on, son?" the general asked Trey as they finished an early morning swim in the hotel's indoor pool and then sat on the pool's edge.

He was in his military mode, Trey sensed, general to subordinate. Not father to son. Trey experienced this persona before when he was a much younger kid and progressed through adolescence to his teenage years. Although older now, his father's tone and demeanor didn't allow for prevarication. So, he didn't pretend ignorance of the reason for his father's question.

"I have a female friend who needed help to get out of the country covertly. So I asked General Alexander and Admiral Alexander for help. The Admiral arranged to have my friend's credentials pushed through in a few hours, and then the general flew her off the island in a private jet he keeps here in Japan. He took her to an undisclosed location where she boarded a flight to the states."

"Who is this woman to you?"

"Just a friend now. However, when she was younger, she was kidnapped by a human trafficking ring. You may have read about it or seen it on the news when the ring was arrested. Before the arrests took place, I helped her and ten other young girls escape, give evidence to the authorities, then sent them to a private boarding school. Over the years, I've kept an eye on their progress. They are out of school now, working in various careers or pursuing advanced degrees. I still help when and where I can. One of the women from the group is a musical virtuoso. I encouraged her studies and she and I became lovers for a brief time.

"A few nights ago, I accidentally ran into her at a club where she was performing. She told me that a young but powerful Yakuza attorney is infatuated with her. She doesn't share his feelings and fears that he would force her into another form of involuntary sexual servitude as his concubine. She asked for my help. I gave it."

"I applaud your altruism, son. Under similar circumstances, I likely would have done the same thing. Still, what you did, getting her out of the country without going through customs, is unlawful. It could place the Alexanders in jeopardy, not to mention what could happen to you if the Japanese government finds out about this. It might also spark an international incident or open you up to retribution and danger from the Yakuza criminal organization."

"I know who they are, Dad. The Yakuza are notorious for their strict codes of conduct, organized fiefdom nature, and unconventional ritual practices. Their members are often heavily tattooed and wear their hair slicked back, which is rather thuggish. Yet, they are still regarded as being among the most sophisticated and wealthiest criminal organizations in the world."

"They are everywhere, son. Therefore, threats from them are to be taken seriously."

"I'm not a fool, Dad. I understand the risks from the Yakuza and the Japanese government. So do the Alexanders. They readily agreed to help and rushed paperwork through the proper channels to prepare identification and a passport. There was nothing underhanded about it other than the speed with which it was accomplished. The credentials aren't fraudulent. They contain her legal name, just not the assumed name she was given when she was abducted. The small island where she was born barely has a government structure and certainly doesn't have an embassy here in Japan. However, because it's among the tiny islands in the archipelagos, which may constitute a part of the State of Hawaii, the American Embassy can legally issue a passport for an American citizen."

"I see. You used your eidetic ability to figure that out, didn't you?"

"What good does it do me not to use it when it could help save someone's life?"

"You cannot risk anyone finding out about your total recall abilities, son. You could disappear into some black site where you'd be studied as if you were a specimen in a petri dish or abducted by some despot and forced to do things against your will. What I don't understand is why you didn't ask me for help?"

Frowning, Trey looked up into his father's eyes. "I, frankly, didn't think of it."

"Just as you didn't think to tell me that you were going to be knighted by the King of England." His tone was dry as dust.

Trey saw the hurt his benign neglect caused his father and was surprised by it. "You're right. I apologize. Fiona asked me the same question after the event. I'll tell you what I told her. I didn't think about it likely because I didn't think you would find it relevant. I've received other awards since I was in elementary school. Still, neither you nor other relatives showed up for any of those events, not even my graduation from the academy or college. So, it didn't cross my mind to invite you to that event."

"Yet, you included Fiona, a woman you've known for less than three months."

"Although I'm your son, you and I have spent less than that amount of time together during the whole of my life." He shook his head in regret. "Look, I didn't tell her either. It was a surprise for her. Only Sandra and Hugh knew about it and I asked them not to tell anyone."

The general nodded in understanding and looked away. "We don't know each other. I get that, but it's still my duty as your father to protect you. I want to know you, son. I want you to know me." He turned back to look into his son's eyes. "I've made a mess of our relationship, yet, even if I could go back all of those years to your early childhood and do it all over again, I don't know whether I would know how to do anything differently. I'm trying to fit a round peg into a square hole which is your life and mine. We are such different people. It's as if we don't share the same gene pool." He remorsefully shook his head again. "I envy few people in my life, but I do begrudge my friend, Al Lowry's life. He married the first woman I ever loved and raised a loving, close-knit family with her and their seven children. There is mutual love, trust, and respect between each one of them. Fiona is among them and is an extraordinary young woman. You're over thirty years old now and I wish you and I had an inkling of the family unity the Lowrys share."

"Father, I don't know how to get to where you want us to be in our relationship. I've grown up not depending on you or any other family member. Even now that I'm an adult, you and I occasionally see each other, but I haven't made time to talk with or visit either set of my grandparents. I know that they have siblings, nieces, and nephews, and those nieces and nephews are married and have children in my generation, but I wouldn't know who they are if I met them on the street. They haven't reached out to me or I to them. I don't fit into their world because I've not served in the military. the way that most of them have.

"The Lowrys celebrate their family connections in ways that I don't understand. What they share wasn't a part of my early childhood or socialization even before mother died. I can only live vicariously through Fiona much the same way you do through your friendship with her parents. Still, their relationship hasn't inspired me to want a child of my own. I wouldn't know how to teach what I never learned."

"I understand. I never learned the need for close family unity as a child either, so I had no frame of reference when I married and you came along. Your grandparents selected your mother to be my wife and I dutifully married her as instructed. I was deployed and rarely saw her or you once you were born. I'm trying to restart my life by getting to know someone I believe I could care about. I want to push the reset button with you, too, son. Are you willing to give me a second chance?"

Trey negligibly shrugged. "I can't promise I'll be any better at forming a relationship, but I'll make the effort."

Fiona awoke, shockingly aroused, and fisted her hands in Trey's long hair as it spilled over her thighs. Then, on its own volition, her body heaved up, levitating off the bed where only moments earlier she'd been sound asleep. When Trey nibbled his way up her body and found her mouth, she smiled against his lips.

"Good morning," she pleasantly sighed and stretched as he slid inside her moist heat. "You're awake early. Did you go swimming?"

"I did, yes, with my father. How did you know?"

"Your hair is still wet and it smells of chlorine."

"Ah, you're very observant." He began to move inside her, rocking her world.

"Sometimes," she said cryptically. "Other times, I simply ignore what I observe."

Trey stopped moving, leaned away, and looked into her eyes. "What does that mean?"

"I trust you to tell me when things begin to change between us. I will do the same for you when that happens. I don't want any secrets between us while we're together like this."

"You said 'when,' not if. What do you think will change other than we could get closer together?"

"You were with another woman yesterday. Probably the same young woman you spoke with at the club who you didn't bring to the table to introduce her to anyone. You usually make a point of introducing anyone you're talking with to me. At least you have since the very first night of this tour. Then when your friend, Daniel Connor, mentioned that he spotted you early in the morning with a young woman, you didn't react by so much as a blink, yet you smoothly changed the subject. I want you to know that it's okay, Trey. I'm not insecure and I don't need to be involved with every aspect of your life. You had a life before me and you'll likely have one after."

Uncoupling, he rolled off Fiona and lay on his back, palming his face with both hands. Then, on a frustrated breath, he turned his head in her direction. "It's not what it looks like on the surface."

"Regardless of what *'it'* is, if *'it'* impacts the relationship between you and me, that's the only time I need a heads-up. When it's time to walk away, no harm, no foul."

A fissure of fear streaked up his spine at the thought of losing her. He turned completely toward her, reached out to caress her face. "I know we've been very casual about this relationship, but I don't want anything to come between us. Especially not something to do with me and any other woman I may have known intimately.

"Yes," he continued on a windy sigh, "I was with a woman—"

"Amiria Kono."

Surprise covered Trey's face as he searched Fiona's countenance but found no censure in her demeanor. "Yes, Amiria. She asked for my help and I gave her what she needed."

After a beat, when Trey offered nothing more, Fiona nodded. "Okay." She rolled out of bed.

"'Okay'? That's all you have to say?" He leaned on his elbow, and his brows narrowed at her dismissive tone.

She shrugged and continued into the en-suite bath.

Trey didn't know what to do with her nonchalance over an issue that would have had most women of his acquaintance screaming at him like banshees. Instead, her dismissive behavior had him even more concerned than before. When he started to rise to follow, her cell phone charging on the nightstand chimed. He picked it up and noted that it wasn't a text message but an incoming call from her uncle, Jake Hawkins. He started to rise to take the phone to her. However, another came on the heels of that call—this one from Aiden McKenna. Trey decided to let both calls go to voice mail and follow Fiona, as was his original plan. He and Fiona needed to talk without outside interruptions.

Fiona was brushing her teeth when he entered and the shower waters were running, steaming up the elegant space. The light green mask on her face and neck smelled pleasantly of limes and lemons. Reaching into his toiletry kit, he began his daily routine first with his electric shaver. Moments later, he stepped into the dual shower stall behind Fiona as she began running conditioner through her long hair. Next, he poured rich, foaming, fragrant shower gel into his loofah-gloved hands and began to scrub Fiona's back, a task she performed for him as well. He used this time to think of what he and Fiona needed to discuss to clarify and reinforce their relationship.

They had become so natural with each other, enjoying their daily ritual together. Trey didn't want to disturb their routine. Generally, it included shower sex. However, Trey surmised that their conversation about Amiria and the one they needed to have about their relationship going forward didn't bode well for a continuation of that pleasure this morning.

He was right when Fiona simply thanked him for rinsing the conditioner out of her hair and stepped out of the shower. Trey knew Fiona well enough to know she was holding out on him. This situation was a sensitive area of his clandestine life, and Trey wasn't sure how much he could tell her. So, he didn't immediately follow her into the dressing room. Instead, Trey leaned his outstretched arms against the shower wall and bowed his head in thought, letting the spray hit his body from three directions, drenching him. When he entered the dressing room, prepared to discuss how he felt about her, Fiona was gone.

Chapter 23

The group formed early and started their day at Innsyoutei, a unique restaurant specializing in traditional Japanese kaiseki cuisine and situated beside a beautiful temple. Sitting on Tatami mats, the atmosphere was engaging; and the service was superb. Fortunately for Fiona, the staff spoke English and described each of the colorful dishes Trey ordered for breakfast. However, Trevor and Kyle didn't need descriptions. It was simply open mouth and insert food.

After breakfast, they abandoned the car service again and took to the subway system, which, Maxwell explained, served upwards of seventy million riders daily. For Fiona, who admitted she was a country girl, those numbers staggered her imagination. Charlotte agreed. However, in the subway station, there were people whose job was to literally push people into each railcar tighter than sextuplets in a womb.

Once onboard with no room to move and hardly any space to breathe, they were off at breakneck speeds to the Ueno Zoo in Taitō, Tokyo, Japan's oldest zoo, which, Fiona learned, opened in 1882. It was a five-minute walk from the subway system's Park Exit of Ueno Station, with convenient access to the Ueno Zoo Monorail, the first monorail built in the country. Fiona's architectural and engineering expertise had her nodding, impressed with the quality of the structure, which had been in existence for more than one hundred years. It was a smooth ride connecting the eastern and western parts of the grounds. They started at the farthest point and worked their way back to the entrance.

Sandra and Fiona walked arm-in-arm, following behind Maxwell, Charlotte, and Harriet. "Something is wrong, isn't it? Between you and

Trey, I mean." Trey, Hugh, and the boys were leading the pack, excitedly darting from one exhibit to the next.

Fiona shrugged. "Nothing to worry overmuch about."

"You and Trey have been out of sync since Daniel mentioned seeing him with a woman early the other morning. I presume the woman in question was Amiria. If so, you're right not to worry. There is nothing between them now except friendship."

"Perhaps, but Trey had a blueberry shade of lipstick on his clothes that day in some interesting places."

"He doesn't do serial dating, Fiona, of that, I'm sure. Right now, he's off a step or two. I believe it's because he's worried about your reaction to what you witnessed. You two are good together and good for each other. I just hope you two will be able to work through it and get back on track. I'm not going to stick my nose into your business."

"Thanks, Sandra. I don't want to be a distraction to him, particularly since we've only got three weeks to go before the end of his tour, and he still has work to accomplish."

"What are your plans after we leave Japan?"

"My Uncle Jake is in the Republic of Seychelles, Africa. He and my Aunt Kelley want me to come to Africa to visit with them for a few weeks before I head back to my home in Maryland. According to my dad, we're about three weeks ahead of schedule on Trey's project. Both the studio and his residence are under roof. So, now that I have a much clearer idea about Trey's tastes, I've started ordering the furnishings for his home and studio. Everything will be delivered to my warehouse for storage until I can get home and make sure the décor fits his needs."

"I just received word from his agent, Bill Chandler, that several of Trey's musical scores are up for awards, Academy Awards and Grammys. So, we'll have to stop in California before heading back to New York. I'm sure he will want you to accompany him."

Fiona shook her head. "I've never been to Africa and now that I'm this close, I want to see as much of it as I can. My family wants to rendezvous there for a few weeks. It will be the first time we will all be together in a sort of family reunion. I don't want to miss this."

"I understand. Have you told Trey yet?"

"I haven't, no. It just happened today. My uncle called me this morning to tell me he's making the arrangements. My Hawkins cousins are also going to join us."

Sandra frowned. "Is your uncle African?"

"He's an American of African and Creole descent. He's currently the US Ambassador to Seychelles."

Sandra stopped walking and just stared at Fiona. "Wait. Your uncle wouldn't be Jake Hawkins, would he?"

Fiona frowned and nodded. "Yes, he's my mother's brother. You've heard of him?"

"Of course. Who hasn't? He's as wealthy as Jeff Bezos, Bill Gates, or Warren Buffett. He heads one of the largest corporations in the world and has his fingers in a lot of pies."

Fiona laughed at the analogy. "Well, right now, his holdings are being managed by my cousins, who are three of his four children, while he's in the Foreign Service. He and his second wife, Kelley, just had a baby boy who is less than a year old. Everyone, except my cousins, Jacob Junior and Adam, who you've met, was there for my mother's birthday party before I joined you and Trey. They encouraged me to accept Trey's offer to spread my wings and travel. I've thoroughly enjoyed my time with you, Trey, and Hugh, but I miss my family fiercely. So, I'm looking forward to this family gathering."

Still arm-in-arm, they started walking again. "As well as you should. Just give Trey a heads-up as soon as possible."

Fiona nodded. "If you think it's that important to him, I'll talk with him today."

Lunch was hot dogs, French fries, and soft drinks at the zoo before the group headed off to spend the afternoon and early evening at the Tokyo_Disney_Resort, a one-hundred-fifteen-acre theme park in Urayasu, Chiba Prefecture near Tokyo. Again, they opted for the subway system since the theme park's main gate was directly adjacent to Maihama Station and Tokyo Disneyland Station.

Only Sandra, Harriett, and the boys had been to a Disney Park, so it was an adventure for the adults as well as the boys. They visited each of the seven themed areas: the World Bazaar; the four traditional Disney lands: Adventureland, Westernland, Fantasyland, and Tomorrowland; and two mini-lands: Critter Country and Mickey's Toontown. The boys were overjoyed and their energy levels didn't diminish until after dinner in the hotel suite. Then, they were sent off to baths and bed while the adults rested with after-dinner drinks before preparing to dress for another night on the town. This time, the general arranged for two American teenage girls, whose mother was an officer in the Army Rangers, to stay with the boys overnight so the adults could go out and play.

"Trey," Fiona began as she scrubbed his back in the shower. "I understand that you have to stop in California before going back to New York."

"Yes, Sandra told me. We'll be in California for less than a week. So, we'll cut our visit here in Japan short, so it shouldn't be a problem for our schedule."

"That's just the thing. I'm not going back to the states right away."

Trey stopped scrubbing his hair and turned around, his facial expression troubled. "Why? Where are you going?"

She told him about her family's plan to meet in Africa for a few weeks. "We've never done anything like this before. It's just that my mom and Uncle Jake don't have any other siblings or relatives. My Aunt Skai Littlefeather was Uncle Jake's first wife. Unfortunately, she died, but her mother is still alive. Her name is Kiavi Littlefeather, and she's a noted author of Navajo children's literature. She recently married a close family friend, Ezra Neal. Although he's not a blood relation, we call him Uncle Ezra because he practically raised Uncle Jake and my mom. Uncle Ezra and Aunt Kiavi have never traveled, but they are also going to join us, too."

"I had hoped to show you my New York studio and condo before you returned to Maryland."

"I didn't know that. However, I do want to see as much of the African continent as I can. So, I may extend my trip there beyond the family reunion. Uncle Jake has some diplomatic missions to attend to in different African countries. He's asked me to go with him."

"Yes, I remember hearing him mention some of the work he's doing there. I wish I could, but I can't go with you."

"I understand. You still have a lot of work to accomplish before you leave Japan, and more things have been added to your schedule. I have a few more weeks before the family reunion and quite a bit of architecture to photograph and experience. Then I'll be back in Maryland to finish your home and workspace. I'm pleased with the progress we're making, are you?"

"Could we talk about the construction later? First, I want to address the elephant in the room."

"We don't have time for that discussion right now, Trey. Everyone will be waiting to go out for the evening. According to Sandra, you have six clubs on your schedule tonight."

"Then when can we make time to talk about it?"

"Let's talk after lunch tomorrow, okay?"

He nodded but was far from satisfied with the delay.

Little did either of them know, they would not have time for that conversation.

<h1 style="text-align:center">Chapter 24</h1>

The sounds outside Fiona's bedroom window were unlike any she had ever heard before. The ocean, with huge waves curling up high in the air, loudly crashed against the shore. The night before, there had been a severe storm out in the ocean, causing the waves to come in hard and strong against the island's sandy beach. Turning to look at the clock on the nightstand, she noted that it was still very early. The sunrays were just beginning to peek over the Indian Ocean, causing a gradual lightening of the sky.

One hundred fifteen islands constituted the Republic of Seychelles, a country in the archipelagos, considered a part of Africa. Her Uncle Jake is the US Ambassador to the country. When she and his sons, her cousins, landed the day before, the islands, which lay east of the African mainland, were a stunning sight speckled on the seemingly endless deep blue waters. In addition, there were other nearby country islands and territories they flew over, including Comoros, Mayotte, Madagascar, Réunion, and Mauritius to the south, as well as the Maldives and British Indian Ocean Territory to the east.

The plantation house her uncle and aunt used as a residence looked like a resort. The official US American Embassy with a rooftop helicopter landing pad was on the property, closer to the public road in another grand building. Other outbuildings he used for specific purposes, including a spa, a huge horse stable, and an eighteen-hole golf course with a clubhouse. There was also a tennis court, basketball court, volleyball court, and plenty of other grassy spaces to play other sports like baseball, football, or soccer. The land was lushly landscaped with pine trees, flowers, and plentiful hideaway alcoves, but so large that they used golf carts to move from some venues to others. However, when Fiona went inside the primary residence, there was a panoramic view of the Indian Ocean through continuous glass walls on all three levels of the mansion. All forty bedrooms were suites with a picture-perfect view of the ocean and the wide sandy beach. Water sports of every type and description took over the rear of the house. It took a while for Fiona to figure out which set of three elevator bays were closest to her bedroom suite.

Seychelles, Fiona learned from her cousins, Jacob and Adam, on their flight from Japan, developed from a predominantly agricultural society to what was now a market-based diversified economy. Agriculture was being supplanted by rapidly rising service industries and tourism. In recent years, island officials' plans had encouraged foreign investment, and BlackHawk Global, Fiona's uncle's company, was among the most prominent investors. Jacob and Adam's youngest sister, JaiHonnah, and her husband, J. Roderick Baylor, co-chaired the monolith BlackHawk Holding. Jacob was the president of BlackHawk Global and Adam the director of the not-for-profit BlackHawk Foundation.

Adam explained that poverty was still widespread, although Seychelles boasted the highest per capita GDP in Africa and economic prosperity. The BlackHawk Foundation was gearing up to begin the process of turning the country's economy around through education and teaching skilled trades like plumbing, electrical engineering, and carpentry, which have a future. Coupled with the proper education, these skills could spawn small businesses and cottage industries.

Adam headed the philanthropic foundation NGO only part-time. His deal with his father, Jake Hawkins, was that he could spend half the year with his Formula One race cars and the other half of the year managing foundation projects all over the African continent. Since his racing season was over, he told Fiona it was now time for him to get back to work. So the family reunion his father planned was shaping up to be a welcomed respite for him before the hard work began.

Adam and his brother, Jacob, were in Tokyo to handle business for different aspects of BlackHawk Global and the Foundation. They knew Fiona was there, so they swooped in and scooped her up when they were ready to leave for Africa. When Adam and Jacob arrived, Trey and Hugh were away from the hotel, working at a studio. They convinced her to fly to Seychelles with them a few weeks early before they were scheduled to meet the rest of the family for the reunion.

Since there wasn't any reason for her to stay in Japan, she prepared to leave. She had accomplished what she joined the tour to achieve. However, Fiona did regret that she had barely enough time to say her farewells to Sandra, Harriet, the boys, Charlotte, and Maxwell Kennard before her cousins had her out the door and headed for the airport.

When they got to the airport, she had to stop and laugh. The BlackHawk supersonic jet was painted to resemble a black hawk in all its fearsome majesty. Her uncle was a character, but this was beyond comical. Like the bird, the plane's fuselage was stark black with expansive wings and a short tail with a single broad white band and a white tip. The cone-shaped bill tipped down in front, and the windows formed the eyes. It was a formidable sight to see.

Fiona called Trey and Hugh before the private plane lifted off the runway, but her calls went to voice mail. She knew they were working and generally didn't take calls during that time. Finally, she called Sandra, who agreed to give Trey her message. That was the best she could do, but so far in the last twenty-four hours, Trey had not called.

Sighing, Fiona stood and put on a robe before opening the accordion-like, French doors spanning the sleeping area and sitting room and leading to a private patio overlooking the ocean. It was early still, so she leaned against a post and just breathed in deeply the ocean air. The property, one of her uncle Jake's retreats, was a palatial plantation house and outbuildings situated on a beautiful, private, sandy beach, all with incredible views. She stood for quite a while, enjoying the magnificent scenery and solitude. The sun was still coming up with fingers of light over the horizon when Fiona walked across the sand down to the water's edge. It was surprisingly warm and calmer now as it gently lapped against the shore.

What a glorious morning, she thought, walking out further until she was waist-deep in the clear waters of the Indian Ocean. She leaned back, lifted her legs, and, with arms outstretched, floated there as the tide rocked her and the sky continued to lighten more. Her mind drifted to the wonderful experiences she'd had over the past three months and the amazing people with whom she'd shared time.

Sandra was a joy, as were her wife, Harriett, and their boys, Trevor and Kyle. Then there was Hugh Howard, a warm, caring man who was the perfect guide for all things English. Spending time with Charlotte Everson, her former teacher and her mother's close friend, showed a side of her Fiona would never have imagined. Although the general, Trey's father, was somewhat of an enigma still, she liked what she saw developing between him and Charlotte. Of course, the person who brought all the people and magical experiences together, Trey Kennard—

"Hey!" someone yelled, breaking into her thoughts. *"Hey there! Are you all right?"*

Jolted, Fiona opened her eyes to see a man swimming fast toward her. She righted herself, treading water, and called back. "Yes, I'm fine."

Just before the man reached her, he said, "You shouldn't be this far from shore this early in the morning. Sharks feed in this area. Please, let's head for the beach."

"Okay." She began to swim along with him. She didn't realize she had drifted that far offshore. When they climbed out of the water, Fiona's robe clung to her body like seal skin. The man, she noticed, turned his back to her and pretended not to notice her transparent robe as he bent and picked up a pair of running shoes. He fit them on his feet, and then, without so much as a wave, he ran on down the deserted beach at a quick pace.

Odd, Fiona thought, *he didn't even introduce himself*. She shrugged it off and headed back into her suite to shower. However, just as Fiona entered the en-suite, the in-house phone rang. "Yes?"

"Hey, are you up for a ride along the beach?" It was JaiHonnah Hawkins Baylor, her cousin.

"Sure. When?"

"Now. Meet up at the south side, by the stables."

"Okay."

Fiona dressed in jeans, a white T-shirt, and riding boots. Though her hair was still wet, she didn't take time to dry it. Instead, she twisted as much water out of it as she could and let it hang loose to air dry. She would wash and condition it later; a task Trey enjoyed performing for her, she recalled with a bit of sadness. After brushing her teeth and washing her face, she left her suite through the sitting area and went into the wide hallway.

It took time to walk the long, convoluted halls to the south end of the mansion. It had more than forty bedroom suites and so many common areas, nooks and crannies that a person could get lost without a good sense of direction. When she made it out to where the horses were stabled, JaiHonnah and four of her children: nine-year-old twins, Shelly and Shelby, her husband's daughters from a previous marriage, were helping their four-year-old twin brothers, Rodney and Reese, mount up. Jefferson Junior, Miles, and Stephen Logan, Ambassador Emeritus Jefferson Logan, Senior's sons from his previous marriage, were already mounted. They were taking their horses around the corral and putting them through their paces. The siblings, LaiLoni Skai Hawkins Logan, Adam, and Jacob Hawkins, led four saddled thoroughbreds out of the barn. Fiona's six brothers followed them. All were dressed and ready to ride.

"Here, try this filly on for size," Adam joked. "She's got agility, speed, and spirit. Her name is Sparkle."

"She's a beauty." Fiona took the horse's reins and inspected her, as Mrs. McKenna taught her and her brothers to do before riding. Her brothers were going through the same process of examining their mounts. She lifted the horse's feet to inspect her hooves, shoes, and legs. Satisfied the horse was in excellent shape, Fiona swung up onto the saddle and leaned forward to rub the horse's long neck. Looking around, she asked about her cousins' husbands. "Where are Roderick and Jefferson?"

JaiHonnah laughed as she and LaiLoni Skai fluidly mounted their horses. "They have daddy duty with the little ones along with Jake. Kelley is staying behind to supervise with Ezra and Kiavi,"

"Let's go, girl," Fiona crooned to Sparkle, and the group left the corral at a swift trot.

Excellent riders all, they had ridden more than ten miles down the south end of the beach and were walking the horses back through the surf at the water's edge at a much slower pace to cool the horses down.

"I presume you had a good time on your European and Asian tours?" LaiLoni Skai asked as she, her sister JaiHonnah, and Fiona rode three abreast. Jai's four children rode ahead, four abreast with Adam and Jacob flanking them. Fiona's brothers were leading the pack much further forward.

Fiona sighed in appreciation. "It was an unbelievable experience. Every day was like a new adventure. I have to admit, I never spent so much time in clubs or bars in my life, but the nights were magical. Trey, you met at my mother's birthday party. He and his music consultant, Hugh Howard, worked all night going from one club to another, looking for talent and new music, and then spent most mornings until lunchtime working in studios."

JaiHonnah nodded. "I remembered Trey Kennard from my Miss America pageant. He was one of the judges."

Fiona nodded. "He mentioned it to me the day before Mom's birthday. While in London, I ran into your brother, Jacob, at the club Heaven the first night we were in England." She avoided mentioning that Jacob was with JaiHonnah's loathsome nemesis, Geneva Simpson.

JaiHonnah shook her head in wonder. "That's one hell of a schedule. When did you sleep?"

"After lunch or later if we went sightseeing. We were up again and out by eight or nine for dinner and in the first club by eleven. Sometimes they changed the daily schedule to take me sightseeing earlier in the day. On most weekends, we headed out of London and drove into the countryside. Trey and Hugh were still working, but the country bars or pubs had different types of music. We spent a wonderful time in Truro, a beautifully quaint village in the south of England." She went on to tell them about the other sights she experienced, including meeting the King and Queen of England.

LaiLoni Skai nodded. "Aunt Mavis shared pictures of it with us. Based on what I saw, you really got to see some incredible places in England,"

"We did, yes, and it was very educational. Trey was able to wrap up his work early in England, so we made it to France for nearly a week and met the incomparable French Mariah. Trey recorded a show in her club with the sensational songstress, Loretta, her sister, Kayla Hill, and Vivian Alexander Montgomery's younger sister, Aretha Grace Alexander. That was an incredible experience, too. Trey made a side trip possible so that I could see Adam race in the Grand Prix. Unfortunately, we could only stay a few hours.

"Then, we were off to Spain for four weeks. We drove all over the country, visiting clubs and listening to unique music. At La Masquerade, one of many popular nightclubs in Murcia, the place was packed. There were dazzling lights and loud music, but the cigarette smoke was so thick I could barely breathe. Still, Trey and Hugh picked up two acts they took into a studio the next day.

"The food and iconic sights were awe-inspiring. The pre-Romanesque architecture of Santa María del Naranco in Oviedo, the bronze statues of Don Quixote and Sancho Panza in the Plaza de España in Madrid, the modern Hemispheric at the Ciutat de les Arts les Ciències in Valencia, and the Hanging Houses of Cuenca were even more fascinating than I expected. Pictures, even in three-dimensional, paled by comparison to actually seeing these sights up close

"I could bore you to tears with everything we did and places we went. Places like Madrid, Barcelona, and Seville were all great with incredible historic charm. However, my favorite place in Spain is the City of Murcia. It's the place where time stood still. Buildings seemed as old as time itself but still solid and functional. I couldn't believe there were flower boxes in office windows. Palm trees in the parks. Narrow cobblestone streets and little shops of antiques which I wasted no time exploring.

"It's a charming, walkable community located in the southeast of the country between Andalusia and Valencia on the Mediterranean coast. If I ever wanted to leave the United States, I believe I could live there for a lifetime. It has plenty of landmarks I found myself lingering over—from Moorish gardens and other influences to the ornate architectural blend of Plaza Cardenal Belluga.

"Festivals of various types and descriptions were being held in the Mediterranean valleys, mountains, and coastlines. I think we visited each and every one, including the luscious Playa La Manga Del Mar Menor." Fiona laughed. "We never stopped moving over the entire region."

"You really must have enjoyed it."

"I did. Trey leased this small but opulent villa that was right on the coast. The Mar Mediterranean stretched out before us just below the terrace, yet we could see the Sierra Nevada mountain range. Trey and Hugh told me they went skiing there many times. I shipped home more pieces I found there than any other place we visited." Fiona laughed. "Not everything was for clients or gifts. I believe if we stayed in Spain longer, I'm afraid I might have become a hoarder."

JaiHonnah smiled. "Not likely. You're too organized for that. I spent some time in Spain, too. I found the people to be friendly."

Fiona nodded in agreement. "Little old women with aprons around their waists and scarves around their heads were a real dichotomy to the very stylish women in the latest couture designs we had seen elsewhere in the country. They are small-statured people with ready smiles but big, voracious laughter."

JaiHonnah nodded. "That's what I remember most about them."

"Trey found this quaint hotel on the Plaza del Generalissimo where we had several fine meals, and then we walked around the mostly deserted streets. Several days, we would sit at sidewalk bistros amid orange groves and have lunch. Oranges grew in abundance on trees lining the streets around the Cathedral de Iglesias, the city's centerpiece. The bells of the Cathedral rang twice, signaling the beginning of siesta. Shops and stores closed. School children went home. Offices shut down. Everything stopped, except us. We wound our way through the cobblestone streets to the Teatro de Romea and saw musicals performed in rehearsal many days.

"Another day, we drove up a steep and narrow winding road into the mountains to see the Santuario de la Fuensanta Christiania Delagardo Diega. When I tell you it gleams, I'm not exaggerating. It's a white, Gothic building perched on a hillside plateau overlooking the City of Murcia. Two widely spaced bell towers stand sentry beside it. The majesty and magnificence of the golden interior of the Santuario are overwhelming. There's a single full-sized figure of a woman clad in the finest silk and gold with a child standing in the palm of one hand. The Cross of San Christobal is missing from the chain that hung from her neck. I read that it was found several years ago on the Navajo Reservation where your mother was born, and your grandmother lives now. The story of how it got from Spain to America has to be an interesting one. I meant to ask your grandmother about it. Anyway, the face of the statue is blank, like the face of a porcelain doll. Looking at this piece of art, I felt as if, at any moment, silent tears would fall without any other show of emotion."

Fiona joyously laughed. "Next, after such a moving experience, we were off to LaManga Del Mar Menor on the coast in the Costa Calida district, where we ate cheese, freshly baked bread, fruit, and olives and drank wine on a terrace overlooking the sea. We had several more stops before we left Spain, but I'd really like to return and do it all over again."

"It sounds as if you and Trey Kennard became close."

Fiona sadly nodded and then shrugged. "We did. Perhaps closer than either of us thought at the time. In Japan, I believe we were about to have *The Talk* before your brothers snatched me up and brought me here." She laughed. "I think it was a good thing they did. I needed to put some distance between us to get my perspective back in working order. Initially, I joined Trey on tour in part to get an idea of how he worked and lived so that I could design his home and studio space. It was also an opportunity to see places I had only read about and to do things I had never done before. It was everything and more than I expected.

"What was unexpected was that Trey and I would become intimate. So, it was a good thing that Uncle Jake asked me to come here earlier than originally planned."

JaiHonnah nodded. "Dad wanted you and your brothers to see firsthand a project he has underway here. That's why he wanted all of you to come early, before the official start of the reunion. He's planning to expand this project to the other islands of Seychelles."

"He mentioned something about it when we talked at Mom's birthday party and when he called me about coming here for the reunion."

"It's important to Dad," JaiHonnah smiled. "We've never had a true family reunion after Mom died. Before we found LaiLoni, we would sometimes get together someplace to share a meal, but someone was always missing, had to come late, or leave early. Dad wants us to be closer, like Vivian's family is. They have a dedicated ten-day annual reunion in Summer County, South Carolina, around the Juneteenth holiday. Dad wants us to do that type of thing. Put the two-week family reunion on the calendar to be held somewhere in the world each year without fail."

"It's a great idea," Fiona nodded. "My dad and mom don't get out of Bay County often for long periods of time. As you know, Dad's family all live in the area, and we're in and out of each other's homes all the time. So, this will be good for Dad and Mom and the rest of us, too. Although I missed my family, I enjoy seeing iconic places I've only seen in pictures. There are innumerable places I'd like to visit."

"I know what you mean. I lived in several places on the European continent when I was training to be an engineer and architect. Now I want my children to see the world with Roderick and me."

"I want the same thing for my family with Jefferson," LaiLoni Skai smiled. "He and his three sons have traveled extensively, but not together as a family the way they are now. The boys are getting older now, and soon they'll be off to college. Our two daughters, who are no longer toddlers, are curious about places I read to them about. We also have the African refugee girls we adopted. So, this renewed sense of family relationships is essential for them and me, too.

"For most of my life growing up on the reservation in North Dakota on the Canadian border, I didn't know I had a family. So, spending the time now shouldn't be passed by without celebrating where we came from. This time will never come again. We need to make these lasting memories for our children and for us. So, I'm going to start chronicling our events to pass down for future generations."

They continued to talk and brainstorm about ways to enhance their times together as they rode the horses along the beach.

Breakfast was served on one of the upper-level verandas overlooking a two-tiered pool lagoon and the Indian Ocean. Jake and Kelley sat two abreast at one end of the wide table, while Alroy and Mavis also sat side-by-side at the opposite end. Their offspring and the rest of the family fit into spaces along each side of the table with the little people seated among the adults. The seat and place setting to Fiona's right would have been filled by one of her brothers, she thought, but instead, a man she recognized from her early morning swim took the seat. "Well, hello," she said to him.

"Hello," he nodded and immediately began a discussion with Adam on his right.

Well, not the social type, Fiona assumed by his curt response to her. Studying him, she noted he was a very tall man of about six feet, ten inches, most of which appeared to be solid muscle, long legs, and no fat. His skin tone was in the olive-brown range, with a bearded face and long black curly hair tied in a rawhide band at the nape of his neck. Indigenous American, if she had to hazard a guess. His facial features were remarkable and, for some reason, reminded her of the actor Keanu Reeves. His eyes were sharp but seemed to have a bit of sadness there. Yet, powerful energy seemed to radiate off him even while sitting relatively still and eating breakfast. Maybe she was projecting, but there seemed to be more to him than what was on the surface.

After breakfast, her uncle called her, her brothers, JaiHonnah, Adam, Jacob, and Jefferson Logan, into one of the libraries. International attorney Thomas Ashton Marshall and the stranger were already there talking when she arrived. She had read about Mr. Marshall, whom friends called Ashton. He arrived the day before and brought his wife, Circuit Court Judge Kristen Catherine, and their three children with them. While Kristen, who everyone called KC, and her two boys and a girl took advantage of the beach, the rest of them settled around a large library table bearing a scale model of what appeared to be a three-level hospital.

"Some of you have met Dr. Noah Mikasi, but for those who haven't, he's a physician who has worked all over the African continent and much of Asia, training others to perform basic medical services for indigent people. Most recently, he was with the NGO Doctors Without Borders. I've asked him to head up a task force to evaluate the medical services here in the Seychelles islands and build clinics where necessary. He will also take on the task of building a cutting-edge hospital, the prototype I had my daughter, JaiHonnah, design for me, and staffing it with forward-thinking doctors, nurses, and other medical professionals.

"To aid him in the process of staffing the hospitals, I've asked my son-in-law, Jefferson Logan, to head an education task force to evaluate the state of the academic systems in the islands. He will be making recommendations for schools and library programs necessary to raise the literacy quotient through the unique program he manages at Summer County Academy in South Carolina.

"To assist the overall efforts, I've purchased transponders on Nicholas Collins's satellite so that both the medical and education programs will be interactive. Medical facilities on the islands will be linked with experts in the flagship hospital. The same will be true of the schools we will build and link together. The schools will also have exchanges with Summer County Academy and others like it in Washington, DC, Mitchell County, Maryland, and Chicago, Illinois.

"Fiona, I need for you to take time out of your schedule to stay here and work with both programs. First, on the plan, each one needs facilities to accommodate the education and medical programs. I'd like for you to identify those facilities on each island and have them retrofitted for the services they will provide. Boys," Jake referred to Fiona's brothers, "I'm asking you to pledge a part of your time annually to come here to teach your skills and train workers and help complete the facilities your sister will design and build. I'm designating this project: Operation: Uplift.

"Because this affects your businesses, I've talked this over with your parents before I raised the prospect of doing this with you. I know I'm asking a lot of each of you, but I also know your skill sets, and I trust the quality of your work. To be sure, nothing comes for free, but with Operation: Uplift, the expense is not an issue or a question. There is no such thing as a budget for this undertaking. Simply tell Adam what you need or want, and it's his responsibility to get it for you; no questions asked.

"Everything we do for Operation: Uplift will be under the BlackHawk Foundation umbrella, which you know Adam heads. In six months, we'll evaluate where we are and what we need to do going forward. I'll tell you now, this is a prototype test area. If we are successful here, I intend to replicate this program in the poorest countries in Africa, starting with Burundi, Malawi, Niger, Mozambique, and The Central African Republic. Because of the multitude of legal systems associated with each country, Thomas Ashton Marshall and his law firm, Marshall and Associates, have agreed to spearhead that aspect of the project. He has offices in Washington, DC, and can work with the Ambassadors of each country who have an embassy in DC or representation with the United Nations in New York City.

"I've given you a lot to think about, so I won't press you for an answer now. Dr. Mikasi, Ashton, Jefferson, Adam, and I have been working on Operation: Uplift for nearly a year. So, if you have questions, which I'm sure you will, don't hesitate to ask any one of us. We'll meet again in a week to discuss it, and you can give me your answers then. For now, let's join the rest of the family and friends poolside."

Fiona sat still, stunned at the extraordinary task her uncle was asking her to spearhead. One hundred fifteen islands made up the African country known as The Republic of Seychelles. If he wanted her to find, build or retrofit a medical clinic and school facility on each island, she would have to spend time here year-round. Quickly, she rose and went in search of her parents.

On an oath, Noah slowly rose from his seat to follow the others out of the library. *When you assume, it makes an ass out of you and me*, he thought morosely. Mainly him, but, well, it wasn't exactly his fault. How was he to know that the red-head, raving beauty he rescued from the Indian Ocean before she became fast food for the sharks was not some brainless woman trying to commit suicide? There he was, running his daily ten-mile exercise routine on the beach, and he sees a silky white piece of cloth far out in the ocean. When he realized the fabric was wrapped around a female form, his instincts from his SEAL team training took over, and he dove in to try to save her.

Then, when they reached the shore, that white piece of clothing was as transparent as clear glass against her skin. She might as well have been wearing nothing at all. He couldn't just stand there and stare the way he wanted to because the bulge in his wet jockstrap and running shorts would have been evident. The woman had sex appeal galore with the dark red hair that was so long it skimmed the top of her beautiful rear end. That, along with the long legs, hourglass figure, grapefruit-sized breasts, and a face that should have been on a movie screen, came together and screamed **DO NOT TOUCH!** She was simply gorgeous. That was why he assumed she belonged to either Adam or Jacob Hawkins. He had known both for a while, and they tended to associate with beautiful women; Jacob more than Adam. She seemed to fit their mold.

Now, to find out that she's their unmarried cousin, an architect and engineer, and the person he would have to work closely with over the next six months? This factor was a killer on steroids. Life couldn't be this cruel.

Still, he had tried to ignore her and failed miserably. As she sat beside him at the breakfast table, her warm, fresh, and unique scent wrapped around him like a siren's song. She captured his attention from the moment she walked into the room. In the library, he sat as far away from her as possible. Otherwise, his concentration on Operation: Uplift would have been for shit. Now he had to think of her not as a very desirable woman, but as a colleague. He hadn't had sex in quite a while, so he had to pledge to remain celibate for the time he would be around her or find a substitute to slake his needs.

Chapter 25

*D*amn it! *Fiona is gone, and I can't get my head back in the space where it belongs,* Trey thought as he paced. When he returned to the hotel, Sandra told him Fiona tried to reach him. He hadn't picked up the call because he was at a critical point in recording the Alexander children's voices, looping it into the audio presentation he recorded in Paris. Hugh had found old recordings done by the original vocalists for most of the songs the four women sang. Sandra obtained the necessary copyright permissions. Hugh did an imaginative job blending those earliest songs in with the new ones and did the voice-over with Ivy's songs.

Then Sandra confided that Fiona found lipstick traces "on some interesting places on his clothes." Initially, Trey was confused about that before realization dawned. Amiria put her head in his lap, and he covered her up with a blanket to hide her as he drove from her flat to the Air Force base. He remembered she was wearing lipstick and, at the time, considered it strange that she would have on makeup at that early hour. *Who stops to put on lipstick when she's trying to escape a dangerous situation?* He dismissed the thought until she tried to give him a blow job while he was driving. He stopped her before she could get him into her mouth. She made a joke of it at the time, saying she had nothing better to do while her head was in his lap.

T Then, just before Amiria boarded the flight with Benny Alexander, she tried to kiss his mouth. He turned his head, but her mouth must have grazed his clothing. Again, he thought nothing of it at the time. Rather, he was in a hurry to get back to work so he could finish up early and spend more quality time with Fiona. They planned to have a serious conversation about their future…together.

No wonder Fiona had been so casual about his explanation regarding Amiria. He hadn't realized there was questionable evidence of a sexual encounter on his clothes. Now that he had time to consider it, he'd bet real American money that Amiria's behavior was calculated toward destroying his relationship with Fiona. *Hindsight is always twenty-twenty.*

Come to think about it, Amiria asked him about Fiona, and he admitted that he was involved with someone very special to him. Amiria wished him well and then began to reminisce about their brief interlude before she asked for his help in escaping the clutches of a Yakuza criminal. Now he wondered whether that had been a ploy to get back into his life. Even now, she was staying in his New York condo until he had time to get her to someplace relatively safe. To make those arrangements, he needed to talk with Tina Justice Collins. Yet, he could easily have Amiria join the tour with History. At least they didn't know her connection to him, and their tour schedule took them all over the United States. History was also booked for places in Canada and South America. That would give him time to work out a solution for Amiria's safety, and it would get her out of his condo.

Wasting no time, he instructed Sandra to handle Amiria's travel and introduction to the band. He'd bring the band into the New York studio and work with them on new music in about six months. Then he could send them out again on a European tour for another six months. As long as Amiria was with them, he could not chance to bring her anywhere near his home in Bay County. Hopefully, Fiona would be back in Maryland, and they could clear up any misgivings between them. He had to hope that would be the case. Any other option would have been disastrous for him.

"Trey?"

"Yes?"

"Your friend, Daniel Connor, left a message asking you to contact him to arrange to meet. Do you want me to make time in your schedule and coordinate it with him, or will you call him back and do it yourself?"

"If you'll text his number to me, I'll contact him and handle it. I'll let you know what we decide so you can make any necessary reservations."

"Okay, good. Texting it to you now," Sandra put action to words. "Now, have you spoken with Fiona yet?"

"No, I haven't." He dialed Daniel's number, dismissing the issue involving Fiona. At the moment, it was entirely too distracting and hurtful. After all the time they spent together, it was apparent Fiona believed he had slept with Amiria and lied to her about it. She told Sandra about finding the lipstick on the fly of his pants and his shirt but hadn't mentioned it to him. "Yo, Danny Boy," Trey joked when his call went to voicemail. "Let's do this. Call me." He disconnected.

On the surface, the situation might look suspicious to Fiona, but he was innocent. If he had known about the lipstick traces at the time that he and Fiona discussed his relationship with Amiria, he could have explained it—. On an expletive, he realized any explanation would have sounded lame even to his trained ears. What could he say about the lipstick on his fly? Amiria tripped and fell face-first into his lap? Yeah, that would go over like a lead balloon. He certainly couldn't tell her the truth about what he had done. The fewer people who knew, the better. That kind of information could put Fiona in danger from the Yakuza if it ever got out what he had done to help Amiria. He had to hope that Fiona would come to realize, on her own, that he would not disrespect their relationship by having an affair with another woman right under her nose. She meant entirely too much to him, more than any other woman ever had.

When his cell phone rang in his hand, he checked the number and grinned. "Danny Boy."

"Yo, Three I's, I guess I'll never live that name down, huh?"

"Hey, what can I say? You were pitch-perfect when you sang 'Danny Boy' for the school extravaganza."

"Yeah, yeah, yeah, that was before my voice changed. When and where are you buying my lunch?" Daniel joked.

"One hour. Fuku-Fuku."

"Yeah? Fuku, too, because you definitely are buying. That place costs real American folding money, not chump change. I'll have to put on a clean shirt and tie and wear real shoes to be admitted to that place. Have you checked the cost of the yen on the big board today?" He laughed.

"On a bet, we'll flip a coin to see who pays," Trey said and disconnected.

Over an hour later, Trey and Daniel enjoyed Asian and Korean barbecue, grilled mackerel, chateaubriand steak, and miso-chicken steak while they caught up on old times at the restaurant Fuku-Fuku.

"Are you still playing soccer?" Daniel asked.

"I am, yes. I played while I was in England a few months ago, and I'm with a men's soccer league in New York at the fitness center I use, INDULGENCES. How about you?"

"Hey, yeah! I've heard of INDULGENCES. My brother-in-law, Jackson Chase, has a membership there. Jackson took me to work out there once or twice. So yes, I still gear up with several military guys I do physical training with. Most like to play football, but some of us prefer soccer."

"You were a natural back at the academy."

"You taught me everything I know, Trey. It was good having you as a mentor to look up to. Have you gone back to the campus for reunions?"

"No, that was more than ten years ago. Those are days best left behind. I was there for a very long time year-round before you came, and I didn't enjoy it the way you did."

"Yeah, I know, but I was thirteen when I enrolled. We had just lost our father to cancer. He was a Master Sergeant, and I had this need to be around military men after his death. The academy was the perfect place because they had all military services represented. My sister, Jacqueline, worked hard to find the right place for me, and to pay for it, too."

"I remember her. She's a very attractive woman. She's married now, right?"

"Yes, she married Jackson Chase. They have triplets: two boys and a girl, and twins: a boy and a girl. As I've said, Jackson's the one with the INDULGENCES membership."

"I remember reading about him. He's some kind of Wall Street Wizard, I believe."

Daniel shrugged. "He mostly works at his bank in Mitchell County these days, although he's still a member of a brokerage house in New York City. He's a venture capitalist, a developer, and he and his brother, have a boat-building business."

"You have another sister, too, don't you?"

Daniel nodded. "Leigh Ann. She's getting her doctorate at Stanford in California. She's engaged to Brian Mitchell."

"Wasn't your sister, Jacqueline, married to his brother, Robert Mitchell?"

"Your memory is still phenomenal. Yes, she was. They married right after she graduated from college, but we called him Bobby. His death was a blow to everyone. Brian is at Stanford, too, studying engineering.

"Here's a news flash. My mom remarried and lives in Arizona with a really nice guy who worships the ground she walks on."

"Wow, that's great. With all the new and extended family, I'll bet they keep you busy."

Daniel smiled as they continued to eat. "They do, yes. What about you? Anyone special in your life?" Daniel smiled as they continued to eat.

Trey shrugged. "Maybe. At this point, I'm not sure."

"Is she the woman I met with you at the club? The supermodel?"

Trey laughed. "Yes, Fiona Lizette Lowry, but she's not a model. She's an architect and engineer who designed and is building a new place for me in Bay County."

"Wow, we'll practically be neighbors. I remember you said that she lives in Bay County, right?"

"Yes. Fiona was born and raised there. She's one of seven, and before you ask, she doesn't have sisters."

"Beauty and brains, wow. She is gorgeous. Hey, I hope I didn't screw anything up when I mentioned seeing you at the Air Force base with a different woman."

"It's okay." Trey shrugged.

"I did put my foot in it, didn't I?"

"Let's just say I should have been a bit more forthcoming with details before we ran into you that night."

"Sorry, man. I didn't even think before I opened my mouth. I hope I didn't create any permanent damage."

"Me, too." Trey laughed as he and Daniel continued to catch up on each other's lives.

Chapter 26

"So, you two really think I should do this?" Fiona asked her parents as they strolled up the beach arm-in-arm. The warm tide flooded in around their bare feet.

"We do," her mother said as they matched footfalls in the ankle-deep water and sand. "We told your brothers the same thing when they asked. Bay County will always be there, and you will always have a home to come back to, but you and your brothers are young yet. There is a big, complicated world out there.

"When I graduated from nursing school and joined the Army, it was in part to see the world. I was younger than you then, only twenty and so naïve. Still, what I did helped thousands to survive when they might have died were it not for the service we performed. You have the chance to do the same thing here. What my brother is attempting to achieve is important now and, if he is successful, which I have no doubt he will be with you and your brothers' help, you will impact millions for the common good."

Alroy squeezed his daughter's hand. "Don't worry about us, Fiona. Your mother and I handled things before you seven showed up, and we're well situated to take on fewer projects or to hire more workers if we choose to. JaiHonnah and Roderick promised to loan any help we need while you're away. Your brothers have good people who can take over whenever they need to travel, but unlike your brothers, you're the key to Operation: Uplift. To build the clinics and schools, Dr. Mikasi and Dr. Logan will have to have places their people can live and work on each island. Your uncle could afford to hire a whole battery of architects and engineers to do this, but you're his blood, and he trusts you. He is depending on you because you know what needs to be done to get this plan off the ground as a practical matter."

She squeezed them both as she continued to walk between them. "I can't say that I'm not excited by the prospect; any architect would be. Traveling these past three months has given me a new perspective on life and living. I've seen what endless generations before me have built which still survive. I want to do more with my life than design and build custom homes and silly tree houses for spoiled kids. I want to see and experience other countries. The idea of working in different African nations is intriguing."

"It's important work, Fiona. Your mother and I have developed a bit of wanderlust, too, so we plan to do more traveling. I want to go to Ireland and take your mother to see where my ancestry came from. Your mother wants to go to Louisiana to see what she can find out about her ancestry. Although your uncle wants all of us together to start a family reunion tradition, your mother and I want all of you home for the Christmas holidays."

"I can do that. I'll talk with my brothers and see whether we're all in agreement about our existing projects and then come to a conclusion. I can make Trey's project my last major one for a while."

"What about your personal life?" Mavis looked at her daughter. "Aiden still wants you to come home to marry him."

"I know, but we had a conversation before I left to go on tour. I love Aiden, and I always will, but I don't want to be a politician's wife. I predict important things will happen for Aiden over the next ten years. I can give him my moral support, but I can't be the type of wife he needs to enhance his career. So, I won't marry him."

"What about Trey Kennard? From what his father and Charlotte tell us, you two have become very close."

"That's true, but just as Aiden's life is moving in a trajectory I can't follow, Trey's career is all-consuming, too. He thrives on the music he creates because of the genius he is. I'd feel as if I would be such a distraction to him that he would not be able to create great music." She shrugged and continued. "Yes, he'd make the time to work on a solid relationship between us, but his first love is now and will always be his music. I just don't know whether we have what we'd need to sustain anything long-termed and committed. However, I don't want to get ahead of myself because I don't know his feelings at this point. We never talked about a future together for us; we were living in the moment. So, he may not be thinking of a committed relationship with me. When I left Japan, there were some unsettled questions between us. If it's important enough, we'll find a way to have that conversation sooner or later.

"For now, I'm excited about using my training, experience, and education for something very important to me and, as you so aptly put it, 'for the common good.' I have a chance to spread my wings and help people improve their lives. This opportunity is as important to me as Aiden's career aspirations are to him and Trey's musical creations are to him. If there is a future for any of us down the road, time will tell."

The first annual Hawkins family reunion was in the history books, and the real work had begun. Over a month had passed, and Fiona and the two assistants she hired were well into their tasks of locating facilities that they could retrofit to accommodate the medical facility and the school on several islands so far. She decided upon that approach because it was quicker to take an existing building and reimagine it rather than constructing it from the ground up. She hired real estate agents on each island to find suitable properties for her review and inspection.

Fortunately, Dr. Mikasi had a pilot's license, and Adam provided a BlackHawk seaplane he used to fly to each island with them. Because of the islands' proximity, they could visit at least two and sometimes as many as four islands a day. They were met by the real estate agent at each location and driven to several locations. Jointly, they evaluated the structures recommended and came to a swift decision about the suitability of the buildings. If none of the buildings were acceptable, they scanned the area for building sites.

Fiona took advantage of Roderick and JaiHonnah Hawkins Baylor's advice to use shipping containers to get the necessary buildings under roof at nominal costs swiftly. As their contribution to Operation: Uplift, the Baylors purchased hundreds of used and abandoned steel containers from Hawaiian docks. They had the containers transported via BlackHawk Shipping to Fiona.

When the first of many BlackHawk cargo ships arrived stacked high and wide with used steel shipping containers, Wesley and Roselyn Hunter Greenfield and their six children were there to meet it. Wesley was the Baylors' foremost authority on building structures using containers. For more than five years, Wesley managed the construction of an entire community in Washington, DC. It was the prototype for their unique homes, offices, schools, and other types of businesses.

In addition, Wesley's wife, Roselyn, a Ph.D. educator, managed the new educational program, which saw inner-city kids graduate in the highest echelons of academia and compete with other countries. It was the same program Dr. Logan managed at Summer County Academy. Fiona appreciated their hands-on help for the month they were able to be there. However, they pledged to return in six months for another extended stay.

Once the structures were agreed upon, Adam had the foundation's attorneys purchase the properties. Then, based on Fiona's recommendations, the lawyers began obtaining the necessary construction licenses and permits from local authorities.

Close on her heels, her brothers came in and prepared the lists of materials they needed to complete the projects. If some of the finished materials were not readily available, like windows and doors, and it was more cost-effective to do so, they started little cottage industries to manufacture what they needed locally. Those small manufacturing businesses lifted the economy in useful ways.

The Operation: Uplift team worked with men and women, teaching the building trades and skills the workers would need to perform each aspect of the construction. They would provide a turnkey facility for Adam to have outfitted for medical devices purchased from Dr. Mikasi's list of recommendations and education furnishings and tools like flat-screen televisions and iPads Dr. Logan ordered. Adam added human and electronic security to each facility as the staff Dr. Mikasi and Dr. Logan hired took up their positions.

Adam held a celebration when the first co-located medical and educational facility went operational. Ambassador Jake Hawkins came to the celebration, as did his son Jacob. They brought American businessmen and women and US ambassadors to other African nations to witness what could be accomplished. Jake wanted them to put skin in the game, too. Among the hundred or so business people in attendance were Gregory Alexander and Jackson Chase representing their Wall Street investment firm, Compliant Trading and Investment, Inc. Also, among the invitees were the power couple, Nicholas and Tina Justice Collins. Several such parties were held as progress on Operation: Uplift continued.

Selina Mattawa rolled off of Noah and onto her back, still breathing hard. "What's wrong, Noah?" She looked up at the ceiling and not at him.

Dragging the palms of his hands down his moist face, he didn't otherwise move. "I have some problems I need to solve at work on my mind." Frustration was evident in his voice.

"Again? You called to arrange to see me tonight, but you can't relax? There's something wrong with this picture," she groused and rolled out of bed, grabbing up her robe as she purposefully strode out of the bedroom to her kitchen. Grabbing a couple of water bottles out of the refrigerator, she sat at the center-post island and drank half of one bottle in one long swallow. The other bottle she left for Noah.

Noah was in the act of putting on his shirt when he came out of Selina's bedroom.

Selina admired his ruggedly handsome face and body, a more beautiful specimen she had never seen before. He had broad shoulders, muscular arms, pecks of steel, defined washboard abs, a flat stomach, strong thighs, and long, strong sculptured legs. His phine physique was why she took the initiative when he came to her office to discuss the purchase of medical equipment manufactured by the company where she worked.

Several times she suggested dinner meetings in the fervent hope that he would want to take their business relationship outside the office. It took a while, nearly six months, but she finally got him into her bed, and what a gift that was. He was well worth the wait. However, recently he hadn't called often, and when he did, his performance between the sheets was lackluster at best. He never kissed her, but she accepted that as just his way. They didn't date in the traditional sense. Yes, they would occasionally go out to dinner, but more often, he would pick up groceries and cook them at her place. That, too, she considered simply his way, but they always ended the evening or occasional morning tryst with satisfying sex.

He never introduced her to any of his acquaintances or invited her to parties at the forty-acre plantation on the beach. He lived and worked there in a mansion with members of the wealthy Hawkins family and others.

Noah didn't talk about himself. So, what Selina learned about him and his background came from reading about him in the local newspapers. The media referred to him as Doctor Mikasi. So, she assumed that he was a medical doctor because he knew what types of medical equipment he wanted. However, she didn't know where he was from or whether he had any family. She couldn't even determine his approximate age from looking at his handsome face. She could only guess he was over thirty because of the long history of work recounted in the news when he was interviewed. For the most part, the articles were about the work he and his team were doing under a project known as Operation: Uplift. It was all anyone talked about these days. That was especially true when she broke sales records with his purchase of the medical equipment he needed to use for the project. She received a nice bonus because of it, too.

Still, the benefit of having Noah in her bed outweighed the benefit of the money she received. At thirty-three, she was open to a relationship that could lead to marriage. Noah did fit her requirements perfectly. However, Selina wondered about Noah and the beautiful architect and engineer, Fiona Lowry, the niece of Ambassador Jake Hawkins. Ms. Lowry and Dr. Mikasi were often interviewed together or written about in the same articles. Yet, no one in the press or news media hinted at a relationship between them other than business.

Instead, some of the gossip mags recounted Fiona Lowry's apparent relationship with musical genius Trey Kennard. The articles were complete with pictures from a recent trip they were on together several months earlier. So, if that relationship was still ongoing, it probably wasn't good form for Noah to screw the boss's niece. Especially not when Fiona's six older Lowry brothers were on the island, too. They were all handsome men and causing quite a stir among the single women on the kitchen island, as did the brothers, Jacob and Adam Hawkins.

However, to Selina's way of thinking, if Noah was in the mood, this Fiona didn't know what she was missing. His shirt and jeans were still unbuttoned as he sat across from her at the island and uncapped the water bottle to take a long swallow. There were visible scars on his beautiful body, the origins of which he wouldn't discuss with her. Still, again, they didn't share much more than a business relationship with occasional side benefits. She wanted more, but Noah wasn't a man who could be manipulated on any score. In any event, Selina felt that she was in it for the long haul. So, she would bide her time and hope Noah would begin to see her as wife material.

Noah knew he should end this relationship with Selina. It had no place to go, and, at this point, he was just going through the motions. Tonight, like others of late, thoughts of Fiona were screwing with his head—both of them. He could psych himself up to have sex with Selina, but he knew she was only a substitute for the woman with whom he wanted to make love.

His desire for Fiona Lowry surprised him. It hadn't been anything that Fiona had done to invite his attention. Rather, she was scrupulously all business in every instance where they were together. She still referred to him as *Doctor* Mikasi whenever she addressed him. They weren't even on a first-name basis. Because of his uncharacteristic desire for her, he encouraged that distance between them. He always regarded her as Ms. Lowry and rarely let himself spend time in her presence if it wasn't business-related.

Mealtimes were a different situation. The house staff served breakfast, lunch, and dinner at pre-arranged times. Usually, fifteen to twenty project workers ate together with whomever else, like family and friends, and were in the household at specific, designated times of the day. There were also people from the embassy who would sometimes join in with the Project: Uplift teams. People who were designated to work on different aspects of Operation: Uplift were also coming and going. Discussions around the table were usually about the project and rarely strayed to personal matters. Noah had a working relationship with others but didn't join in for purely social gatherings. Of course, when business-related social affairs were held on the plantation or elsewhere in the City of Victoria, his attendance was expected, and he complied.

Then again, if others knew of his background, they probably wouldn't have wanted to associate themselves with him. Only one person, his team leader, Wind Breeze, aka LaiLoni Skai or Dakota Sinclair, knew his story as a US Navy SEAL or his Code Name: Stinger. She had lived his story with him in the orphanage where they both grew up in the North Dakota mountains on the Canadian border. When she brought him into the super-secret world enforcement organization created by the G7 and known as The Nursery, as one of her recruits, he had just completed medical school. He worked under her tutelage and on her team to complete many successful missions for years until a severe injury sidelined her career. Noah was there when she fell forty feet because her parachute got hung up in the trees on a nighttime helo jump into Afghanistan. He stayed with her, rendering aid, while her second-in-command, Stallion, took over the operation and led the other forty covert agents to complete the mission. Still, because she wasn't one hundred percent anymore, she was put on inactive duty as an outlier, someone called into active duty if an operation required specific skill sets. At his request, he was now also an outlier.

Wind Breeze still looked after every member of her team, although she was outside of regular duty. When she selected him for this operation, she did so because of his knowledge and expertise with all things Africa-related. He spoke the languages and dialects and several others and was an expert on the political landscape of each country. More importantly, he could act with swift and deadly force to protect her family members if or when necessary. Her family had been terrorist targets before. Since her father wanted to remain an ambassador, she was taking no chance that her family could be harmed again. Noah could kill or maim with a flick of his wrists. At six-ten, two hundred pounds, he was a lethal weapon who could also heal a severe injury or ailment with the same ice-cold ministration. She had never known Noah to let emotion cloud his judgment. Wind Breeze would have been surprised to learn that her cousin, Fiona, was unknowingly doing just that.

This project was one about which he had long been interested. So, when his handler learned that Jake Hawkins was interested in sponsoring the same type of plan, she put them together with her brother, Adam, and her husband, Ambassador Jefferson Logan, to collaborate. They were of one mind, and the project came to life. What was unexpected was the appeal and impact Fiona Lowry had on him.

Selina sighed. "Is it only work that's on your mind, Noah?"

He had been so deep in his thoughts that he had zoned out. "No, it's not the only thing."

She stood and came around the kitchen island to stand between his open thighs. "Then it's a simple case of mind over matter," she crooned, smoothing her hands over his chest and tweaking his flat nipples. Noah permitted Salina to lay her lips on his body and suckle while one of her hands slipped down into his jeans. He didn't wear Jockeys in the tropical heat, preferring to go commando as he was in The Nursery. So, her efforts to arouse him were unencumbered. After exercising him, she bent to take him into her heat, but he remained unaffected. That was test enough for him to realize that it was best to end this relationship now.

With his hands on her forearms, he pried her away from him and simply looked into her eyes.

When she sighed in frustration, he knew no words needed to pass between them. It was over. So, he stood, zipped his jeans, and buttoned his shirt. Moments later, he straddled his Harley, revved the engine, and sped off into the darkness.

Chapter 27

Christ! Noah thought, watching Fiona execute another perfect dive off the twenty-foot-high platform into the lower-level lagoon and swimming pool. It was an extreme water-feature structure with a lazy river, grottos, multiple water slides, lounge areas, surfing, and spillways over the infinity edges. It was an awesome sight in daylight, but even more spectacular at night, with blazing fire pits and colorful lights creating a spectacularly magical environment.

Jake Hawkins spared no expense when it came to his family's entertainment. His daughter, JaiHonnah, designed the plantation more like a lavish resort than a single-family mansion. The Hawkins family members took advantage of the lush environment several times a year. Jacob and Adam made it their primary residence since their father is the US Ambassador to the Republic. Now more of their family members would be in residence.

Fiona's cousins, LaiLoni Skai's stepsons, Jay, Miles, and Stephen Logan, followed her onto the high diving board, attempting to perform as perfectly as she had. *Her form was poetry in motion,* Noah thought, *an Olympic-class swimmer.* She wasn't doing anything to attract his interest except having fun with her cousins and teaching them how to dive safely. Nevertheless, she had his undivided attention.

The Logan boys weren't the only fearless ones. JaiHonnah's twin stepdaughters, Shelly and Shelby Baylor, were also lined up to take the plunge with Fiona's encouragement as she floated in the water.

The sisters, LaiLoni Skai and JaiHonnah, two gorgeous and physically stacked women, were in another section of the mid-level pool with their under five-year-old children, helping them navigate the less challenging water features. They didn't draw his undivided attention. Yet, the dental floss Fiona wore as a bikini had Noah fixated. She resembled someone out of a Disney fantasy with her long, flowing, thick, dark-red hair and sun-bronzed skin. It was understandable that Fiona would wear clothes appropriate for the climate in the heat of the tropics. Still, the micro shorts and tops she habitually wore were enough to give eunuchs a hard-on. Generally, she wore no bra or panties, he could tell, and the only other nods to convention were sunglasses, tennis shoes, and a baseball cap turned backward on her head. The majority of all that smooth-looking skin was exposed.

He suffered every time they had to work together. Closing his eyes, he leaned his head back against the cushioned deck chair and let his sunglasses further block his ability to see the walking wet dream that Fiona personified. Beside him, Adam took a call concerning a shipment of supplies they needed for the main hospital, which was nearing completion.

"That was Bronson in Shipping," Adam said after he disconnected the call and relaxed against his comfortable deck chair. "He's got everything you asked for and wondered whether I would authorize a flight to bring the supplies here from Seattle, Washington, rather than wait and have them arrive via cargo ship. So I told him to fly them in. Are you going to have time to get the clinic set up before the holidays?"

"That shouldn't be a problem. Thanksgiving isn't a holiday here in the islands."

"You're right. Are you going to the states to visit family or friends?"

"No, I'll be here for the duration."

"If you don't have holiday plans, why don't you come with us to Hawkinstown, Texas? My father has a home there."

"Thanks, but no."

"You never said, but where is your family from?"

Noah shrugged. "I don't have a biological family that I know of. I grew up on the Canadian-US border."

"I didn't know. The offer is open to come to Texas with us when we leave."

"I've got more than enough work to keep me busy here. I also want to get started on plans for—"

Adam shook his head. "Man, take a break. This project is a process, not a race. We can't afford to have you burn out on this prototype. Of course, we all want it to be a success, but taking a break once in a while is necessary. So I'm going to take a six-month break to hit the Formula One race-car circuit when it begins."

Noah knew that, but nothing else in his life was more important to him than this project. He didn't have family or close friends to spend his time with during holidays or for vacations. The people he knew best and were like family to him were still in The Nursery, fighting to separate the good from the evil. They occasionally had downtime when they could socialize, but for the most part, the men and women in that struggle were like him. With no families to speak of, they bonded together closer than any siblings would be.

Adam shook his head. "You're not going to listen to me, are you?"

"I'll take some time when I feel it's necessary. While the momentum is high, I want to take advantage of the situation."

"You and Fiona must be made from the same gene pool," Adam said wryly and shook his head again as he got up and headed for the upper pool.

Noah watched him go and chanced to see Fiona do a double backflip and smooth dive into the lower pool. *Yeah, no,* he thought, *me and Fiona Lowry are nothing alike.* He was from Vulcan with Mr. Spock, and she was from Venus, the goddess of love and beauty. She could have been the Greek Aphrodite.

"I'll catch up with you in a few days." Fiona hugged each of her six brothers before they got into the limo to leave for the airport. She waved as the limo pulled around the circular driveway, headed for the gate, and pulled out of sight. She watched the gate close and lock, feeling a little melancholy before she turned away to go into the mansion. It was still early in the morning, but the heat was oppressive. Stretching and swinging her arms over her head to release the tension in her neck and back until her bones cracked, she headed inside to the relative silence except for the waves pounding against the shore.

Since the family and friends left for the states, most of the servants had gone to spend time with their relatives for the Christmas and New Year's holidays. Only a few remained to tend to the house. She and Dr. Mikasi would have to fend for themselves until they finished setting up the clinic on one of the distant, remote islands. The supplies were due to be delivered to the island tomorrow. She and the doctor needed to be there when they arrived to ensure nothing went missing like the delivery the week before, with the same type of supplies. The truck carrying those supplies had been left parked fully loaded overnight outside the clinic gates. Before morning, it had been vandalized, and thousands of dollars' worth of equipment had vanished along with the supplies. They were taking no chances this time.

Inside the front vestibule, the air was extremely cool, giving her skin a chill, but she still had tension in her neck and back. So, instead of putting on something warmer, she kept stretching to warm her muscles as she headed to the shared office to get some work done. When she entered, Dr. Mikasi briefly looked up from his work and then continued a conversation on his headphone.

Fiona didn't disturb him, but went to the four library tables they had installed to hold the three-dimensional maps of the Seychelles islands involved in their project. The models took up most of the space on the co-located tables, giving them an overview of their progress since the project began. Then, keying into the computer, Fiona began to add to her notes. Because she still couldn't release the tension, she raised the computer to standing height instead of sitting.

Through the glass walls of his office, Noah watched Fiona work. Her back was toward him as he finalized plans for the following day. He would meet the cargo plane and see to its unloading himself. Then he would follow it back to the clinic and make sure the gates were open and the truck was not left unprotected. The crew he hired would be on hand to ensure nothing would go missing. The vandalism had delayed their efforts by two weeks, which meant everything else on the schedule was delayed also. He knew the Hawkins and Lowry family members were anxious to get back to the states for the start of the holiday season, so he assured them he could handle what needed to be done until they returned in mid-February. Everyone left, except Fiona, as she had details to handle on another island that couldn't wait for several months to be addressed.

So, here he sat, watching as she stretched her neck from side to side and her arms up and back. He recognized the stress points she was attempting to alleviate. He had them, too, and more from his need to mate.

"Yes," he said into the headset and got up to go to the map on the library tables, "I'm here. Let me look at the map. I believe the dock area is deep enough to accommodate the load." He bent over the map to check the depth of the water indicated on the map. "Yes, it looks like ten meters give or take at low tide. Is that sufficient?" He nodded and said, "Okay, I'll see you tomorrow by ten," and disconnected.

Fiona briefly looked up from her computer. "Was that the cargo pilot?"

"Yes. He's coming in by ten in the morning, but he has other stops, so his plane will set down heavier in the water. Also, he's never flown to this island, so he wasn't sure how close to the dock he could get to unload."

She nodded and continued entering data, but stopped long enough to stretch her arms toward her back.

Noah noticed and stood on the other side of the table regarding her. "Tired?"

Fiona shook her head. "No. I must have slept wrong or something. My back, arms, and neck are cramping."

Noah came around the table to stand behind her. "May I?"

She shrugged. "Sure." She stood still. As soon as he put his hands on her, his ministration was like magic. She nearly melted at his touch when he abruptly stopped.

"Come with me." He led the way out of the office and down the steps to one of the interior rooms outfitted with medical equipment. "Would you take off your shirt and lay face-down on the table?"

Given the relief his short ministration gave her, when he turned his back, she eagerly disrobed. She shrugged and used the shirt to cover her naked breasts. After all, he was a medical doctor.

Noah poured a fragrant oil into his palms, briskly rubbed them together to create warm friction, and began at Fiona's lower back, giving her a deep tissue massage. He could feel the knots giving her the most discomfort and went to work on them. Slowly working his way up her back to her shoulders, his thoughts didn't stray from a doctor administering aid to a patient. He could switch off his desires as he touched her warm skin and focused on taking away her tension.

Fiona was having a difficult time staying coherent while Noah's clever fingers worked magic on her. She stifled more than a few moans as his hands glided over her, providing the relief she needed. However, when she closed her eyes, she had visions of him touching her more intimately. That caused her eyes to pop open just as he laid a hot towel over her back and shoulders.

"Let that heat soak into your muscles for a while, and then let me know how you feel."

"I feel like your hands are magic. You could work on me anytime." Suddenly, she flushed. *"Whoa!* That didn't come out quite the way I meant it."

Leaning against another bed with his legs crossed at the ankles and his arms akimbo, he shrugged. "I understood what you meant. It wasn't personal, and my touch was intended to relieve your stress. That's all."

"It did. Thank you." She noticed the towel had cooled. "I think you can remove the towel now."

He did and put it in a laundry basket. He heard Fiona slide off the padded table but didn't immediately turn to regard her. "Are you better?"

"I am, yes."

"Good." He turned, but she had her head bent as she tied the ends of her blouse up under her breasts to form a makeshift bra. "I'm, uh, going to make something to eat. I'll only be a while," he awkwardly said, as if she cared where he was going or for how long. He strode out of the medical office.

He moved so quickly that it caused Fiona to frown after him. *He is a strange one*, she thought. He barely spoke to her when they were working unless it had something to do with their tasks. His offering to give her a massage surprised her, and she hoped it would lead to a real conversation between them that didn't involve their work. She wasn't surprised when it didn't. From what she read of his bio, he was an extraordinarily competent and highly regarded physician. They were lucky that he agreed to spearhead the medical aspects of the project. Still, he wasn't very friendly around her.

Well, we don't have to be pals to get our work done, Fiona thought. Not feeling very hungry, she didn't follow him to the kitchen and headed back to work instead.

Cooking relaxed him, so Noah spent the next hour making shrimp gumbo. He poured the vegetable oil into the pot to season it before adding the flour to make his rue. While that slowly simmered and reduced, he peeled and chopped two good-sized onions, green peppers, and celery. He added chicken broth and his vegetables to the rue and sniffed. Smiling, he continued cutting Italian sausages into chunks and setting them to heat before adding them to the pot.

While that simmered, he baked a crusty loaf of onion bread, tossed a green salad, and selected a white wine to accompany the meal. Finally, he added peeled and deveined fresh jumbo shrimp, chopped fresh okra, and his blend of Louisiana spices to the pot. The aroma filtered through the kitchen as he got dishes out and prepared a place setting for his lunch.

When he turned, Fiona was leaning a shoulder against the kitchen doorframe with her arms crossed over her full breasts and her shapely legs at her ankles.

"I came to get a snack, but what you have seems more appealing."

"Uh, thank you?" It was more of a question, as he was at a loss as to what to say next. *What does she mean? Is that some sort of double entendre?* He had a lightbulb moment. *Food. She is talking about food.* He needed to get his thoughts out of his need for sex…with her. "Uh, I have enough…I mean, there's more than enough if you'd like some…something to eat, I mean." *What the fuck is wrong with me?* he wondered. *Have I lost my ability to think and talk to a beautiful woman?*

"I would, yes." She moved to get her dishes since he didn't seem inclined to do so. "I didn't know that you could cook. Where did you learn?"

He shrugged. "Uh, here and there."

Well, that was as clear as mud, Fiona thought, with a slight smirk. He was so articulate when discussing Operation: Uplift, but so disinclined for social activity. He seemed such a solitary, reserved person except sociable in any other context. She tried several times to engage him in conversation, to no avail. Then, like now, when they were the only two people around except for a few security staff and servants, he clammed up and became very distant.

She was not a person to force herself on anyone, so she stacked her dishes on a tray, served herself of the food, and left him in the kitchen to return to the office to eat.

Way to go, Noah thought, slouching. Now Fiona couldn't even stand to spend time in his company. It certainly wasn't her fault he found her so attractive that he could not carry on a conversation in her presence. Yeah, he didn't know anything about who his family might have been, but he and Mr. Spock were definitely from the same gene pool.

Chapter 28

The sky was a cloudless, brilliant blue when the BlackHawk fixed-wing amphibious aircraft lifted off the water. Fiona paid little, if any, attention. Noah was an exceptional and capable pilot who, like always, kept his own counsel. So, she didn't disturb him with inane chatter as he cleared his flight plan with the area's air traffic control towers.

She sat tailor-style, strapped into the cockpit seat, reviewing her notes for the day. They had a few stops to make, so she expected they would be island hopping until late in the evening. Based on her tasks and the days it would take to accomplish everything on her To-Do list, she calculated that she would be able to leave on vacation and fly to the states in five days. That would provide ample time to shop in San Antonio, Texas, for gifts. She was going over her list when her phone chimed.

Without looking at the screen, she said, "Yes?"

"Fiona?"

Her head came up and focused on the voice she hadn't heard for many months. "Hello, Trey," she said, but the connection wasn't clear.

"Hello, Fiona. Where are you? It's hard to hear you."

"I know. I'm in the air right now. May I call you when I land?"

"Yes, that would be best. I'll wait to hear from you."

"Okay. Soon." She disconnected the call and looked at the phone for a long moment as if she didn't quite know what it was. After radio silence from Trey for all this time, he would call when she was unable to talk with him. She would make time to call him back on a landline when they landed. For now, she had to stay focused on her tasks.

Noah sensed the call Fiona received had her temporarily out of sync. Her voice changed from her first utterance of a name. Trey. She sat quietly, looking out of the window for a while, but didn't immediately resume working on her iPad.

He couldn't ask her about the call or whether it upset her, as he had to report his position to the tower and receive permission to land. Within ten minutes, they were on the water, floating on pontoons toward the dock. He could see the truck and workers he hired waiting for them. They were early, which pleased him, but he still had his thoughts on Fiona.

Shortly after he and Fiona secured their plane at the dock, the cargo plane landed and floated toward them. It was a much bigger seaplane than theirs, and it took time to position it for unloading. He and Fiona worked in tandem, checking the deliveries against their manifests. When everything was accounted for, Noah and Fiona co-signed the bills of lading, and the laborers they hired began to load the truck. The eighteen-wheeler pulled away from the dock a few hours later and headed for the clinic and co-located school.

Just as they finished placing the last box in the clinic, the ground began to shake.

"Earthquake!" Noah yelled over the loud noise and grabbed Fiona, shoving her under a table as crates stacked high in a storage room began to shift and tumble to the floor. Noah grabbed as many as he could and held them in place until the after-shock-waves began to dissipate. "It's all right now." He looked down. Fiona lay sprawled halfway under the table with blood streaming from a cut on her forehead. *"Fiona!"* He immediately went to his knees to push the large, heavy crate away from where it pinned her shoulder and arm under its crushing weight.

Quickly, Noah managed to examine Fiona for other injuries. Finding none, he searched the storeroom for a neck brace. Once he found one, he stripped away the packaging, pushed her heavy braid aside, and gently fastened the brace around her neck.

Operating on autopilot, Noah cleared the table of debris and gingerly lifted Fiona onto the table to better examine her head injury. Superficial, he hoped, but the falling crate had knocked her out. Grabbing a box of gloves and a suture kit, he proceeded to clean the wound and stitch five sutures into her head at the hairline. Blood still caked in her hair, but the bandage would keep the cut clean for now. Next, he examined her extremities more carefully, bending and flexing her legs. When he palpated and then flexed her right shoulder, Fiona moaned, and her eyes popped open in pain.

"You're going to be all right, Fiona. An earthquake hit, and you were pinned to the floor under a large crate. Your right shoulder is dislocated. I need to pop it back into place now." Noah put action to words. She screamed once and then moaned long and loudly when her arm was reset. "I know that hurt, Fiona." He continued to examine her arm, hand, and fingers. Once finished and assured she had normal blood flow to her arm and hand, he slipped a sling over her head and around her neck brace until he had her arm immobile against her side.

Helping her sit up on the side of the table, he noticed tears clinging to her long eyelashes. The sight of them broke his heart, but she looked up at him with such trust that he could do nothing but frame her face in his hands and kiss her mouth. *Oh, God! Oh, God! Oh, God!* he thought and moaned as a mantra. Her head was only inches away from being crushed by the crate instead of just grazed. When his lips left hers, with his eyes still closed and his hands still palming her face, he placed his forehead against hers, breathing her in.

Fiona was more than a little out of it, with pain and confusion, but the kiss with which Noah Mikasi captured her mouth brought the situation back into stark relief, and a constellation of stars swam in her head. *Whoa!* she thought. *His kiss was unexpected, but packed an astonishing punch.* When she closed her eyes, she could still see the intensity in his eyes and taste it on her lips. Bewildered, she was about to comment when they heard shouts in the hallway.

"*Docteur! Docteur! Vous êtes ici, docteur?*" several voices yelled.

"*Yes, I'm a doctor!*" Noah quickly entered the darkened hallway. "I mean, *Oui. Qu'en est il?*"

"Vous venez! Vous devez venir! Maintenant! Ils sont mal! Ils ont besoin d'aide!" Frantically yelling, several people pulled him toward the front exit.

"Attendez! J'ai besoin d'un sac medical." Noah went back to the storeroom, where Fiona still sat on the side of the table.

Fiona looked up at him. "What do they need? I don't understand the dialect."

"It's Creole French. I'll explain it another time. Right now, people have been hurt. They need me to come to see what I can do to help."

Fiona tried to stand up and support herself.

"No, Fiona! You stay here. I have to go, but you stay here where you'll be safe. If there are more aftershocks, crawl under the table."

"No, I'll be fine. I want to do whatever I can to help, too." She tore off the neck brace. Her right arm and shoulder she left in the sling.

Stubborn woman! Noah silently fumed but didn't waste time arguing with her. In any event, he preferred having her where he could keep an eye on her and monitor her head injury. Moments earlier, she'd been out cold. At least, if she was with him, he could make sure she didn't collapse. After grabbing a bag and filling it with the essential medical supplies he might need, Noah and Fiona followed the anxious men and women out of the clinic.

The devastation is horrendous, thought Fiona. Poorly constructed homes and businesses had collapsed, leaving a trail of dangerous obstacles and debris in the roadway. People were pawing at the ground, trying to rescue those trapped inside the damaged structures. Babies and toddlers screamed and cried unrelentingly while men and women wept as they tried to rescue family members or others from the rubble.

There was no time to waste. With no concern for her injuries, Fiona worked her right arm and shoulder out of the sling and went to help dig.

Hours passed relatively unnoticed when a young boy of about ten years old came to find Fiona. *"Le médecin, il dit à venir. Il a besoin de votre aide."*

Fiona could barely understand him, but one of the people working with her translated what the boy said. She followed him about a quarter-mile through the devastated streets to a building that was once a school.

There, she found Noah conferring with a local government official. When he turned and spotted her, he frantically waved her forward.

It took her only a few seconds to see why he summoned her. The school had been demolished, but there were children still alive and trapped. One false move and the entire structure would pancake, crushing out the lives of those still inside. Quickly evaluating the engineering angles needed to shore up the building and looking around for what could be useful, she began instructing the able-bodied to gather chunks of sturdy beams she could use to stabilize the sagging roof.

When she started toward the structure, Noah stopped her. "What do you think you're doing?"

"What needs to be done. I'm small enough to crawl through this opening to get to the children. None of you can. You're too big. Once I'm inside, I'll be able to further evaluate the situation. From what I can see out here, I need support beams, like Lincoln logs, to shore up critical points until the children can be rescued. You and others can push these beams to me so I can leverage them up to reinforce the ceiling."

"You can't do that! You were seriously injured. You probably shouldn't be walking around right now."

"I am walking around right now, and I don't have time to argue. If another quake hits or we even have an aftershock, what's left of this structure will come down and kill those people inside. If you can come up with a better engineering plan, *doctor*, I'll listen. Otherwise, you see to your patients, and I'll handle this." When he just looked at her with heat, she proceeded to work her plan.

Noah wanted to follow her, but he was triaging patients right there in the rubble. He'd been back and forth to the clinic to administer aid to those more seriously injured. Fortunately, three med students, who pledged to work for the clinic for three years in exchange for tuition assistance, were home on school break. They were working in the incomplete clinic with patients they could not treat and release. Four nursing students were lending aid and identifying the more critically injured for priority treatment.

A cheer went up when Fiona carefully led twenty-three children and two teachers through the rubble to safety. All were filthy dirty with nicks and scratches but alive. Thanks to her engineering skills, other willing hands made their way inside to shore up the school and continued to search through the night, looking for those who may have still been trapped or buried. They could not save them all, but the effort continued for the next three days. Fortunately, the island was small, with a population of fewer than two thousand people.

Noah and Fiona slept when they could and ate on the fly. He tended to the patients while she guided local officials on how to save structures or to safely take down those which were too dangerous to rescue. Noah arranged for tents and portable toilets to be flown in with other rudimentary supplies. Without basic amenities, such as running water or a sewer system, he and Fiona established places to wash and take care of personal hygiene to keep unsanitary conditions down and the possibilities of diseases from going rampant.

Fortunately, Fiona had designed the clinic and school to withstand nature's challenges of high winds and earthquakes. The steel shipping containers she used to construct the facilities were bolted to thick concrete slabs on rubber foundations. The rubber absorbed the shock waves and kept the buildings from being severely damaged. When the relatively undamaged clinic reached its capacity with patients, the co-located school was pressed into service to handle the overflow. Volunteers helped to nurse, clean, and feed the patients, many of whom were family members and were incapacitated. Noah and his med and nursing students did regular rounds twice a day, visiting patients and seeing to the walk-ins.

By day seven, after the quake, services were significantly under control so that Noah and Fiona could prepare to leave. During the seven-day ordeal, neither said anything about the kiss Noah initiated on the day of the quake. Rather, they focused on whatever came next to the exclusion of all else. They had to wear surgical scrubs after the first few days, and by day three, their cell phones had died without them noticing. Fortunately, when they boarded the seaplane, the engine roared to life.

So, they plugged in their dead cell phones, filed the flight plan, and lifted off, headed back to the plantation on Victoria.

After assuring her worried family members that she was all right, Fiona arranged for a flight back to the states the following morning on one of her uncle's private jets. Two hours into the flight, she contemplated what work she would have to leave undone until her return when she heard Noah attempting to contact the radio tower for clearance to enter the airspace over an area.

"Victoria tower, this is BlackHawk 2021, over. Come in, Victoria tower, over," he kept repeating, but received nothing but static in response.

When Fiona looked up and out of the cockpit windows, all she could see were ominous-looking, spinning thick black clouds. "Is this as bad as it looks?"

"Worse. It's a cyclone. It wasn't there when I filed the flight plan, or I would have been notified. So I'm going to have to find someplace to land where we can take cover."

"Land?" Fiona asked skeptically, observing the tense expression on Noah's face. "There is no *land* in sight."

"Hold on." Noah executed a sharp turn to the left and headed back the way they had come just as the wind picked up. "This weather system is too large and dangerous for me to fly through, over, or around. We don't have enough fuel for any of those maneuvers. However, I think I spotted an island about ten kilometers back. It didn't appear to be inhabited, but it may be able to provide us with the necessary shelter until this weather system passes over."

Noah scanned the water until he saw the cone-shaped island of about a mile in circumference. As he circled the island, looking for the best place to put down, he sought to allay Fiona's fears. He began to talk inanely to her as his mind calculated a million other scenarios. "Did you know that the Seychelles plateau, together with India, Madagascar, Africa, South America, and Antarctica, formed Gondwana about one hundred sixty-five million years ago? Together with Madagascar and India, Seychelles drifted away from Africa, leaving Madagascar behind about eighty million years later and following India to the north. It stopped its voyage about fifteen million years later.

"During this period," he continued as the wind picked up, causing turbulence to rock the plane from side to side, "one of the most significant volcanic eruption events in world history took place and dominated Seychelles and the whole region. The volcanic remains at Pointe Zeng Zeng and Pointe Ramasse are the only evidence of this volcanic activity in the earlier Seychelles. Probably there was a crater southeast of La Passe. I've dived in that area with Dr. Cecile Jordan Dixon and her son, Donald. They are both oceanographers. We did a six-week training session with members of her family who are in the Alex-Mont Ranch Academy somewhere near your home in Maryland. The Grand Barbe basin is one of the most exciting and unexplored. We're scheduled to do another dive next year during school break in March. You should join us.

"Some theorists say that the catastrophic impact, making an end to the dinosaurs' era, should have placed Seychelles, forming the Amirante Basin, which, for the moment, is only half a circle, but at that time Seychelles and India were still together. So, the other half drifted away so that India should now lie in front of Bombay," he finished as he set down on the water's edge.

When she turned her head away from him to look ahead, the strong tides were wafting the plane into a dark, open maw between sheer rock faces. Stunned, she turned back to see Noah concentrating on shutting down the plane's gauges and functions. "You did that on purpose," she accused.

"Did what?" He began to unlatch his door.

"You distracted me while you landed."

He shrugged. "I thought I was giving you interesting facts about the formation of this region of the world. You're a strong swimmer. You might enjoy diving in the various areas of the basin before corporations start drilling for oil and spoiling the natural beauty of the under-the-sea world. Now, since I've added to your education, I need your help to secure the plane further into this cave before the weather sets in. I don't want gale-force winds to lift the plane and destroy it. If the wind destroys our only means of transportation, we'd either have to take up permanent residence here on this rock or it would mean we'd have one helluva swim home." He bounded out of the plane to stand knee-deep in the water and began to push the aircraft further into the cave.

Fiona got out on her side of the plane and began to push the struts that held the wings in place. The pontoons helped to make it easier to float the aircraft out of the wind and storm surge.

Fiona got out on her side of the plane and began pushing the struts that held the wings in place. The pontoons helped to make it easier to float the plane out of the wind and storm surge.

"This should be safe enough." Noah climbed up and into the plane to turn on the lights and retrieve a high-powered flashlight. The plane's lights helped illuminate the cave's interior, but Noah carefully checked the ceiling for bats and other dangerous creatures, such as poisonous spiders and snakes. "This is a good example of what I was saying. This island was once underwater. You can see that by the striations of water levels on the walls. Global warming has now lowered the water level, revealing more of the surface. Give it a couple of million years more and this island may reveal enough of its surface to become habitable." Finding no evidence of a threat, he tethered the plane's wheels with blocks to prevent it from moving as the water continued to surge onto the sandy floor of the cave.

"It would help if you would check the plane for supplies. I'll be back. I need to find rocks and dry wood on this rock before the storm hits us in about an hour." He draped a coiled rope over his shoulder, followed by a duffel bag. Then he was gone, disappearing up the sheer rock face.

Fiona found an assortment of things on the plane that may not have proven useful individually, like a stainless-steel wok complete with cover and cooking utensils. She had no idea why it was on board and didn't think about it over much. However, the case of twenty-four water bottles would be beneficial. At least they wouldn't die of thirst. Water surrounded them, but they couldn't use it as drinking water. There were canned beans and other staples that would not prove useful unless she found a can opener. There were other things, including two blankets bound in shrink-wrap, which she stacked on the sand.

When she checked her watch, the light was fading fast as the storm approached. The water level was rising, but, so far, it didn't threaten to flood the cave. Still, it allowed her to pull the plane further into the cave's shelter and out of the wind. What concerned her more was that over an hour had passed, and Noah had not returned. By the end of hour two, she feared something may have happened to him.

When she thought she should go to try to find him, as if he were Spiderman reincarnate, he swung down on a rope a foot away and nearly scared the life out of her. She didn't even hear him coming down from above. One moment she was looking out at the boiling ocean vista and worried. The next, he was there, close enough to touch, frowning at her. Then, without a moment's hesitation, Fiona launched herself into Noah's arms.

"*Whoa!* What's this?" Noah frowned, confused as he held Fiona's trembling body in his arms. "What happened? Are you all right?"

She held on tightly to him, burying her face in his broad, firm chest. "I was afraid something happened to you. I was about to come to look for you."

"It's okay. I'm fine." He was relieved that nothing had happened in his absence.

"Okay," she said on a shaky exhale of breath. "I know that you don't particularly like me, and this is an inappropriate request, but would you mind just holding me for a moment or two more while my nerves settle?"

Frowning again, he held her at arms' length and looked into her eyes.

"Guess not." She huffed in frustration.

"No, that's not it. What gave you the impression that I don't like you?"

"Oh, I don't know. Maybe it's because you avoid me like I'm carrying the plague. Unless it's business, you don't talk with me. Then, if I enter a room, you leave shortly after that. What else am I supposed to think?"

With one move too swift for her brain to register completely, he jerked her to him and covered her mouth with his. When he didn't detect resistance, he deepened the kiss, plundering her mouth with his tongue. Then, quite unexpectedly, she came alive in his arms, circling his neck and eagerly participating. He dropped the things he was carrying, including her shorts and his, and hiked her up until her legs clamped around his waist like a vice. Then, when he plunged into her moist heat with more speed than finesse, he had her pinned against the wall of the cave while the typhoon raged outside.

Fiona couldn't get enough; she couldn't get close enough when the madness overtook her, and she lost her mind. Finally, she gave up and gave in to the moment with Noah repeatedly retreating and then pounding deeper and deeper inside her. He was a big man, more muscular, lengthier and larger than either Aiden or Trey, but she rode him like an out-of-control jackhammer.

Noah didn't think he'd felt anything this glorious in his entire life. She locked around him like a fist in a silken glove. He found that Fiona had incredible control of her inner canal muscles. Each second he knew it couldn't get any better, but then it did when she tightened those female muscles even more, and he found himself near asphyxiation from his heavy breathing. Noah had never experienced what his SEAL buddies called the Singapore Kiss before. Now that he had, he didn't know whether he would ever be satisfied with ordinary sex again or with any other woman.

She palmed his face, ravished his mouth, and pumped him harder and faster than before, sliding back and forth, giving herself the friction she needed. Then, grabbing her hips, he helped her glide, his member slick with her creamy moisture.

Pulling up his T-shirt, she tossed it away. He did the same with the shirt she wore tied under her bountiful breasts. His reward was her unbound, stiff nipples teasing his chest while her long, strong legs chained him to her. Each time she cried out in climax, it drove him just that much more along a thin rail of sanity and escaping control. It was like being an out-of-control train rolling downhill without the ability to slow or break. There was just so much of that long, lean, naked skin that deserved to be worshiped and savored. She wasn't an insubstantial woman, but in his arms, she felt weightless. Her long, thick hair was loose around her, around him, curtaining them from the flashes of light, booming thunder, and the furious ocean crashing against the short beach. The sounds matched the runaway beats of his heart and loins.

Fiona lost her breath again and panted unsteadily. His mouth fused with hers; their tongues dueled in an age-old rhythm of lust. He repeatedly ignited her body with his ability to piston against her erogenous zone with precision and regularity. Though her back was taking a beating against the smooth wall, she trembled at the thrill of it all and didn't want him ever to stop.

Noah leaned back and looked into Fiona's eyes as her breath hitched and he repeatedly filled her. With their focus intent on each other, their breaths labored; they watched each other's eyes go opaque. His nuts contracted into him before he lost control and came again, harder on a strangled cry than he ever had before. The spasms went on for what seemed like an eternity, his heart thundering in his chest and his muscles bunching taunt against the exquisite pain of a hard, pleasurable release. The next time his strict control snapped, on simultaneous strangled cries, it dragged them both off the precipice into oblivion.

When Fiona woke, she realized she was naked, laying on a blanket. Her head was on Noah's right arm. They were covered by the other single blankets she found on the plane. Nearby where they slept, a fire pit burned around jagged rocks where the wok sat heating with the top on it. She tilted her head up and to her left to look at Noah's right profile. For a moment, Fiona watched his rapid eye movement slow, and then his eyes opened. He lifted his left arm to check his watch for the time before he turned his head to look into her eyes.

They stared at each other until Fiona sensed movement in the knapsack. Then, quickly sitting up, she grabbed the blanket to cover her breasts and pointed. "Something moved in or under that sack!"

"Dinner." Noah moved to a kneeling position. He wore nothing, not his shorts, shoes, or shirt. Opening the sack, he retrieved a large lobster. Lifting the top of the wok, he dumped the first and then a second crustacean into the boiling water and secured the lid back onto the base. The lobsters thrashed about but eventually stopped moving.

"I see you went on a deep-water shopping spree." Fiona looked at him wryly as she began to braid her hair and watch him work at preparing a meal. It was as distracting as hell to watch him move around without the benefit of clothes on his beautiful body. She did, however, notice what looked like a branded wand of Hermes or Mercury consisting of a winged staff with two serpents entwined on his left upper arm. She recognized that it was a symbol of the medical profession and as the emblem of most military Medical Corps. Many people wore ink, but to be branded had to be even more painful. When he turned, she noticed that his other arm was also branded. She wasn't quite sure of its origin, but it appeared to be a trident, a unique warfare insignia emblem of the US Navy SEALs. Fiona was curious, but despite having mind-blowing sex, she didn't feel that she knew him well enough to ask him personal questions.

"I had to make several dives to find these two lobsters. The light was fading, which made it hard to see underwater." Noah added more seasonings he had gathered from his foray over the island and closed the lid. He retrieved the can of beans and, using a multifaceted Swiss Army knife, efficiently opened the tops of the cans before placing them on the hot rocks to heat. Then he used the corkscrew to open holes in several coconuts to drain the juice before he cracked open the shells to get at the meat. He used the halved shells as bowls to hold their meal. Finally, he sliced pineapples and added them to the top of the wok to heat.

Curious, Fiona carefully watched. "You're very handy. Where did you learn to do this?"

"I grew up in an orphanage in a rural area on the Canadian-US border. It was a hike into the closest town on either side of the international boundary, so we learned several survival skills. Foraging for food was one of the skills we had to learn to stay alive. Coconut and pineapple were not on the menu. Instead, we found apples, but more vegetables, like carrots, celery, and squash."

"I didn't know. Is that what convinced you to become a medical doctor?"

"No, we rarely came in contact with medical professionals. When I was small, I learned to read. One of my spelling words was doctor. When

I tried to sound the word out, for some reason, I could never make it work phonetically. I thought it should be dock tore." He shrugged. "It was a word that stuck with me. I learned about herbs used for seasoning food and medicinal purposes so that when I went to college, I decided to pursue a career in medicine. Initially, I thought I would become a pharmacist based on my early experience, but I needed more of a challenge. So, I got to be the thing I couldn't spell when I was four or five years old." When he thought about it, he had never told anyone that story or any other about his life. *Odd*, Noah ventured silently. He found her easy to talk with when he had never felt that way with other women.

"Was that before or after you became a US Navy SEAL?"

He should have been surprised that she knew him to be a Navy SEAL, but he learned that Fiona Lizette Lowry was a highly intelligent woman. So, he answered her without a filter. "During."

"Where is home for you?"

"Wherever I am at the time is home. I don't have a street address."

"You've obviously traveled extensively. Is that why you speak the languages so well? You promised to tell me, remember?"

He nodded. "I remember. The native population of this country speaks Creole."

"My mother is of Louisiana *gens du couleur libre* creole ancestry. I can converse with her in her tongue, but this is different."

"The majority of people living in Seychelles are principally of African and Malagasy origins. However, today's Creole people also include mixed-raced African, Malagasy, Indian, Chinese, French, and British origins.

"Just as in the Americas, Africans and Malagasy were brought here as slaves to work on sugar and coffee plantations. Being enslaved isn't unique to the United States. These slaves were the last to be introduced to the Indian Ocean. Their origins lie in East Africa and, to a lesser extent, Madagascar. Today, Creoles are found throughout Seychelles, numbering nearly eighty thousand. They are the dominant group in politics and are proud of their African/Malagasy heritage. Seychelles has made Creole one of the three official languages of the republic, along with French and

English. Just as in Louisiana, Creole developed from the amalgamation of French and other dialects of the original settlers. Here, the Creole vocabulary is prinmarily French, with a few Malagasy, Bantu, English, and Hindi words. Most Seychellois can speak and understand French. Younger Seychellois read English, the language of government and commerce. French is the language of the Roman Catholic Church in the Seychelles Islands."

"It seems you like to study different cultures."

"I do. It helps when I have to determine and respect someone's religious beliefs or ask medical questions. I think you have the same interest from an architectural perspective. You like to see what others built centuries before."

She nodded and was a little surprised that he had nailed her interests. "Where did you go to medical school?"

"Johns Hopkins and Harvard." He continued to answer her questions without filters, but she didn't know the salient questions to ask. Those would be the questions he wouldn't be able or willing to answer for her. Hours after his birth, he was found in a men's room of a hospital clinic and wrapped in a terrycloth bath towel. His DNA confirmed he was of so many origins that he could not be identified as a member of any one prevalent source. So he and the other children in the orphanage formed their own family, their cabal.

As they grew up and out of the orphanage, most were chosen because they had no family ties and enlisted in a super-secret, worldwide enforcement organization created by the G7. It was known only to a select few as The Nursery. It took care of their needs, including a wide range of educational tracks. He chose medicine as his career trajectory with side specialties in languages and cultures. When he finished medical school and his residency program, he attended the US Navy's Officer Candidate School, where he sharpened his knowledge and skills. There he trained as a Navy SEAL and saw combat in several military theaters and campaigns.

When his handler and fellow resident of the orphanage deactivated, he did so as well. Few people knew of his history or his Code Name:

Stinger. So, for the time being, he was safe. He didn't have to provide any information Fiona couldn't read off his public biography. So, they continued to talk easily until the meal was ready.

With her gaze directly on his, when there was a lull in the conversation, Fiona took a deep breath before she admitted, "I shouldn't have done what we did."

Noah couldn't help but notice that Fiona drew her long, strong, shapely legs up to her chest and loosely circled them with her arms. She was still nude, as was he, and he recognized hers was a protective gesture.

Comfortably relaxed, sitting tailor-style with his elbows on his widely spread knees, his phallus aroused, he met her gaze and didn't look away. "I know I should apologize for it. I initiated it when you said you thought I didn't like you. Generally, I'm not concerned about what people think of me. I simply don't give a damn, but with you, it's different. So, here's the thing. I care very much what you think. You see, I've never slept with a woman I respect or admire more for her intellect, tenacity, and courage. I've never made love to a woman I've wanted more until I met you." He negligibly shrugged. "Don't misunderstand what I'm saying. I've had sex with women, but for me, in the past, it was purely a physical release and vastly different from the type of intimacy I want to share again with you...and often.

"Still, I recognize that it was an overabundance of adrenalin that got us started—first, the earthquake and then the weather emergencies. You may not have felt more than a physical need to release stress. We were bound to have some type of proof-of-life episode."

For some unknown reason, his confessions had thrills skittering through her, causing her blood to go hot and her breasts to peak, but she had to exercise control with this man more than she had with Aiden or Trey. "You said you should apologize, but you haven't."

"No, I haven't, and I won't. Why would I lie and say I apologize for something I wanted to do? Something I still want to do with you. Something I enjoyed doing with someone I've wanted to make love with since I forced you out of the Indian Ocean? What I will apologize for is not wearing a condom. It's not like I don't have one. Like most men, I carry at least one condom in my wallet, but with you, I didn't think about it. I've never done that before. It's likely one of the reasons why I enjoyed loving you so much well into the night until we fell asleep. I was unable or, more to the point, unwilling to pump the brakes and stop myself before I touched you. If we hadn't fallen asleep from sheer exhaustion, I'd still be inside you, but not using protection was wrong. I'm safe, health-wise. If there are consequences, such as a pregnancy, without question, I want you and the child we may have made."

"I appreciate your honesty, Noah. I'm safe, too, and there should be no chance of a pregnancy. I'm wearing an IUD. I agree with your rationale for our behavior. We'll just leave that interlude as an overreaction to stress. I'm in a relationship of sorts. I don't do recreational sex with multiple partners. In fact, I've never done this before, either. You're only the third man I've ever been with."

"Look, Fiona, if you tell me that you don't want me to touch you again, then I won't. I won't like it, but I don't force myself on women. I'll respect your boundaries. However, since we're being honest here, I want to make love with you again and again, but that's not all I want with you. Sex is easy. It's a physical manifestation of a prelude to lovemaking and intimacy. Sex is not the majority of what I want with you, but it's my baggage to carry, not yours. So, I can't make the same pledge to you that we shouldn't have done what we did. Instead, I believe we should make at least a daily habit of it. Considering you haven't said that you don't want me to touch you again, it leaves the question open and on the table for consideration once you resolve whatever existing relationship you're involved with now.

"So, Fiona Lizette Lowry, if you come to me for stress relief or any other reason once you return from your holiday sojourn, know that I will be here for you, and I will make love with you often and continuously until you tell me to stop."

Three days later, an emotionally and mentally confused Fiona finally boarded a private jet headed for Texas to celebrate the holidays with her family. Then she would be off to see Aiden and then Trey. Hopefully, by her return to Seychelles, her confusion would have cleared.

Chapter 29

"Congratulations, Mr. Attorney General," the Maryland State Supreme Court Chief Judge said with a firm handshake and a broad smile.

"Thank you, Sir." Aiden stood on the stage with his family. He turned to shake the hand of the governor, who had held the Bible on which he had sworn his oath of office. He wished that Fiona had been there for that occasion, but the heavy snows in the area prevented her arrival at the statehouse in Annapolis, Maryland. So instead, when Fiona landed in Baltimore, where the snow wasn't quite so bad, she would meet him there at his condo in the city. He couldn't wait to see her.

"The next step for you, Mr. Attorney General is, no doubt, to seek election to my office as Governor. However, I'm warning you that I'm not ready to give it up quite yet," he joked.

"Not to worry, Governor, I'm a patient man," Aiden returned, clamping his hand on the Governor's back.

They both chuckled, but the battle lines had been drawn. Aiden was coming after the governorship. This governor would have only one term in office before Aiden planned to take his place.

Aiden's family enveloped him, passing him from one person to the next. Then, finally, he was able to get free to wave to his audience of faithful supporters and step to the podium to deliver his speech. He took a moment to savor the boisterous applause and congratulatory shouts. This wasn't his first election win, and it wouldn't be his last, but each time it bolstered his spirit toward the time when he would be the President of the United States of America. When the din finally lessened to a dull roar, he smiled and said simply, "Thank you to my family, friends, and fans, but our work is just beginning."

Right down front stood Chevon Ellis and her father, grinning up at him and enthusiastically applauding. This was the time the Ellis' were waiting for. Either he would marry Chevon before the end of the month or they would release the video of him having sex with her on every Internet and media platform. Her pregnancy was noticeable at this point, so he didn't doubt she was pregnant. The only question on his mind was whether her fetus was the result of their apparent sexual encounter. He still didn't remember sleeping with her, but they had the video evidence that he had. The video was real and not doctored, he confirmed. They hadn't used someone who looked like him either. The close-ups were dispositive of the sexual act without evidence of a condom.

Chevon refused to have an amniocentesis test done to determine the DNA properties of the fetus. He had informed his immediate family and his campaign manager, Harris Charles, of the circumstances. His family urged him not to buckle under Chevon's threat. They wanted him to wait until the child was born to make any decisions and, if the child was indeed his, to go to court for full or, at a minimum, joint custody.

On the other hand, Harris was gearing up for the next election so that Aiden would be primed and ready to become a candidate for the governorship. Harris thought that with all the political power Chevon's family's media holdings, the Ellis News Group, brought to his campaign for Attorney General, he should go ahead and marry her. Harris believed her to be the perfect political wife for him and an asset to the next campaign.

Harris argued that Chevon was attractive, personable, and knew how to work a room full of political donors. She was also on the national news as a reporter every day. Her Q rating was high, so she had name recognition and national appeal. That would be a benefit as the governor's wife and far more useful when he ran for the presidency and her to be the First Lady. According to Harris, Chevon Ellis brought many assets to the table, and it was a win-win situation, one which Fiona couldn't guarantee for him.

Aiden was in love with Fiona. He didn't even like Chevon Ellis. Because of her treachery and malice, her appeal to him was nil to none. He couldn't even conjure up a scenario where he'd want to have sex with her. If he were forced to accede to her demands, he'd live only a half-life, one of misery and despair. He wasn't willing to put himself through that. So, he had a possibly life-altering decision to make.

Fiona was coming home. She had planned to be there to celebrate his victory. He would discuss his dilemma with her when she arrived. After all, she was still his best friend, and he would ask her again to be his wife. However, he had to make the rounds of all the parties given in his honor before he met Fiona at his condo in Baltimore. While he continued delivering his prepared remarks, he looked out into the audience again. He was pleased to see that Chevon and her father were nowhere in sight.

"Thank you," Fiona yelled to the chopper pilot over the noise of the blades as she got out of the helicopter. Then, bending low, she made her way to the rooftop access door to Aiden's building. The building supervisor smiled and held the door open for her.

"Welcome back, Ms. Lowry."

"Thank you. I hope you and your family had a wonderful holiday."

"We did, and thank you for the fruit and wine basket you sent to us for the occasion."

"You're welcome. Has Mr. McKenna arrived yet?"

"No, ma'am. Not yet. Do you still have your access key and code?"

"I do, yes." They entered the elevator.

Fiona had been back in the states for almost a month, and her body had yet to acclimate to the change. She and her family spent the Christmas and New Year's holidays in Hawkinstown, Texas, at her uncle's ranch near San Antonio. It hadn't been cold there, about forty degrees, but she had to put on more clothes than she had to wear in the last eight months.

Now, as Fiona waited for the elevator to take her down to Aiden's condo, she missed the balmy weather in Seychelles. They had made good progress on Operation: Uplift and the tasks her uncle had laid out for her. So, she was anxious to get back to work. However, she had several promised visits to make before she returned to Africa. She also had to have a battery of medical checkups before her return. Since she would be in New York, she arranged to have all the tests done there. It was relatively easy to arrange the dental, eye exam, and physical in the same medical building on the same day. Her friend, Angelique Alexander, a supermodel and Le Cordon Bleu-trained chef, made the arrangements with the specialists she used.

However, Fiona's first stop after the holidays was to see Aiden. She was happy for him. He handily won the election as she predicted he would. Fiona wanted to be there when he took his oath of office, as she had been for every milestone in his life. He was still her best friend, but weather conditions in and around Annapolis were not conducive to landing there. So, she directed the pilot to take her to Baltimore International Airport instead. The rest of her family went on to Bay County. Her brothers would stay there for a few months to catch up on their projects and then join her in Africa when they could.

At Baltimore Airport, Fiona chartered a helicopter for the short ride to the landing pad atop Aiden's condo building. Unfortunately, she would only be able to spend a few days with him before she caught a flight to New York to see Trey. When Aiden asked her to come, he intimated that there was something very important he needed to talk about with her. She pressed him to discuss it over the phone, but he wouldn't relent. Nevertheless, it sounded serious, so she agreed to spend a few days with him.

When the elevator doors opened, Fiona stepped inside, inserted her key, and added her access code to the panel on the elevator wall. It was a short ride down to the Penthouse level. Still, when the doors opened to his flat, romantic music played, the lights were low, the aroma of delicious food permeated the air, and a woman stood silhouetted against the panoramic glass doors leading to the terrace. Fiona could see that the dining room table was set for two and chafing dishes were on Sterno pots, heating food for an intimate late evening meal.

For a moment, Fiona thought she had the wrong condo, but as she looked around, she recognized the furniture and art on the walls she helped Aiden select for his new place. Just then, the woman turned, and a smile slipped slightly from her face.

"Oh my, you're not who I was expecting. Are you in the wrong place?"

"Is this Aiden McKenna's condo?"

The woman came toward her. "Yes, it is. I'm Chevon, his fiancée, and you are?"

"I'm Fiona Lowry."

"Of course, Aiden has spoken of you often. Is he expecting you?"

"Yes, I was supposed…" she trailed off, noticing the woman was very pregnant. The sexy lingerie left nothing to the imagination. "I must have misunderstood his message."

"Oh." Chevon smiled and rubbed her abdomen. "He probably wanted us to meet and get to know one another. He neglected to mention it to me this morning when he left home. I'm sure he must have forgotten that you were coming. He's visiting with supporters at different parties. After his swearing-in, I came home to make a special dinner to celebrate his success. He should be home any time now. As you can see, we're expecting, and with the campaign wrapping up and our wedding plans in the works, we've been a little scattered."

"Obviously." Fiona nodded. Something about the woman seemed familiar, but in the lowered lighting, she couldn't place her. "Look, I don't want to intrude on your celebration, so I'm not going to stay to wait for him to arrive. However, I'd appreciate it if you would tell Aiden I came by and that I wish you both the very best." She moved back into the elevator with her luggage.

"I'll be sure to do that, Fiona. He'll be disappointed that he missed you. Travel safely." She waved as the doors closed.

Confusion covered Fiona's face as she rode to the lobby level of the condo. *So this is what Aiden wants to talk with me about?* she wondered. *He is getting married and has a baby on the way?* It seemed so out of character to her that he would invite her to come to stay with him and his fiancée. She had to admit that it was a rather tactless way to do it. If anything, as a politician, Aiden was the very soul of tact. *Is this invitation geared to hurt me?* she wondered. Then again, she wondered why no one in her family or his mentioned that Aiden was getting married. Especially since her mother specifically told her that Aiden still wanted her to be his wife. The more she thought of it, the more confused she became, but when the elevator doors opened, she made her way to the concierge station to arrange for a van to take her back to the airport.

For now, she'd just wait to hear from him.

Taking out her phone, Fiona called the pilot to alert her that she was on her way back to the airport and to ready the plane for a flight to New York City.

When Aiden stepped off the elevator, he smiled. The lights were low, romantic music was playing, and the smell of delicious food filtered through the air. *Fiona is finally home,* he thought. He heard her moving around in the kitchen and decided to slip into the bathroom for a quick shower. He needed to wash off the perfume smells and lipstick. After that, they would talk over dinner and then make love the way they had for years. He missed her so much, but now that she was home and the election madness was over, they would use this time to work on their future plans together.

He was heartened that Fiona had not invited Trey Kennard to travel with her and spend the holidays with her family in Hawkinstown, Texas. Maybe he had been wrong about accepting what the press and news media reported about the relationship between Trey and Fiona. What did it matter in the big scheme anyway? Instead, he needed to focus on trying to explain Chevon's claim that he had sex with her and that they were expecting a child together. He stepped out of the shower, dried his hair, and slipped into a short pair of drawstring pants. With his feet and chest bare, he went in search of Fiona.

He frowned at the silhouette of the woman standing at the terrace doors, looking out at the snowy panoramic view of the night's cityscape. She wasn't a tall woman or shaped like his Fiona. Then, turning on a brighter light, his frown deepened. "Chevon? What are you doing in my home? How did you get in here past security?"

"Hello, darling. I didn't hear you come home." She moved toward him. "Would you like a drink? I know it's been a tiresome day, Mr. Attorney General. Let me be the first to say how proud I am of you. However, as you said, 'It's only the beginning.' In two years, your campaign for the governorship will be well underway. Then in eight years, you'll be situated perfectly to run for the presidency. Of course, we'll have more children by then and make a lovely family portrait.

"Aiden? Who are you calling? We need to talk about—"

"Security? Yes, this is Aiden McKenna. There's an intruder in my penthouse. Send a security team immediately to remove her and notify the state police." So saying, he disconnected the call.

"What are you doing?" Chevon fumed, yelling at the top of her voice. *"You can't have me thrown out! I won't allow it! After all, I'm the mother of your child!"*

When the elevator doors opened and the security team entered, Chevon was in full rant mode. She scurried around and tried to evade them, but they were quicker than she was in her condition. They were mindful of her pregnancy, but still got her handcuffed and into the elevator just as the building supervisor stepped off.

"I apologize, Mr. McKenna. We didn't know anyone other than Ms. Lowry was here in your home. When she left, we assumed she was meeting you somewhere else, or she had some type of emergency. She seemed upset when she left."

"What? What are you talking about? Ms. Lowry was here?"

"Yes, sir. She was. You said she always had permission to come and go as she pleased whether you were here or not."

"That's correct. Ms. Lowry has unfettered access. When was she here?"

"It was a little over an hour or maybe as much as two hours ago."

"Where did she go?"

"She had one of the vans drive her to the airport."

"Where was she going?"

"That I cannot tell you. The van's driver mentioned that he dropped her at the private jetport for Adventurer Executive Airline. She didn't tell him where she was going."

Aiden gave the building super a dispirited "Thanks" and ushered him to the elevator.

When he was finally alone, he shut off the music and turned off the warming trays in his kitchen. He realized Fiona was likely here at the same time as Chevon, and, given the romantic images, Fiona probably believed whatever the manipulative woman told her. Aiden tried calling her cell phone, but his message went to voicemail. If she were already on a flight, her phone would be on airplane mode.

Frustrated, he took a deep breath and knew what he had to do.

He speed-dialed his campaign manager. "Harris, I've just had Chevon Ellis arrested for trespassing."

"You did *what?*" Harris fumed.

"I had her arrested. This incident will probably be all over the news tomorrow, so I'll prepare a statement—"

"You've just made a career-ending decision, Aiden! Her father and his cronies will crucify you in the press and news media. As a result, you won't be able to run for dogcatcher in your own county."

"None of that matters to me now. Fiona was here. There is no question in my mind that she didn't wait for me to get home because Chevon was here and fed Fiona some cock-and-bull story about us. How Chevon got in is a mystery, but—"

"Are you crazy? I gave Chevon the code for your condo. I've been working with her and her family's media group to get you elected. How do you think we got all of that positive media reports on the front page

news? Chevon is the best thing that could have happened to you, not Fiona! She doesn't have—"

"Harris?"

He sighed in frustration. "Yes, Aiden?"

"You're fired!" Aiden disconnected the call. He knew what having Chevon arrested would do to his aspirations, but nothing was more important to him than Fiona.

He made another call to his parents and siblings. "Dad, Mom, we are going to have some difficult days ahead. So, effective immediately, I'm resigning my office, and as soon as I can manage it, I'm going after Fiona to beg her to forgive me for my arrogance."

<h1 align="center">Chapter 30</h1>

The flight from Baltimore to New York City was a quick one-hour-thirty-minute trip. A car service waited at the baggage claim at the private jetport and, within moments, Fiona was headed for Trey's business office. Fiona was earlier than she told him she would be by two days, but she needed to finally have this face-to-face conversation with him.

Trey warned her he would try to convince her to stay with him for longer than she originally planned, but he also made it clear he wanted to take their relationship to the next level. Trey wanted permanence and a commitment Fiona wasn't sure she was ready for. She also owed him the truth about what happened between Noah Mikasi and her six weeks ago.

When the car service stopped in front of his building, she noted it was next door to the trendy restaurant, Angelique's Place, and her nightclub, The Runway. Both places were owned and operated by her friend, Angelique, formerly Menendez-Gaza, now Alexander. She was now married to the basketball icon Gregory Alexander. At last count, they had three children. She met and became friends with Angelique when she helped her cousin, JaiHonnah, reimagine the prima ballerina Linda Lewis' private library building into a residence and dance school. Now Linda was married to baseball legend Will Hamilton. They had two sons.

Though they were all about the same age, both Angelique and Linda were happy and starting families. Fiona wondered whether she would ever find that special someone and fall in love enough to want to make that kind of commitment. She wasn't thirty yet, so she thought she had plenty of time. For now, as her mother had advised, she'd *Never see the wonders of the world if she only looked out of one window for the whole of her life.' Isn't marriage like choosing to see life out of one window for the whole of my life?* she wondered. Odd that she should be thinking of such things. Especially at a time when she was on her way to see Trey, the man who had opened her world for her and laid it at her feet. She owed him so much, but did she owe him the rest of her life?

She let the thought pass as the doorman held open the door for her. In the lobby, the desk clerk gave her the access code for Trey's office floor. When the elevator doors opened, Sandra was there with open arms to welcome her.

"Oh, it's so good to see you, Fiona! You look wonderful."

"Thank you, Sandra. It's really great to see you, too. How are Harriet and the boys?" Arm-in-arm, they strolled through the halls to Sandra's office and sat to chat.

"Wonderful. They wanted me to let them know when you came to town. We hoped to have a chance to hear all about your time in Africa. We've never been there. Is it really as beautiful as we hear?"

"Even more so. We'll have to make time while I'm here. I have several reasons for being in the city. First, tell me, how is Hugh?"

"Oh, he's doing just great. Unfortunately, he's out on a date. If we had known you were coming in earlier than you said, I'm sure he would have been here."

"The general, I hear, is doing well. My parents told me that Charlotte and her family joined him here in New York City for the holidays."

"Yes. We had a big Christmas dinner and a great New Year's Eve party, but I could go on and on about that," Sandra said as she and Fiona continued to catch up.

Amiria Kono passed by Sandra's office and caught a glimpse of someone she hoped never to see again. Fiona Lowry. The woman was all Trey talked about. Amiria was displeased that Trey sent her to tour with the musical group History. They had returned only a few weeks ago. When Trey returned from receiving awards in California, he refused to see her alone. With him, she was strictly a colleague. He channeled all his interests toward Fiona Lowry.

Maybe if Fiona weren't around, Trey would finally want to rekindle their love affair. Well, according to him, it wasn't a "love affair" per se. Rather, he saw it as "an affair," which never should have started, and he would not repeat. However, she wasn't willing to give up on Trey Kennard that easily.

Amira knew he wasn't expecting Fiona for another few days because he cleared his schedule so he could spend all his time with her. She knew Fiona had designed and built a home and studio for Trey somewhere in Maryland. Now that the house was completed, Trey often went there. The day after New Year's, Trey returned to Maryland for an extended stay for rest and relaxation. He was thrilled with the property and hoped that Fiona would join him. That didn't happen, but Trey planned to spend more of his time in Maryland than in New York to be with her. If that happened, there would not be an opportunity to put a stop to Trey's infatuation with Fiona Lowry.

Amiria knew Trey was upstairs working in his residence. She made it her job to keep tabs on his every move so she could be close to him as often as possible. Since it appeared Sandra and Fiona were settling in for a long chat, Amiria slipped out of the office and hurried to Trey's residence. She had all the codes for access since she stayed there while he was still on tour. As Amiria entered the lower level of his residence, she went into the laundry to find one of his shirts. She quickly disrobed, put on his shirt, left it unbuttoned to the waist, and left her feet bare. Next, she tousled her hair, slapped some color into her cheeks, and dampened her face to make herself appear as if she had just rolled out of bed with him.

She crept up to the next level, hiding and waiting for Fiona to arrive. Her timing was perfect. Trey was up on the third level. She could hear the shower running when the elevator pinged. She opened the door just as Fiona stepped out and plastered a sleepy, confused smile on her face. "Oh, you're not the delivery person, are you? When the concierge said the food was here and he was sending him up, I thought it was…oh, never mind. It's not important. You must be here to see Trey?"

"I am, yes." Fiona looked at the scantily-clad woman she remembered from the club in Tokyo. The shirt she wore open down to her pubis was one of Trey's monogrammed ones. Fiona shook her head at the realization. "Trey wasn't expecting me today. I'll contact him at a later time."

Amiria pursed her lips and tilted her head as if listening. "Yes, that would be best. We just got out of bed, and he's still in the shower. Who should I say stopped by?"

Fiona shrugged. "It really doesn't matter. Goodbye." She returned to the elevator.

Amiria, filled with glee, did a little triumphant dance until she heard the shower turn off. Then, hurrying to get out of the condo before Trey found her there, she didn't bother to put his shirt back in the laundry. It smelled of his unique scent, so she would keep it until she had Trey back in her life and in her bed again.

At midday, during a lunchtime meeting, Sandra asked Trey, "Isn't Fiona going to join us?"

Trey frowned. "Fiona? Why would you ask me that? She's not due to arrive until tomorrow."

Sandra looked at him with a confused expression on her face. "Tomorrow? Fiona came in last night. She and I had a conversation for about thirty minutes before she went up to your residence. I saw her to the elevator and punched in the code myself."

"*What?*" Trey was stunned.

"What's going on, old boy?" Hugh joked. "You've been talking a blue streak about Fiona, and you didn't see her in your place?"

"No, I didn't." Trey was perplexed. Rising from the lunch table, he dialed Fiona's number, but his call went to voice mail. "The hell with this!" Trey fumed. "Sandra, would you arrange for a flight for me to Seychelles as early as you can make it?"

"Sure, Trey, but I'm not sure when Fiona plans to leave to go back to Africa. She said she had several things to take care of here before she left."

"Here? As in New York City or Maryland?"

"Both or either. Fiona didn't specify what she had to do."

"Okay, hold off on chartering that flight. I'll keep trying to reach her, but I wonder why Fiona changed her mind and didn't come to my residence."

"That I couldn't tell you. Fiona was definitely on her way up to your place the last time I saw her. When she left, she didn't stop to say goodbye to me. That's why I thought she was still here in your residence."

"I wonder why Fiona would leave without seeing you?" Hugh questioned.

Trey wondered the same thing.

When Fiona walked out of the doctor's office after the third and last medical appointment of the day, she was in more of a daze than she had been when she left Trey's residence. What was it with the men in her life? Were they all out to make her suffer? If so, for what, she didn't know or understand. She thought them both to be friends first and lovers second, but the friendship must have only been in her mind. First, with Aiden and Chevon Ellis, the woman she now remembered as a national political news reporter. Then Trey and Amiria Kono, his musical protégée.

Still, she wouldn't focus on Aiden's or Trey's behavior. There were more important things to focus on, and the sooner she did so, the better. Finally, the car service pulled to the curb. The door automatically opened and she got in.

"Where to, Miss?"

"The McCoy Grande Condos and Hotel, and would you mind waiting? I'll only be a few moments. Then I need to get to the airport."

"Yes, Miss." He began to drive to the hotel.

Two hours later, the private BlackHawk jet lifted off, headed for The Republic of Seychelles and a very uncertain future for Fiona Lizette Lowry.

Epilogue

Fiona Lowry sat tailor-style on the rear terrace of her uncle's mansion and watched the sun breaking the dawn over the Indian Ocean. She sat troubled by her thoughts and the decisions she had to make. Fiona recognized that she was committed to seeing this project through to its conclusion, and she was proud of her contribution to the better good. However, Fiona wondered whether staying here was a good decision.

As she looked up the beach, she saw a figure running in the surf and recognized Noah's sleek form cutting down the distance at a rapid pace. He hadn't been at the mansion when she arrived yesterday, but the staff said he should return late last night from a trip he made to France. Fiona didn't stay awake to wait for his return because what she had to discuss with him could wait another day. So, instead, because she was weary from her long flight from New York, Fiona turned in early. Of course, Fiona knew that Noah usually ran a ten-mile stretch of the beach twice a day; she only had to sit and wait for his return. The closer he got, the more rapidly her blood rushed through her body.

Noah had a lot on his mind. A secret rendezvous of the Nations United in Security and the World Security Network, known to only a few as The Nursery, was called together in an installation in France. The Nursery is a covert entity created by the nations that constitute the G7: France, Germany, Italy, Japan, the United Kingdom, Canada, and America. The President of the United States, no matter who that person is, holds the leadership role in perpetuity for twenty-five years. The sole purpose of the unit is to secure peace worldwide within that time frame—by any means necessary. When it is achieved, all nations will disband their military forces and weapons systems, and then the job is over. A smaller unit will be formed under the aegis of the United Nations to police the countries and assure no other aggression occurs.

The clandestine meeting was called because factions of a white slavery group were in business again on the European, Asian, and African continents. The Nursery had decimated a league of wealthy participants several years earlier, but apparently, a new group out of Russia was starting up again. Since the Outliers were spread around the globe, they were being tasked to work their networks of confidential informants for any information they could gather on the growing problem. The Nursery task force had been investigating white slavery among the Baltic states of Estonia, Latvia, and Lithuania. They found that Estonia was a significant source country, trafficking women to Norway, the United Kingdom, and Finland for forced prostitution. Some Baltic countries didn't have or didn't enforce criminal laws against white slavery. However, the United Nations banned the practice, and The Nursery, as a creation of the G7, was expected to take action to stop the crimes against girls and women.

The task force was also surprised to find that Estonian men were being trafficked within the country for forced labor, too. Specifically, the men had been forced into committing criminal acts and had been shipped to Ukraine for forced delivery in the construction industry. Healthy men were forced to impregnate young girls on baby farms and for ethnic cleansing. The babies were being sold to the highest bidders internationally. What happened to those babies after that was anyone's guess.

Noah recalled that the head of The Nursery, Delta Dawn stated that "We know that Russian oligarchs are behind the human trafficking crimes in the United States. We also suspected that white babies and children were kidnapped from the Baltics and trafficked for high-cost adoptions and pedophiles. Until recently, we didn't know that South and North American criminal cartels also sell children to the highest bidder. We believe that's what was recently unwittingly uncovered in New England. We want to rescue as many children as possible and try to reunite them with their parents. What concerns us is that, in many cases, the parents may be illegals who are hiding from the authorities and are not likely to complain that their children have been kidnapped.

"We need your ears and eyes focused on this regardless of what other projects you have in the works. This threat to world security is a priority all-hands-on-deck mission. No exceptions. We are dedicated to crushing these criminal activities and bringing those responsible to justice with all due haste and by all means necessary."

Noah had his marching orders and, as an Outlier in The Nursery, knew that he would have to take time away from Operation: Uplift to perform his duties. He didn't want to do it, but as in his years as a US Navy SEAL, he never failed to answer the call. He hoped that Fiona would return before he had to leave. They had unfinished business to discuss. His need for her, while she was away, was like a never-ending ache in his gut. He feared that she would reject him, and if that happened, he wouldn't know what to do to save himself. She was beginning to mean so much to him. He had never been loved by anyone, and he had never loved another soul. However, with Fiona, what he felt for her, he feared was love in scope and depth that defied logic. So, when he looked up and saw her sitting on the terrace, his heart hammered just that much harder in his chest.

Walking across the sand toward Fiona, he steadily watched her stand and watch him with the same amount of intensity. Finally, when he would have ravished her mouth, she held him off with one hand. Then, searching his eyes, she said, "Noah, I'm pregnant with your child."

From the Author

Greetings family, friends, and fans!

I'll wager you never fathomed you would become the determining factor in one of my novels, but here you are, poised to write the ending story for our gal-pal, Fiona Lizette Lowry. She has lived such an uneventful life until her parents encourage her to see the world. To do so, she has to leave her first lover and best friend, Aiden McKenna, at a time when he believes he needs her and her moral support the most.

Then there's new friend, Maxwell "Trey" Kennard, the musical genius who opens up the world for her in England, France, Spain, and Japan. For him, she brings another type of music into his rather solitary life. What's a woman to do with two dynamic men at her fingertips?

Get another one in the person of the taciturn Dr. Noah Mikasi. Unlike Aiden, who has deep family roots or Trey, who has shallow family roots, Noah has no roots whatsoever.

Okay, pals-of-mine, who shall it be that our fair maiden, Fiona Lizette Lowry, gives her heart to and why? It's your choice and I will reveal the winners in an upcoming novel, featuring some of the characters from *City Chic, Country Cool, and Worldly Wise* and new people we will meet. Post your decisions and comments on Facebook @Ann Jeffries, Amazon.com, BarnesandNoble.com, Goodreads.com, at Annjeffries.net, or send them directly to me at AnnJeffriesAuthor@gmail.com.

Until then, I remain faithfully yours,
Ann Jeffries

About the Author

Ann Jeffries, the critically acclaimed author of the Family Reunion—Wisdom of the Ancestors Series, is a native of Washington, DC. As an only child, she enjoyed the benefits of a private school education at Allen in Asheville, North Carolina, and a public education at the University of Maryland. Ann began writing fiction for her own amusement.

Ms. Jeffries is the recipient of many awards for leadership and public service. A keynote speaker at colleges, universities, conferences, and conventions, she has extensively traveled the North American continent, Asia, and Europe. Among other endeavors, she is an entrepreneur, an avid supporter of public television, a genealogist, and a voracious reader.

Her pride and joy are her family members, particularly her Fabulous Four grands. She lives in Maryland and South Carolina.

Follow Ann on her website: www.annjeffries.net, Facebook @ Ann Jeffries, on Twitter @Ann Jeffries and her publishing house site: www.newviewliterature.com. Her novels are available in both e-book and paperback. Her autographed copies can be found on her website: annjeffries.net and also unautographed on Amazon.com and BarnesandNoble.com. All of Ms. Jeffries' novels are available in audiobook format through Audible, iTunes, and Amazon.

www.ingramcontent.com/pod-product-compliance
Lightning Source LLC
Chambersburg PA
CBHW030804200726
48285CB00014B/609